Readers have lost their hearts to

Always,
in
December
x

'A poignant, heart-tugging, life-affirming story that
will wrap around you like a hug in any season'
JOSIE SILVER

'Tender, uplifting and gorgeously romantic.
I already want to reread it. I loved, loved, LOVED it!'
CATHY BRAMLEY

'A sweepingly romantic, heartbreaking love story, packed with Richard
Curtis-style moments, and an ending that took my breath away'
HOLLY MILLER

'Absolutely gorgeous. A compelling and pull-at-the-
heartstrings read. Kept me reading late into the night'
JO LOVETT

'My favourite read of the year so far . . . if the rights to turn *Always, in
December* into a film aren't snapped up immediately, there's no justice'
5* NETGALLEY REVIEW

'I absolutely adored this book and was totally invested in Josie
and Max's story. Heartbreaking, beautiful and life affirming'
5* NETGALLEY REVIEW

'It made me laugh, it made me cry . . . it is a fantastic debut
and I can't wait to see what Emily produces next'
5* NETGALLEY REVIEW

'Wow, I'm at a loss for adequate words. Highly
recommended read, but have the tissues at the ready!!'
5* NETGALLEY REVIEW

Emily Stone lives and works in Chepstow and wrote *Always, in December* in an old Victorian manor house with an impressive literary heritage. Her debut novel was partly inspired by the death of her mother, when Emily was seven, and wanting to write something that reflected the fact that you carry this grief into adulthood, long after you supposedly move on from the event itself.

Keep up with Emily on Twitter @EmStoneWrites.

Always, in December
x

Emily Stone

REVIEW

First published in 2021 by
HEADLINE REVIEW
An imprint of HEADLINE PUBLISHING GROUP

Cataloguing in Publication Data is available from the British Library

ISBN 978 1 4722 7960 6

Typeset in Garamond by CC Book Production

Printed and bound in Great Britain by Clays Lrd, Elcograf S.p.A.

Headline's policy is to use papers that are natural, renewable and
recyclable products and made from wood grown in well-managed forests
and other controlled sources. The logging and manufacturing processes
are expected to conform to the environmental regulations
of the country of origin.

HEADLINE PUBLISHING GROUP
An Hachette UK Company
Carmelite House
50 Victoria Embankment
London EC4Y 0DZ

www.headline.co.uk
www.hachette.co.uk

To appreciate the beauty of a snowflake it is necessary to stand out in the cold

Aristotle

Part One: December

Chapter One

Josie stood in the doorway of her flat, under the mistletoe that Bia had insisted they hang 'just in case' and stared mutely at the box Oliver was clutching. One of her hands was still resting on the door, and for a moment she nearly gave in to the urge to slam it in his lying, cheating and, she realised now, far too symmetrical face.

Oliver cleared his throat. 'I know you wanted your stuff back so I just thought I would . . .' Something about the expression on her face caused him to trail off and he looked down at the box of her belongings instead. He fumbled with it as he tried to hold it out to her, awkwardly bumping into the doorframe instead.

'Right.' She gave in and took it from him, deliberately manoeuvring so that she avoided touching his hand. She grunted at the sudden weight of it – it was far heavier than it looked. She supposed that made sense – two years' worth of stuff left at his flat, forgotten about or left there deliberately to make life easier. Stuff she'd presumed, up until a few weeks ago, wouldn't be leaving there for the foreseeable future, given she'd assumed that she would, sooner or later, be moving in. What had he been thinking, as he packed it all away? He'd pleaded with her not to end things, initially, but now here he was, determinedly marking the end of the relationship.

She pressed her lips together firmly to stop them trembling, and turned her back to Oliver. Right at the top of the box, rolling around on one of her books, as if thrown in as an afterthought, were the flashing reindeer earrings he'd given her three weeks ago, ahead of their work Christmas lunch. The lunch where, instead of coming back with her once the desserts were out of the way, he'd stayed on to drink and flirt with a colleague of theirs. The lunch where, instead of coming home within the hour, he'd gone round to said colleague's house. And slept with her.

She set the box down on the vinyl floor, just outside Bia's room. She supposed, then, the earrings had been his farewell gift to her, though neither of them had known it at the time. The thought that had flared up time and time again since the morning after, where, still in bed, he'd told her what he'd done, stabbed at her mind now, even as she tried to repress it. The idea that, if she hadn't gone home early after the lunch, then maybe they wouldn't be stood here now. Maybe she'd be curled up next to him on his tiny red sofa watching reruns of *Line of Duty* and ordering a Thai takeaway and bottle of white wine. Maybe he wouldn't have given in to temptation, also known as Cara. Or maybe it would have only been delayed, until the next time there was Prosecco and a skin-tight red dress involved.

She took a deep breath through her nose as she stood up, vowing to throw the earrings in the bin the first chance she got. He was still standing there when she turned back around, and she fought hard to keep her face impassive, to force down the angry lump in her throat. He shoved his hands in the pockets of his too-tight jeans and rocked back on his heels, looking over her head and around the flat as if admiring it for the first time. She folded her arms and raised her eyebrows. No way was she making this easier for him.

'So are you . . . ok?' He finally met her gaze and seemed to flinch back a bit from whatever he saw there. Good. It meant she'd nailed the drop-dead glare. She raised her eyebrows further. She wouldn't be surprised if they'd disappeared under her fringe by now, but she didn't care. She refused to be dragged into any form of small talk, not after what he'd done to her.

'I mean, after what happened in the office today, I just wanted to make sure . . .' He trailed off again, apparently losing the ability to speak in full sentences. Josie kept her arms tightly crossed, desperately hoping that the heat she felt pulsing under her cheeks wasn't showing on her face. Of course he'd bring that up. Of course he'd figured out why Janice had wanted to talk to her. One of the serious drawbacks to sharing an office with your ex, on top of the fact you had to see them every day, was the fact that you couldn't lie and say everything was going just *swimmingly* at work.

'I'm fine,' she said shortly, though from the way his brown eyes turned soft as his gaze lingered on her face, she knew he didn't buy it. She shifted her weight from one foot to the other, wishing she'd changed out of her black-and-white-striped work dress, which felt too tight now, and too exposing, like she'd got home at two in the afternoon and been sat doing nothing for four hours. Which, to be fair, she had. Though maybe he wouldn't notice – he'd never paid much attention to what she'd worn when they were together, something she'd found incredibly charming, the fact that he'd genuinely seemed not to care whether she was in a tracksuit or heels. She wondered now if that had all been put on, given the girl he'd slept with.

Oliver opened his mouth, shut it again and nodded, clearly thinking better of whatever he'd been about to say, whatever condescending support he'd been about to offer. 'Alright,' he said evenly. He ran a hand through his dark brown hair, which lay flat against his head, almost like it was stuck in place, though the side parting that she knew he combed into place every day was slightly ruffled. 'But you know you can still talk to me, right, babe? I still—'

Josie held up a hand. 'Don't call me babe.' She sighed. 'Please, just don't.' She didn't want to hear it. The offer of a shoulder to cry on, telling her that he still cared about her. Because surely if he cared about her that much, he wouldn't have slept with someone else. And certainly not someone they both worked with, someone she had to face in the office, who walked around the place in completely impractical heels like she owned it.

'Right,' he said, and rubbed a hand across the back of his neck, looking away from her and glancing around the dull hallway. One of the lights was flickering weakly down the other end, the effect somehow highlighting the ugly, stained carpet which contrasted sharply with the vinyl inside the flat that Josie made an effort to keep clean and shiny. He took a breath, looked back at her with those brown Bambi eyes, the ones she'd fallen for two and a half years ago, when he'd first swanned into the office, just confident enough for it to be attractive and not annoying. 'Jose, look, I know I hurt you, and I know you don't think you'll ever be able to forgive me, but I hate the idea of you sitting here alone, trying to deal with this. I just think if we could talk, we—'

Josie shook her head. 'Oliver, I can't do this right now.' His hand dropped to his side and he looked so damn pathetic in that moment, shoulders hunched under his black North Face coat, that she almost gave in and rested a hand on his arm. Almost. Until she remembered that he was not the wronged party in this situation. He had no right to keep trying to worm his way back in, to make her feel like she was overreacting. 'And I'm not alone,' she said, her voice clipped. 'I have Bia.'

'Right.' He nodded a few times, looking like that bobbing-head dog she'd got in this year's office secret Santa. She'd had it on her desk since, trying to show she appreciated the gesture, even though the fact that every single bloody person that stopped by bopped it when they left her desk and then she had to watch it slow down its nodding out of the corner of her eye while she tried to type. 'Alright.' Oliver cleared his throat. 'Well I guess I'll see you at the party on Tuesday then?' He tried a hesitant smile, showing off the crooked teeth she knew he hated.

'I guess you will,' she said, trying not to sigh. The party

that they all had to go to, despite the fact that it was on Christmas Eve.

He hovered in the doorway for a moment longer, and she wondered if he was waiting for her to give in and hug him, or invite him in or something. After all, throughout the course of the relationship it had always been her making the compromises, her staying out late because he wanted a night out, or agreeing to go on a hectic city break rather than a retreat to the country. They both knew it, both had their roles to play. But this was different. Oliver glanced up, saw the mistletoe hanging sadly above them, and turned a little pink. Josie grimaced. She was going to kill Bia.

'Well,' he muttered, 'until then, I suppose.' He shuffled away from the door, but glanced over at her before she could shut it. 'I'm sorry, you know.' His eyes, almost exactly the same shade of brown as hers, didn't blink once. 'I know it's crap timing and I really . . .' He shook his head. 'I'm just sorry.'

She hesitated for half a second, her lips pressed tightly together, wondering whether she should say something to make him realise that sorry wasn't good enough, to ask him why, and why now, at a time of year he *knew* was difficult for her. To ask him if he'd slept with Cara again, if he would move in on her, now that Josie was out of the way. But she couldn't bring herself to, wasn't sure she actually wanted to know the answer. So instead she nodded once, then let the door click shut.

She allowed herself a moment to close her eyes and rest her head back against the door. She refused to let the tears come, though, taking slow breaths and screwing up her eyes to banish back the burning. *He's not worth it*, she told herself. And she'd been through worse and survived, hadn't she?

She pushed away from the door and sighed as she hauled the box of her stuff to her room at the far end of the corridor. The bigger room, because Bia had insisted she take it, even though they paid the same amount of rent. She grimaced at the purple tinsel Bia had put up around her doorframe. She had half a mind to tear it down, but wouldn't because, despite her feelings on the subject, she knew it would upset Bia.

She'd only just dumped the box on her bed when she heard a key in the front door. Speak of the tiny she-devil.

'Jose? Josie!' The sound of Bia's voice was followed by the sound of various objects falling, including the clanging of a set of keys, and Bia swearing, loudly. Josie huffed out a small laugh despite herself as she stuck her head around her bedroom door to see Bia's multicoloured handbag on the floor, contents strewn everywhere, and one of Bia's arms stuck inside her coat as she flapped around to try and get it off. Bia caught her eye and held up a bottle of wine in her non-trapped hand. 'I saved the essentials, and that's what counts.' She carefully set the wine down on the step that led up to the kitchen, then manoeuvred her way out of her coat and flung it into her bedroom without looking. 'Come on, you look like you need a glass.'

Josie followed Bia obediently to the open-plan kitchen-slash-living room and perched on their secondhand sofa while Bia clunked around in the kitchen for glasses. The living room was currently cosy and festive – fairy lights across the top of the fake fireplace and around the windows, a bowl of nuts on the coffee table in the middle of the room and a small Christmas tree in the corner, decorated erratically with blue, silver, red and gold baubles and tinsel, so that if you stared at it for too long you felt dizzy. All Bia's handiwork, except for one decoration on the tree – a small wooden swan – which Bia had given Josie the first year they lived together and forced her to put on the tree every year since then.

How lucky Josie was that Bia had been one of the four people she'd shared a house with when she first moved to London. She'd known no one here, so had to opt for the SpareRoom option, making a decision on which place to rent based on a twenty-minute viewing and awkward chat with the other housemates. It had been Bia's sparkle then that had sold her on that first place and now, eight years later, they were still living together, albeit in a different flat.

'So,' said Bia, setting down a glass of red in front of Josie, before leaning against the counter which separated the living room and kitchen, 'I passed short-arse coming down the stairs.' At four foot nine, Bia was hardly in the position to call anyone short, but she'd always been sure that Oliver had a complex over being just a few centimetres shorter than Josie. Maybe she was right, thought Josie, given Cara was perfectly petite and not long and gawky like her.

Josie scowled her displeasure to Bia, who already knew all about the break-up and how he'd told her he'd slept with someone else while she was still in bed, barely awake and not yet dressed.

'Want to talk about it?' Bia asked.

10

Josie shrugged. 'Nothing more to say. He was just dropping back my stuff.'

Bia snorted. 'Nice of him.'

'Quite.'

Bia took a gulp of wine, closed her eyes and groaned in not entirely faked pleasure. 'Thank God for that,' Bia sighed. 'I swear to God, Jose, if someone offers me one more glass of mulled wine, I'm going to throw some goddamn mulled water in their face.'

Josie raised her eyebrows. 'What happened to the jolly, festive you?'

'Oh, she's still here, but she wants champagne, not stewed alcohol.' Bia took another grateful gulp of wine and Josie sipped hers too.

'It's nice.'

'Malbec.' Bia grinned. 'To get me in the mood for my flight tomorrow.'

Josie frowned. 'What?'

'Don't tell me you've forgotten.'

Josie hesitated, caught in the headlights.

'Argentina!' cried Bia, her wine sloshing dangerously close to the surface of the glass as she punched it in the air. 'Remember? You were the one who told me to go for it. I'm going to go, find the lust of my life, spend Christmas on the beach, then party in Buenos Aires for New Year. I told you this,' she insisted.

'Yes, but I didn't think . . .' Josie didn't finish the sentence. She'd told Bia to go for it, yes, assuming, at the time, that she'd be spending Christmas with Oliver like they'd planned, but she hadn't really thought she'd book it. Bia was constantly announcing grand plans and then never

11

following through – over the summer she gave up on a month-long yoga retreat in Spain because she decided she didn't really like yoga, then there was the time she signed up for acting courses in London before figuring out she couldn't afford them, or when she thought it would be brilliant to make some more money selling beauty products from home, until she discovered that actually involved quite a lot of effort.

'. . . and when I come back, I will miraculously have figured out what I want to do with my life and can quit this terrible PA job.' Josie nodded, and tried to look like she'd been paying attention to everything Bia had just said. 'That's how it works, right? Life-changing holiday, life epiphany?'

'What? Yeah, that's how it works, for sure.'

Bia twisted her lips, clearly unimpressed with Josie's lack of enthusiasm. 'Unless you think I should be a PA for the rest of my life?'

'No, don't be silly,' Josie said. Though in all honesty, it was relatively hard to keep up with what Bia was doing for work at any point in time – she hadn't stuck to the same job for more than eight months since Josie had known her, though she didn't look at it as being flaky, just as figuring out what she wanted to do. Living that way would give Josie near constant heart failure, she was sure, but it worked for Bia.

'Jose, are you ok?' Bia frowned down at her.

'Yeah,' said Josie, taking a big gulp of wine as a distraction. 'Just, you know, Oliver.' Bia nodded sympathetically. In truth, Josie hadn't quite realised she'd be spending Christmas alone until just now. She hadn't given it a huge amount of thought, trying to put off thinking about the day as she always did, but if she had, she'd have assumed Bia would be around for most of it at least, given Bia's parents lived in London too. Now, she was facing the quite grim prospect of spending over a week alone in this flat. She glanced automatically to the coffee table in front of her, to the three envelopes there that she'd been preoccupied with before Oliver had interrupted. The first, unopened, was a formal letter from her company. The second, a Christmas card from her grandmother, reminding her, again, that she was welcome to stay with them for Christmas. And the third, the same letter she wrote every year without fail, to her parents.

Bia followed Josie's gaze, but didn't ask, and for that Josie was grateful. She couldn't face telling Bia about her job yet, and Bia already knew why Josie couldn't bring herself to spend Christmas with her grandparents. But she didn't know about the last letter. Josie hadn't ever told anyone about that – it was something private, something she did just for herself.

'You could come with me, you know,' Bia said softly. 'The offer's still there, I'd love to have you with me.' Josie looked up, and hated the understanding she saw on Bia's face. It made her head hurt, trying to stop herself from giving in to the urge to cry all over again. Today had been a rough day, that was all.

Josie hesitated, then sighed. 'I can't. I'm sorry.' Because the thought of booking a ticket to fly tomorrow was too much, given how drastically her life had already changed in a matter of weeks. She'd seen first-hand how impulsive decisions could lead to devastating consequences, and while that sort of spontaneity seemed to work for Bia, it wasn't something she'd ever been able to do. Just the thought of it sent a writhing ball of anxiety through her stomach.

'Well, what about Laura then?' Bia asked, referring to Josie's self-proclaimed work wife. 'You know, for Christmas?'

'She's off to Scotland with her hunky Scottish fiancé.'

Bia shook her head. 'Typical. Ok, well, look, I've got another bottle of this hiding in my handbag . . .'

'Of course you do.'

'So let's drink our way through this and the next one, order a takeaway and maybe put on *Love Actually*, or, as it's your pick, like *Pride and Prejudice* or something.'

Josie wrinkled her nose. 'Not really in a romantic film kind of mood.'

'*Lord of the Rings*?'

Josie laughed. She looked from Bia, her heart-shaped face currently framed with curly bright red hair, hair which she'd dyed to go with the festive period but was liable to change at a moment's notice, to the over-decorated Christmas tree, and felt her chest tighten painfully at the thought of a Bia-free flat as of tomorrow. The burning behind her eyes was back. God, she needed to get a grip on herself. She glanced down at the envelopes on the table again, thought of everything they signified, and knew she had to get out of the house.

'Hold that thought. I've just got to post this letter, then I'll be back.'

'Now?' Bia exclaimed incredulously.

'I'll be back,' Josie repeated, pushing to her feet and

14

setting the half-empty glass of wine down on the kitchen counter beside Bia before she grabbed the three letters. She dropped two of them on her bed beside the box of her things while she grabbed her phone, bike lock and bank card – just in case – from her room.

When she strode back along the corridor towards the front door, Bia was standing at the top of the step in the living room, watching her over the rim of her wine glass. 'If this is you bolting because you smell smoke and I don't or something, then I'm definitely going to come back to haunt you after I burn alive.'

Josie rolled her eyes as she slipped on her coat, put on her trainers and tucked the last letter inside her pocket. 'Lovely, graphic image there.'

'Alright, but hur-ry,' Bia said, drawing out the syllables on the last word. 'If you're not back soon, I'm finishing the rest of your wine. I'll drink it out of your glass, no shame.' Josie waved a hand over her shoulder at Bia as she let herself out of the flat.

As soon as she was the other side of the door, she allowed her face to crumple and screwed up her eyes. Of the last twenty years, there had never been one where she'd looked forward to Christmas Day. She'd long since forgotten what it had been like to be a child, desperate and excited for Santa to come, listening out for the creak of a parent's footstep. And though she liked the break from work every year and enjoyed the extra time to spend with friends, who were inevitably in better moods and looking for excuses for fun as the day grew nearer, she dreaded the countdown to Christmas itself, to the reminders it brought. The last few years, she'd got through it in London by keeping busy and distracted, which had been made easy by good friends, especially Bia and Laura, a demanding job, and, more recently, Oliver. And now, at least two of those things had been taken away from her. Josie slid a hand into her coat pocket and ran two fingers over the smooth envelope. Christmas, it seemed, was looking very bleak indeed this year.

Chapter Two

The cold, damp air whipped past Josie's face as she let her bike whizz down the side of Streatham Common, past the runners trudging their way up the other side of the road, her gloved fingers resting lightly on the brakes. Her breath misted out in front of her, the puffs soon disappearing into the little bubble of darkness around her – darkness that never extended too far here with all the lights and people, not like the little village she grew up in, where she'd learned to take a torch every time she stepped outside at night. Her cheeks were already freezing, and it felt like little misty water droplets were clinging to her skin, though it wasn't raining. There had been a lot of talk of snow recently, in the office and on the news, the whole country getting excited about the prospect of a White Christmas, as it seemed to do every year. Josie would much rather take the rain, though she knew that was a controversial opinion and one often best kept to herself. But for her, the snow only brought on painful memories of Christmas Day twenty years ago, of watching

17

through the window as fluffy snowflakes fell onto an empty driveway outside her grandparents' house, a full but unopened stocking lying next to her, listening to her grandmother stifling sobs from where she made Josie a hot chocolate in the next room.

Josie screwed up her face against the stinging in her nose and gulped in more air, coughing on the car fumes that she accidentally swallowed at the same time. She turned right at the bottom of the hill and pedalled faster, past the train station, past the first post box she saw. She wasn't ready to post her letter and turn back yet, was desperate to forget about the terrible day she'd just had.

She was forced to come to a stop at the next set of traffic lights, panting harder than she should be, given how short a time she'd been on the bike. She waited while the man changed from red to green and a surge of people crossed the road in time to the beeping, heads down, keen to get home into the warm. But there were three people who didn't rush like the others, who strolled across smiling, oblivious to the commuter chaos around them. A family – mum, dad, and little boy of about five or six, Josie would guess. The boy was laughing, a reindeer head-band on top of his sandy hair, the horns flopping with the movement of his head. Both of his parents gripped one of his hands, and he swung back and forward, using their arms as levers to propel himself in whatever game he was lost in.

It reminded her so much of her and her parents, on evenings like this one, only quieter, without the buzz of traffic, the annoyed car horns, the people tssking when someone got in their way. The streets of her village may have been easier and safer to walk down, but she used to do that too, hold both her parents' hands, demand to be swung up on the count of three until she'd got too tall for them to manage it. That's how they'd walked down to the post box on the week before Christmas, every year since she could remember, and all the years she couldn't, according to her grandmother. Hand in hand, her in the middle with a letter to Santa tucked into her coat pocket, ready to send to the North Pole.

It was her ninth year that stuck out in her memory. It had snowed that year and she'd been delighted, running around leaving fresh footprints in that way you can only do in the countryside, demanding to pick up a carrot from the shop for the all-important nose of a snowman. None of the carrots they had at home were right – it had to be perfect, she'd insisted. So they'd posted her letter on the way to the shop, and she'd only stopped swinging on her parents' arms when her mum nearly lost her balance on the icy side of the pavement. For some reason that particular moment was imprinted on Josie's mind – the way her mother's fluffy brown boot had slipped, how she'd grabbed Josie's hand to right herself, nearly pulling her over as she did so. How her mother had laughed at herself for being so silly, how she and Josie's dad had grinned at each other over the top of Josie's head. A premonition of what was to come a week later, Josie often thought now.

What had she written in her letter to Santa that day? She remembered the way the snow had felt crunching underfoot, the way her fingers had started to feel numb as they neared the post box, even through her red gloves. She remembered her mum's silver bobble hat, pulled over her long mousy-brown hair, making her look like a princess, Josie had thought at the time. And she could hear her dad's voice, listing silly things she could have put on the list – a left sock, an onion, a new dishwasher. But she hadn't the faintest clue what she'd actually wanted for Christmas that year, what her nine-year-old heart had craved.

She'd still believed in Santa then, though. It wasn't until the year after, when he didn't bring her the one and only thing she wrote on her list, delivered to the post box as usual, with her grandmother holding her hand where her mum should have been, that she stopped believing.

That didn't stop the tradition, though. After that year, she carried on writing a letter every Christmas, still took it to the post box. It was something she'd never been able to let go of. Only now the letter was very different, and it said the same thing every year.

Dear Mum and Dad, Missing you always. Merry Christmas and lots of love, Josie.

A loud beep of a car horn jolted Josie back to reality. She realised she was in the way – the lights had changed, but she was holding up traffic behind her because she was waiting close to the middle of the road, rather than off to the left as she should have been. She grimaced and fumbled to get her trainers on the pedals, pushing off and getting quickly to the side of the road, deliberately not looking at the car behind her for fear of seeing the glare of the driver. She brushed away a tear that had escaped without her notice, took a breath to stem the flow, and started pedalling again. She passed another post box, but she wasn't ready to go back to her flat, wasn't ready to smile and drink and talk about what a wonderful time

Bia would have on her adventure. She needed to get her head on straight first. Think about something else, she told herself firmly. Automatically, her mind turned to work, which wasn't overly helpful right now. Because all that did was conjure up an image of her boss, flicking back her dead straight black hair, having pulled her into one of the little glass cubicles, which everyone could see straight into, for a 'chat'.

Josie, I'm afraid there's something we need to talk about.

Josie gritted her teeth and pedalled faster, overtaking the cyclist in front of her. She was on Streatham High Road now, underneath the Christmas lights that, while nowhere near as impressive as those on Oxford Street, still put to shame the little display that her village had been so proud of. She wondered if they still did that there now, and how much the Christmas tradition had changed. Everyone used to gather together to watch the lights switched on, with people handing out homemade mulled wine and mince pies, using it as an excuse to catch up on the latest gossip. She'd gone with her parents every year, disappearing with her best friend from school the moment they got there, hunting out the chocolates that were always inevitably left somewhere unattended. Her grandparents had tried to take her along that first year after it happened, but she hadn't stop crying the whole time, and they'd stopped going after that. She wondered if they'd started going again after she'd left for university, staying away for the Christmas holidays without fail, or if it was too painful for them, too. She'd never been able to bring herself to ask.

She scowled at herself as she swerved to avoid a

pedestrian who wasn't looking when they stepped onto the road. She wasn't supposed to be thinking of that, that was definitely not distracting herself. Fine, then, if not work then something else. But of course, the something else was inevitably Oliver. Oliver, telling her he had something to talk to her about while she was sat in his bed. Oliver, laughing off her comments about Cara giving him the eye during their Christmas lunch, telling her he'd be back soon, he was just staying for one more. And Cara herself, tossing back her soft curls, watching Oliver with those bright blue eyes, framed with gold eyeliner and wearing that stunner of a red dress.

A red dress, just like her mum's red dress, the one she wore to the Christmas Eve party. The party her parents weren't going to go to, but changed their minds about at the last minute because Josie's grandmother persuaded them. Her mum had been wearing red lipstick to match the red dress, which she'd let Josie apply.

'Be good, won't you, Posie?' Her dad's voice, fuzzy in her memory because she couldn't quite recall the way it sounded. His arms grabbing her sides and swinging her up and around, her squeals of delight, her mum wincing because she was really too heavy to still be doing that. *'There's still time for Santa to change his mind, you know.'*

Josie hit the traffic lights just right this time, getting through just before they changed to amber. Her breathing was coming faster and faster, but she pushed on, needing to feel the burn in her thighs.

Her grandmother, patting her mum's hand. *'You go and have a good time, love, we'll be fine here, won't we, Josie?'*

Josie nodded, her hair plaited, ready to sleep in it like that so it would go curly for Christmas Day, because her hair looked best curly, and everyone knew you had to look your best on Christmas Day. She didn't really want her parents to go, she wanted them to stay and watch the film with her, but they'd promised they would be here in the morning, that she could go to their bedroom the moment she woke up to open her stocking.

Josie's vision was blurry now, the headlights of cars looking more like flames, dancing out to other parts of the road, encasing everything in an orange glow.

The police on the doorstep, speaking to her grandfather, who was still wearing his tartan dressing gown. Josie creeping downstairs, wondering how everyone else could be up before her, wondering if she'd already missed the pancakes her mum made every year for Christmas breakfast. Her grandmother's face, pale, eyes red, as she turned to look at her.

'Let's go upstairs for a minute, shall we, Josie love?'

The tears were coming freely now, no chance of stopping them. They traced paths of heat down her cold cheeks and she tasted the salt of them as they pooled in the corner of her mouth.

Lights flashed again as she tried to clear her vision, unsure if the flash was in the present or in her memory. A car horn echoing round her mind. Her parents' faces, illuminated in the headlights. She hadn't been there, but that didn't stop her from imagining it, over and over.

The horn again, louder now. She gasped, swerving back into the cycle lane, and looked down to change gear as her gloves slipped on the metal.

She looked up to see a black cab pulled over on the road right in front of her, across the cycle lane, hazard

23

lights flashing. She fumbled with her brakes but the door to the taxi was already opening on the pavement side. She swore, swerved, and had only a fleeting impression of a man's face as he got out of the taxi and slammed the door behind him, glancing towards her just in time to see her coming at him.

Her brakes screeched painfully, and she tried to swing the bike left, out of his way. But it wasn't enough. Her heart gave a warning slam in her chest, and for a paralysing second she met the man's confused gaze, the light of her bike reflected in his eyes.

Then he was slammed backwards, and her bike skidded away from her. She shoved her hands out and pain shot through her wrists as she landed on the tarmac with a thump.

Chapter Three

Josie stayed sprawled on the ground, her heart pounding, ears ringing. Her knees stung and she could feel the dampness of the road seeping in through her tights. As she pushed herself into an awkward kneel, she realised her hands were shaking.

There were several people clustered around her, one of whom was shouting, she noticed now, the sound finally getting through the buzzing in her ears. She focused in on a figure marching around from the other side of the taxi – a woman. A short, slightly plump woman. Why was she shouting at her? Then she got it – this was the taxi driver.

'Didn't you see me here?' she screamed, her voice disproportionately deep compared to her size. 'What the hell were you thinking, coming at us at that speed? Do you not have eyes? Do you not think it might have been sensible to slow the bloody hell down?'

Josie scrambled all the way to her feet, wincing a little. She wasn't seriously hurt, but her arm had twisted awkwardly from where she'd tried to cushion her fall, and she was pretty sure she'd have a bruise on her hip when she checked later. And her tights had laddered. Great. Well, that's what you got for cycling in completely impractical clothes, she supposed.

One of the passers-by who had stopped to witness the spectacle asked if she was ok, and she nodded, dumbfounded, while taxi woman continued to rant, her eyes skimming over Josie to a spot behind her. Josie jumped, remembering, far too late, about the man she'd hit. She spun, her heart renewing its gallop.

Her breath loosened a little when she saw him. Another man, slightly balding, had stopped to help him, and he was already getting slowly to his feet, his movements slow and awkward. She jerked towards him, her nerves fizzing, mouth dry.

'Are you ok?' she blurted out, but he didn't seem to hear her above all the interested chattering of the little group around them. The balding man was now holding out to him a wallet, and a few stray bits of paper he must have dropped. She stumbled forward another step, earning an evil glare from taxi woman. God, what if he was hurt? He was up, but he looked a bit unsteady on his feet – what if he had a broken rib or something?

'I'm . . .' She tried again, but stopped, sucking in a tight breath when he finally looked at her. She couldn't quite make out the whole of his face, only got an impression of a somewhat chiselled jaw and messy hair, but she swore she saw it darken, the night's shadows winning out over the pockets of light from the streetlamps and headlights. She took another wavering step towards him, wrapping her arms around herself. 'I'm so sorry,' she breathed. He said nothing, just dismissed her with a glance and turned instead to Balding, who was helping him to take the last of his belongings.

Josie became very aware of the clamminess of her palms. 'I really, I don't know what to say, I can't apologise enough,' she babbled, wishing he'd just meet her gaze, rather than now looking at the tarmac, frowning, as if she weren't worth paying attention to. 'I just, I don't know what happened, I wasn't concentrating, it was completely my fault and I—'

He held up a hand as the crowd around them began to disperse, losing interest now the drama of the moment was over. He looked her up and down, as if weighing up the sincerity of her words, taking in her laddered tights, the skirt of her work dress poking out beneath her blue winter coat, purple and white trainers that definitely did not go with the outfit. Her body felt stiff and when his gaze travelled up to her face, she felt her cheeks warm. She had no doubt she looked a total mess – he probably thought he'd been run over by a complete lunatic.

'It's fine,' he said, his voice clipped and low enough that it barely carried over the sound of the traffic. He turned away from her again to thank the balding man, who nodded, glanced at Josie in a curious sort of way, then headed off up the street.

'It is not bloody well fine,' taxi woman muttered. But she'd already turned her back on them both, apparently deciding that, now it was clear no one was seriously injured, she was better off out of it.

Josie hovered awkwardly. Her knee was throbbing now, but she didn't want to bend down to check it in case that

27

looked like she was more concerned with herself than the stranger she'd just knocked off his feet. Now that they were the only two people left, he glanced over to her and his eyes flickered briefly, as if he was surprised to see she was still hanging around. She couldn't quite make out the colour, wasn't sure if they just looked dark because of his expression. He was about her age, she realised, and a couple of inches taller than her.

'I'm really, really sorry,' she said again, aware that she sounded like a broken record, but completely at a loss as to what else she could say that wouldn't sound utterly wrong, given the circumstances.

'I said it's fine,' he said on a tired sigh. Not as clipped as before, but still not quite what she was after. Josie bit her lip, but before she could say anything else, the taxi driver wound down the window on the passenger side.

'All good here then?' she asked, clearly making an effort not to look at Josie, seeming to decide this was a better form of punishment than shouting at her.

The man nodded. 'All good, cheers.' Oh sure, with the taxi driver he was perfectly affable. But then, Josie supposed she'd been helping him get to where he was going, not knocking him over the moment he got there.

'Right-oh.' And with that she rolled up the window and pulled back out onto the road behind a bus.

The man frowned again the moment the taxi drove away, and turned his attention back to the road. The way he was determinedly ignoring her, she could probably have got away with just leaving him, but it felt wrong to abandon him. She glanced down at the road too, and noticed what he was looking for before he did. She grabbed his phone, a metre or so from where he stood, and her stomach twisted as she saw the screen was completely smashed.

'Shit,' she muttered, grimacing apologetically as she held it out to him. 'I'm so—'

'Sorry?' He raised his eyebrows as he took it from her and she felt herself flush. His eyes were green, she realised now she was closer, though they were those fancy two-toned kind of eyes, with a ring of something lighter around the edges. It felt wrong to describe the second colour as 'gold', given the way his eyes seemed to scowl without so much as a furrow of eyebrows.

'I'll pay for it,' she said immediately. She wondered what model of iPhone it was, how much that would set her back, whether she'd have to use her credit card to pay for it. He didn't reply, just pocketed the phone and grabbed her bike from where it was still strewn across the cycle path, pushing it up the kerb onto the pavement. She should have done that, she realised. The bike was in the way, and she hadn't even thought to move it.

She stepped up beside him. 'Seriously, let me pay for it. Maybe there's a phone shop near here that's still open and we can—'

'Stop.' He said it in such a final way that she did. 'I've said it's fine. Besides, we were parked on a cycle lane, weren't we? So you're not the only one to blame.' He jiggled the handlebars of her bike a little, as if impatient to be rid of it, and she took it awkwardly.

'I just . . .'

He sighed, slipped his phone out of his pocket, switched it on and held it out to her. It lit up to show his home screen, still visible beneath the cracked glass. 'See?' The word was a little aggressive. 'Still works and everything. And besides,' he carried on, overriding her protest, 'my contract's up soon. So if I'm not bothered about living with a smashed screen for a few weeks, then you really shouldn't be either. Ok?' It was a demand, more than a question.

'Well,' she said slowly. 'If you're sure. . .' The problem was, although he said it was all fine, he really sounded as though it was not in fact fine in the slightest. She bit her lip, trying to figure out what she was supposed to do now.

'Look, thanks for the concern and all, but I could use a pint after that, so I'll just . . .' He trailed off, looking up and down the road, then huffed and looked down at her. 'Do you know where the nearest pub is, by any chance?'

'I'll show you!' Josie knew she sounded far too enthusiastic, but she was determined to make him not so pissed off with her. He frowned and she nodded vigorously. 'I know a good one around here.' Well, 'good' might be a bit of an overstatement, but she'd been to one round the corner with Bia a few times on a Friday night. She started walking, pushing her bike in a way that made her have to hunch over awkwardly, and he followed along beside her.

'You don't have to walk me there,' he grumbled, shoving his hands into his coat, which was reminiscent of Benedict Cumberbatch's in *Sherlock* – long, grey and expensive-looking. 'You could just point me in the right direction.'

'It's no trouble!' she said, a little too squeakily, despite the fact that she was pretty sure that he wasn't really concerned with *her* trouble so much as didn't want her tagging along. Well, too bad. She'd show him the damn pub and maybe that would even out her karmic bad luck or whatever. He made absolutely no effort to start a conversation, seeming to be particularly focused on the pavement in front of them. She fought the scowl that wanted to settle on her face. She knew she'd run him over and all, but he didn't need to be such a prick about it – she'd have forgiven someone for doing it to her, she was sure. It wasn't like she'd done it on purpose.

After a full minute of silence, she was severely regretting not just giving him instructions and hopping on her bike. She tried desperately to think of something to say – but what did you say to the stranger you'd just knocked over in the middle of the road? She needed Bia. If Bia had done the same, she'd have this man laughing in two minutes tops.

'So, umm, were you on your way home from work?' she asked.

'No,' he said slowly, and the look he gave her was a little incredulous. She pushed her bike a bit faster. Well, no, ok – if he was on his way home from work then he would probably know the area, and therefore know where a pub would be. But, in her defence, he could be a hot-shot businessman or lawyer or something, living in a big house in the country and down in London for meetings. Besides, he didn't have to be so damn rude about it – he could show *some* appreciation for the fact she was trying to show him around. She sneaked another glance at him, but couldn't guess anything else about him, everything hidden under that damned coat.

'What about you?' he asked after a moment, with the distinct impression of someone forcing himself to continue the conversation.

She started, caught in the action of surreptitiously studying him. 'What?'

'Were you on the way back from work?'

'Oh right. No.' God, this guy must think she was a total idiot. She cleared her throat. 'No, I was just running a few errands.' She took the handlebars of her bike in one hand, felt automatically for the letter with the other, then jolted when she realised it wasn't there. She must have lost it in the road somewhere and not noticed.

'Everything ok?'

'Yeah. Sorry. It's just . . . I was sending a letter, I think I must have dropped it.' That was ok, though, she told herself. She'd write another one tomorrow and post it then.

'A letter?' His voice was a little less clipped this time, almost incredulous instead. 'People still write those these days?'

She shrugged. 'Well yeah, I guess so. Memo – my grandmother, that is – is always writing letters, even though she's the most technologically savvy person I know.' No need to tell him that's not who she was writing to this evening.

He stepped out of the way of a jogger, quiet for a moment. 'When I was a kid,' he said slowly, 'I used to try and get my friends at school to write me letters in the summer holidays, but it never quite caught on.'

He said the whole thing completely deadpan, but Josie let out a snort of laughter. 'Really?'

'Mmm. My best friend at the time, James Winterbourne, kept the letter I wrote to him and then read it out to everyone at school once we got back in September.'

She laughed again. 'That's so mean! What had you written?'

'God, I don't remember. It was just the principle of the thing that stuck with me more than anything. I never did quite forgive him for it.'

'Aha. So James Winterbourne has been struck off the wedding guest list for a letter-writing faux pas.' Though he met her gaze, her smile wasn't reflected.

'Quite.'

Damn, maybe she'd put her foot in it. Maybe he'd been married and it had all gone terribly wrong, or maybe he'd been jilted at the altar, or James Winterbourne had married the love of his life or something.

'So how come you're out this way then?' she asked, her voice cringeworthily jovial at the forced change of subject. 'Do you live in London?'

'No.' His voice was a little distant, but he shook his head and when he spoke again it was with a little more purpose. 'No, I'm from Bristol actually. Well, from a few places, I suppose, but I grew up in Bristol, and live there now.'

'So you're down here for Christmas?'

He grimaced. 'No. Well, I wasn't supposed to be.' He pulled a hand through his messy hair, and the coppery highlights in the brown caught the artificial light a little. 'I was due to fly out to New York today, but my flight has been cancelled because of some bloody storm.'

Josie frowned, looked up at the sky. It was cloudy, for sure, and the echo of misty rain still hung in the air, but it didn't exactly seem stormy. She glanced at the man to see him raising his eyebrows.

'There's obviously not a storm *here*,' he said, in a way that seemed condescending enough to make her flush again. 'But somewhere over the Atlantic or something. Anyway. I'm now on standby for a new flight, but looks like I'm stranded here for now.'

'That's so crap,' Josie said, hoping her voice was conveying adequate sympathy. 'So will you go back to Bristol now then?'

'No, I need to be here in case of flights, so I checked into a hotel I've stayed at before around here.'

She nodded as they came to a stop and gestured to her right at an old building. 'It doesn't look like much on the outside, but they do good beers, I think, and there's a nice garden out back.'

'Ah yes, useful in this lovely English summer we're in the midst of.'

It sounded like a joke, but if he'd bloody smile or something, then she could be sure. 'If you don't like the look of it, I can . . .'

'I'm not fussy.' He turned to face her. 'Thanks.' He pulled his hands out of his pockets and held one out to her. No wedding ring, so maybe the stolen love of his life theory was more likely. 'I'm Max, by the way.'

She took his hand in her gloved one. His grip was firm, sure, and though she wasn't exactly doll-sized like Bia, his hand made hers feel small. 'Josie.'

He smiled, finally. Just a small softening of his lips, but it made his chiselled face look less sharp. 'Well, it was nice to meet you, Josie, even if the manner of our meeting left a little to be desired.' She grimaced, though there was no venom in his voice.

He'd let go of her hand and turned away from her by the time she blurted out, 'Why don't I buy you a drink?'

He looked back at her, his brow furrowed over those shifting eyes. She rolled the bike back and forth on the pavement, pinpricks of heat travelling uncomfortably over her skin from the way he was considering her.

'I mean, as an apology. A drink in exchange for a phone.' And yes, that was part of the reason, because really, buying him a drink was the least she could do, but it wasn't all. Stranded here, he'd said. Alone at Christmas, though he hadn't explicitly said that. And right then, she didn't want him to be lonely, at least not in that exact moment, not when she knew exactly how that felt.

He cocked his head, as if weighing up her offer. 'A drink in exchange for a phone . . .' He shrugged. 'Ok.'

She bit her lip – he hadn't exactly sounded enthused by the idea. 'Ok?'

'Ok,' he repeated, completely deadpan, his expression giving nothing away.

She locked up her bike, already slightly regretting the impulse, being as how they seemed to have already run out of things to say to each other, then led the way inside. She immediately had to strip off her coat to deal with the onslaught of heat from the fire in the corner and the impressive mass of bodies crowding the place. She headed to the bar, decorated with that fake green tinsel and jars of fairy lights, wishing right then that she had a local pub she could have taken him to instead, one where the landlord knew her name, where she could be chatty to the staff, rather than risk being stilted and awkward, as she was feeling now. The closest thing she had to that in Streatham was the little pizza place down the road from her flat, which she and Bia often went to, where the waiters greeted them politely, but with an undercurrent of suspicion, like they were wondering if they had a secret, pizza-eating agenda.

A woman behind the bar, her hair in bunches despite the fact she'd got to be in her mid-twenties, sidled up to them, and flicked her gaze over Josie to settle on Max. She beamed widely, more at Max than Josie, and Josie looked at Max for the first time since entering the pub. Well, of course he'd have to be bloody attractive, wouldn't he? He'd taken off his Sherlock coat and was wearing a petrol-blue jumper underneath, which fitted his body snugly enough to make it obvious that he spent some time working out. The two-toned eyes were more obvious now in the light, the dark green merging subtly into amber. His hair was ever so slightly wavy, though she wasn't sure if the windswept look was something natural, or because of their little accident just now, and there was exactly the right amount of stubble grazing his jaw.

'What can I get you?' the barmaid asked.

'Umm, I'll have a glass of house red,' Josie said, looking questioningly at Max, who shrugged.

'Sure, I'll have the same.'

Drinks in hand, Josie managed to find a small corner table and slipped into the booth, leaving him to take the chair opposite. Max grimaced as he sat down. 'What's wrong?' Josie asked quickly. If he was in pain from the accident, maybe she'd allow him to be a bit pissed off with her.

Max raised his eyebrows in a way that suggested she might have sounded a bit too concerned, and nodded up towards the ceiling. She frowned and looked up, but he shook his head. 'No, the music.'

She listened. 'God, terrible,' she said. 'Impossible to escape the endless Christmas songs at this time of year though. You just have to grit your teeth and block it out.'

His lips twitched as he met her gaze, not quite giving in to a full smile or, God forbid, the hint of a laugh. 'Cheers to that,' he said, and they clinked glasses. She took a sip. It wasn't as nice as the wine Bia had brought home, but it wasn't bad.

Max relaxed back against his chair, his eyes fixed on her face in a way that felt a little intense. 'So, Josie. Tell me. What is it that you do, when you're not off kamikaze bike-riding, running down strangers on the road?'

She took another sip of wine. 'Oh that's my main profession actually.'

'Aha. That would explain the expert way you did it then. A lot of money in it?'

'Tons.' He did that lip twitch thing again. 'I'm in marketing,' she admitted.

'*In* marketing,' he mused.

'Yeah, I work for an agency.' She paused, then added, in a slightly put-on voice, 'Peacock PR and Marketing.'

He let out a short burst of laughter, which surprised her so much that she jumped a little. 'Peacock PR? Are you serious?'

'Unfortunately, yes.'

'So what kind of thing do you work on?'

She waved a hand in the air. 'All sorts. At the moment we're rebranding a "luxury" beachwear company.' She

37

did the air quotes around 'luxury', because she was very aware that if she didn't, she sounded far too much like Janice.

He nodded sagely. 'Busy time of year for them, is it?'

'You'd be surprised. All the rich people going on beach holidays, getting a dose of winter sun and all that.'

'Or Christmas presents,' he pointed out.

'Exactly.'

'Or, you know, people who want to look sexy in their bikini on Christmas Day. To make a change from the sparkly dress.'

'Right,' she said. 'We did some market research a few years ago, turns out a lot of the British population actually swan around eating their roast dinners in bikinis. So my company was like, there's an untapped market right there.'

He nodded seriously, taking a sip of wine. 'Genius. So do they do Christmas swimwear? Themed things like Santa or snowmen or something?'

She laughed. 'No, but I'll pitch the idea to the client.' Her phone buzzed from inside her coat on the booth seat, and she slipped it out of her pocket. Thank God her phone, unlike his, had survived the fall. She definitely did not have any spare cash to be buying a new one right now.

Where are you? Did you get lost?

Bia. Josie tapped out a quick reply.

Just picking up a few things, back soon.

Because, somehow, explaining that she'd nearly run over a strange man and was now having a drink with said man didn't feel like the kind of thing you relay over WhatsApp. Even if, for Bia, the fact that he was hot would probably be enough explanation.

'Everything alright?' Max asked.

'Yeah. Just my flatmate.'

'Just the one?'

'Yeah, for the last few years. How about you – do you live with anyone?'

He frowned, like the question was unnecessarily intrusive, despite the fact he'd just asked the exact same thing. 'No,' he said slowly. 'At the moment it's only me.' She wondered again about her jilted lover theory, but her phone buzzed again before she could answer.

What things?? Whatever it is, stop it and come home. I'm drinking all the wine alone and it's making me sad.

Josie snorted.

Stop it then! You'll be hungover for your flight tomorrow.

Exactly. You need to come and save me from myself.

Smiling, Josie tucked the phone away, and looked up to find Max watching her in a way that made heat trickle down the back of her neck. 'Sorry, I'm going to have to go. My flatmate flies to Argentina tomorrow and I want to say bye . . .'

'Of course.' He glanced to the bar, which had filled up quite dramatically since they'd been sitting here, the after-work crowd arriving in force. 'Well, I'm not facing that queue for a solo drink.' He got to his feet and finished the last of his wine as she gathered up her coat. Together, they pushed their way through to the front door. Outside, Josie took a breath of cold air, enjoying the feel of the breeze as it whisked away the heat from her neck even as it made her shiver.

Max turned to face her, slipping on his coat. 'Well, thanks for the drink. You've more than made up for trying to run me over.'

She wrinkled her nose. 'I really am sorry about that, you know.'

'Really? You should have said.'

She let out a little laugh, then crossed the pavement to where she'd locked her bike around a lamppost. 'So how come you're supposed to be going to New York?'

'My parents live there. Said I'd spend Christmas with them this year.' His voice was light enough but there was something there – something oddly similar to the way her voice sounded when she talked about Christmas plans. Though maybe she was just reading into it or projecting or whatever. And even if not, it was hardly her place to ask.

'They live there? So did you grow up there or something?' She cocked her head. 'You don't sound American.'

He smiled. 'No, I got stuck with my sexy British accent. My mum's American, but she moved here when she met my dad, so two years ago she made him move back to New York with her in payment.'

She turned her attention to her bike. 'I guess that sounds fair enough. So what will you do, while you're stuck in London?' She frowned in concentration as she tried to unlock her bike. She'd stupidly put her gloves on before she tried to do it, which made the whole thing slightly trickier.

40

He leaned against the lamppost, watching her struggle. 'Room service and films is my current plan.'

'Well, why don't you do some of the Christmassy things in London while you're here?'

'As in Winter Wonderland and all that?'

She laughed. 'You don't have to sound so scathing. It's actually not that bad. I usually hate all that stuff too, but my flatmate made me go a few years ago and it was actually a lot of fun and . . .' She trailed off. The only reason it had been fun was because Bia made it so, getting really excited by the whole ordeal and dragging Josie from one thing to the next. But Max would be doing it alone, stuck here without friends or family. She cleared her throat and glanced up to see him watching her, with that same intense gaze. 'It, ah, has drinks and food and ice-skating and stuff. Or stalls to do last-minute Christmas shopping, that kind of thing.'

He nodded slowly. 'Alright. I think you should take me, then.' He said it evenly, but it still made her jolt.

'What?'

'I think you should take me,' he repeated, slipping his hands into his pockets. 'To make up for running me over.'

She cocked her head. 'Didn't you just say the drink had made up for that?'

He shrugged. 'I changed my mind. So, I'll meet you there at two?'

'Two?'

'Yeah. That way, if we hate it, we won't have to spend the whole day there.'

She could only stare at him, not really sure how she'd

got herself into this. Her plans for tomorrow had consisted of watching TV and crying over Oliver with copious amounts of chocolate. It was probably because of that, that she squared her shoulders. 'Ok.'

His lips did that twitchy, almost a smile thing again. 'Ok?'

She nodded. 'Ok.'

Chapter Four

'Josie I can't see you, where did you go?' Josie glared at the back of the stranger who had just bumped into her then lifted her phone up again so she could see Memo's face – and half of her grandad's.

'Sorry,' Josie said. 'The joys of walking through Central London on a Saturday.' The Saturday before Christmas, no less, when everyone seemed to be in a general rush and panic, or too caught up in the bloody festive spirit to notice when someone was walking towards you. Mind you, Josie thought, trying to be reasonable, she was hardly one to talk – holding her mobile in front of her was hardly conducive to paying attention to where you were going, but Memo had insisted on sticking with the FaceTime call as planned.

'I do wish you'd stand still, my love, your head moving like that is making my eyes go funny.'

Josie laughed as she crossed the road from Green Park station. 'Come on, Memo, you're not that old. And I can't anyway – I'll be late to meet my friend.' Something in Josie's stomach twisted at the thought of *who* she was going to meet, but she tried to keep any trace of that from her face.

'Bia?' her grandad asked, popping his head into full view of the screen and making Memo tssk at him as he invaded her space.

'No, not Bia,' Josie said, shaking her head slightly. Her grandad had met Bia once at Josie's birthday party a few years ago, and had been slightly enamoured with her ever since.

'Who then?' Memo demanded, pushing Grandad back to his side of the red sofa – the one that they'd had ever since Josie was little, the one that had a permanent indent from where her grandad sat in the same spot every evening without fail to watch the local news.

'I do have other friends, you know,' Josie said, by way of a non-answer.

'Of course you do,' Memo said. Her eyes – brown, like Josie's, like her dad's – sparked in that defensive way of hers, the spark that used to come out whenever Josie had said someone was mean to her at school. The spark that Josie saw a bit too much recently – a sure sign that Memo wasn't convinced that Josie was 'totally loving London life', as she so often claimed.

'Where *is* Bia?' her grandad mumbled, the half side of his face that Josie could see looking slightly forlorn.

'She's . . .' Josie hesitated. 'On her way to Argentina, actually.'

'Argentina!' Memo smiled, and reached up to pat her hair – grey, because *there's no point pretending I'm anything but ancient, my darling,* but neatly styled into a bob that she had cut and blow-dried in the local village salon every week. 'Do you remember when we went to Argentina, John?' She prodded Josie's grandad in the ribs and elicited a grunt, then turned back to Josie, while Josie waited at a traffic light to cross the road. Nearly there now. Her stomach jumped again and she told it, silently, to calm itself down. 'It was such fun, we did it on our tour around South America. Did I tell you about that, Josie?'

'You did,' Josie confirmed. Back when Josie had first left school, Memo had relayed every single travelling story she could think of, in order to try and convince Josie to take some time out to study, but Josie had never really been the travelling type.

'Wait,' Memo said, frowning. 'If Bia's not there, then who will you be spending Christmas with?'

'I . . .' Josie made a show of looking away from the phone and around her, as if she was checking for traffic as she crossed the road.

'Are you . . . You're not still planning on spending it with Oliver, are you?'

Josie wrinkled her nose. 'No. Absolutely not.'

Her grandad muttered something that sounded like, 'Ought to give him a piece of my mind.'

'But then, oh Josie, please don't tell me you'll be spending Christmas alone in that little flat of yours?'

'Memo, I've told you so many times, I *like* spending Christmas alone.' That was only sort of a lie, Josie reasoned, because she'd still rather spend it alone, pretending that it was a normal day, than go back to the village where her parents were killed. 'And I like my flat,' she said, a little defensively.

45

Memo waved a slim hand in the air. 'Yes, yes, it's a lovely flat, but why don't you come here, my love? Helen's coming and we'd all love to have you here.'

'I can't,' Josie said firmly. 'And I have a work party on Christmas Eve anyway,' she added, talking over whatever protest Memo was about to mount. 'So it just wouldn't be practical.' She swiped down to check the time on her phone and bit her lip. She'd be early at this rate, and she couldn't be having that. She slowed her pace considerably, which was probably for the best anyway – the cold air was stinging her cheeks right now, but she was starting to get warm inside her coat from hurrying, and she didn't want to arrive all hot and flustered.

'So how come Helen is spending Christmas at yours? What happened to spending Christmas with Mike's family?'

Memo rolled her eyes. 'Oh, she broke up with Mike, didn't she tell you?'

'What? Are you serious?' Mike was her aunt Helen's third husband, and Josie had really thought it might last this time. She sighed. 'So, you were right then. What did you give it, six months?'

'I'm always right about Helen, my love – a mother knows her daughter.' It hung in the space between them for a moment – the fact that Josie's mother wasn't here, the fact that Josie's mother would never get to know her the way her grandmother did. Then Memo smiled and the tinge of sadness between them was gone, taken away in that way that only Memo could do. 'Did I tell you I bumped into Pippa Cope the other day? Do you remember her – Beth Cope's mum? You went to school together.'

'I remember,' Josie said vaguely.

'Well, Pippa told me that Beth is pregnant again! Isn't that nice?'

'Sure,' Josie agreed, though in reality, being as how she hadn't spoken to Beth since she was about fifteen, and hadn't even known that she'd had a child already, the news was somewhat hard to get excited about.

'It's such a nice place to raise children here, don't you think?'

Josie huffed out a laugh as the sound of tinny Christmas music wafted over to her above the sound of engines and car horns. It was getting busier now, hordes of people clogging up the street. She stopped, leaned against the railings of the park. No point in trying to keep up FaceTime against this tide. 'Yes, I'm sure it is a lovely place to raise children, Memo, but I don't *have* any children, so let's not go there just now, ok?'

'I'm just saying,' Memo said, with a little eyebrow raise to underline the point. 'And even if not, you might be a bit happier here around your family, don't you think?'

'I am happy,' Josie said automatically. Memo pursed her lips and looked like she might argue the point further, but Grandad helpfully chose that moment to get up off the couch, groaning slightly as he did so.

Josie frowned. 'Is your back playing up again, Grandad?'

'It is,' Memo answered. 'I've told him to stop using that bloody ancient lawnmower as it weighs a ton, but you know what he's like.'

Josie glanced up the road, towards Winter Wonderland. 'Memo, I'm really sorry but I have to go, otherwise I'm going to be late.'

'But we haven't done the quotes yet! It's my turn this week.'

'Right, ok.' Josie gestured for her grandmother to go ahead.

Memo paused and held her hands up for dramatic effect. 'I'll have what she's having.'

Josie rolled her eyes theatrically. 'Come on, we watched that together!' Memo just waited expectantly. '*When Harry Met Sally.*'

Memo nodded. 'That was your mum's favourite film, you know.'

Josie smiled. 'I remember, you told me.' Her grandparents were her dad's parents, but that didn't stop Memo from providing her with just as many memories about her mum, and Josie loved her for it. 'But now, I really have to say goodbye, ok?'

'Fine, fine. I love you, my darling.' A muffled sound from off screen. 'Grandad says he loves you too, he's just got a mouthful of biscuit.'

Josie laughed. 'Glad to know where I stand in the pecking order of granddaughter versus Hobnob. I love you both too.'

Josie hung up and shoved her phone in her pocket, then braved the chaos as she fought her way to the gate where she and Max had arranged to meet.

Max was waiting for her, standing casually, hands tucked into the pockets of his Sherlock coat, by one of the barriers next to the slightly tacky golden arch. The words *Winter Wonderland* were emblazoned on it, with a bespectacled

Father Christmas on one side of the lettering, smiling benignly down on those who walked underneath him. Max hadn't noticed her yet – unsurprising given the crowds of people jostling for space around him. Jesus, she'd forgotten the sheer number of people from last time she'd been here with Bia. She clocked a couple of girls going in, walking through the archway, both of whom looked back at Max to give him a second glance. He seemed totally oblivious, and Josie wondered if that was because he was used to it, or because he really had no idea how good looking he was.

She kept her head down, glancing up every few seconds as she walked briskly towards him, trying her best to avoid that awkward eye-contact thing where you spot each other from a distance and then have to keep away and back again until you reach each other. Unlike the other loners around him, Max didn't have his phone out as a prop, but was stood quite still instead, apparently content to watch the people around him drift through the arch. The music from inside was louder now, not one harmonious tune but a collection of tinny Christmas jingles, blended together to form something that was both instantly recognisable and impossible to name.

Max noticed her when she was a few metres away from him, and shifted his position to face her, taking one hand out of his pocket and touching it to his temple and then out towards her in a sort of mini-salute.

Josie fixed a bright smile on her face as she stopped in front of him. 'Hi!' Her own hands, both in black gloves, one clutching her handbag to her shoulder and the other flopping uselessly at her side, felt suddenly redundant as she tried to work out what to do with them. She gestured feebly towards the entrance the other side of the metal barrier, determinedly keeping her smile in place. 'Shall we?'

Max nodded his assent, and followed her around the barriers, joining the queue, which thankfully seemed to be moving quickly. 'So did your flatmate get off today ok?' he asked, glancing down at her as they shuffled forward, trying to keep a polite distance between the two Puffa jackets and their pram in front of them. His hair was just as messy today, proving that it wasn't just being knocked off his feet that made him look a little dishevelled in a way that was undeniably sexy.

'Huh? Oh, right.' Josie cleared her throat, feeling like an idiot. 'Yeah, she left this morning.' She smiled slightly at the memory of Bia stumbling back into the flat in her leopard-print heeled boots for the fourth time and declaring that she'd forgotten a vital *possible* outfit for New Year, then swearing as she tried to make it fit into her already over-large suitcase. Her luggage definitely weighed more than the allowed twenty-three kilos though Bia had brushed Josie off when she'd tried to point that out. *They don't really* mean *that, Jose, I'm sure they'll let me on.* And Josie was sure they would – Bia would no doubt somehow talk her way out of any fine for the extra weight.

The sounds of the toddler in the pram ahead filled the resulting silence between them, a mixture of crying and shouting, with one of the Puffa jackets bent over the pram, trying desperately to convince said toddler that everything was alright. The owner of the Puffa jacket looked over their shoulder, revealing a woman with short, tufty, white-blonde hair. She glanced around before smiling apologetically at Josie, who smiled back, trying to convey reassurance. Had her parents ever taken her to something like this as a child? She'd often thought they must have, because every time she smelled those sugary nuts you get at the Christmas Market, she had a fleeting impression of laughter, hot liquid and butterflies in her stomach. One of the many memories of her parents she must have lost from her childhood, stolen away from her immature brain before she could fully cement them there, despite Memo's efforts to the contrary.

When the lady, wearing a Santa hat and looking extremely pissed off about it, at the next available box office signalled impatiently, Josie and Max stepped forward together. The lady stared at them balefully, clearly wishing she'd opted for a less Christmassy temp job.

'Err . . .' Josie hesitated, and glanced at Max. She wasn't sure whether she should ask for one or two tickets. Was she supposed to pay for him?

'Two tickets?' the lady prompted, looking at Josie as if she thought she was an invalid.

'Yes, please,' Max said, sliding his wallet out from his coat pocket. Josie wrinkled her nose at the old leather and the sheer number of cards, receipts and bits of paper sticking out from inside the wallet. Surely he must lose things like that? He handed over his bank card to pay and the lady handed them their tickets without glancing up from her screen.

'Here,' Josie said, fumbling in her handbag, 'I think I have cash, hang on.'

Max shook his head, slipped his wallet back in his pocket and without even touching her managed to manoeuvre

Josie out of the way of the trio of girls who stepped up behind them. 'Don't worry about it.'

Josie hesitated, then nodded and smiled her thanks, figuring it would be rude to argue. She tucked a strand of hair behind her ear, wishing that she'd opted against Bia's advice and gone hat-free. It was a crisp day for sure, but not cold enough to see their breath, the clear sky above allowing the sun to warm the chilly air. Soon, once the sun set, she was sure she'd be thankful for her hat, gloves and scarf, but right now she felt too warm as they walked down the first makeshift street, with food stalls either side of them. She couldn't take her hat off now though, because she was sure that her hair would be plastered to her head, something that Bia clearly hadn't thought about when she'd dressed Josie in her *winter chic* outfit this morning before she'd left.

Max glanced down at her as he set the pace, his long, leisurely stride covering the ground in a way that made her feel she had to rush to keep up with him. 'So . . . What now?'

'Well,' Josie said, blowing out a breath. 'I thought we could go ice-skating?'

'Ice-skating . . .' Max frowned immediately and Josie resisted the urge to grit her teeth. It had been his bloody idea to come together, he could at least *fake* the enthusiasm.

'Yes,' she said more firmly. 'Ice-skating.' She made herself smile brightly again. 'It'll be fun!' *And maybe break the ice,* she thought to herself, smirking a little at her joke, though she wouldn't say it out loud. 'Come on, I think it's this way.' She took the lead and marched on, even as she saw his expression twist sceptically.

'I'm not actually that good at—'

'Doesn't matter!' Her voice came out in that same forcibly jovial tone, like an over-excited shop assistant, but she couldn't seem to stop it. 'It's all part of the experience,' she insisted. And it would be better, she was sure, than walking around in awkward silence for the afternoon.

They managed to get in on the next 'round' of ice-skating, which, she was told by plump, finger-waggling ice-skating man, was very lucky indeed. They pulled on their skates in the locker room, the white plastic skates refusing to give so much as an inch to mould to her feet. There was still five minutes before the changeover, so they hobbled awkwardly to the side of the ice rink, Max pulling a face as he tried to walk, and leaned against the barrier to watch the remaining people from the last group.

Josie watched a young girl with blonde hair in two plaits, around seven or eight, she'd guess, being pulled around the ice rink by her dad, face set in concentration, legs barely moving as she tried to keep her balance. She smiled as the girl stumbled, wide-eyed, and grabbed hold of her father for support, who laughed a little and said something to her before starting up again, slowly.

Almost unconsciously, Josie rubbed at the scar on her left wrist, hidden by her glove. She'd been ice-skating with her own parents once, she remembered. It was an indoor rink, nothing like this one, but her dad had been holding her hand, just like this girl's. She remembered he'd had to get off the ice for some reason, and had handed her over to her mum. She'd refused to skate with her mum at first, telling her that she *just wasn't as good as Daddy,* but had been cajoled into it by laughter and teasing. And then her mum had fallen, just as Josie had been afraid of. And instead of letting go of Josie's hand, her mum had grabbed hold of it, trying to keep upright but pulling them both over in the process. Everyone had been so worried, Josie remembered now, because she hadn't said anything, hadn't even cried as she'd smacked her wrist on the ice. They were worried it might be broken at first, but it turned out to be just a sprain. It had left a round, puckered scar on the top of her wrist, though, which she'd used to learn left from right as a child.

'Josie?' She jolted a little at the sound of her name and looked up to see Max watching her. 'You ok?'

'Yes.' She smiled, trying to let go of the twinge of sadness. 'Sorry, in my own world.'

'They're letting people on now, so if you want to . . .' He gestured at the gate to the ice rink.

'Right. Yes. Yes, come on then.' She started her awkward, clunky walk to the gate, thankful that she was not the only one looking like she was walking on precarious stilts.

'You sure you're ok?' He tripped over his skates as he shuffled along behind her, having to grab hold of the side to stay upright. God, and they hadn't even hit the ice yet.

'I'm sure,' she said lightly. Because explaining that she'd been hit by a memory of her dead parents seemed just a tad too much for a first date. Not that this was a date, she told herself firmly. Attractive he may be, but he also seemed like he never laughed, and she couldn't be doing with that. Besides, she'd literally only just broken up with Oliver.

Josie stepped onto the ice first, and immediately clung to the barrier at the side as she shuffled forward to make room for Max. She turned her head to see him following her tentatively, staring at his feet as he slid forward. His expression of unrelenting concentration made her laugh and he looked up at her and smiled sheepishly in response. 'I did try to tell you I was no good at this.'

She just shook her head, still smiling, and risked a few more awkward shuffles forward. Most of the other people were on the ice now, and the ones left clinging onto the edges were almost uniformly under the age of twelve.

She glanced back at Max. 'Ok, come on, we can do this.' She made herself push away very slightly and attempt to copy the woman in front of her. Right leg, left leg, right leg, left leg. Max had followed her – she could see him in her peripheral vision, though she didn't dare turn her head in case it diluted her focus.

She was halfway around the rink when she lost him. She risked a glance back, having to flail her arms when she nearly fell. Max actually *had* fallen, apparently – she could see him getting to his feet the other side of the rink, and grimaced to herself. Great. She should have listened when he said he didn't want to do it. But by the time she completed her first loop he was up on his feet, clinging to the barrier. She met his gaze, and he raised his eyebrows as she headed for him, waving her arms as she realised she had no idea how to stop. She hit the barrier with a gentle thump and laughed a little, despite herself. He smiled too and it lit up his face, his eyes crinkling in a way that softened them. The wave of warm relief that ran through her was almost intoxicating. 'You're a pro,' he said with another grin.

She flicked back her hair dramatically. 'Well, I *was* due to compete in 2012, but my marketing career got in the way.'

He shook his head in mock sadness. 'An unsung champion.'

'Tell me about it.' She cocked her head. 'Are you ok? I saw you fall.'

He wrinkled his nose. 'So much for getting away with that unseen. I'm fine – balance just not really one of my strong suits.'

They leaned back against the barrier, earning a glare from a girl who couldn't have been older than four, being as how they were blocking the route round. Max took Josie's hand and pulled her gently back onto the ice, letting go as soon as they were out of the way. A couple in their twenties skated past them, towards the centre of the rink, their strides in perfect unison, her bright blue coat perfectly offsetting his grey.

'They look like something out of a bloody Coca-Cola advert,' Max muttered, watching them too, and Josie laughed, causing Max to smile, a little reluctantly she thought, again. 'Come on, then,' he said, holding out his hand.

She batted it away playfully. 'I'm not holding onto *you*, you'll just pull me over.' Exactly like her mum had, she thought to herself, though the memory made her smile now.

They attempted another circle before Max declared that they had to have a break from all the hard work. They were both still smiling when they stepped out of the locker room, a full forty-five minutes ahead of the end of their allotted hour, and Josie felt something shift, like they'd managed to fumble their way through the initial awkwardness a bit. The fact that he was proving he was actually able to have fun helped a little, she admitted.

'So, mulled wine next?' Max asked. 'That's Christmassy, right?'

'Right,' Josie agreed with a nod. They glanced around at the various stalls, both of them seemingly lost as to where to start.

'One of everything' Max declared, and set off in the direction of the nearest wooden hut, the smells of cinnamon and orange peel getting stronger as they neared it. He handed her a branded *Winter Wonderland* cup, and they sipped the mulled wine as they walked down, now clearly in the market section. Even Josie, who had practically made it her mission not to enjoy this kind of thing in the past, couldn't resist eyeing up the trinkets – beautiful earrings and handcrafted woodwork.

When Max headed off to the next available drinks stall to get them a top up, Josie checked her phone and saw a message from Bia.

Are you having fun? Did he like my outfit???

All good. He loved the outfit, hasn't stopped complimenting it.

I knew it!!! Send a pic. Want to see him.

Josie snorted, and as Max walked over to her she managed to surreptitiously take a photo of him, which she sent to Bia. She got a set of three heart-eyed emojis back.

'They have mulled *gin*, Josie,' Max said, wearing a look of clearly exaggerated amazement. 'Something about cherry and cinnamon, and I sort of lost track after that, but I figured we had to try it.'

Josie smiled a little as she remembered Bia's mulled water comment but she took her cup and sniffed before taking a tentative sip. It wasn't bad, though it was a good deal stronger than the mulled wine. They passed a flower stall next, and Max doubled back, then reappeared with a single rose. He snapped off the end of it, then tucked it behind her ear, fastening the stem in place with her hat.

'As a thank you, for bringing me,' he said. He shrugged like it was no big deal, but Josie couldn't help reaching up to run her fingers over the rose's petals, then tracing the place where he'd touched her ear.

'So, umm, what do you want to do next?' she asked, partly to cover up the flush that she was sure was creeping into her face. 'We could—'

'Josie!' A squeal to her right cut her off and she spun to see none other than Claire bloody Burton rushing towards them, arms outstretched, her dyed red hair bouncing around her shoulders. 'I *thought* it was you!' She practically leapt on Josie, pinning her arms as she hugged her. 'Oh it's been too long, I can't *believe* we bumped into you like this.'

'We?' Josie asked weakly.

'Oh, Oliver's just over there, getting us a drink,' Claire said, gesturing behind her without looking. *Well great*, Josie thought. That was just fantastic, wasn't it? Of *course* she'd have the bad luck to bump into her ex at Winter bloody Wonderland. Claire glanced at Max, but then steamrolled on without waiting for an introduction. 'Yes, I dragged him along, you know, to cheer him up after . . .' She broke off on a cough, her pale cheeks turning a little pink. It didn't deter her though – from Josie's experience, very little could deter Oliver's big sister. 'He was just *devastated* when you ended things, Jose.' Claire glanced over her shoulder, then dropped her voice. 'He's been moping around for days without you, can't seem to break him out of it whatever I do. I just *wish* you two could make it up, you were so

58

good for him, kept him on the right track, you know?'

'He slept with someone else, Claire,' Josie said shortly. Josie saw, out of the corner of her eye, Max raise his eyebrows at that, but he said nothing.

Claire grimaced, and reached up her hand to toy with the frayed ends of her hair. 'Of course,' she said quickly. 'Of course, it's not that I think you should forgive him right away, or ever,' she added quickly at the look on Josie's face. 'I just, well . . .' She trailed off and Josie's stomach squirmed. She shouldn't have been so short with her – it wasn't Claire's fault that her brother had decided to throw away their relationship for a pair of knockout heels and a tight red dress.

Claire turned around and waved, and Josie saw Oliver walking towards them, hair fixed in place as always, chest pushed out in the way it always was when he walked. She tried desperately to think of something to say, something to excuse her and Max before his imminent arrival, but came up blank. She glanced up at Max, but he said nothing, only glancing between Oliver and her. No bloody help at all. Claire turned back to face them, and this time looked at Max. She smiled. 'I'm Claire, by the way,' she said.

'Right,' Josie said quickly, the back of her neck far too hot. 'Right, sorry, Claire this is—'

'Josie?' Too late. Oliver was here, standing frozen with his arms at ninety-degree angles, a cup of steaming liquid held stiffly in each hand. 'What are you doing here?' He said it like an accusation, like she'd planned this somehow, deliberately to spoil his fun.

She tucked her hair behind her ear, which dislodged the rose, so that she had to fumble to put it back in place.

Oliver's gaze followed the movement and he frowned when he saw the rose, glancing ever so briefly at Max by her side, who just stood there, hands in pockets, a benign expression on his face. 'Oh, you know,' Josie said vaguely, trying to figure out what she should look at and settling for his Adam's apple. 'Just fancied a day out.'

'But you hate this kind of thing,' Oliver said, still frowning, eyebrows pulling down towards his sharp nose.

Max raised his eyebrows. 'You do?' Both Claire and Oliver snapped their focus to him immediately, the fact that he'd spoken for the first time making him impossible to ignore now.

Josie cleared her throat. 'I, well . . .'

Oliver was staring at Max, his gaze flickering to the top of his head, and Josie just knew he was measuring up the height difference between them. Max smiled, an easy, charming smile, one that he saved for strangers other than her, apparently, and held out a hand to Oliver. 'Max,' he stated.

Oliver stared at the outstretched hand for a moment before fumbling with the cups he was holding, taking a good few seconds to offload one to Claire. 'Right,' he said, grasping Max's hand, his eyebrows still pulling together as he looked from Max to Josie and back again. 'Right, I'm—'

'Oliver,' Max said cheerfully. 'I gathered.' Josie jolted as Max swung an arm around her, the weight of it settling on her shoulders. 'It's so good to meet you at last.' Josie glanced up at Max, trying very hard not to look stiff and awkward, but he gave nothing away, still smiling amenably at Oliver. 'I've heard all about you of course.'

Oliver's frown intensified, making his face look even

more angular than usual. Claire was still smiling, but she looked uncertain and her gaze was now darting around the three stalls immediately behind them, selling Christmas decorations, jewellery and paintings, maybe wondering if she could make an escape from the meeting she'd initiated.

'You have?' Oliver asked, looking at Josie this time, who tried to arrange her expression into something between a smile and an apology, and ending up doing a weird jerk thing with her head in the process.

'Oh yeah,' Max continued. 'Couldn't believe it when Jose told me about you guys breaking up.'

Jose? She risked a glance up at Max again, but he didn't meet her gaze.

'I'm sorry,' Oliver said, biting out the words, 'but who exactly are you?'

'Max,' he said slowly, and Josie had to suppress the completely inappropriate urge to giggle at the way Max managed to make it sound *that* condescending.

'Right,' Oliver huffed, 'but—'

Max drew away from Josie slightly so he could look down at her, scandalised. Josie shook her head ever so slightly as she did her best to return the look. 'You didn't tell him about me?'

Josie cleared her throat. 'I, err—'

'Me and Josie go way back,' Max continued, giving Josie's shoulder a little squeeze as if to emphasise the point. 'Met at a club, oh I don't know, what was it, Jose, about . . .?' He looked down at her, his lips twitching as he waited for her to finish the sentence.

'Err, five years ago?' Josie offered, taking a sip of her cinnamon gin, which was already cooling down dramatically.

'In a *club*?' Oliver asked, looking at his sister, who merely shrugged, and focused her attention on whatever was inside her cup.

'Yeah,' Max said breezily, 'can't remember the name of it now, but we hit it off and have been friends ever since. She never mentioned me?' He rolled his eyes at Josie as if to say *come on now* and she fought to keep her face straight.

'No,' Oliver said shortly. 'And we've been together two—'

'Years,' finished Max, nodding, filling in the blank with the obvious guess. 'Yeah, I know. I've been in New York most of that time, you see, moved there a few years ago, but Josie and I stayed in touch. I was hoping to meet you on this visit, but, well.' He pressed his lips together and Oliver flushed. Claire took an extra-large gulp of her drink, which brought on a minor coughing attack, though she waved Oliver away when he tried to thump her on the back. 'Anyway,' Max continued, 'I'm back in London for a bit, so I thought I'd drag Josie to this.' He winked at Claire, using her own phrase from a moment ago, and she smiled feebly back, before wiping her chin with her hand. 'You know, get us in the mood for Christmas.' He raised his gin in a salute.

Oliver stared at Max mutely for a moment before looking directly at Josie, who was doing her best to look at ease, pressed against Max's side, the heat of his body travelling between both their coats to get to her. 'Josie, what—?'

But Max had slipped his phone out of his pocket and was making a show of looking at the time. 'Oh, Jose, look,' he said emphatically, shoving the phone under her nose and tapping the top corner where the clock was.

'Oh damn,' Josie said, trying to sound confident. 'We'd, err, better go otherwise we'll miss the . . .'

'Ice Bar.' Max saved her from having to make something up. Max let go of Josie to pat Oliver on the shoulder, who was clearly trying, not very successfully, not to glare at him. 'Great to meet you both, at last,' Max added, with a final, winning smile for Claire, who couldn't seem to help beaming back, though she straightened her face when Oliver glanced at her.

'Bye!' Josie called behind her, as Max steered her away, linking his arm through hers and dragging her determinedly the other way, which may or may not have been the way to the Ice Bar – she had no idea.

'Did you really live in New York?' Josie whispered the question, though that was probably unnecessary given how loud this place was.

'Nah. Like I said, my parents do now so I've been to visit a few times, but thought it would be difficult to explain why he's never met me unless I was abroad somewhere.'

Josie was quiet for a moment, then, unable to contain it any longer, she burst out laughing. Max stopped, looking down at her, and she slipped her arm from his to clutch her side, not sure why exactly she found the whole thing so funny. Max's lips twitched slightly. 'Thought you might need an out,' he said.

'Yes,' Josie agreed, still laughing. 'Yes, thank you, that was . . .' – she straightened up and beamed at him, Oliver's incredulous expression imprinted on her mind – 'brilliant.' She sighed, and downed the rest of her gin. 'He cheated on me,' she explained with a wave, glancing over her shoulder to check they weren't following.

'I gathered.'

'At the work Christmas party.'

'Ouch.'

'With a mutual colleague. Cara.'

He shook his head. 'What a bitch.'

She let out another little laugh. 'Well, it was more his fault than hers, but still.' She sighed. 'So thanks, again.'

'You're welcome.' He glanced behind them. 'I know what it's like – the whole ex thing.' She looked up at him. It was the first real bit of information he'd offered voluntarily. 'My girlfriend . . . She broke up with me earlier this year.'

Josie nodded slowly. 'When?'

'May.'

She nodded again. Maybe he was still getting over her, if he'd really loved her. Maybe that partly explained why he'd been so short with her at first. Well, that and the whole knocking him over thing. She wanted to ask more, but Max squared his shoulders.

'So, Ice Bar?'

Josie shrugged. 'We can try. I doubt we'll get in, I'm pretty sure Bia said you have to book.'

'Nah, I'll sweet talk them.' Max linked an arm through hers again, and when she looked up questioningly said, 'They might still be watching.'

Somehow Max did manage to talk them into the Ice Bar, though she had no idea what he said, because he made her wait behind him. So after a few more drinks, which they drank huddled in Inuit-style overcoats, the two of them meandered back towards the exit, in much easier company than when they'd first set foot inside. It was dark now, and Josie had to admit the whole thing was rather festive, the lights of the stalls glowing, the smell of chestnuts, spices and candyfloss washing over them, people laughing as they passed makeshift bars.

It might just be because she was feeling pleasantly buzzed, but she really could, in that moment, see why people got all excited about it. She smiled up at Max, who grinned down at her and took her hand, swinging it as they walked. He'd been like that since they'd bumped into Oliver, like he'd decided they had something in common, both having to get over someone in their past. She smiled to herself a little at the thought that Oliver had inadvertently made her not-quite-date so much more fun.

'So,' Max said, 'are you heading out of London soon for Christmas?'

She tried and failed to keep a smile on her face. 'Nope. Staying at my flat this year.' No matter what she might have told Memo, her stomach dropped a little as she imagined the day, at home next to Bia's Christmas tree, eating Deliveroo for one, which was even *worse* than those people working at Deliveroo, because at least they got paid. She tried to think of something else, and deliberately made her voice bright as she said, 'I've still got to go Christmas shopping before that though. Such a nightmare.'

He glanced down at her. 'Not a fan?'

She wrinkled her nose. 'Well, I usually have it all done in September, and order everything online but this year I . . . didn't.' No need to say the reason – that Oliver had kept telling her they'd do all theirs together, had insisted that she had to be more creative, that she couldn't just order everything online because it was *impersonal*. And now she was stuck having to cram it all into one day before her aunt Helen came to visit her and collect the presents for herself and her grandparents, as she did every year. She sighed as they walked back under the archway, leaving the lights twinkling behind them.

Max let go of her hand, and even through her gloves her fingers registered the loss of warmth. He turned to face her, studying her. 'Well, in a twist of fate, turns out that I'm an excellent Christmas shopper.'

She cocked her head. 'Are you now?'

'Mmm-hmm,' he nodded sagely. 'So how about I take you tomorrow? We'll make a day of it, and I'll help you.'

She frowned up at him. 'What, really?'

'Sure, why not?'

She tucked a strand of hair behind her ear. 'It's just . . . isn't there something else you'd rather be doing? Not that I don't want you there,' she said quickly, concerned then that it sounded as if she was trying to ditch him. 'Only . . . Well, I'm not exactly known for my enthusiasm when it comes to any kind of shopping, let alone Christmas shopping.'

He looked like he might smile, but seemed to deliberately pull his expression into something serious. 'Ok, consider me duly warned. But given the fact that the majority of my mates are either up in Scotland or in Bristol, and my family is in New York, it's either invite myself along with you or hole up with a crate of beer in my hotel room, and no one likes a day drinker.'

Josie laughed. 'Well, when you put it like that.'

Chapter Five

'What about this?' Max asked, holding up a shower cap with little ladybirds on it.

Josie laughed. 'I'm not sure my grandmother's really the shower-cap type.'

'What are you talking about? Everyone is the shower-cap type.'

Josie raised her eyebrows. 'Even you?'

'*Especially* me.' He put the cap on his head for effect and Josie burst out laughing, earning a disapproving look from a middle-aged woman perusing the washbags next to them. She could hardly blame her, though. She'd usually be that woman, glaring at anyone who dared to look like they were enjoying themselves in a crowded store this close to Christmas. Well, ok, she probably wouldn't be glaring, but she'd certainly be *thinking* mean thoughts.

Josie looked down at the price tag. 'Forty-five pounds?' she asked incredulously. 'For a shower cap?'

'But look, it has pretty ladybirds on, they're worth at least a fiver each.' Max tapped one of said ladybirds as if to emphasise the point, then shrugged as he put it back. 'Alright, maybe not.'

'I thought you said you were good at this,' Josie said with a smirk.

'Hey, it's not my fault that you have no taste.' He walked on, giving the middle-aged woman, who studiously ignored him, a polite nod as he passed. Josie followed, manoeuvring herself carefully down the aisles so that her shopping bags didn't accidentally knock anything off the shelves. Shamefully, given she'd lived in London for eight years, this was her first time in Fortnum & Mason. It had been Max's idea to come here, at least to 'look', and she had to admit it was beautiful, with perfectly decorated Christmas trees on each floor, each themed around a certain colour scheme, the closest one showing off blue and silver baubles with intricate designs on each one. No doubt Bia would call it boring, Josie thought wryly. There was a giant golden crescent moon hanging above them from the ceiling, with twinkling gold stars on varying lengths of thread cascading around them, and despite the number of sweaty bodies all pushed in here, it still smelled sweet, chocolate mixed with a flowery perfume.

'Ok,' Max said, glancing at her to make sure she was still following him, 'we can do this. Tell me about your grandmother.'

'Don't *you* have to do any shopping?' Josie was aware that there was a faint whine in her voice, but she couldn't quite stop it. He'd come out all guns blazing, lighter today than the last two days, like he had decided from the get-go to be his most charming self for whatever reason. As such, he had powered her through the day so that she was nearly done with the shopping. She'd got her grandad some nice gardening gloves and a sign saying 'My Garden, My Rules' and she'd settled on a Space NK voucher for Helen, figuring she was bound to get it wrong if she tried to buy Helen something specific. So that left only Memo to go, which was always the most difficult present even though she knew her so well.

'Nope,' Max said easily, stopping to look at the scarves and giving Josie a questioning look. She shook her head. She'd got a scarf for her two years ago. 'I did all mine ages ago.'

Josie huffed, feeling like he was taunting her. 'Well, aren't you organised?'

He grinned at her, seeming to find her annoyance incredibly amusing – indeed, the more reluctant she'd been throughout the day, the more fun he'd seemed to be having, like he was determined not to let her mood affect him. Or maybe, because she wasn't being forcibly cheery like the last two times she'd met him, he'd decided that role needed to be taken up by him. 'Not usually,' he admitted. 'I just knew what I wanted to get everyone this year.'

Josie side-stepped a woman with a buggy, who'd stopped to pick up something her toddler had thrown onto the floor. The Christmas music got louder as they neared the other side of the shop – they must be near a speaker. 'This year? What's so special about this year?'

'Huh?' He frowned over her shoulder, clearly distracted by something, but when she turned to look she couldn't figure out what it was. 'Oh, no, nothing special,' he said breezily. 'I just had specific ideas, that's all.'

'Are all your family in New York this year?' Josie put her bags containing her other presents down and brushed a hand through her hair. She was too hot, but couldn't seem to motivate herself to take her coat off, knowing she'd only have to put it back on as soon as they stepped back outside.

Max picked up the nearest photo frame, examined it, then put it back down again. She wondered if he genuinely enjoyed the shopping or if it was all put on, like her enthusiasm for Winter Wonderland yesterday. If it was faked, she thought he was better at hiding it than she'd been. 'My parents and my sister, yeah.'

'Sister?'

He looked at her, smiled, and his eyes crinkled in that way that made him seem warm. 'Yep. My baby sister,' he said, chuckling a little. He noticed her slight smile as she tried to figure out the joke, and elaborated. 'She hates being called the baby, which I suppose makes sense given she's twenty-seven. She's four years younger than me, but has forever been the one taking care of me.' His voice softened as he spoke of her, and his eyes turned a little sad. She cringed internally – no doubt she was only reminding him that he was stuck this side of the Atlantic, away from his family. 'And you,' he said, his voice firmer now, 'are clearly trying to distract us from the task at hand. Your grandmother. Go.'

'I don't *know,*' she complained. 'She's . . .' Josie waved a hand in the air. 'Classy, I guess. Likes to bake, though she's actually terrible at it – she never manages to follow the recipe right, but she doesn't give up.' Josie smiled at the teenage memories of coming home after school to be greeted with overly chewy biscuits, or cake that tasted just a bit too strongly of egg.

Max frowned for a minute, then headed off with a new determination, so that Josie had to grab her bags in a fluster, and really did knock off the nearest photo frame this time, muttering an apology even though there was no shop assistant in sight. She caught up with Max next to the homeware section, and scowled at him for the unnecessary sprint – wasn't shopping supposed to be relaxing? Though maybe not, considering the frantic way everyone else was sorting through the shelves. This was precisely why she usually did hers online, in plenty of time to return things if they weren't right.

Her phone beeped from somewhere in the depths of her handbag, and she fished it out, expecting to see a message from Bia, who *still* hadn't told her she was there safe, despite having landed several hours ago. Her heart gave an extra-large thump when she saw Oliver's name pop up instead.

Can we talk? Please?

She scowled at it for a moment. He was probably trying to figure out if she'd already replaced him with Max, after yesterday's encounter. Well, too bad. She was tempted to reply with a simple *No,* but figured that she should just ignore it for now. No doubt she'd have to talk to him at some point, and maybe it *would* be better to just get it over with so he'd stop asking, but for now, she was enjoying the fact that she didn't have to sit around thinking of him – she was entitled to distract herself, wasn't she? And Max was proving to be the perfect distraction.

Having spent the morning telling Max she'd never buy

anything from Fortnum's, Josie ended up buying a little tea set for Memo – white with a turquoise and gold border. It was a little out of her budget, but her grandmother deserved something special, and whether it was because of Max talking about his sister or the memory of her grandmother's baking, she was feeling particularly nostalgic. She had a moment of doubt when she wondered whether it would go in their kitchen, given she hadn't been to their house for years, but it was understated and she was pretty sure it would go with anything.

'Yes,' Josie said decisively after she'd paid. 'I think she'll like it.' She took the bag the shop assistant handed her. 'Though I'll be able to tell either way – she's got a terrible poker face.'

Max laughed. 'Are you spending Christmas with her then?'

'No,' Josie admitted after a beat, 'but we open our presents from each other over Facetime every Christmas Eve. It's like a ritual.' One that Memo had started when Josie had stopped coming home for Christmas, so that they still had some 'family time'.

'A very modern day ritual,' Max commented, and Josie grinned.

'Quite.'

They passed the jewellery section on the way out and, even though it was such a girly cliché, Josie couldn't help being drawn over to have a look. She noticed a pair of big star earrings, dangly ones that sparkled in the Christmas lights around the casing, and laughed a little.

'Yeah, I've always found jewellery quite funny,' Max said, deadpan.

She pointed the earrings out. 'These are *exactly* like a pair I got given for Christmas when I was nine.' The last Christmas she'd shared with her parents, she thought before she could stop herself. 'They were in my stocking,' she explained, smiling at the memory. 'Clip-on, obviously.'

'Obviously.'

'And plastic.'

Max raised his eyebrows. 'But apart from that, they were exactly the same? I'm not sure you should let Fortnum's hear you say that.' He glanced up to the nearest shop assistant and flashed her a grin, which made her beam and go a little pink. Clearly, he'd learned how to use his looks over the years.

Josie rolled her eyes at him as they walked away from the jewellery. 'Well, they were gold and stars and dangly. And they were my favourite thing for a while.' She remembered how she'd asked her mum to put her hair in a bun every time she'd worn them, so that they were even more obvious.

'Do you still have them?'

'No. I lost them a few months later.'

'Shame. I'm sure you'd look great with plastic golden stars in your ears.' He glanced at her earlobes and she touched one absentmindedly.

'Not really my style anymore.' She was wearing studs, as usual, little daisies. She couldn't imagine wearing something so bright and *out there* now, even if it was just a pair of earrings.

They made their way back outside, and the cold wind actually felt like relief as it brushed the back of her neck, after the toasty warmth of inside. She grimaced at the sound of her phone vibrating. Surely Oliver wasn't ringing her now too? But it wasn't Oliver.

She bit her lip and glanced at Max, who gestured for her to answer. She turned away a little bit, trying to keep her voice down. 'Aunty Helen?'

'Josie!' Her aunt's husky voice boomed down the line. 'Darling! How *are* you?'

'I'm—'

'Now, look,' Helen continued, talking over Josie. 'I know we said tomorrow for supper, but I got my dates mixed up and I'm actually here in London today. I don't suppose you can meet me today instead, could you, darling?'

Josie looked over at Max, who was politely studying the street, rocking back and forth on his heels. 'Well, I'm—'

'I *know* it'd be an inconvenience, darling, but I've double-booked myself tomorrow and I'd *hate* to miss our annual supper, I've been *dying* to hear all about your year.'

Josie grimaced at the thought of having to tell Helen just how wrong her year had turned out. 'Well, the thing is—'

'I've got us a table at the Ivy Market Grill,' Helen continued. 'You know it, don't you? In Covent Garden.'

'I know it, yes, but the thing is,' Josie said, talking as quickly as she could to avoid being interrupted again, 'I'm actually out with a . . . a friend at the moment, so I'm not sure I could—'

'Oh bring her along!' Helen exclaimed, sounding delighted. 'I'd love to meet one of your friends, darling, I do worry about you here all alone sometimes.'

'Well, I . . .' Josie trailed off weakly. She couldn't really say no, even if she did want to prolong the day with Max.

But this was the one time of year she and Helen saw each other without fail, and it would surely make her a terrible person to refuse to go just for the sake of a few more hours with a man she'd only just met. She sighed, and Helen sensed victory.

'Wonderful! I'll meet you there in an hour.'

'An hour?' Talk about last minute. Josie wrinkled her nose. She bet Helen was lying – she must have other plans that had fallen through today and was trying to rearrange things so as not to have an evening in a hotel alone.

'Yes, we'll have an early supper, shall we? Can't wait to see you, darling!' And with that, she hung up, leaving Josie staring mutely at her phone.

'Everything ok?' asked Max, coming up to her.

Josie tugged a hand through her hair. 'Yes, I . . .' She blew out a breath. 'That was my aunt. She's in London and wants to meet me for dinner in an hour – she booked a table but forgot to tell me, apparently.'

'Dinner at five p.m.?'

'Apparently, yeah. I'm so sorry. She said you're welcome to come, though?' Max frowned, then smoothed out his expression so Josie couldn't tell what he was thinking. Which maybe was just as well, because she wasn't actually sure what she wanted him to be thinking in that moment. She would have been happy to spend the rest of the day with him, but the thought of him sitting next to Helen and having every inch of him examined over a three-course meal was enough to make her cringe.

'I'd love to,' Max said, perhaps a touch too evenly, 'but it actually works out well – I've got some errands to run and I said I'd Skype my parents later.' Josie nodded, not sure why she was suddenly finding words hard to come by. 'Where are you meeting her?'

'Covent Garden.'

'I'll walk you – might as well walk rather than get the tube if you can bear it.'

She nodded, then looked down at her cluster of bags, sighed and hauled them off the pavement. Lips twitching, Max took two of them off her, and Josie didn't even try to protest.

'So,' Max said as they neared Covent Garden tube station, the sound of people clapping making its way up to them over the general chatter. Someone must be performing further down. 'Tomorrow.'

Josie glanced up at him. His hair was sticking out at odd angles from the wind, which had died down as it grew darker, like the darkness had chased it away. 'Tomorrow?'

He didn't look at her, his attention on a busker playing 'Feed the World' on the corner. 'Plans?'

'Plans?' Josie took the lead, heading towards the Ivy Market Grill.

'For tomorrow. What are your plans?'

'Oh.' Josie felt the tell-tale heat creep up her neck and resisted the urge to rub at it, though, really, he could have found an easier way of asking her. She wrinkled her nose. She didn't have anything concrete planned for tomorrow even though she'd booked the day off from work weeks ago, but it seemed a bit pathetic to say that, this close to Christmas. She'd already given two days to him at short notice – the weekend, no less – was it tantamount to admitting that she was a loner with no friends if she was available for a third day at the drop of a hat? Or did he even mean that? He hadn't actually asked her out, maybe he was just making polite conversation. *Or maybe you're just overthinking it, Josie.* She sighed. 'I've got a few things I have to sort out,' she hedged.

'Things.' Max nodded.

'Stuff I need to get done before Christmas. I've got a work Christmas party on Christmas Eve I need to . . . get ready for.' True, given she hadn't even thought about what she was going to wear to their *charity event,* to quote Janice. 'And other . . . stuff,' she finished lamely, coming to a stop outside the restaurant.

'Stuff and things,' Max said slowly. 'Sounds boring. Come out with me tomorrow instead.' Josie tried very hard not to smile, to keep her expression neutral to match his, even though a little thrill went down her spine. *Not a date,* she told herself firmly. He was just looking for friendly company, that was all. She wasn't even sure she *wanted* it to be a date, not this soon after Oliver, not with someone who lived in Bristol. 'Come on,' Max said evenly. 'You're not going to leave me hanging while I'm all alone in London, are you?'

Josie laughed and relented. 'Fine. What do you want to do?' She shifted the bags to her other hand and shook out her arm, which was starting to feel numb.

'I'll pick you up at nine.'

She narrowed her eyes. 'You'll pick me up?'

'Well, in a manner of speaking. I don't actually have a car, obviously. Here,' he added, fishing out his phone and opening up Notes, 'give me your address.'

She did as he asked, only belatedly thinking that she

should maybe be more cautious about giving her address out. 'Where are we going?'

'It's a surprise.'

Josie sighed. 'I'm not a huge fan of surprises.'

He rolled his eyes. 'Don't be such a cliché. Everyone likes surprises, they just don't like the possibility that it's a *bad* surprise.'

She contemplated this for a moment, then shook her head. 'Regardless, I like to know what's going to happen next.'

He considered her for a moment, his expression unreadable. He was really bloody good at keeping what he was thinking off his face. He 'pffed' and waved a hand dismissively. 'Boring,' he declared again. But then his voice softened a little, a hint of sadness creeping through. 'You can't plan your whole life that way, it has a habit of not cooperating.' She thought unwillingly of her parents, deciding last-minute to go to that party, but pressed her lips against that thought. This was not the same thing.

'This is where you're eating, I take it? Fancy.' And just like that, he was back to an easy, jokey tone. He walked her to the door, holding it open for her, and a wave of heat hit them, along with the smell of garlic, mussels and, she was pretty sure, port. It was dimly lit in here, which worked for the festive theme, with green tinsel decor around the side of booths, though she couldn't quite imagine how it would feel in summer. She'd been in here only once before, and that had been in winter too, for a work lunch.

The hostess took her coat and bags, and was in the process of instructing a waiter to take them to the table, when Helen's voice boomed out. 'Josie!' She was walking briskly towards them from the other side of the restaurant, etiquette be damned. She was wearing an extravagant purple dress that showed off an impressive figure, given she was in her sixties. Her blonde hair, dyed religiously every six weeks, was in a new style, shaped around her face in a way that accentuated her cheekbones. Josie glanced at Max, but it was too late to tell him to get out quickly. Helen pounced, drawing Josie into a tight hug. Josie caught a faint whiff of tobacco, as she always did, even though Helen insisted she'd given up smoking *years* ago. Helen was a good few inches shorter than Josie, but you wouldn't know it unless they were stood right next to each other – Helen had a way of carrying herself that made her seem like the tallest person in the room. She was Josie's dad's older sister, and though Josie often tried, she found very little of her dad in Helen, although she often wondered if she would have seen more of the similarity, had she had the chance to know her dad as an adult.

'And who is *this*?' Helen demanded, wasting no time, and eyeing up Max critically with no hint of shame.

Josie cleared her throat. 'Max, Helen, Helen, Max.'

Somehow instantly guessing what type of person she was, instead of shaking her hand, Max brought it to his lips and kissed it swiftly. 'Delighted to meet you.'

Helen's eyes narrowed, reserving judgement. 'Are you the "friend" Josie was with? Are you staying for supper?'

Max ran a hand across his stubbled jaw. 'I wish I could, but I have other duties to attend to, unfortunately.'

'Hmm.' Helen glanced between the two of them before

whispering to Josie, perfectly audibly, 'What happened to the other one? Oliver, wasn't it? I liked him.' Which wasn't entirely true – Helen had only decided to like Oliver after the fourth time she'd met him, a year and a half into the relationship.

Josie sighed. 'I'll tell you later.'

Helen turned back to Max. 'And what is it that you do?'

Max said, 'I'm an architect,' at the same moment that Josie realised that she hadn't even *asked* him what he did for a living in the last two days. God, he must think she was so self-involved.

Helen was pursing her lips, clearly deciding whether she thought 'architect' was a good career choice. 'For which company?' she asked, and Josie suppressed a snort. Like she'd have any way of telling the good companies from the bad. Josie smiled apologetically at Max over Helen's head.

'ALA,' Max said. 'Do you know them?'

Helen didn't seem to read the slight joke in Max's voice, thankfully, and just sniffed slightly.

'Ladies, if you're ready to be seated . . .' The waiter was hovering uncertainly next to them, and Josie became aware that they were very much clogging up a walkway, though everyone was too polite to tell them explicitly to get out the way.

'Yes, yes,' Helen said, waving a hand and taking Josie by the elbow, abruptly ending the conversation with Max.

'I'll see you tomorrow,' Josie said over her shoulder.

Max nodded. 'Nine a.m.'

Josie was steered abruptly around a corner, and Helen let go of her elbow when they reached a corner table. 'Sit on my right, won't you, darling? My ear is playing up again.'

Josie seated herself and smiled her thanks to the waiter as he handed her the menu, noticing that Helen already had a bottle of sparkling water and a bottle of Chardonnay on the table.

'Nightmare at the hotel,' Helen was saying. 'No record of my reservation, and then Susan has come down with a terrible headache so had to cancel our plans, and well anyway, how are you, darling?' All without pausing for breath.

Josie smiled despite herself, taking a sip of the wine her aunt had poured. 'I'm good.'

Helen eyed her appraisingly. 'You look peaky.'

'Well, I suppose it's cold today.'

'Hmm. And who's that chap then? How did you meet?'

'In a club, five years ago,' Josie said promptly.

Helen looked up from the menu and frowned. 'In a *club*?' Like she was one to judge: she'd met the husband she was now on track to divorce – the third – at a cocktail bar when out with one of her friends.

Josie shook her head. 'It was a joke.'

Helen's eyebrows shot up as she returned to the menu, one finger scrolling down the options. 'Not a very funny one, darling.' But despite what Helen said, Josie found herself laughing, and for once the sound of an instrumental version of 'Silent Night' did not annoy her.

Chapter Six

The icy wind whipped Josie's hair around her face, all efforts to tame it long since abandoned, and there was the taste of salt on her tongue as she sucked in a breath against the cold. Sand had made its way into her boots - completely impractical for walking along the beach, but she refused to go barefoot like Max. Honestly, she'd be surprised if he didn't get frostbite. He was actually *in* the water now, allowing the foaming white hands of the waves to creep up around his ankles, trousers hitched up as he paddled like a toddler on a summer's day. He grinned over to where she stood a safe distance back, camera in her hand.

'Come and play,' he said, his voice barely making it over the sound of the wind and waves. A little way down there was another couple, walking hand in hand, wrapped up in big waterproof coats and scarves, and Josie could see both of them looking at Max like he was a madman.

'No way. And I won't be taking you to hospital later to get your toes sewn back on, just remember that.' His only answer was to grin at her again, and she felt her face fighting the stern expression she'd adopted. He seemed genuinely happy here – from the moment they'd stepped off the train, his step had become more bouncing, his expression more animated. Despite the freezing temperatures, it was infectious.

Josie lifted her camera, twisting the lens to focus in on Max, who now had his back to her, looking out at the horizon. It was a wonderfully clear day, a few wispy clouds the only marring of the vast expanse of blue above them. The water sparkled, ripples of diamonds that constantly adapted to the swell of the ocean. Josie took her time with the photo, wanting to get it just right, then snapped a few shots, catching Max's outline as he turned to look at her, his jaw soft, the hint of a smile evident in the photo. She'd brought her camera on a whim, being as how Max had refused to tell her the plan until they got off the train, but she was glad now that she had.

Max trudged up the sand to join her, flexing his toes when he stopped. Josie shook her head. 'You're mad.'

His eyes were bright, and although they were a far cry from the blue of the ocean, they seemed to absorb some of its shimmer, the green outweighing the amber today. He ran a hand through his hair – it was the kind of hair that suited the wind and salt, and the sparkle of the sunlight today made it look more coppery than usual. 'Well, you never know when you'll have the chance to do something again, right?'

'Mmm, I'm not sure having your toes frozen off is on anyone's bucket list.'

He prodded her in the ribs and she laughed, batting

his hand away. She lost her footing slightly as she did so, stumbling backwards on the uneven sand, and he grabbed her free hand – the one not holding the camera – to steady her. Only, of course, being *her*, she overbalanced too much the other way and practically fell into his chest. He laughed softly and took the sides of her arms in his hands, cocking one eyebrow as he looked down at her. She cleared her throat, suddenly intensely aware of how close they now were, and how her heartbeat had picked up, ever so slightly.

She took a step back. 'Thanks.'

He bent down and rubbed his feet dry before slipping on his socks and trainers again. When he stood up, he hooked his arm companionably through hers as they walked. She fell into the rhythm of his long stride and slung the strap of her camera over the other shoulder. It felt so easy to fall into step beside him, and unlike the last few days she didn't feel the pressure to say anything, comfortable to listen to the waves lapping the shore, the laughter of a child behind them.

'Get any good photos?' He nodded at her camera and she shrugged. 'It's an impressive beast, I'm not even sure I'd know how to work it – it's an iPhone camera all the way for me.'

'I love it,' she admitted. 'I brought it last year. It cost far too much money to justify, but I did it anyway.' She couldn't really explain it, how *right* she felt behind the lens, how she felt like that was when she was most relaxed, and most herself. 'I used to dream of being a professional photographer,' she said, smiling a little at the memory – when her friends at school were planning on being vets, doctors or actresses, she was instructing people where to stand so she could take photos of them. The one time she was really bossy, her mum used to say. She preferred wildlife and landscape photography to photos of people now, but it was one thing that hadn't changed as she'd grown up.

'What stopped you?'

Josie gave him an incredulous look. 'Well, it's not exactly a stable career path, is it?' Max gave a little half shrug, like it shouldn't matter, though Josie knew that was a romantic's view of the world and had no place in reality.

'Do you like what you do now? Marketing?'

Josie hesitated, then sighed. 'No, I guess not. Not really. I went into it because it can be creative sometimes – the social media stuff especially – but my company is quite strict on what they want out there and it sort of . . . takes the fun away, I guess.' She brushed her hair away from her face – they were walking with the wind behind them so it kept flying around and blocking her line of sight. She probably would have tied it up if she'd known where they were going, but still, it was actually a nice sensation, the wind tangling its fingers through her hair. 'Currently, my job seems to mainly involve looking at different shots of models in swimwear.'

'Doesn't sound so bad.' She poked him in the ribs with her elbow and he laughed. 'Still,' he said, 'if you hate it, why do you do it?'

'I don't *hate* it.' She paused, staring out at the sea for a moment. 'Actually, they're making my role redundant as of January, so I might not have a choice whether to hate it or not.' Her stomach squirmed uncomfortably – it was the first time she'd actually allowed herself to say it out loud, and though it wasn't right to say that this made it feel more *real,* it certainly made it feel like more of a problem.

Max frowned, and didn't answer right away, like he couldn't quite figure out what to say. 'That's shit,' he said eventually, which made Josie laugh.

'Quite. I have a choice, though.' She scowled when she thought of Janice's face, teeth showing in a fake smile, as she'd offered her said choice. 'I can take a "sideways"' – she struggled to get her hands up to do the air quotes because one of her arms was still entwined with Max's – 'move, or I can take the redundancy package.'

'What's the "sideways"' – he copied her air quotes – 'move?'

Josie waved her free hand, wishing she'd remembered gloves as her fingers sliced the cold air. 'They're calling it an Exec, but basically it's doing the same job for less money, with more of a focus on the digital side of things.'

'Sounds like you should get out while you can.' He steered her up the next ramp onto the pavement, heading towards the pier.

'Yeah, but then I'd have no job and no money . . .' The circle was going round her mind in a loop, continuously playing in the background. She could take the new role they were offering and look for other things at the same time, or she could take the package and just hope she got offered something before her money ran out. But then what if the new job was worse than her current one? At least she knew what she was doing there, and had friends, including Laura, which sort of counterbalanced the Oliver issue. She hadn't figured out yet if she was brave enough

86

to take the risk, though saying that out loud would sound all kinds of pathetic.

'Life's too short to not do what you want,' Max said simply, as if it were that easy, as if everyone did something they enjoyed.

'Do you love being an architect then?'

He smiled, though for some reason it didn't seem as bright as before, like he was losing some of the ocean's energy now they weren't down on the sand. 'I do. I geek out on buildings. And I do get the creative thing. It took me a while to get to the point where I was allowed to . . . imprint . . . my own personality on a building. But I knew I'd get there, so I didn't mind the grafting so much.' He glanced down at her. 'Sounds to me like you don't envisage your future in marketing, though, so it's different.'

She chewed her lip as she considered it. She'd just assumed she'd work her way up through the ranks, but did she really want to be a Marketing Director in ten or twenty years? She shook her head. So not today's problem. 'Did you always want to be an architect?' she asked, trying to steer attention back onto him.

'Well, it's not like I was announcing in the school playground aged six that I wanted to design buildings, but I got set on it as a teenager, I guess, and never looked back. My mum and dad hated the idea at first,' he added, but as a smile was playing round his lips, this clearly wasn't cause for resentment anymore.

'Really? Why?' It seemed like a perfectly respectable career choice to her, and wasn't it one of those careers where you could make loads of money?

'They're the cliché, my parents. Both doctors – that's

how they met. They're both great at what they do – and my mum loves it so much that she's keeping up some consultancy work in New York. They assumed I'd go into medicine too, and had to suffer the disappointment when they couldn't impart all their wisdom, I suppose.'

'But they're ok with it now?' Max was now steering them to the other side of the road, towards a run-down-looking fish and chip shop, the faded blue and white lettering on the shopfront a testament to better times gone by.

'I used to get fish and chips here as a kid,' he said by way of explanation. 'We came on holiday here every year without fail, the week of the August bank holiday. Haven't been here in years,' he said, sounding slightly nostalgic. He held the door open for her, and she stepped in, surprised that it was even open in the middle of December. The smell of grease filled the air, and, while it couldn't be described as toasty, it was still warm enough to be a welcome interlude from the chill outside. There was a skinny man behind the counter, who certainly mustn't try much of his produce, with a sharp angular face and a receding hairline. 'Chips as we walk, or are you hungrier than that?' Max asked her.

'No, that sounds great.' She smiled at the angular man, who grunted in response as he turned to carry out Max's request for two cones of chips. Couldn't be much fun, she supposed, sat here waiting for the odd tourist on the day before Christmas Eve. She glanced around the shop – there was a small reindeer at one end of the counter, the only nod to the festive season that she could see.

'Sorry, what were we talking about? Ah yes, the classic teenage angst as I searched for a different identity to that which my parents thrust upon me.' He nodded thoughtfully and Josie laughed. 'They're alright with it now – for the most part. They still occasionally like to bring it up. It came up on my thirtieth birthday two years ago, as if I'd magically grow into my medical career once my twenties were done with.'

The chip man presented them with two greasy parcels and told them to add their own condiments at the end of the counter. Josie went a bit overboard with the salt, but, hey, it was Christmas, and winced when Max doused his in vinegar. 'Not a fan?'

She made a face. 'Didn't your parents tell you that too much vinegar makes you sour?' It had been Memo's favourite saying as Josie was growing up, though she'd used it out of context all the time, so that it never actually made any sense.

His turn to laugh. 'I suppose I am a bit sour at times.'

They ate their chips as they walked up the pier, though Josie bit into the first one a bit too enthusiastically, so that the fluffy inside burned the inside of her mouth. They found a bench to sit on, and though it was damp from condensation and sea spray, Josie found she didn't care as she relaxed against it, Max shielding her from the worst of the wind.

'So why are you going to a work party, if they're making you redundant?'

Josie paused in the process of licking salt off her finger. 'Huh?'

He scrunched up the greasy cone in one hand, already finished with his chips. 'Didn't you say that's what you were doing tomorrow? Work Christmas party?'

89

'Oh.' Josie frowned, trying to remember when exactly she'd mentioned it. 'Right. Well, I haven't decided if I'm staying on, remember.'

'Ah.'

'So I've got to keep in the good books to keep my options open, you know?' She picked up another chip – a thin, crunchy one, the kind she liked best – and popped it in her mouth. 'It's a charity event,' she explained, then made a face. 'We're all being forced to go – our parent company is putting it on for all the companies under their "umbrella", as well as a bunch of clients, and for a reason only known to them, they decided to do that on Christmas Eve.' She didn't add that, until recent events, she'd actually been glad of it, because it gave her a purpose other than general 'Christmassy' activity. Now, though . . . 'I'm dreading it, to tell you the truth,' she said on a sigh. 'But it's important to *network* for the future, isn't it?'

He grimaced. 'I remember those events.'

Josie cocked her head. 'You don't have to go to them anymore?'

He hesitated for a fraction of a second. 'No, not anymore, thankfully. I'm guessing the pixie will be there too?' Max added, before Josie had time to question him further.

She frowned. 'The pixie? You mean *Oliver*?' She snorted at the description. She supposed he did have a slight pixieish quality, what with his height – or lack of it – and thin chin, but while she wasn't sure if Max meant it as an insult, she was sure Oliver would take it as one. 'Yeah,' she sighed. 'Yeah, he'll be there, as will the girl he cheated on me with.'

'Ouch. Don't go then.'

She rolled her eyes and popped the last few chips into her mouth. 'I told you, I have to.'

He nodded slowly. 'Is it a closed event, or are you allowed a plus one?'

Josie's stomach jumped, but she kept her expression carefully neutral. 'I'm allowed a plus one, yeah.'

'So I'll come then,' he announced, not making it into a question. She wondered briefly if she should be offended by that, but was too focused on trying not to grin too broadly to properly consider it. 'We'll make it fun.' He took the greasy paper from her hands, then tucked a stray strand of her hair behind her ear before throwing the paper in the bin to his left. She was glad he'd turned away from her, because she was pretty sure his touch had brought a flush to her cheeks.

'I said I'd meet a mate who's passing through on the way home tomorrow during the day, but in the evening we can . . .' He trailed off, reached into his pocket and brought out his phone, which was buzzing, the name *Chloe* flashing on the screen. He glanced at Josie. 'My sister,' he explained. 'Sorry, I'd better answer, she'll just keep calling if I don't.'

Josie nodded her acceptance and watched as he walked away from her in that casual stroll, then leaned against the railings. She shivered, the wind biting at her face again now that she didn't have Max's body as a shield. She got up and walked around the bench to the other side of the pier from Max, clenching her fingers to her palms to try and warm their icy tips. There was a little boy on the beach just below her, laughing as he ran after a shaggy, golden dog. The dog's tongue was lolling, its tail in the air as it ran towards the waves, barking like it was trying to ward them off, then lapping at the water when that achieved nothing. Wanting to capture the moment of the dog on the seaside, she unhooked her camera from her shoulder and adjusted the settings again, just as the boy's mother, she presumed, came walking up behind them, wearing bright red wellies and a big, puffy coat, clearly no stranger to the coastline.

She was deliberately standing at the other side of the pier from Max, but the wind carried his voice over to her regardless, so that she could make out snippets of his phone call. 'I promise I'm alright.' A laugh, then, though Josie thought it sounded slightly bitter. 'It's not like it's my choice.' 'Chill, ok? I'm not going to do anything drastic.' He went quiet for a moment and Josie realised she'd paused in the action of taking the photo, her attention on what he was saying despite herself. 'I know, I know.' A sigh, then, 'Well, I'm not alone, exactly.' Josie immediately started fumbling with her camera, suspecting that he would be glancing over at her. 'No, look. Josie!' She started, then turned to see him gesturing her over. She hesitated, then walked across to him.

He held out the phone to her as she approached. 'Say hello to my sister, won't you? She thinks I stuck with the room-service plan.' He thrust it into her hands.

'Hello?' she said cautiously.

'Hello?' A sharp, direct voice came from the other end. 'So you're the—?'

Max snatched the phone away before she could finish. '*See?*' He rolled his eyes at Josie, as if they were both in on his sister's behaviour. 'Anyway, I've got to go, I'm having a lovely time with Josie at the beach.' Josie didn't catch what his sister said, but Max cut her off anyway. 'Yes, the beach. I'll call you all later, ok?' And then he hung up, slipping his phone immediately back into his inside pocket. 'Sorry about that. She's just worried about me.' Though he smiled, it held a tight quality, not the relaxed, open smile she'd seen when he'd played in the water.

Josie nodded. 'Nice that she worries though.'

'Yeah. I suppose.' He sighed, shook his head. 'She's the golden child, followed in Mum and Dad's footsteps and is now a junior doctor. We both try not to resent her for it.'

'You *both* do?'

'Yep.' He leaned back against the railings. 'It's just as hard *being* the golden child as it is living in their shadow, don't you know?'

'Hmm, wouldn't know anything about that, being an only child and all.'

Max looked down at Josie's hands and she realised she was still clutching the camera. 'Can I see some of your photos?'

Josie bit her lip. 'I suppose so.'

He chuckled. 'Don't sound too enthusiastic.'

'Sorry,' she said quickly. 'Yes, sure.' She handed over her camera and showed him how to flick back through the recent photos, twisting her hands as she stood a little behind him, her gaze flicking between him and the viewer. It was a personal thing, more than she suspected he realised, to share them with him. 'They need editing,' she said. 'And they're just fun photos, you know, not—'

'I like this one.' It was one of him, with his face partially turned towards her, the contrast between the sea and sky perfect without any enhancements, the photo somehow managing to capture the icy chill of the day while keeping a warm feel to the composition.

Josie smiled a little. 'Me too.'

He flicked through a few more. 'They're really good. Not that I'm the best judge, I guess, but it's like I can feel you in the photos.' He handed her back the camera, and she felt herself blush. It was the best thing to say. Oliver always used to say that she was hiding behind the lens, and got grumpy with her because she didn't like to be *in* the photos, just take them. He hadn't ever seemed to totally get that, even if she wasn't visible in them, she still was very much a part of every photo she took.

'My mum bought me my first camera,' she said with a little smile. He took her hand as they walked back along the pier, and it felt so easy, so natural.

'Really?'

She nodded. 'When I was nine. It was a cheap Kodak one, you know, one of the disposable ones, and I was *thrilled.*' She grinned at the memory, at how excited she'd been. 'Mum used to take all the photos too, I guess that's where I got it from.' The smile faded as she thought of it, of how her mum had always taken too many family snaps on holiday and at parties, how her dad had complained but gone along with it, how her mum had to take several before she managed to get her thumb out the way and everyone's eyes open. Josie was glad of it now, because it meant she had memories of her childhood, but there were too few photos of her mum actually in the shot, like her childhood was documented without her.

'Used to?' Max asked.

Josie hesitated. 'They died,' she said softly. She felt his head whip round to look at her, but kept her gaze firmly on the ground in front of her. 'In a car crash when I was nine, driving back from a party on Christmas Eve.' She felt his grip tighten on hers for a moment. He was still staring at her.

'Jesus,' he said. 'That's . . . Jesus.' She finally looked up at him. His eyes were round, his lips pressed together as he took it in, clearly trying to figure out what to say. This was the worst bit, when you first told people, because they never knew how to react. 'That's awful, Josie – and I know it's a cliché, but I'm sorry.'

She nodded. Funny, how it was the done thing to apologise, to take responsibility for it. 'It was a long time ago,' she said, which was what she always said.

He squeezed her hand. 'Doesn't make it ok,' he said softly.

She felt a lump in her throat and forced it down. She was not going to start crying. 'No, I suppose it doesn't.'

The sun was setting now, a blaze on the horizon, the orange glow reflected on the water. 'It changes you, that kind of loss,' Max said, his voice husky now, like he was voicing his own feelings and not hers. She wondered who in his past he'd lost, or if he was thinking only of her. 'But you get through it, learn to live with it.' His gaze was intense on hers, so that she felt she couldn't look away. It wasn't a question, but it was like he was seeking her reassurance then, like he needed her to tell him she was ok.

She tucked a strand of hair behind her ear. 'Yeah.' Her lips threatened to tremble but she kept them still. 'It's a part of me now, I guess, something that will always be there, but I came through the other side, for sure.' She squeezed his hand and gave a little head toss. 'I mean, you've seen me with my sunny disposition and all that.'

He smiled, but it still looked sad, like he understood the weight of it still hit her sometimes, the fact that she'd never got to really *know* her parents as people, before they were taken from her, the fact that they lost their lives all too soon, that it could have been different, if only they'd stayed at home that night.

Max was quiet and a little distant as they made their way back to London, sitting in the window seat of the train and staring out at the passing landscape as the sky grew dark. It was like she'd upset him, talking about her parents, like she'd reminded him of something, and now he was lost in thought. She was too unsure to ask outright, not wanting to force him to relive a traumatic memory if he didn't want to. He'd talked about his parents in New York, about his sister, but she knew that losing a close family member was not the only kind of loss.

He came with her all the way to her flat, and walked her up to her floor, the light still flickering in the corridor. It was cold enough in the corridor that they could see their breath. Josie turned to him and smiled as she fished for her keys. 'Thanks for today. I suppose you were right – some kinds of surprises are ok.' The hint of a smile he gave her didn't reach his eyes and she looked away from it, back down at her bag. She found her keys, then hesitated. 'Do you . . . want to come in for a drink or something?'

'I'd better not,' he said, and even though she left a short pause for him to elaborate, he said nothing more. She tried not to feel stung by that. Maybe he thought that she was too damaged, having become an orphan at nine. Maybe he didn't want to get in any deeper into whatever it was they were doing here with someone who had that kind of trauma in their past. She focused intently on unlocking and opening the door. She shouldn't have said anything. But then, maybe *she* didn't want anything more to do with *him* if that was the way he felt.

'Well,' she said, as she stepped inside and turned to him, forcing a bright smile even though it felt almost painful to do so. 'Thanks again.' He didn't mention the party tomorrow so she didn't either – she certainly didn't want to force him into something he didn't want to do.

Max nodded, glancing briefly into her flat before looking up at the mistletoe still hanging above the doorway. Josie followed his gaze. She should have just taken the damn plant down the moment Bia was out the flat. When she looked back at Max, she jolted as his gaze met hers, his eyes still holding that same sad, intense look. He frowned ever so slightly as he looked at her, like he was trying to decide something. Then he stepped forward, closing the distance between them, and tucked her hair behind her ear, his fingers leaving pinpricks of warmth behind them.

'And thank you,' he murmured.

She felt her heart stutter and took in a breath. 'For what?'

Just the hint of a smile grazed his lips. 'For keeping me company.'

He leaned into her, brushing his lips against hers gently, offering up the mere whisper of a kiss. It was enough to make the nerves along her forearms prickle. He pulled away, only to rest his forehead against hers for a moment. He sighed softly. 'Goodnight, Josie.'

Chapter Seven

Josie's phone buzzed and she reached across her dressing table to grab it, sucking in a sharp breath as she accidentally brushed the corner of her ear with her hair straightener. She set the straightener down carefully on the heat mat as she read the WhatsApp from Laura.

What are you wearing??

Josie glanced in the mirror briefly before replying. She'd spent longer than usual on her makeup, using her special Charlotte Tilbury eye palette, a present from Helen, and following the tutorial only to create the *'Sophisticate'* look, but she still thought she looked plain and boring. It was stupid to think it mattered, she knew that. It wouldn't make her any less redundant or Oliver any less of a cheater. But still.

My blue dress, she typed back – the blue dress she always fell back on, skater style. She'd decided to play it safe on that front. At least she *knew* she looked nice in that. *Are you not already ready?*

Course, came back the reply. *John and I are getting a drink just across the road so we're there on time.* Josie snorted. Laura had literally never been late to anything as long as she'd known her. *Just checking you're actually still coming.*

As if I'd bail on the free Prosecco.

Laura sent her back a line of strong arm emojis.

Josie went back to straightening her fringe, her stomach twisting and churning as she thought about braving the event. The toast she'd just had to line her stomach now felt like a bad idea. Because on top of the Oliver and Janice issues, she didn't actually know if Max would show. She'd told him to meet her here at five originally, but that was before he'd got all weird with her, and they hadn't exchanged numbers, so she didn't even have the option of sending him an ever-so-breezy text message.

She jerked the straighteners again when her phone started flashing so that she hit her scalp. She winced as the heat seared it. *For God's sake, Josie, get a grip.*

'Hi, Memo,' she answered, deciding to quit while she was ahead and switch the straighteners off.

'You're not on FaceTime!' Memo said, her voice ever so slightly accusing. 'Didn't we say five p.m. today, before you left for your party?'

Josie hit her head with one hand. 'God, sorry. We did, I just completely spaced.' That, or she'd been distracted by the thought of whether or not Max would show up this evening. 'Hang on, I'll switch now.' She faffed around with her laptop and, when Memo answered the FaceTime call, Josie saw both her grandad and Helen squeezed in on each side of Memo on the red sofa, peering into the screen. Helen and Memo looked all glammed up with what Josie thought must be identical red lipstick, both with sparkling studs in their ears. Her grandad's one nod to the occasion was a smart tweed jacket – the one jacket he wore for everything from dinner at a friend's to weddings and garden parties.

'Happy Christmas Eve!' they chanted together, like they'd actually *practised* it, and Josie laughed.

'Don't you look beautiful?' Memo said, smiling broadly at Josie. 'All ready for your party?'

'Just about,' Josie said, trying hard to sound breezy.

'Why do you look worried?' Memo asked, her gaze fluttering across Josie's face. So much for the breezy, then.

'I'm not worried,' Josie said evenly.

'You look worried. Doesn't she look worried, John?'

Her grandad peered into the screen, making Josie feel hot around the collar of her dress. 'I'm fine, Memo,' Josie insisted.

Memo shook her head. 'You're too pale.'

'Well, I'll put on some more bronzer, then.'

She huffed out a breath. 'You're always looking pale these days. I don't think you get enough sleep.'

'Leave the girl in peace, Cecelia,' her grandad said gruffly. 'She's got a lot on her plate, that's all.'

Memo scrutinised Josie for a second more, then smiled, conceding the point, thankfully. 'Well, we're all very jealous here about your party, aren't we?' She looked from Josie's grandad to Helen and back again. Her grandad agreed with a grunt – though Josie knew he'd like nothing less than to be in London going to a party – and Helen nodded vigorously, taking a sip of something that looked like sherry.

'Very jealous,' Helen repeated, leaning across Memo to give Josie an appraising look. 'You've straightened your hair, have you? You should put some hair spray in it, darling, it looks a little flat.'

'Oh shh,' Memo pushed Helen away with her spindly fingers. 'Ignore her, Josie love, you look stunning.' *Just too pale*, Josie nearly said, but stopped herself. 'Oliver will be so sorry he ever even *looked* at another girl when he sees you.'

Josie knew this was supposed to make her feel better, but all it did was tighten the knot of anxiety in her stomach. She tapped her nails against the dresser next to her laptop. She should have painted them, she realised now.

Helen pushed her way back onto the screen. 'Oh there's no point crying over that now, Josie. Move on to bigger and better, that's what I say. Though he *is* a very nice young man, and maybe if you—'

'Helen!' Memo leaned forward and snatched the laptop onto her lap, if the change in angle was anything to go on. 'Josie, go and get your present, let's do that now. We'll have to be quick, we're off to the Copes's for drinks this evening before the carol service in the square.'

'That's nice,' Josie said, turning to grab her present from Memo and Grandad off her bedroom floor. She remembered that carol service – remembered playing with Beth Cope while everyone sang and drank mulled wine. She'd gone with her parents, the night they died, before they'd headed off to their party.

Frowning away the tears that burned the back of her eyes, Josie turned back to the laptop. 'It will be nice, I think,' Memo was saying, patting down her grey bob. 'I made some brownies to put in bags and hang on the big Christmas tree – you remember the one?' Josie nodded. 'Well, anyway, I really think this batch turned out quite well – less salty than the last batch. Your grandad ate two, didn't you, John?'

'What?' His bushy eyebrows pulled together as Memo turned the screen towards him. 'Oh, yes. They were very, umm, pleasant.'

Josie laughed. 'Very convincing.'

Memo sighed. 'He's hoping the baking will replace smoking.'

'Well he's right about that – you *should* stop smoking, it's bad for you.'

Memo's hand fluttered across the screen. 'Josie, whatever damage is done is already done by my age, there's no point in changing it now.'

Josie frowned, but heard Helen, out of sight, say, 'Hear, hear', and knew she was fighting a losing battle with the two of them.

'Anyway,' Memo said. 'Presents!' They opened their presents in front of the screen in a way that had long since stopped feeling weird, and Josie beamed at the beautiful jewellery box Memo and Grandad had got her. Her grandad laughed a little at the sign she'd got him, which was a surefire acknowledgement of a job well done, Helen started listing all the new skincare products she had her eye on at Space NK, and Memo genuinely seemed thrilled by the tea set. She'd have to remember to tell Max, Josie thought. If he showed up. God, there went her stomach again. She checked the time, trying to control the urge to do something, anything, with her hands.

'I'm really sorry, guys, but I've got this party and I—'

'But the quote!' Memo said. 'Helen's got one this time, haven't you, Helen?'

Josie raised her eyebrows. 'I thought it was my turn?'

'Yes, well, you wouldn't have done a Christmassy one, would you? And Helen wanted to get involved.' She turned the screen towards Helen, leaving no room for argument.

Helen cleared her throat dramatically. 'To me, you are perfect.'

Josie smirked. 'Why thank you.'

She heard her grandad laugh in the background, but Helen tssked impatiently. 'Well?'

Josie hesitated. Christmassy, they'd said. 'Ummm . . .'

'Oh come on,' Memo said, and Helen turned the laptop back to her. She'd gotten herself a glass of red wine since Helen had taken over the screen. 'You must know this one, love?'

Josie saw her phone vibrate next to her laptop and started, then remembered that *obviously* it wouldn't be Max, being as how he didn't have her number. Laura, she saw. God, she needed to get going, she wanted to make sure she found Laura in time so she didn't have to walk in alone.

'Well?' Helen was demanding.

'I don't know,' Josie said, and it came out more impatiently than she meant it to. 'Sorry, I mean, just let me think on it, ok? I'll text you.'

Memo frowned. 'Why are you so flustered?'

'I'm not,' Josie insisted. 'I'm just worried about making the party on time. On which note . . .'

'Actually, I wanted a word with you quickly,' Helen said. Josie watched as Helen stood up and moved across the living room and into the kitchen. Something she couldn't say in front of Memo then – that did not bode well. 'Darling, I just thought you ought to know . . .'

Josie's stomach jolted. 'Ought to know what? Has something happened?' She dropped her voice, glancing behind Helen on the screen to check her grandparents hadn't followed her into the kitchen. 'Is Memo ok?'

'Oh no, no, it's nothing like that, don't you worry. Your grandparents are fine.' Funny how she never seemed to refer to them as 'Mum and Dad' in front of Josie. 'It's just, well, I did a little digging online into that new man that you're seeing.'

Of course she did. 'I'm not really "seeing" him, Helen. And—'

'Anyway,' Helen continued, breezing over Josie. 'I found his architect firm, the one he said he worked for, ALA, and I hate to tell you this, darling, but he is not listed on their website *anywhere*.'

'Ok,' Josie said slowly. 'But that doesn't necessarily mean anything. Maybe they just don't list all their employees on the website, or they haven't updated it or something.' It had taken a good year, after all, for the internal system at her company to update her title after she'd been promoted.

'Well, yes, I considered that, but I called them to ask and they said he hasn't worked there in two months.' She let that hang for a moment.

'Two months?' Josie repeated, frowning. So he'd lied to Helen about where he worked? That was strange. Or was it? Maybe she was just letting Helen get to her.

'Yes,' Helen said, leaning towards the screen and dropping her voice like she was in on a conspiracy. 'And they wouldn't tell me why he left. I did ask.'

'It might not mean anything drastic, Helen.'

'Hmm. Well yes, maybe.'

'Why did you even go looking?'

'Because I'm *worried* about you, darling! You show up with a new man right after you break up with that lovely Oliver' – Josie gritted her teeth at that – 'and you look all flustered. I just don't want someone to swoop in and take advantage, that's all. I saw a dreadful article online the other day about a man who took everything from a young man right in the dead of night – he'd created a false identity and everything.' Josie allowed herself a small, wry smile. She knew why her aunt kept it vague with the 'online' – she was the type of person who pretended to read the *Guardian*, but in reality got everything from the *Mail*.

'Look, I appreciate you worrying about me, honestly I do.' The doorbell rang, and Josie's heart did a semi-painful jump. She stood up, taking the laptop with her, and started walking towards the door, dropping her voice slightly. 'But I don't think it's anything like that. I'm being careful, I promise.'

'Well, just have it in mind, won't you?'

'Fine, sure,' Josie said, knowing that agreement was the only way to stop her going on about it. 'But right now, there's someone at the door and I'm already running late, so I've got to go, sorry. Say goodbye to Memo and Grandad, won't you?'

'Bye, my love!' Memo called from the living room. 'And your grandad says bye too.'

'I can speak for myself, Cecelia,' she heard her granddad grumble distantly. Josie shook her head. She'd bet anything they'd both been listening to every word Helen said, and no doubt the three of them would be gossiping about it for the rest of the evening.

'Well, alright, bye then, darling. Have a wonderful time tonight,' Helen said.

'I'm sure I will,' lied Josie, now right by the front door, her bare feet making the lino floor creak ever so slightly. She shut the laptop screen, tucking it under her arm, then took a breath, willing her heart to calm down.

She opened the door to see Max standing there, wearing dark jeans, a blue shirt and a sleek, well-cut black jacket, his coat over his arm, even though it was bloody freezing outside. He looked incredible, his muscular body filling out his jacket perfectly, and she only realised she was staring when he smiled at her, the smile reaching up to warm those eyes which seemed to shift colour constantly, more amber now to match the lighter bits of his hair. His gaze travelled up and down the length of her body in a way that made her skin beat, before resting on her eyes.

'Hi,' Josie said, wishing her stomach would calm down. She shouldn't feel *this* nervous. It was just Helen – she'd thrown her, that was all.

He leaned against the doorframe and ran one hand over the stubble on his jaw. 'Hey,' he said easily, whatever had soured his mood yesterday clearly a thing of the past. 'Ready?'

'I, err . . .' She brought a hand to her hair but dropped it, remembering not to mess it up after she'd spent so long taming it. 'Yes, in a minute. I wasn't sure . . .' She trailed off, but he got her meaning anyway.

'If I was coming? I wouldn't abandon you like that,' he said, with a casual shrug. 'Besides, it was my idea in the first place.'

'Right,' she said, for some reason hyperaware of the

fact she was barefoot. 'I'll just grab my shoes, give me a sec.' He nodded and stepped inside so she could shut the door on the draught from the corridor. So what if he'd lied about where he worked? she thought. Maybe he'd been fired or something and didn't want to admit it in front of Helen – she wasn't exactly the type of person you immediately wanted to open up to. She put her laptop back, grabbed her heels and sat on her bed to slip them on, then checked the mirror one last time before picking up her bag and heading back out to meet him. She didn't really know much about him, though, and here she was, letting him into her house. She bit her lip. No. She couldn't let Helen get to her, even if she did mean well.

Max straightened up from where he'd been leaning against the door when she came back into the hallway. God, should she have told him to sit down or something? She offered him an overly bright smile in some effort to compensate, feeling incredibly self-conscious as her heels clicked on the floor, like she'd for some reason suddenly forgotten how to walk in them. And it was like he bloody *knew* that, the way his gaze dropped to her shoes, lingered on her legs.

His eyes sparked when she reached him. 'I got you a present,' he said, producing a box from his pocket and holding it out to her. His brows pulled together slightly when she didn't immediately take it.

Her stomach did a small somersault. 'You didn't have to do that!' She wasn't sure where to look, now that he was looking right at her.

'Here,' he said, a little aggressively. He thrust it into her hands.

107

She opened it, feeling incredibly self-conscious and trying to arrange her face into a suitable expression. When she saw what was inside, she stared mutely for a moment, then picked one up to examine it. The earrings. The big, dangly star earrings she'd pointed out at Fortnum's. She shook her head – she remembered the price tag on these. 'I can't . . . I mean, these are amazing, but I can't accept this, it's too much.'

He shrugged, and that little frown returned. 'Well, either you have them or I'll have to get my ears pierced – there's a no-return policy on earrings.' She bit her lip. He sighed. 'If you won't take a Christmas present, then consider it a thank you.' She met his gaze, and it was almost like he was staring her out, daring her to refuse. But when he spoke, his voice was soft. 'If it weren't for you, I would have just been sat around moping these last few days.'

She hesitated, but, at his encouraging nod, took the earrings out of the box and replaced her studs with them. She touched one of them. 'Thank you,' she said. 'They're beautiful.'

He reached out and traced a finger along her earlobe, down the sparkling earring. 'They might not shine as brightly as you, but at least they're pretty.' For a moment, he held her gaze, and even though his touch was light, Josie found herself flushing. She looked down quickly, but when he held the door open for her, she touched the place on her ear where his fingers had been, her skin still tingling.

It was just a short train ride from Josie's flat to Battersea, where the party was, so they arrived at the venue promptly at six p.m., right on time. It was being held at Battersea Arts Centre, a grand, impressive building from the outside, with mini turrets out of the roof giving the impression of a small castle. There were two Christmas trees either side of the pillared entrance, decorated simply in silver and gold, and there were fairy lights just below the archway. Josie smiled at Max as he opened the door for her, trying to control the squirming in her stomach that had only got worse on the journey over here.

A man, dressed smartly in a black suit, smiled at them as they arrived. 'The Peacock's party?' Josie nodded. 'Please check your coats just here, then you're in the Grand Hall.' The man indicated where he meant.

Josie glanced around but there was no one else she recognised in the entrance hall. She should have timed it better – deliberately arrived twenty minutes late or something. Although surely Laura, at least, must be inside somewhere. They checked their coats, and Josie felt a shiver run down her spine as she gave up her extra layer. When Max touched her bare shoulder to steer her in the right direction, she jumped, and he raised his eyebrows.

'Sorry,' she said, trying to smile even though her mouth was dry. 'Just cold.' She glanced at him as they walked, though his attention was on the interior of the building, not her, looking up and around them, his lips occasionally moving as though he was silently talking. She realised she was twisting her hands in front of her and dropped them, deliberately flexing her fingers at her sides. She shouldn't have brought Max with her. Now she had to try and pretend she was all breezy, at the same time as worrying about what he was doing and whether he was having a good time.

Josie led the way into the hall, and, like Max, she couldn't help looking up as she did. The ceiling was phenomenal, arched over them like a dome in a beautiful lattice design. The windows were huge, the tops of them domed to match the ceiling, each one decorated with fairy lights, and there was a Christmas tree in each corner. There were circular tables dotted around the room, with what looked like a mini stage down the other end, and a large buffet-style table on one side. And there were people here, thank God. Josie let out a slow breath as she realised they were not the first ones to arrive, that the room was already filling up, people milling about with glasses in their hands or sitting at the tables in small groups, heads bent towards each other.

'I knew they'd renovated it in here, but I haven't ever been in,' Max muttered, and Josie cocked her head up at him, not totally sure he was talking to her, given his gaze was still flicking around the building. 'It's impressive.'

'Prosecco?' A woman, dressed smartly in black and white, held out a tray to them and Josie took one of the glasses gratefully, taking a sip immediately.

They walked a little further into the room, and Josie felt heat from somewhere caress her skin. There was music in the background, she realised now – not the usual Christmas tunes but something instrumental and classical; she could hear the violins. She searched the room for someone she knew, someone from her own company, and pressed her lips together when she saw Janice, sleek black hair twisted into a bun, sitting on one of the tables near a makeshift stage.

Josie stopped as Max turned in a small circle to admire

the room a little more, and felt her face soften into a small smile. At least if the evening was a complete fiasco he'd at least have appreciated the architecture. He grinned a little guiltily at her when he saw her watching, then looked over her head, his gaze sharpening.

'Where are all the bikini models then?' Max asked, taking a sip of Prosecco. 'It's the only reason I came.'

'I *knew* there was an ulterior motive.'

He shrugged. 'Of course.'

She laughed, then jolted, nearly spilling her drink, when she felt a tap on her shoulder. She turned to see Oliver, smiling in a way that looked painful. He *was* a bit pixieish, now that she thought about it, all clean-shaven and perfectly smooth hair, his frame quite obviously petite in his smart black jacket and maroon shirt – a nod to the festive season, she supposed. His eyes – the ones she'd described as *chocolate* when she'd first gushed about him to Bia, didn't sparkle with pixie mischief tonight though, but rather looked a little mournful.

'Hey Jose,' he said. 'Happy Christmas Eve.' He reached out for a hug and, feeling it would make a scene if she refused, she returned it, trying not to think of how comforting and familiar he smelled, how her body remembered exactly where to fit against his. She pulled away as soon as she reasonably could. She glanced up at Max and though his expression gave nothing away, the perfect poker face, she was pretty sure he'd seen Oliver coming and made her laugh deliberately.

'Nice to see you again,' Max said affably, shaking Oliver's hand.

Oliver frowned. 'I didn't know you'd be here.'

Max smiled easily, a direct contrast to Oliver's tense jaw. 'It was a last-minute decision.'

Josie was saved from having to try and bridge the conversation when she saw a blonde, broad-shouldered woman by the tray of Prosecco and waved her over, trying not to look desperate. Laura marched over to them at a speed that indicated she hadn't broken her no-heels rule even for the party, with her fiancé John, only ever known as Scottish John in the office, following just a step behind her.

'Thank God you're here,' Laura said as she approached. She dropped her voice so that only Josie could hear. 'I was dreading having to make small talk with Accounts.' She jerked her head behind her where two women and a man stood huddled together. Laura took the glass of Prosecco that John handed to her and took a glug. She was wearing a very un-Laura like dress, black, sparkly and floor length, which worked because of her enviable flat stomach. 'It's my sister's,' she said, noticing Josie's appraisal. 'Thought I'd best make an effort what with all our shareholders here.' She fluffed up her hair, then, sparing no more than a nod for Oliver, smiled at Max. 'Sorry, I'm Laura, I'm in the PR team at Peacock's with Josie.' She had her formal work voice on, all brisk and efficient.

'Max.'

'And which company are you with?'

'Actually, I'm with Josie,' Max said easily, toasting Josie with his Prosecco as he did so.

Laura's blue eyes, as usual framed only with mascara, turned appraisingly. '*Are* you now?' Laura raised her eyebrows at Josie, and Josie shook her head, giving her a look to tell her she'd explain later. She hadn't told Laura ahead of time that she might be bringing someone, in case he hadn't actually shown up. Laura smiled at Max. 'Well, it's nice to meet you. This is my fiancé, John,' she said, indicating the tall, just-as-blond man beside her. Luckily, John was more olive-skinned than Laura's pinky tone, and had brown eyes rather than her blue, otherwise they might well have been mistaken for siblings.

'At least I'm not the only tagalong,' John said, grinning through his beard, his Glaswegian accent still strong despite his years in London. Max and John struck up an easy conversation while Laura sighed, nodding to where Janice was waving her over.

'I'd better go see what she wants.' Laura headed off at that same clipped speed, leaving Josie alone with Oliver. She tried to take a sip of Prosecco to distract herself, but found her glass empty. John was now explaining to Max that he worked as a freelance journalist, and Josie tried to think of something to say to insert herself into the conversation, but she wasn't fast enough – Oliver grabbed her wrist and pulled her away a step.

'Josie, I really need to talk to you.' He glanced at Max and John. 'Privately.'

Josie shook her head. 'Not now, Oliver.'

'Please.' He looked at her with those big Bambi eyes, adopting the puppy-dog look he always used to try and get his own way. 'It's not about what you think, I promise. I just . . . I don't want you to hear it from someone else, that's all.'

Josie's stomach twisted, making her feel a little sick, and, like she was somehow a beacon, Cara was immediately obvious. She was standing towards the stage area and, like a taunt, was wearing that same red dress she'd worn to the Christmas lunch, the one that showed off a slim, perfect figure and toned, tanned legs – even if the tan *had* to be from a bottle. Cara's gaze flicked towards Josie, then away quickly, and Josie felt sure she was watching them, waiting to see her reaction.

At that moment, Max laughed at something Scottish John had said, and Oliver scowled over at them. 'Seriously, Jose,' he muttered, 'who *is* that guy?'

Before Josie could say that it was none of his business, that he had no right to look so angry when he was surely about to tell her that he and Cara were an *item* now, that he could very much go to hell, Janice got up from the table and swept over to them, her stiletto heels clicking on the wooden panel flooring.

'Josie, don't you look wonderful?' Janice said, barely sparing her a glance. 'Oliver, a quick word?' She left him no option, gripping his forearm and steering him away from Josie and back towards the entrance.

Josie hesitated, feeling the need to check Max was ok.

'You're kidding!' John was saying to him as she rejoined them. 'One of my old school friends is an architect. Erin Fuller – don't suppose you've ever come across her?'

Max was shaking his head. 'You've got to be kidding me. You're mates with Erin?'

Deciding they were getting along well enough and sufficiently engaged in a game of Kevin Bacon, Josie silently walked over to the table where Laura was sitting, now alone, and collapsed down next to her. Laura frowned. 'What's up?'

114

Josie hesitated, then shook her head, but couldn't help the scowl towards Cara even though she *knew* she should be more pissed off at Oliver than at her. Still, she didn't have to make it so damn obvious, did she? They could at least have waited until after the Christmas break, was that really so much to ask? Laura grimaced sympathetically. 'Ignore Cara Drama, she's just trying to get attention because she's bored and knows she'll never amount to anything more than a mid-level exec, and therefore knows she needs to lock in a guy before she loses her looks and they figure out that's all she's got going for her.'

Josie snorted, then immediately felt harsh for doing it. She grimaced. She hadn't told Laura yet that she'd been made redundant – maybe *she'd* never amount to anything either.

Laura pursed her lips, studying Josie's face, then glanced over her head. 'The boys are coming over.' She leaned in a bit closer. 'Speaking of which . . . Don't waste any time, do you?'

'It's not like that, it's . . .' She twisted the stem of the Prosecco glass on the table. 'I don't know what it is.'

'When did you meet?'

'Three days ago,' she admitted.

Laura gave Josie an incredulous look. 'And he just happened to be free on Christmas Eve to come to a party with someone he's only just met?'

'He's stuck in London waiting for a flight,' Josie said defensively. 'Stop making it sound bad.'

Laura looked over Josie's shoulder at Max. 'He's pretty dashing.'

Josie raised her eyebrows. 'Who says "dashing" these days?'

'Seems nice,' Laura continued, ignoring Josie.

'Yes,' Josie agreed. He was nice, she thought, though she hadn't figured that out at first, being as how he'd almost tried to hide it from her.

'And he's been making John laugh, though I'll admit that's not all that difficult.' Josie knew Laura was building to something so said nothing, waiting for her to get to the point. They both glanced over to John and Max, who had stopped a waitress to get more drinks. John was broader than Max, but somehow Max still seemed to have more presence. It was the way he carried himself, Josie decided, like he'd learned the way to move through a room with purpose, and so that people moved out the way for him, rather than the other way around. Laura lowered her voice. 'So what's the damage, then?'

Josie huffed out a breath. 'Why does there have to be damage?'

'Is he married?'

Josie laughed. 'No.'

'How do you know?'

'Well, there's no wedding ring, for one.'

'Right, because people never take those off.'

'He's not married,' Josie insisted, though she remembered again what her aunt had told her. He'd lied about where he worked – could there be more he was lying about? Without really thinking about it, she lifted a hand to run her fingers over one of the star earrings he'd given her. Laura watched her do it.

'Nice earrings.'

'Thanks.' She decided not to own up to the fact that Max gave them to her, given she could see him and John

116

approaching now. John casually rubbed Laura's arm as he sat next to her, handing her a new glass of Prosecco just as Max set one down in front of Josie. She smiled up at him, perhaps a touch more enthusiastically than was really necessary, but the smile he gave her back was quick and efficient.

He held up his phone. 'I just have to call the airline, they've left me a message. Be right back.'

Josie nodded, and tried to ignore the *I told you so* look that Laura was giving her. Before Laura could start up again – the presence of John wouldn't stop her – Josie asked Laura about how the wedding planning was coming on, which distracted her enough that she launched into a story of how difficult the events manager at the venue – a Scottish castle no less – was being and how she was paranoid about there being a train strike around that weekend, which would mean that no one from London could make it. A waiter came round with canapés, and Josie took an arancini ball, taking little bites as she listened to Laura's story and trying very hard to stay present, rather than keep scanning the room for either of the two men who were preying on her mind.

Max came back after about ten minutes, sliding into the chair next to her. She caught a subtle whiff of his aftershave – something expensive, she reckoned. 'What did they say?' she asked.

He picked up his glass and took a sip. 'They said they've got me on a flight on Boxing Day.' He shrugged. 'We'll see, I guess.' Josie nodded and smiled, because it seemed like the appropriate reaction, but before she could ask anything more – like how long he was actually going to be away for and if he'd be coming back to London at any point after that – someone tapped the microphone on the stage area, and the chatter in the hall died down briefly as everyone looked at the man on the stage, clearly a technician.

'Speeches already?' John asked.

'They'll want to get them out the way so they can get drunk with the rest of us, I imagine,' Laura said.

Max grinned appreciatively as the CEO of the company, a man in his sixties who Josie had only seen once in the four years she'd worked for them, took to the stage – a little platform that raised him ever so slightly above everyone else. He cleared his throat, touching his glasses and nodding to the guy in black who was adjusting the microphone to his height. 'If you wouldn't mind, I'd like to say a few words before we all get stuck in to the festivities.'

There was a shuffling around the hall as people found seats or quickly grabbed another drink, then turned their attention to the stage. 'Thank you so much for joining us this evening, and for giving up your Christmas Eve to support our sponsored charity for the year.' He indicated a table behind him, which was home to various items – a bottle of champagne, a hamper basket, and photos of what looked like a helicopter and the Eiffel Tower, amongst other things. 'Please do take the time to bid on the items here and show your support – Christmas is all about giving, after all.'

Laura made a derisive noise. 'The whole charity thing was supposed to get us press attention,' she explained in a subtle whisper to the three of them. 'That's why it's on Christmas Eve too, the board thought it would mean we got some mentions in the diaries, and that a few mags might cover it which *obviously* they haven't done because the whole thing has been handled terribly. I did try to tell Janice this, but instead of listening to common sense and years of experience, she chose to ignore me.'

'It's been a good year,' the CEO continued, 'and we've seen some growth, which is excellent news, but there's still room for improvement and we've been looking for ways to expand and restructure each individual company to make sure that we stay strong players in the market.' Josie clenched her teeth at the word *restructure*. Here he was, talking about how good the year had been – if it had been so good, then why were they trying to make a bunch of people redundant?

'I'm going to let each company tell you their most exciting news themselves. First up, from Peacock PR, is the lovely Janice Evergreen.'

Janice swept onto the stage immediately, and Josie knew she must be loving this – the chance to stand up in front of everyone and prove how important she was. She went on again about the positive year and Josie took a gulp of her Prosecco, glancing at Max, who, though he was wearing a polite expression, had to be regretting his decision to come right now.

'But the *most* exciting thing we have to look forward to,' Janice was saying, 'something which we're so pleased to be announcing at last, is that we'll be opening up a New York office early next year, which will be headed up by none other than our own Oliver Burton.'

It took a moment for the words to sink in, for Josie to notice that Laura was leaning in, frowning at her. 'Did she say . . .?' But she didn't need to finish the question because there he was, on one of the tables closest to the stage, raising his hand at the polite applause that echoed around the hall.

'Did you know?' Laura whispered. Josie could only shake her head mutely. No. She hadn't known that while she was being made redundant, her ex-boyfriend was being made the head of a new branch. Across the other side of the Atlantic, no less.

Chapter Eight

Josie didn't hear the rest of the speeches. Occasional words, like *celebrate, congratulate* and *financial,* got through the dull ringing in her ears, but she didn't bother to concentrate to make sense of the wider context. Laura kept flicking her glances, but Josie just stared straight ahead, focusing on making sure she was blinking so that she didn't look vacant or bored, if anyone important were to glance at her.

How long had he known? Surely he couldn't have just found out? This was the kind of thing you knew for months before it was announced – you had discussions over the starting date, negotiated a better salary. Which meant he must have known while they were still together, must have been talking to Janice about it in private meetings at the office where they both worked, then just failing to mention it when they got home for the evening. He was planning to uproot his entire life, and he hadn't even bothered to discuss it with her. She wondered if he'd known Janice was planning to make her redundant too, if that had come up in all their secret talks.

Her eyes were stinging now, though she couldn't work out if she was angry or sad. She took a steady breath and tried to keep blinking. She felt a warm pressure on her right hand and looked down to see Max squeezing it. 'Are you ok?' he whispered. Josie nodded, but couldn't bring herself to look at him directly. God, what must he think? He'd come along for a fun Christmas party and here she was, trying not to cry. Laura shoved a drink into her other hand – Josie suspected it was Laura's second, untouched glass of Prosecco – and Josie took a sip, grateful to have something to do.

The CEO finished off the round of speeches and, after announcing the bowl food would be out shortly and wishing them a happy Christmas, left the stage to a polite round of applause, which died off soon enough to be taken over by chatter and laughter. Josie dimly heard the violins start up again in the background.

There was a crowd of people surrounding Oliver now, shaking his hand and thumping him on the back. She shouldn't watch, she knew she shouldn't. It would only make her feel worse. But before she could make herself look away, his head swivelled around and his gaze locked on hers. She stood up abruptly, and Max, John and Laura all followed her lead so that the people on the neighbouring table gave them odd looks.

Oliver was coming over to them now, taking short, quick strides as he weaved his way around the white-clothed tables. Laura swore under her breath, then shot off to intercept him, jerking her head at John as she did so. Josie didn't understand the gesture until John walked away from them too, splitting off from Laura and stopping right in front of Cara, who had clearly been on her way over as well, though God knew why. Even feeling as she was, Josie had time to marvel at the silent communication between the two of them – they'd only been together eighteen months, less time than she'd had with Oliver, but she and Oliver had never been able to do that, to know what each other were thinking like that.

It took Josie a moment to realise that Max had hold of her hand and that he was squeezing it gently, trying to pull her along, to get her moving. 'Come on, Josie, let's go.' She gave in to the pressure, tripping slightly as she went with him. Everything around her felt strangely distant, like someone had pressed the mute button and turned down the dimmer switch.

'We can't just leave,' she mumbled as he dragged her along behind him, back to the entrance hall.

'Why not? You showed your face, didn't you? Can't say fairer than that. Besides, everyone will be too hungover tomorrow to remember exactly what time you left anyway.' Josie just nodded, her brain apparently unable to focus on more than one thing at a time, still thinking of all those nights she and Oliver had talked about work, bitching about Janice and lamenting the fact that both of them were overdue a promotion. Nothing. He'd said nothing the entire time.

'Stay here,' Max commanded when they reached the hall. 'I'll get our coats.' Again, Josie just nodded, staring down at the mosaic floor.

'Josie.' She winced at the sound of Oliver's voice. She looked up to see him walking towards her, breathing a little heavily, like he'd genuinely run after her. She wondered vaguely how he'd got away from Laura. For a moment they stared at each other, then Oliver shook his head. 'I'm so—'

'I am so fucking tired,' Josie hissed, 'of hearing how sorry you are.' He flinched at her uncharacteristically harsh tone and she took a breath through her nose. She needed to get control of herself – the last thing she wanted was for him to know how much this was getting to her. She crossed her arms. 'I suppose congratulations are in order.' Perhaps if she were a stronger person, she'd even mean that. He'd always wanted to work abroad, after all. Was always talking about Sydney, New York, Toronto. She supposed, if she'd really thought about it, she should have known he'd never be content to just stay in one place, not like her.

'I wanted to talk to you before the speech,' Oliver said, raising his hands in a sort of helpless gesture.

'Yes, because telling me right before Janice announces it to the whole company is *so* much better.' He said nothing and she forced herself to lower her arms, drop the defensive pose. 'It doesn't matter, Oliver,' she said crisply. 'We broke up. It's none of my business what you do now.' He grimaced and she felt just a tiny bit harsh. This was his big night, and she was ruining it.

'I was going to ask you to come with me,' he said softly, his gaze never leaving her face. 'I just . . . I couldn't figure out how to do it, how to convince you to leave your life here, which is why I never brought it up before . . .' Yes, she thought bitterly. Before.

But despite herself, she had a flash then of being in New York, her and Oliver out at fancy restaurants or posing by the Statue of Liberty. She'd never been, so the images

124

were a little fuzzy, things she'd seen on films or TV merged in with bits of London. She sighed. 'Not really my thing, is it, packing up for some adventure in the Big Apple? We both know I'm more of a fan of the safe option.' Which is exactly why he hadn't told her, apparently. She was too damn predictable and he'd known, presumably, that she wouldn't have been excited by it, would have tried to convince him to stay in London instead. She liked to think she would have considered it, but the truth sat uncomfortably in her stomach, weighing it down – she would have hated the idea, hated the risk of it.

Thankfully, Max came back with their coats at that moment. Oliver frowned at the sight of him. 'You're leaving?'

Max handed Josie her coat and she slipped it on. 'That's my fault,' he said cheerily, a benign smile on his face. 'I'm stealing her away.' Oliver actually glared at him then, before struggling to control his facial muscles. Max pretended not to notice. 'Congratulations, by the way. New York – you must be excited.'

'Yeah, I guess,' Oliver mumbled.

'Surprised you didn't bring it up the other day, when I mentioned New York.' Max raised his eyebrows in question, and let it hang in the air for a moment. 'But then, I suppose I didn't really let you get a word in, hey?' Max's voice was perfectly friendly, the jibe so subtle that Oliver had no reason to get wound up. He flushed instead, and Josie felt impossibly grateful in that moment that she was not the most awkward one in their little trio, that the attention was very firmly off her and how she was taking the news.

'Babe—'

Josie turned to glare at Oliver as he followed them. She shook her head. 'Don't.'

He stopped in his tracks, but she could feel him watching them as they walked away.

Max bundled her out of the entrance hall, away from the allure of the domed, stained glass ceiling and straight into a car that was waiting outside for them. Clearly he'd taken the time to order an Uber at some point, though she hadn't seen him do it. She stared out the window as they drove, not saying anything, happy just to let Max get her home, if that's what he wanted to do. She wondered what he thought of her now, if he thought she was pathetic – losing her hotshot boyfriend who was off to swan around in New York, while she had to decide whether to take the crumbs that Janice threw at her feet. She thought again of his reaction, after she'd told him her parents had died. If he'd thought she was damaged goods after that then this had certainly done nothing to alleviate that impression, now had it?

It took her a good ten minutes to realise they were not heading back to Streatham. She took her attention off the endless headlights and frowned over at Max, who was looking out the window. 'Where are we going?'

'Just to a bar I know,' he said, with a glance at her. 'I want to say a quick hello to the owner while I'm in London. Is that ok?' He said it all casually, like it had absolutely nothing to do with her, and she couldn't help the smile that pulled at her lips.

'Sure,' she said, just as casually, not letting on how grateful she was not to be shipped back home. She didn't think she could face it, alone in that flat, waiting for Christmas morning to creep in on her. Not just yet, anyway.

She gave up trying to figure out where exactly they were going – she wasn't used to driving around London, sticking to the train and tube mostly, so it looked different from this angle, the landmarks all wrong. There were plenty of other cars on the road, people on their way back to their families before Christmas Day. Max made small talk with the driver and Josie allowed the conversation to wash over her like background music, the rise and fall of their voices strangely soothing. It was at least forty minutes before the car pulled over, down a little street off the main broadway.

'Thanks, mate,' Max said, and hopped out, holding the door open for Josie so she could shuffle out to avoid a puddle the other side of the car. It was a moment before Josie realised that there was a small gathering of people down the end of the street, huddled together under a lamp, their breath clouding together with smoke from their cigarettes. Josie hunched her shoulders against the cold as she followed Max towards them, to the building behind them, with subtle lighting in the windows, and a crooked sign above the door. It was a bar, she realised now, but the entrance was barely noticeable, so much so that you could have easily walked past and missed it, if you weren't paying enough attention. She followed Max to the door, feeling like she was being led through some kind of secret entrance, away from the bigger pubs and excitement on the broadway.

She ducked her head under a wooden beam that she was sure must have seen a few casualties in its day as they made their way inside, then had to blink a few times to

127

figure out exactly what kind of place they'd come to. There were three adjoined rooms, with the bar seeming to be in the middle one, dim lighting meaning there were plenty of secret corners to hide away in, the whole place giving off the impression that it was lit by flickering candlelight alone, which just couldn't be true. The rooms seemed lopsided somehow, like they were on different levels, though there were no steps between them. Each room was relatively small, yet the place didn't feel crowded, even though there were plenty of people here, the murmuring voices offset by classical music.

'How did you even know this place was here?' Josie asked as Max led her towards the bar.

'I know the owner,' he said, doing a quick scan of the room.

'How?'

He gave her a little guilty smile. 'I, err, designed the remod of the place actually.'

Josie started, then looked around again. 'Wow. That's so cool. *This* is so cool.'

He grinned, his eyes flickering a little in the moody lighting. 'It was one of my favourite projects, because there were so many rules about what we could do with the building and the owner had such a specific idea of how he wanted it to feel. It was a lot of fun.'

Josie made a mental note to tell her aunt that Max was very clearly not lying about being an architect, even if he'd given her a different company name, just as a short, slim man cut in front of them, beaming. 'Max!' He clapped Max on the back, standing on the balls of his feet to do so. 'What on earth . . .? Well, this is just a marvellous surprise.' He clapped his hands in front of him. 'It's been too long, my friend.'

Max smiled that smile that Josie was learning was the genuine one – unlike the charming one he'd used on Helen or put on deliberately for Oliver, this one softened the lines of his sculpted face. 'Sorry, mate. You know how it is when life just gets in the way.' He gestured towards Josie. 'This is Josie. I brought her along to show off the place.'

'As indeed you should!' The man's voice was musical, and seemed to have an exceptionally large range, the intonations bouncing up and down in pitch as he spoke. 'Welcome, Josie, it's a pleasure.'

'George is the owner,' Max explained. 'And a friend,' he added at George's scolding look.

'A drink!' George announced, putting a finger in the air in a way that would have been comical if anyone else did it. 'I shall return.' He swept away with a flourish, and Max chuckled quietly beside her.

'I like him,' Josie said decidedly.

'Most people do.'

He found them a space at the rather full bar, right against the wall, and insisted she take the stool while he stood beside her, leaning against the wooden bar top, which, instead of being the usual blunt rectangle, moved in and out in non-uniform waves that almost seemed to ripple in the candlelight effect. Josie ran a hand along the side of the wood, noticing the differences in the grain.

'It was hand crafted,' Max explained. 'Like I said, very specific ideas.'

George returned, as promised, with a drink for each of them – a spiced Christmas cocktail, though he wouldn't tell them what was in it. It was red, and tasted of cherry and ginger, and Josie was pretty sure there was brandy in there somewhere. Whatever it was, she'd finished it in the time it took George and Max to have a quick chat, and another one was placed in front of her without so much as a look from her. She pulled it towards her – it was Christmas, after all.

George went off to the other side of the bar to chat to someone else, and Max shifted his position, his arm brushing hers as he did so. She felt the flash of heat, and became acutely aware of how tiny she felt, perched on the stool next to him – which was saying something as she usually felt too tall and awkward wherever she went. There was more stubble on Max's jaw than there had been a few days ago, and it made him look even sexier, especially in the candlelight, which, she thought decidedly, suited him, like it set his hair and eyes alight. She realised she was studying him and cleared her throat. 'Not a fan?' she asked, gesturing towards his cocktail, which he was only halfway through.

'Sure.' He took a sip as if to prove it. 'But I know George, and this'll be five times the strength of your average cocktail.' Josie paused in the act of taking another sip, not entirely sure if he was joking or not. He laughed at her expression, which made her think it *was* a joke, but she put it down to have a little break, just to be safe.

He hadn't asked, and Josie knew he wouldn't, that he wasn't expecting any explanation, but now that they were here, huddled up in their little corner with the sound of George's laughter reaching them from the other end of the bar, Josie found she actually wanted to talk about it.

She lifted the wooden straw in her cocktail and gave it a little stir. 'He never told me,' she said on a sigh.

He nodded, that poker face already in play. 'Yeah, I got that impression.'

'I think he tried to.' Josie stopped playing with the straw, glanced up at him. 'I'm not sure how I feel about it.'

His eyes were level on hers. 'About the fact he didn't tell you, or the fact he's moving to America?'

Josie pulled a hand through her hair. 'Either. Both. I just . . .' She waved that same hand in the air, then dropped it into her lap.

'I don't think there's a law that says you have to decide how you feel after news like that within the next hour.' She snorted quietly, looking down at her hands in her lap. 'And it's ok, you know, if you both hate him and wish he wasn't leaving at the same time.'

She picked up her straw again, deciding to risk another sip. 'Been in a similar situation, have you?' He shrugged and she immediately grimaced – he'd told her, hadn't he, that his girlfriend had broken up with him in May? 'Sorry,' she said quickly.

But he only laughed, shaking his head at her grimace. 'It's ok. This year has been pretty . . . rough, I'll admit. But then, if none of it had happened, maybe I wouldn't be here with you now.' He reached out, tucked a strand of her hair behind her ear and let his fingertips trail lightly down her neck, leaving little shivers behind. He grinned. 'And then I would have missed out on a fancy work party and free drinks.'

Josie let out a breath. 'Couldn't be having that,' she said, trying to match his easy tone. 'And hey,' she added, gesturing with her cocktail, 'maybe you'll bump into Oliver while you're visiting your parents – at least he'll have one friend there, right?'

'Totally. I'll send him a Facebook message, we can go to a Knicks game or something – I mean, the guy is just dying to be my friend, I could tell.'

Josie snorted and picked up her drink again, realising that her tongue was tingling just a little bit, her head starting to feel pleasantly buzzed. A reason to keep drinking, she decided, all things considered.

'I think you might have gone, you know.' She paused in the act of drinking, the straw still between her lips, to look at him. His gaze was totally locked on hers in a way that made it impossible to look away. His mouth crooked up into a small smile and she felt heat rush to her face. The skin on the back of her neck tingled. 'I think you might have more adventure in you than you give yourself credit for.' Then he turned to nod at George as George held up a bottle of beer, and Josie unfroze, setting her drink down and letting her breath out on a whoosh. 'I mean,' Max said, his voice light again, 'you came to the beach with me, what's more adventurous than that?'

'Well, I suppose adventure's one word for risking frost-bite and pneumonia by paddling in the ice-cold water.'

Max grinned. 'I still have all ten toes, don't I?'

She glanced down at his shoes and shrugged. 'I've yet to see concrete proof of that.'

They stayed for another two drinks, George refusing to let them leave, though Josie switched to one of the mock-tails for the second one, not wanting to get completely plastered and do something embarrassing in front of Max.

She was laughing when they got into the taxi, the chill of the night air slightly taking her breath away. The party now seemed like a vague memory, like it had happened on a different night entirely, though Josie was sure that, if she focused on it, the whole thing would come racing back into humiliating focus. Better, then, not to think of it at all, and to concentrate instead on the way Max was holding her hand, tracing circles on her skin with his thumb, on the feel of his leg pressed next to hers as he sat in the middle seat, right next to her. She should feel tired, she supposed, given the lateness of the hour, but she felt overly alert, like her whole body was waiting. At some point, without her realising it, the haziness of the cocktails had left her, leaving her mind clear and, like her body, intensely focused on the heat of Max's body next to hers.

When they reached her block of flats he got out of the taxi too, and, after saying something to the driver that she didn't quite catch, followed her up the stairs. Neither of them said anything, and now that he was no longer touching her, the air between them felt strangely electric. It seemed to take her several minutes to find her keys in her bag, though surely it couldn't have actually been that long, and she refused to look at him the whole time, not sure what she'd see on his face if she did, not wanting him to kiss her goodbye and then leave, as he'd done last night. When she did eventually find them, it took her two attempts to get the key in the lock because her fingers weren't quite steady, so that Max gave up waiting and did it for her.

He went through the door ahead of her, still holding

her keys, and then turned to look at her. His eyes were measured as he stepped towards her, his expression straight and even as she tilted her chin up to meet his gaze. He reached out, brushed her hair back away from her face. 'You look beautiful, you know.' His voice was low, husky. 'I should have told you that at the beginning of the night.'

'Better late than never.' She was surprised at how level she sounded, given the way her heart was beating right now.

His lips did that twitching that she'd recently decided *was* a smile as he ran his hand down the length of her arm. And then he was kissing her and without even thinking about it she hooked her arms around his neck, pressing herself closer to him. Dimly, she heard the door closing behind her and realised they'd walked back into it, that she was pressed between him and it, his hands now on her bare arms as she stripped off her coat. There was the sound of her keys dropping to the floor and she didn't care enough to look for them, to make sure that the door was locked properly, because that would mean she had to stop kissing him. It was him who pulled away, and she was relieved that she was not the only one breathing heavily.

'The taxi is downstairs, waiting for me,' he said, his voice hitching a little. She felt her stomach drop, her throat tightening immediately, though she managed to press her lips together and nod. He didn't try to move away, though, just reached out to touch her hair again, his eyes on hers the whole time. So, knowing that she may well be setting herself up for a sting, knowing that she shouldn't risk it because she was already vulnerable and a rejection the night before Christmas might well send her over the edge, Josie took a breath, cocked her head, and smiled.

'Or you could stay.'

Max considered her for a moment, then gave her a slow grin. 'Or I could stay.' She laughed, just a tiny bit breathlessly, as he kissed her again.

Chapter Nine

Josie woke while it was still dark – or as dark as it got here, anyway. Max had rolled away from her slightly in the night, but she could still feel the heat of him next to her, his fingers lightly touching hers. His breathing was heavy, so it seemed safe to say he was still asleep. And under the duvet, he was very, very naked. As was she.

She blinked a few times, trying to wake her eyes up, then shifted her body carefully away from his, trying to create as little movement on the bed as possible. She hesitated at the edge of it, biting her lip as she watched the shape of Max's body. He *looked* asleep, and she didn't know why he'd be faking it. So she stepped lightly onto the lino floor, sucking her breath in through her teeth as the freezing temperature outside the protection of her bed hit her. She tiptoed as quietly as she could across the room, grabbing some leggings and a top along the way. When she made it successfully to the other side of the bedroom door she blew out a slightly shaky breath, then pretty much ran to the bathroom, wincing at the cold air on her bare skin.

It was a relief to switch the bathroom light on and see what she was doing as she quickly tugged on her leggings and top. She sighed as she looked at herself in the mirror. She supposed no one looked good the morning after, but it didn't help that her mascara and eyeliner had smudged under her eyes, that her light layer of foundation had cracked in places, and that her lips were slightly swollen. She touched them lightly and grinned despite herself. *That* bit she didn't have as much issue with.

She set to work on her face, washing it clear of last night's residue and applying a light layer of BB cream to smooth out her skin, then attacked her hair and brushed her teeth before nodding to herself. Better. At least when he woke now she wouldn't look quite as much like a dirty stop-out.

She tiptoed back into the bedroom, but there was no need – Max blinked at her through the darkness as she came in. 'It's cold without you here,' he complained, his voice groggy from sleep.

'Sorry,' she whispered, the dark and cold somehow impressing the need to be quiet, like somehow she'd wake the other houses up too early if she spoke at a normal volume. Though she supposed many would be up already, children running excitedly into their parents' room with stockings, determined to start Christmas Day as early as possible. She only had vague memories of doing that, before the accident. She shook her head away from the memory. 'I didn't switch the heating on last night,' she said apologetically. 'I forgot.'

He stretched out his arms above his head and she

traced the movement, running her gaze along the length of his muscled torso. 'Have to say, I enjoyed the reasons for temporary memory loss more than I would've enjoyed the heating.'

She didn't switch the light on, unwilling to break the spell of darkness and catapult them into reality. She felt him watching her as she padded back towards the bed on bare feet, then perched awkwardly on a corner. She didn't know if she should just get up, now she was up, wasn't sure if he'd want to leave right away. He answered that question by grabbing her arm, pulling her across the bed towards him and putting an arm around her. 'I told you,' he breathed into her ear, 'it's cold without you here.' She laughed softly. He kissed the side of her neck and a shiver went through her. 'Bit one-sided though – you're cheating.' He gestured at her clothes and she shifted a little closer, her back pressed against him, tracing her fingers down his forearm.

'Do you want me to leave, so you can get dressed too?' She was aware of the slight smirk in her voice, kind of liked the way it sounded.

He kissed her on the neck again. 'No. I want you to stay so you can get *un*dressed.' She turned her head to grin at him, and he brushed a feather-light kiss on the corner of her mouth. 'Happy Christmas,' he murmured.

'Happy Christmas,' she breathed back. And she realised that, for the first time in a long time, she wasn't sad that it was Christmas morning, that she was actually excited about what the day would bring.

Max relented and used the bathroom to sort himself out while Josie made them coffee, which they drank in bed, chatting nonsense and answering Christmas Day texts until Max sat up straight, seemingly randomly, and announced, 'Right, we're going out.'

Josie raised her eyebrows at him. 'Right. Where, exactly?'

He rolled his eyes and jumped out of bed, seemingly full of energy. 'Come on, take the risk and dig out your adventurous side.'

It was cold and grey outside, hardly picturesque, but somehow the dense, dark clouds seemed to promise something, to hint at something beautiful behind them, so that they made the day feel charged with electricity, rather than oppressive. There was a hint of moisture in the air that clung to Josie's face as the wind kissed her cheeks, but she didn't mind – it felt refreshing, like it was setting her system on fire.

Max made them walk, though he had to follow Maps on his phone and kept stopping to turn the phone in his hand and make sure they kept going in the right direction. Josie was a little out of breath by the time she realised where he'd been leading her, though he didn't seem to find the walk quite so difficult. She grabbed his hand, squeezed, as she looked at the pub.

The pub where they'd had their first drink, after she'd unceremoniously knocked him off his feet. Josie found herself grinning, charmed by the sentimentality of the thought. He smiled down at her, then linked his fingers with hers and pulled her inside. It was busier than she would have thought, given it was Christmas, but everyone was smiling, and each person they passed offered a nod and a 'Merry Christmas', which they returned. The same barmaid was there, and she, too, was beaming, her bunches tied with red tinsel around them so that her hair glittered as her head moved.

'Table under Carter?' Max said.

Bunches nodded, grabbed two menus from behind the bar, and indicated a table in the corner, laid up for two. 'We're eating?' Josie asked. She'd never eaten here before, though she noticed now that there were tables laid up in the next room, crackers on the placemats between the cutlery, a table of four elderly people already sitting through there.

'Well, it was either this or a quick run to the local petrol station to get supplies, I'm guessing.' He raised his eyebrows in question.

Josie wrinkled her nose. 'I have pasta.'

He shook his head mockingly. 'That's just sad.' She punched him lightly on the arm and he laughed as they went to sit down. Bunches took their drinks orders, her eyes lingering on Max longer than Josie thought was strictly necessary, though she supposed she couldn't blame her. Max didn't seem to notice the extra attention and she wondered if it was just because he was used to it, or if he was as distracted by her as she was by him. Given it was Christmas, she decided to go for the latter, just to please herself.

She looked around, noting the fire the other side of the room, the Christmas tree in the corner with presents underneath (presumably fake). The table of four all had Christmas hats on, and were all drinking wine. 'You booked a table,' she stated.

He leaned back in his chair, tilted his head. 'Clearly.'

'When?'

Max just tapped the side of his nose.

They moved on to red wine after their first drink, inspired by the other table. The pub had started to fill up by the time they ordered their food, including a big table of seven, one of the children wearing the type of red velvet dress you can only get away with under the age of six, and a couple who were wearing His and Hers Christmas jumpers.

They were halfway through their roast dinners – Josie had opted for the slightly less traditional beef, which she had to admit was pretty good, tender and juicy, with some of the best fluffy roast potatoes she'd had – when her phone rang. She had to swallow a particularly large chunk of Yorkshire pudding drowned in gravy to get to it while it was still buzzing, and saw that it was a video call from her grandparents. They usually just stuck to Christmas Eve, but having told Memo that Bia was in Argentina, it didn't surprise her that they'd want to check up on her – in fact, Josie was pretty sure that Bia was the only reason she didn't get more sporadic calls from them, worrying about how she was.

She glanced outside, but Max waved a hand at her. 'You can answer it here if you want, don't go and stand in the cold on my account.'

She hesitated, but gave in and accepted the call – it would be unfair of her to ignore them just because she was having a good time. 'Hello, my love.' Her grandmother's face filled the screen, smiling and wrinkled, her grey bob beuatifully curled today and a dash of brown eyeliner under her brown eyes. Her grandad was there too, one bushy eyebrow, half of a stubbly chin, but she couldn't see Helen.

'Happy Christmas!' Josie said, beaming.

'And to you too,' Memo said, raising a glass of some sort of liqueur.

'How's your morning been?' Josie asked.

'Oh, you know, Helen had everyone up early with Bucks Fizz and took us all out on a walk. *How* that woman has that much energy at her age I don't know.'

Josie smiled. 'You're one to talk. Where's Helen now?'

'She's in the kitchen, taking charge of the roast, and I thought it was easier to let her have at it. Do you want to talk to her? I can grab her?'

'No, that's ok,' Josie said quickly, not particularly wanting to risk Helen and Max interacting over video.

'Anyway, how are *you,* my love? I'm worried about you, spending Christmas alone.'

Josie glanced at Max across the table, who was taking a sip of red wine, raising his eyebrows at her over the rim. 'Well, I'm, umm, I'm actually out at a pub with a friend at the moment having lunch, if that makes you feel any better.'

'It does,' her grandad said, moving his head into the frame. 'But we need proof.'

Smiling a bit, Josie turned her phone to Max, who moved his wine glass immediately out of sight, and cleared his throat, giving an awkward little half wave, which made Josie laugh.

Memo made an appreciative 'hmm' noise in the back of her throat. 'So this is your "friend" is it? He's pretty – when are you bringing him to visit?'

Josie laughed again, but they moved on to talk about other things, like what Helen had got them for Christmas – a Kegel exercise set for Memo and a smoothie subscription for her grandad, which made Josie a little nervous about opening her own present from Helen when she got home. If Helen could buy her own mother Kegels, there were no limits. 'I got the quote, by the way,' Josie said, a smile playing around her lips.

Memo raised her eyebrows expectantly. 'Did you know?'

'*Love Actually*?' At Memo's sigh, Josie laughed. 'Thought you'd got me, did you?'

'I have to admit I thought that might be the one to put me firmly in the lead, but alas, there's always next time and I'll catch you out sooner or later.'

Josie was smiling when they hung up, though the interruption meant that her roast had got a little cold. Max, one step ahead of her, ordered a jug of hot gravy.

'How come you're not there?' he asked, then gestured to where she'd put her phone next to her on the table. 'With your grandparents?'

Josie took a bite of beef, chewed slowly, then sighed and picked up her wine. 'It's just . . . it's too difficult. Going back to where I grew up. Especially at Christmas, on the day they died. It makes me sad, and then they get sad that I'm sad and I . . .' She sipped her Rioja, put it down. 'I guess that just seems unfair, on all counts.'

Max nodded. 'I get that.'

When the bill arrived, there was the predictable awkward fumbling with bags and wallets, but Max was insistent that he pay for the whole thing. Just as she'd noticed before, his wallet was chock full of papers, receipts and folded envelopes – his to do list, he said, where he couldn't escape it – which meant that he had to dump several cards and papers onto the table in order to retrieve the card he wanted. One thing in particular made Josie stare, and she reached out to touch the sides of the envelope.

Wordlessly, she picked it up and unfolded it, tracing the writing on the front of it. Her writing.

'Something wrong?' Max asked, after he handed the card machine back to Bunches. Josie turned the envelope around, staring at him. He frowned at it. 'That's not mine.'

'No. It's mine.'

'Huh?'

'It's a letter, I wrote it, and then . . .' She'd lost it, when she'd hit him. He must have picked it up with all his things, shoved it there with everything else without realising. There was no reason he'd have wanted to keep it, surely, and it hadn't been opened. 'You must have picked it up, I guess, in the road. It's the letter I lost that day.'

Max grimaced, and ran a hand across the back of his neck. 'God, I'm sorry, Josie. Was it important? I swear I didn't even realise, I just shoved everything in here, haven't got round to sorting anything out yet.'

Josie nodded – she believed him. Still, the thought of him carrying it around these past few days, of holding on to something so intimate, made her feel a little strange, like she'd given up some part of her without being aware of it. He was watching her, his eyebrows pulled together, clearly worried about whether she was going to be pissed off, so she smiled to reassure him. 'I have this . . . tradition,' she explained, holding up the letter so he could see what was written on the front of the envelope. *Mum and Dad.* She wondered if he'd figure it out. 'And, well, I guess it's been delayed a little this year, but it's still something I want to do. Something I need to do, on the way back.' She took a breath, and he asked no questions. He wasn't the type to pry, she was learning. It was partly that which made it so easy to ask, 'Will you come with me?'

They walked hand-in-hand to the post box, the letter clutched in Josie's other hand. She'd been meaning to write another one, but had let herself get distracted in the whirlwind of Max and the thought of that brought a tug of shame. But she was doing it now, she told herself. It wasn't like she'd forgotten them – she'd never do that.

It was the first time she'd ever shared the tradition with anyone, even if she didn't tell him exactly what the letter was – she thought he knew enough to guess, anyway. It felt more intimate than anything else they'd done so far and as they stopped by the post box there was a lump in her throat that she knew it was ok to feel. He squeezed her hand, saying nothing, just letting her know that he was there.

She heard the gentle thud of the envelope hitting the inside of the post box when she let it go, the sound of something that would never be delivered. She blinked back the tears when Max put an arm around her, stroked her back gently. 'It never goes away, does it, that kind of grief?' he said softly. She wanted to ask him again who'd he'd lost, but it didn't seem like the time. So she just blinked and nodded, leaning into him and wishing she could find the words to tell him what it meant to her, having him there in that moment.

They held hands on the walk back, and Max chatted to her, keeping up a running commentary as he speculated on how Bunches was spending Christmas Day after work, how the couple in the Christmas jumpers met. He gave her the time to get herself together, distracted her enough that, by the time they felt the first drop of rain, she was laughing.

They looked up at the sky together. 'Uh-oh,' Max said. They were still a good twenty minutes from the house.

They had no more warning before it started up in force, and Josie squealed as Max pulled her into a run. For some reason they were both laughing so much that, by the time they reached the end of the road to turn left, Josie had to stop, doubling over as she tried to get her breath back, as much from the laughter as the run.

When she straightened up, Max had his hands out, palms up, and his face lifted to the sky in an almost serene expression. Josie let out another little laugh, and he turned to grin at her. 'No point in fighting it now, we're already drenched.' It was true – Josie's coat was sodden and she could feel the icy water running off her hair and down the back of her neck. So she shrugged and copied him, turning a small circle and closing her eyes as she allowed the rain to drench her face.

She felt Max grip her hand again, pull her round to him. But instead of starting to run, he twirled her under his arm, making her laugh again. He put one big hand on her hip when he spun her back to him, took the other in his. She shook her head. 'What are you doing?'

He spun her in a circle again. 'What does it look like?'

And then they were dancing down the street, letting the rain fall around them, grinning at a woman under an umbrella when she looked at them incredulously. Josie had a feeling that people would be watching them out of windows but she didn't care, she just kept laughing and spinning, deciding that dancing in the rain on a random street in London should be on *everyone's* bucket list.

They were both breathless when they stopped. He smiled, smoothed back her sopping hair, and kissed her, and she did not care, in that moment, that her feet were sodden or her fingers were numb, because she would have quite happily stayed out here, kissing him, until the rain stopped. The cold got the better of them in the end, though, and they were both shivering a bit when they got back to her flat. She switched the heating on, knowing it would take a good hour before the flat was properly warm. When Max pointed out they'd both get warmer much more quickly if they showered together, Josie agreed.

While Josie blow-dried her hair, Max curled up on her sofa, reading the book she'd left there. She came to the doorway of the living room and leaned against it, watching him. He looked so perfect there, next to Bia's Christmas tree, like some sort of TV advert. He seemed to sense her watching and looked up from the book, smiling at her.

She walked towards him, keeping her hands clasped behind her back. He noticed the way she was holding herself, deliberately hiding something, and cocked an eyebrow. She stopped, shifting her weight awkwardly from foot to foot. 'I've, err, got something for you.'

'You have?' He smiled, held out his hands. 'Well, hand it over then.'

She hesitated, then produced the blown-up photograph from behind her back, which she held up for him to see. It was the photo he'd commented on at the beach, the one with him sideways on, almost in silhouette, the smile on his face only hinted at, like it was some kind of secret. She bit her lip as she waited for his reaction. 'I was going to get it framed for you, but, well, I ran out of time, and seeing as how it's Christmas Day today . . .'

He took it from her gently, making sure to only touch the sides. Then he looked up at her. 'I love it.' The smile he gave her was just a little sad, and she wondered if she'd made him feel awkward, giving him something, like he had to give her something in return. 'It's not much,' she carried on quickly, 'not like those earrings, and you don't have to feel obliged to take it with you or anything, I just wanted . . .'

He stood, gave her a quick kiss on the lips to stop her talking. 'I love it,' he said firmly. 'It feels like I have a part of you to take with me now.' She tried to smile at that – after all, that's exactly how she felt about her photography, like she was giving a part of herself, but . . . to take with him. When he left. Did that mean he didn't want to see her again, when he got back from New York? She couldn't quite bring herself to ask, in case it ruined the day, so instead she settled for another glass of wine, for curling up next to him while they watched *Harry Potter*.

Neither of them brought up the matter of him staying over again – it was just assumed. Later, when they were in bed, her back pressed against him, his hand in hers, she remembered that his flight had been moved to Boxing Day. He hadn't mentioned it all day and she wondered if he, too, was pretending that it wasn't happening, was allowing himself to think that it might be cancelled again, that maybe they'd have a bit more time together. He kissed her softly on her neck, running his free hand down her side, and she felt the heaviness behind her eyes taking over. She'd talk to him tomorrow, she thought sleepily, before he left. Maybe she could go with him to the airport. Surely they'd see each other again, surely they could try and make something work, even if it was long distance? Bristol wasn't *that* far away, after all.

She felt her breathing slow, felt the world around her drift. Dimly, she heard him murmuring something to her as she succumbed to the foggy sleepiness, but it was distant, just out of reach, so she couldn't quite grasp the words. He'd tell her tomorrow, if it was important. She was smiling as she fell asleep, thinking of him, dancing with her in the rain.

Chapter Ten

It was the cold that woke her the next day. It took a moment to realise that it wasn't just that the heating had gone off, it was the absence of a warm body next to hers. She sat up, blinking blearily. It was so quiet, like the entire block of flats was sleeping in after a heavy day yesterday. She frowned as she looked over to Max's side of the bed. The sheets were rumpled, the pillow a little dented. She trailed her fingers over the sheet – it felt cool to the touch.

She frowned, sitting up a little straighter as she strained her ears. No sound of running water from the bathroom, no footsteps in the corridor outside her room. Maybe he was just trying extra hard to be quiet. She stood up, shoving on the clothes she'd abandoned on the floor yesterday evening and crossed the room, peering out of her bedroom door before she stepped through it, like she was worried she would be caught spying. She wrapped her arms around her as she walked through to the living room. The bathroom door was open – no one inside. He wasn't making coffee in the kitchen or sitting on the sofa reading her book. He was nowhere.

Her heart thudded uncomfortably in her chest and she forced herself to take a breath, shook her head at herself. He'd probably just popped out to get something, gone to pick up breakfast maybe. He hadn't wanted to wake her up, that was all. She checked the time on the clock over their fake fireplace. Seven a.m. Pretty early to go out to get breakfast, but still. He wouldn't have just *left,* surely – there was no reason to, given he was about to go to New York – that was a pretty easy get-out clause, if he really wanted one. Besides, it wasn't like this was an awkward one-night stand, they'd spent the entire day together after sleeping together, for God's sake – *Christmas* Day. You didn't do that if you didn't like someone, you just didn't.

Still, her stomach wouldn't settle as she set the kettle to boil, and she kept glancing at the door, keeping her ears on high alert as she listened for the sound of footsteps in the corridor. She only noticed the piece of paper when she crossed to the sofa, determined to be found quite content sipping coffee serenely when he returned. It was a page from her notebook, she realised, which she'd left on the coffee table last night – torn out, folded in half, and placed on top of her book. Her name was written on it.

She set the cup of coffee down and snatched the letter up. She had to read it three times before the words actually made their way into her brain, and then she just sank onto the sofa, gripping it tightly in both hands.

Josie, I'm sorry to sneak out on you like this, but my flight is today and I had to get going early to make it — my parents would kill me if I missed this one. I've never been good at goodbyes — who is, right? — so I thought it would be easier for both of us like this. I wish I could see you again, but I doubt life will be that kind to me, so I'll have to settle for these last few days, which have been incredible. You are amazing, and you made missing a flight and getting stuck one of the best things that's ever happened to me. It meant so much to me, spending Christmas with you, and please know that I will be forever glad I met you. Max.

P.S. I hope you don't take the 'sideways move' or whatever that your company offered you. I think you're destined for better than that.

That was it. There was no phone number, no suggestion that they at least *try* to see each other again.

She set the note down on the table, stared at it numbly. She'd known from the beginning that he was only here temporarily, and they'd made each other no promises, but *this*? This felt like a low blow. Because she was sure that he had in no way been thinking of *her* when he wrote this. No, he'd clearly wanted to get out before she could suggest they see each other again, wanted to avoid that awkward conversation, to avoid having to think of an excuse that she'd see right through if he said it to her face.

She swallowed down the rock in her throat and stared out the living-room window. Unlike yesterday, it was a bright blue day, the sun already making its presence known, the sky a beautiful orangey-pink. Like somehow the weather was taunting her. She blinked back the tears, telling herself not to cry. She'd only known him a few days – it wasn't like he'd left her after a year together, after they'd told each other they loved one another, after they'd vowed to spend their lives together. They'd just spent a couple of days together, that was all. The lump grew painful in her throat and she shook her head, trying to block it. No. She shouldn't feel like this. She *shouldn't*.

But she did. She took in a slightly hitched breath. She couldn't help it. And surely, he must have had some inkling of that. She'd opened up to him, told him about her parents, talked about Oliver. She'd shared the letter to her parents with him, for God's sake, the tradition of that. He wasn't thick, he must have known what that meant to her. And then he'd just abandoned her, knowing that she had nowhere to go for Boxing Day, surely knowing that being alone today would not be easy. He could at least have had the decency to wake her – and would it really have cost him so much to let her accompany him to the airport? To let her pretend that it might have meant something to him too?

She stood, grabbing the letter off the table and scrunching it up. She wished she had a fire to throw it into so that she could watch it burn, something symbolic to make herself feel better. Instead she had to settle for tearing it into little pieces, pieces she'd have to vacuum up later.

Her phone buzzed where she'd left it on the kitchen counter and her heart jumped. She practically ran to it, and then had to feel her heart shrink as the weight settled over her once again. Bia.

How was your Christmas?? Is hot guy still there?? Can I call

153

you on WhatsApp or will he be listening in? I want to hear the detaaaaillls.

Josie clutched her phone and pressed her lips together. She couldn't face it, telling Bia, especially when she wouldn't understand that she felt like this – how could she? Memo and Helen had both told her to be careful, hadn't they? They'd both *known* she'd get caught up in it, even if she hadn't recognised the danger herself.

Wrapping her arms around herself, she padded back across the flat. The sun was shining through the window, sparkling like it was encouraging everyone watching it to share in its joy. She should have taken more notice of the weather yesterday – a warning, perhaps.

Leaving the torn-up pieces of Max's letter on the living-room floor, Josie made her way back to her bedroom and, without switching on the light, got back into bed. She closed her eyes and pulled the duvet cover over her bed. And intended to stay there for some time.

Part Two: April

Chapter Eleven

'This. Is fucking amazing.' Max's voice was slightly muffled over the mouthful of hot dog he was chewing.

Next to him on the bench that they'd managed to commandeer in Tribeca Park, Liam rolled his dark brown eyes and snorted. 'Calm down, it's not that good.' Though he tried to dial it down, Liam's accent was typical New York, a testament to the fact that he'd lived here his whole life. He was dressed in what Max had come to think of as a New Yorker style too, a tailored, striped navy suit but with a deep red shirt underneath – bold and expressive, like the city itself, and offset by his deeply tanned skin. To top it all off, he was wearing a pair of stylish black trainers – or sneakers, as Liam called them – rather than the typical business shoes Max himself was wearing. The weather was distinctly warmer than it had been in recent weeks, like the city had finally decided spring was here, and while that was no guarantee that another cold front wouldn't blast in at any moment, for today both of their coats – his old faithful that he thought was suitable for

157

every occasion, and Liam's long beige coat, one of many different coats he owned – were slung over the back of the bench in celebration.

Max swallowed, his throat slightly protesting against the particularly big bite he'd taken. 'It is,' he insisted. 'I'm sure it has absolutely nothing to do with the fact I haven't eaten since yesterday lunch that it tastes this good.' He and Liam had pulled a late one at the office where Max was currently working last night, preparing for today's meeting with a high-profile – translation, complete dickhead – client.

'Mommy didn't leave dinner out for you last night then?' Liam said, chuckling to himself as he spoke, showing a flash of his extraordinarily white teeth.

'She did, actually,' Max said, grinning in a deliberately smug way – the grin he could wind up almost anyone except Liam with. Angel that she was, his mother had taken to cooking for him every night, even when he wasn't sure if he'd be in, and literally never complained about it if the food went uneaten – which is what had happened last night, given he'd been too knackered to do more than change and fall into bed.

Liam rolled his eyes theatrically, but Max ignored him. He knew all too well that Liam bloody *loved* his mother, and the feeling was mutual being as how, on a very loose 'family friendship', revolving around his mother and Liam's father having gone to school together when they were about eight or something like that, Liam had put in a word at the architecture firm where he worked last year, despite the fact Liam had never even met Max until that point. This was before Max had got the – somewhat

158

short-lived – job at ALA and he'd done a bit of freelance for Liam's firm last spring, luckily getting on with Liam immediately. When Max's mother had told anyone who would listen that Max would be in New York a little longer than expected after Christmas, Liam had casually mentioned it to one of the senior partners, who had immediately given Max a six-week contract to assist on a particularly difficult project. Besides, despite the mutual and apparently instantaneous love between Liam and his mother, Max had resolutely decided there was absolutely nothing wrong with a thirty-two-year-old man camping out at his parents' for two months, given they'd practically begged him to do just that and the alternative would be some sort of dump with a nightmare commute.

Max finished his hot dog, brushing a few crumbs off his black jumper – he tended towards the 'casual' of the smart-casual dress code in the office – and sighed. There was literally nothing better than eating when you were hungry. He shifted a little against a cool wind that whipped past them. With a glance up to the sky, he scowled. So much for the weather getting nicer – it was greying overhead, the clouds threatening to steal away the sun's warmth. 'I swear it rains here more than in England,' he grumbled.

'That's definitely not true,' Liam said, his eyes on a runner, tightly clad in Lycra. There were always bloody joggers around here – it was enough to make you feel guilty for just sitting. This particular one was a tall, slim woman this time, and Max's lips twitched. Liam had a weakness for tall, willowy women.

'Feels like it, given the last few weeks. Anyway, how would you know? You've never even been to England.'

'I don't have to have been there to read a weather report.'

'Read them regularly, do you? Weekly check-up on the weather in London?'

'It's a hobby of mine.'

'Is it on your profile on those multiple dating apps you have? Because that's probably why you're striking out there, mate.' Liam only grinned at him. Impossible to rile, was Liam.

Max's phone buzzed in his pocket and he slipped it out. There were a few messages and two missed calls from his mum, but the most recent message was from Erin, telling him she was just boarding the plane and couldn't wait to see him. He stared at it for a moment, then, unable to think of anything better, typed back *Safe flight xx*

After deciding it was safer just to ignore his mum for now, then go in strong with apology and flattery when he got home, he lowered his phone. It lit up immediately again and he looked at it automatically. As did Liam – a reflex, Max supposed. Because it was face up, they both saw the WhatsApp pop up at the top of the screen. Just a line of x's.

'Erin's getting on the plane,' Max said by way of explanation. Though Liam wasn't one to invade his personal life – one of the many great things about him – this subject had come up a few times, just by virtue of working so closely together every day.

Liam nodded slowly. He had a good scalp, Liam. Something that was a bit odd to notice, but it was sort of impossible *not* to notice, given he'd shaved his dark hair neatly around his head – a style which matched his carefully shaven jaw – a bit of stubble allowed around just his jawline and top lip. It looked like far too much effort, in Max's opinion. 'Ah yes,' he said, 'the Edinburgh ex. Worried things will be awkward, after she dumped your ass last time around?'

Max tapped his fingers against his phone. 'I like to think of it more as a mutual decision. And we're both past that – we're just friends now, I've told you that.'

'Suuuure.' The way Liam dragged out the word made him sound even more American, and Max snorted. 'So what, she's flying all the way out here to visit, right before you go back to the UK, I might add, because you're such good friends?'

'You know, you're trying to make that sound suspicious, but it's really not. Just because *you* don't have any friends who would travel a few hours to spend time with you in an objectively cool city, doesn't mean the rest of us live like that.'

'Nah, I'm just more picky than the average guy about their friends – try to avoid any hangers-on, you know.'

'Sure, you keep telling yourself that.' Even though, from what Max had seen, Liam made friends left, right and centre. Probably because he was so easy-going, Max thought. He didn't pry, and it seemed to make people want to be around him. It was that very quality, Max was sure, that had stopped Liam asking him what he was doing back here for another prolonged period of time, having been off to his fancy new London job last time they spoke.

Max slipped his phone back in his pocket and frowned to himself. The thing was, in reality, what Liam said held some truth. Yes, he and Erin were friends. They'd been friends at Edinburgh together way before anything had happened, only actually hooking up in their final year. Thus ensued a classic on-again-off-again relationship that would have made Ross and Rachel proud, spanning about five years until last spring, when she'd called it off again. And now, he was pretty sure she wanted to reverse that decision, given some of the messages he'd been getting. The problem was, it was a different face that flashed into his mind now, one that had been the cause of a fair number of pleasant dreams and not so pleasant awakenings over the last few months.

Max glanced at his watch – some kind of up-and-coming new brand that Liam had told him about – and, without saying anything, they both got to their feet. Hour-long lunchbreaks were frowned upon at their office. Not that Max was complaining. He wanted to be busy, to get stuck into the work he loved again. He'd spent too much time over the last few months either obsessing over the past or worrying about his future, all because of that one fucking day last year – the day that had quite literally made his world tilt on its axis.

No. He closed his eyes very briefly. He wasn't thinking about it. That was the new rule. That was the only way he was going to get through these months – just pretend that it hadn't happened. Distraction – that was the way forward.

They walked back towards the office on West Broadway, dodging a near-endless stream of people, with the grey sky looming ominously above them. Next to him, Liam lumbered along in that way of his that always made Max want to smile – for someone who played as many sports as Liam did, his gait was almost laughably ungraceful, like he was somehow both trying to show off and hide his somewhat built six-foot-three figure, and had compromised with something that did neither. Without so much as a glance at each other, they swung into the Starbucks on the last corner before their office. It was a given that they'd need caffeine to get through the post-lunch meeting, given the way these clients drawled on, and the coffee at their office, despite the fancy building, was truly shite.

They joined the perpetual queue of people, and both smiled at the rosy-cheeked redhead behind the counter, who looked like she belonged in some kind of Irish novel, as opposed to serving coffee to suits in Manhattan. She nodded when Liam ordered his cappuccino with an extra shot of espresso and some sort of fancy syrup or other, then turned her smile on Max. 'Black Americano, please.' He smiled and her dimples winked out.

'You're from England?' she asked as she rung up the order and took payment from Max. Again he nodded, and she beamed, her green eyes creasing. 'That's so cool. I've always wanted to go there. I've been saving up for ages to go. Is London amazing? I'll bet it's just amazing.'

'It's amazing,' Max said, and when Liam snorted quietly beside him, presumed that his voice didn't quite match his words. Seriously though, the number of people who just assumed 'England' meant 'London'. And yeah, ok, he *had* lived in London at one point, but that was really beside the point. Still, he worked up a smile for the cute barista. 'Well, I hope you get to go one day.'

She grinned. 'I'll look you up if I do . . .?'

Liam turned his snort into a cough this time – an overly obvious one – as Max said, 'Max.'

She nodded. 'Max. I'm Amy.' Another smile.

Coffee in hand, they stepped back out to where the first drops of rain were starting up. Though at least that was at the end of their lunchbreak rather than at the beginning. Liam shook his head. 'You don't even have to try, do you?'

Max 'hmm'd' in an innocent way, and took a sip of his coffee.

'You know it's only because of the sexy English accent, don't you?'

Max shook his head in mock judgement. 'Don't be so obviously jealous, mate, it's not an attractive quality.'

Liam held his coffee up. 'Just making sure you don't get too big-headed, that's all. Figure it's my job as your only friend out here.'

Max snorted, but when Liam said nothing more, found himself staring blankly at the pavement as they walked the last stretch to their office, caught in a what-if moment. What if he'd joked, flirted back with the pretty redhead, told her he'd take her out for a drink and give her all the tips for a holiday to London? It would've been so easy, something fun and light. A year ago – presuming it was in the 'off-again' portion of his relationship with Erin – he would've done just that, but now he couldn't even work up the energy to feel bothered one way or another.

'You ok?' Liam asked as they reached the slim brick building that was home to their office. It had been named a New York landmark in the early nineties, having been designed by some fancy architect back in the day, and now had come full circle, housing its own architecture firm.

They stepped through the glass doors to reception and Max took another sip of his coffee, then nodded, pulling himself out of pointless introspection. 'Yeah. Just thinking about this meeting. Should be a laugh a minute, don't you think?'

Liam didn't get the chance to answer, because a woman in her late twenties, dark-haired, slim and toned, wearing tightly fitting gym clothes that left nothing to the imagination, stood up from where she'd been flipping through an architectural magazine on one of the sofas in reception and walked directly over to them. Liam, quite literally, stopped in his tracks as she closed in on them, her dark eyes glinting. She was there to yell at him, Max decided. Perhaps she was pissed off because she'd come out of her way to see him, and he'd not been here. Max had always been able to tell just what she was thinking through those eyes, and she claimed the same about him. They'd become so good at reading each other's minds growing up that their mother had on more than one occasion said that there must be something supernatural going on, and that maybe there was a way they were actually twins – something about an egg separating and remaining in her womb for the four years between them, though the idea had been sufficiently gross to him as a kid, thinking about his mother having eggs and a womb, that he'd tuned out the specifics whenever she went into that rambling theory. They looked nothing alike, though, despite the twin theory. While not short, per se, his sister was petite, and there had always been speculation over why she'd turned out as such, given both Max and their parents were all a bit taller than average. Given she was all dark hair and eyes to his lighter tones, you wouldn't really be able to tell they were related at first glance.

She came to an abrupt stop in front of them, tilting her head up at Max in a way that made the angles in her face even more pronounced – all sharp cheekbones and pointy chin. She'd amped up the look recently by cutting her dark hair short, though Max was pretty sure that she'd done it in part to annoy their mother, who had immediately complained that it made her look boyish. But there was no way you could look at Chloe and think her boyish, whatever she did to her hair – if anything, it had made her looks even more striking. One quick glance at Liam told Max he was thinking along the same lines right now. The narrowed eyes came automatically to Max, and caused Liam to cough and quickly rearrange his expression.

Max could sympathise, to be fair. Chloe had this effect on men, something which had caused him to get into some difficult fights over the years, in order to defend her honour or punish heartbreak, as was the expectation of the big brother. This had culminated in a big argument where he told her to stop putting him in situations where he had to keep confronting people, and her telling him it was *their* honour that he should be worried about. A tacit agreement had then been reached where he looked the other way while she made it through streams of men, leaving a trail of heartbroken bodies in her way when she declared that they just weren't what she was looking for.

'Hello, Chloe,' he said evenly, swigging the last of his coffee. 'Nice of you to drop by.'

She jabbed a finger towards his chest. 'It is bloody nice of me, I'll have you know. I came by ages ago, and when you wouldn't answer your phone I had to just hang around waiting, didn't I?' Max frowned and slipped out his phone. He saw that she'd rung him – barely twenty minutes ago. 'Luckily,' Chloe continued, gesturing towards the reception desk and the college kid who was currently sat there, 'Steve here was nice enough to let me wait for you down here, though he had no idea who you were – you must not have made much of an impression.'

Next to him, Liam bit his lip, and Max got the distinct impression he was trying not to smile. 'Better than your alternative,' Max said, keeping his tone deliberately light to combat her rage, well used to the mini-tantrums that inevitably cooled down as quickly as they flared up. 'The only reason people remember *you* is because you make the wrong impression – hardly something to celebrate.' She waved a hand in the air as if to say 'whatever' and Max sighed. He grabbed her elbow to manoeuvre her to the side and away from the doorway. 'What are you doing here, Chloe?'

She huffed. 'I'm *here* because Mum has been trying to get hold of you for, and I quote, "the whole damn morning" and you refuse to answer her, so she bribed me with a free spin class at one of those fancy Tribeca studios near here. And so here I am. Doing the loving, daughterly thing and coming to check that a) you are still alive and nothing terrible has befallen you – that's a direct quote again, she actually said "befallen" – being as how she couldn't get you on your mobile and the office told her you weren't there when she called them and—'

'Jesus, she actually called the office?'

Chloe ignored him, carrying on in that way of hers, one

word tumbling into another without the need to take a breath, '*And b)* to see what time Erin is landing because she's flapping that the house might not be ready in time, and is worrying that you might forget to pick her up from the airport.'

Liam made a sound halfway through a cough and a laugh, and Chloe's attention shot to him. He actually flushed under her gaze, for Christ's sake, then cleared his throat hurriedly when he saw the look in Max's eyes. One that, he hoped, quite clearly told him he was being pathetic. Chloe, however, gave Liam a little smile, making no secret of the fact that she was weighing him up.

Max took a breath, trying to dredge up some patience and remember that he dearly loved both his mother and sister, and could not blame them for treating him with kid gloves, even though he'd hoped they would have stopped by now. Because, though she'd never admit it, he knew very well that it would not have taken much for their mother to persuade Chloe to come and 'check up' on him, though she'd do her best to hide that under sharp words, as she always had. Which, to be fair, suited them both. Neither of them were exactly great with all that touchy-feely crap.

'Well,' Max said, 'you can tell our mother that I am indeed fine, nothing evil has befallen me, that Erin doesn't get in until this evening and won't care in the slightest what the place looks like, and that I will go and get her myself. *And—*'

'Oh here we go,' Chloe muttered.

'That even if I wasn't going to get her myself, Erin is a fully grown, intelligent woman, who is more than capable of finding her own way from the airport.'

'And boy, is she lucky to have you.' Liam took an ever-so-subtle step back away from them, though that only made both of them glance towards him in unison, before looking back at one another.

'Is that all?' Max asked sweetly.

'Will Erin be needing her own bedroom?' she asked sweetly.

Max scowled. 'Go away, Chloe.'

'What!' Chloe exclaimed, shifting her gym bag further up her shoulder. 'That's a genuine question! And if she *isn't* sharing a room with you, then that means I have to stay on the sofa, which is just so—'

Max ran a hand through his hair. 'God, you're annoying. Why did you decide to come out here for Easter again?'

'For the better weather obvs.' She actually said it – 'obvs' – like she was some kind of teenager.

Both Max and Chloe snapped their attention to Liam when he let out a low laugh. He immediately straightened his face, looking slightly alarmed by the combined force of their gazes, and Max sighed. 'Sorry about this, mate.' He glanced at his watch, gestured to Liam to say that they should just carry on around Chloe to get to their floor.

But Chloe shifted position, making that impossible. 'Yeah, sorry. About Max that is. He's clearly too self-involved to introduce me, but I'm Chloe – his sister.'

Liam nodded, and when he spoke, his voice was ever so slightly huskier than usual. 'Yeah. We've actually met, last year. Your parents' wedding anniversary.'

Chloe gave him an appraising look, then pursed her lips. 'That's right. Sorry, I remember you now. You're my mum's old schoolfriend's son, or something like that, aren't you?'

169

Liam nodded again, giving Max a sort of helpless look. Max wasn't sure if he was asking to be rescued, or asking permission to dive in head-first. Generally, Liam needed no help when it came to women, despite his comments about it being too easy for Max. He also had no idea if Chloe had genuinely forgotten meeting Liam – he could just imagine her playing some sort of game right now, all too aware of the way Liam was looking at her. The problem was, Chloe was good at that bit – too good – but she protected her heart fiercely, so that it made it almost impossible for men to actually get close to her, though she'd no doubt start hissing at him if he ever dared to voice that opinion.

Figuring he'd better move Liam along and out of harm's way, Max groaned. 'For God's sake, mate, pull it together – you'll make her worse, looking at her like that.'

Chloe huffed, swinging her gym bag from one shoulder to the other. 'Stop being deliberately obnoxious and embarrassing. Poor Liam.' She flashed Liam a look that made him clear his throat. 'Next time you try to chat up a girl in front of me, brother mine, I'm going to point out all your flaws in front of them. In excruciating detail.'

Max gave her a friendly pat on the shoulder. 'Honey,' he said with a fake, sarcastic drawl, 'I don't need to chat them up, they all fall at my feet, you know that.' They grinned at each other – both challenge and solidarity. And in all fairness, her arrival had well and truly pulled him firmly out of his self-imposed melancholy. She could be annoying as hell, but Chloe was also the one person who could drag him out of a mood – self-imposed or otherwise. So he kissed her on the cheek to say goodbye before heading through security with Liam.

'Jesus,' Liam said, running a hand along the back of his neck.

Max couldn't help but laugh, and he gave Liam a friendly pat on the back. 'Don't worry, mate, you're not the only one to react like that, trust me.'

Liam shook his head. 'That doesn't actually make me feel better, funnily enough. Not that I . . . I mean, I know she's your little sister and all.'

'Yeah. Just make sure to leave out the "little" if you ever talk to her about that. But don't worry, you'll have the chance to make a better impression tonight.'

Liam frowned as they started up the stairs – a conscious effort on Max's part to try and regain some kind of fitness. 'Tonight.'

'Yeah. I've just decided I need backup, if I have to deal with both my ex and my sister at dinner.'

Liam glanced at him out of the corner of his eye. 'I thought you said she was just a friend?'

'Well, whatever. You're coming.'

'Alright. As long as your mum's cooking, I'm in.'

As they let themselves into their office on the third floor, Max admitted to himself that what he'd thought down below wasn't actually quite true. Chloe wasn't the one and only person who could drag him out of himself. Whether she knew it or not, the other was the one who had, quite literally, fallen at his feet four months ago.

Chapter Twelve

'Erin, let me get you some more. You must be famished after that flight.' Max's mother was already halfway to her feet, her gold necklace swinging with the movement, and was reaching to the middle of the table to the bowl of Spanish rice that had accompanied the roast salmon she'd served. Max resisted the urge to roll his eyes, and deliberately did not look at Chloe, in case he caught a similar expression there. His mum had been trying to force-feed Erin basically since she'd walked through the door, having even gone to this special biscuit shop bloody *miles* away to get some biscuits that she 'thought Erin might like'.

Erin shook her head. 'No, honestly, Valerie, I'm fine.'

His mum pursed her red-painted lips, then turned to Liam, who was sitting opposite Max, black jacket over the back of his chair so his red shirt was firmly on show, and already had a full second helping on his plate. 'Are you alright, Liam?' Her American accent seemed to become stronger when she spoke to Liam, like just being in the same vicinity softened the English edge she'd picked up.

She smiled at him fondly when he choked down his food hurriedly to answer, and Max wouldn't have been surprised if she'd crossed the room to pat his lips with a bloody napkin. Honestly, it was like Christmas for her, with Liam and Erin in the same room – like having her own two children over from England couldn't possibly compare.

Their mum sat back down with clear reluctance and exchanged a look with Max's dad, who smiled at her a little indulgently from where he was sitting at the head of the table, hands resting on his stomach as if it was painful. He worked hard to keep himself fit, Max knew, but despite that there was a slight pouch starting to appear around his midsection, though it was something the rest of the family tacitly avoided speaking about.

His mum's gaze was still flicking between Erin's empty plate and the remaining food on the table, and Max could just *see* she was about to try and get Erin to eat more, having already told Max twice in the two hours that Erin had been here that she was looking 'very slim', as if that was some kind of cause for alarm, rather than something Erin clearly worked hard at. Before he could interject, Erin got there first.

'That was just amazing, Valerie, thanks so much. I'm sorry I couldn't eat more – my body clock is all messed up and I ate on the plane – I wasn't sure that we'd be eating here as I got in so late.' She said it all graciously, but something about it made Max squirm in his seat.

Which wasn't helped by the fact that Mum shot him a glare out of those green-gold eyes – eyes that she claimed he'd inherited and 'made his own', the gold-rimmed irises darker in his than hers. Jesus, it wasn't *his* fault that she'd decided to host a bloody gourmet feast, was it? All he'd said was that Erin *might* be hungry when she got in – which also clearly meant that she might *not* be. How was he supposed to know the inner workings of someone else's internal hunger cues, for God's sake?

'You ate on the plane?' His mum's perfectly plucked – not by her – eyebrows furrowed. 'You did fly business class, didn't you, Erin?'

Max's dad reached out to give her hand a squeeze on the table, at the same time as Max said, 'Mum.'

Chloe, unhelpfully, rolled her eyes, helping herself to a third helping of rice – unlike the two guests, their mum had not thought to offer either of her own children extra helpings. Max noticed the way Liam shifted slightly as Chloe reached across the table, making sure that her arm did not brush his, and couldn't help the little smirk that crossed his face. The two of them had been nothing other than polite to each other – Chloe, he knew, was only behaving so because of their parents' presence, rather than it being her innate nature, like Liam's – and had barely said anything directly to each other over dinner unless it was part of a group conversation. But Max had seen the way Liam kept sneaking glances at her, the way Chloe was almost studiously ignoring those glances. Not that he was one to talk. Just as he was thinking it, Erin shifted position and, for the third time that evening, he felt her knee, clad in those skinny jeans that showed off her epic legs, brush against his under the table. It was brief enough that it could, theoretically, be accidental, and it was certainly something that would go unnoticed by anyone else at the table. But he was sure, by the subtle yet firm pressure, that it was a deliberate move on her part to let him know that while she might be talking to his mother, her attention was on him. Max picked up his drink – non-alcoholic, sadly – and concentrated intently on taking a sip.

'What?' his mother asked, in a tone of voice that reminded Max almost comically of Chloe. He might have got his mum's looks, but Chloe had her personality, through and through, though each of them refused to see it in one another.

His dad cleared his throat, his eyes – brown like Chloe's, though not quite as dark – on the side of his mum's powdered face, and he gave her hand another little squeeze. His mum pretended not to notice.

'Economy is awful these days,' she continued, 'the food especially, and I wouldn't wish it on even Mrs Price on the floor below.' She pursed her lips, her eyes narrowing. 'Well, maybe her. She had the cheek the other day to ask if our cleaner also did our cooking, and I just *know* it was a jibe, because she knows full well that we can't afford both—'

'We wouldn't want a cook anyway,' Max's dad butted in. 'That would mean we'd miss out on your cooking.' He twinkled at his wife, and Max noticed the way his mother tried – and clearly failed – to hide a smile.

'Hear, hear!' Liam said, in his best impression of a British accent.

'Oh Liam, you're such a sweetie.' She gave him a warm smile, her eyes softening as if she was looking at her firstborn. She patted her dark auburn hair, as if checking the curls she'd had put in yesterday were still in place. Like her eyes, Max had got the hair too, though not the curls, given they were artificial, and he had to admit he was grateful for that – he wasn't sure he could have pulled off little ringlets. His was a darker version of hers, too, only really truly auburn in the sun.

Liam's eyes sparkled back, and he raised his glass of Pinot Grigio in a toast to Max's mother. Chloe gave Liam a withering look, which he either didn't notice or chose to ignore, and when she saw Max looking, she mimed gagging into her own wine. Their dad immediately gave Chloe a stern look out of eyes that were eerily similar to hers, and Chloe turned the action into a hacking cough, thumping her chest. Max tried not to laugh.

Luckily, their mum didn't notice Chloe because she was beaming between Liam and Erin, who said, 'Agreed,' with a little smile. Erin took a sip of her own wine, though Max could see her trying to stifle a yawn. She looked knackered – though a polished version of knackered, carefully applied cosmetics blended to cover the dark circles and brighten the pale face he'd seen at the airport, the blue blouse she'd changed into clean and crisp after showering and doing something with her blonde hair to make it more . . . bushy. Though he was pretty sure that wasn't the word she'd use. He knew she must be desperate to get to bed, but wouldn't until she deemed it appropriate to leave the table.

Across the table, Chloe put her knife and fork together, sitting back and patting her stomach. 'Is there any pudding?'

Their mum frowned. 'You've just eaten enough for three people.'

Chloe smiled sweetly. 'But your cooking's just so good,

176

Mum. I barely have time to cook when I'm working, you must remember what it's like, in the early days . . .' She gave their mother a baleful look, and Max saw his mum's expression soften despite herself.

'Alright, but you can come and help me serve it.' Together, Chloe and his mum cleared the table, taking everything to the semi-closed-off kitchen behind them. Chloe shot Max a wink as she walked past. When Max looked back across the table, he noticed Liam's gaze trailing his little sister. Max cleared his throat loudly, and Liam jumped, then shot him a guilty look.

Erin turned to his dad, slipping one slim leg over the other underneath the table. Despite the jet lag, she really did look good, Max had to give her that. 'So, Roger, how's retirement suiting you?'

Given that Erin was already engaging his dad in conversation about life in New York and how he was finding living in America for the first time, Max leaned in to Liam. 'She'll eat you alive, you know.'

Liam swirled his wine in his glass and gave Max an all-too-innocent look. 'I've got no idea what you're talking about.'

Max raised his eyebrows. 'Is that so?'

Liam laid a hand across his heart dramatically. 'Don't you worry, you know she's not really my type.' And it was true – Liam's type tended towards the Erins of the world, long-limbed and sophisticated. Still, he was pretty sure that, if Chloe had decided she was interested, then the man didn't stand a chance.

Max let it drop for the time being, and sat back against the grey chair that was sort of an armchair without arms.

It matched the rest of the apartment, which was mainly white and grey and clearly designed to make the place look bigger than it was. He let his eyes trail around the place: the wooden floors, the corner sofa, the fucking massive windows all around the living room. It was a bit uniform for him, but he could see why his parents liked it here. Though he hadn't been able to quite believe it when they'd told him they were moving to the Upper East Side, of all places – one of the places known across the world for being home to the posh people of New York. He'd known their childhood home had gone for more than they'd thought it would when they'd sold up a few years ago, but still. Not that he knew exactly how much this place cost – but given his profession, he could guess. A three-bedroom apartment in this kind of high-rise fancy building was not cheap. Plus, you got the views across the city here, though currently all you could see were the lights of the other buildings and streets below. The place even had a fancy-arse doorman who greeted Max by name every time he saw him. It made him wonder whether his mother was really doing the hospital consultancy work 'to keep busy' as she claimed, or if they actually just needed the money.

When his mum and Chloe reappeared holding home-made apple pie and the dessert plates respectively, Max noted how Liam suddenly became ever-so-interested in the discussion Erin and his dad were having about the latest Broadway shows. Max let out a soft snort, and Erin briefly flicked a glance at him, eyes questioning. He only shook his head.

After the apple pie was mostly eaten – Erin eating

half of her piece in a clear effort not to offend – Liam announced that he had to go, because they needed to be in the office early tomorrow ahead of a big pitch. Managing to get around Max's mum's protests, Liam said his goodbyes, kissing his mum and Erin on the cheek, shaking his dad's hand, and giving Max a friendly pat on the shoulder. He turned to Chloe last, who was leaning back against her chair, having only got to her feet with clear reluctance because everyone else had. She looked up at him with measured eyes, and he ran a hand across the back of his neck. Honestly, Max felt sorry for the guy – the whole family and Erin were watching the two of them with interest, no sign of embarrassment for doing so. Not sorry enough to distract anyone though.

'Well, it was nice to see you again, Chloe,' Liam said, all airs and graces. Out of the corner of his eye, Max saw his mum give a little nod of approval – politeness went far in her book.

Chloe gave a smile that could in no way be considered sweet. 'You too.' And it was Chloe who straightened and stretched up, giving Liam's cheek a swift kiss, resting one of her hands on his forearm as if to stabilise herself. She pulled back, cocked her head. 'Maybe I'll see you again while I'm here.'

Liam cleared his throat. 'Right. Yeah, maybe.' He gave Max a slightly wide-eyed look at that, and Max only nodded and shrugged, as if to say *I told you so.*

The moment Liam was out the door, Erin took the opportunity before everyone could sit down again. 'I'm so sorry, but I think I'm going to have to call it a night, otherwise I'll be rotten company tomorrow.' She smiled at everyone, and Max's dad and mum both shook their heads as if even the *thought* of Erin being rotten company was unthinkable. Chloe just sat down and dug into a second piece of apple pie. 'Besides,' Erin continued, 'I don't want to oversleep and miss out on anything – I want to make the most of the weekend as it's my first time in New York.'

Another headshake from his mother, her tight little curls twirling with the movement. 'That's a crying shame.' She shot Max a little frown and Max resisted the urge to sigh.

Erin gave Max's shoulder a little squeeze before she left the table. Her touch lingered after she moved on, making it clear to him that he was going to have to make some sort of decision sooner or later, and from the expressions on their faces, the action was one which did not go unnoticed by the rest of the family.

When his mum started to clear the table – party officially over now the guests of honour had left – Max and Chloe jumped in to help, unable to ignore years of ingrained habit. His mum grinned at his dad. 'Trained them well, didn't we?'

His dad stretched back in his seat. 'I take all the credit,' he said lazily.

His mum's eyebrows shot up. 'Is that so?' When his dad only grinned, his mum elbowed him on the shoulder as she walked by, in a way that made Max smile a little. It was nice that some things, at least, remained constant.

It was after he'd set the pile of dessert plates down on the kitchen counter that his mum fixed him with a very direct look. She crossed her arms. 'Are you really going back to the UK, Max?' Out of the corner of his eye, he saw Chloe leaving the kitchen in a move that he had no doubt was deliberate. Bloody deserter. Max didn't answer. He'd long since learned that the best thing to do with questions that his mother knew the answer to was to stay silent. 'But what will you do there?' she pressed. He started loading the dishwasher just so he didn't have to look at her.

'I don't know, Mum,' he said on a sigh. 'But it's not right to stay here with you just for the sake of it either. I've already been here longer than anyone expected.'

He heard the tapping of her perfectly manicured nails on the countertop. 'It won't be good for you. Just sitting around, doing nothing.'

He glanced up at her from where he was putting in the last plate, cocking one eyebrow. 'Who says I'll be doing nothing?'

She bit her lip. 'If you had a plan or a . . .' Max straightened to see her glancing down the corridor, in the direction of Erin's bedroom. At least she never claimed to be subtle. 'A *someone*, well then it would be different, but . . . You can't just go home and do nothing. You can't just let your life stop like that, Max.' Max felt his control slip slightly, enough that he glared at his mother. She winced and he shook his head in apology, pulling one hand through his hair.

Chloe provided a brief distraction, coming in with the remainder of the clutter from the table, but his mum was not giving in so easily. 'What about your old firm?'

Max sighed. 'I doubt they'd take me back now, even for freelance.'

'Well, have you thought about where you'll live?'

'I've got my flat.'

His mum pursed her lips. Her lips were still red, making him wonder just what kind of nuclear lipstick she'd applied. 'Yes, the flat you rented out and, as far as I'm aware, you're doing nothing to end the contract.'

Max gritted his teeth. 'I'll figure it out, ok? Stop worrying.'

'He can stay with me,' Chloe piped up, leaning back against the counter next to Max and giving his arm a friendly punch.

Their mother frowned at her. 'You don't need the distraction,' she said sharply. Then she softened her tone. 'You need to focus, sweetie, your residency is one of the most important times in your career.'

Chloe just rolled her eyes at Max.

Clearly considering it a losing battle now Chloe was on his team, his mum sighed. 'I'm going to bed, I'll see you both tomorrow.' She hesitated before she left the kitchen and glanced back at Max. 'I can't stop worrying, you know.' Her tone was ever so slightly sad. 'It's a mother's prerogative.' She smiled almost wistfully before she left them alone.

Max looked at Chloe, grimacing. 'Am I a terrible son?'

She shrugged. 'Yeah, I reckon so.'

He stared at her a moment, then laughed, turning to put the kettle on to boil. 'Thanks.'

'Any time.' She patted him on the arm. 'So. What's up with the sexy architect?'

Max got down two mugs, smiled at her over his shoulder. 'Well, I'm just fine, thanks for asking.'

She huffed. 'Why don't you bring him along tomorrow?'

He rolled his eyes. 'No. I didn't even invite *you*.' He put a mint teabag in one mug, regular in the other. Held up a third mug to Chloe, who shook her head.

'Don't make it sound like that, you know full well I'm doing *you* a favour by making it a group thing and not a date.'

He chose to ignore that. 'You barely said two words to him all evening, I doubt he'll even *want* to come.'

She shook her head and gave him a wicked look. 'Oh, he'll want to come, trust me.'

Max couldn't help the little wince. 'What's up with that doctor from your course that you were seeing?'

She shrugged. 'He's boring.' She narrowed her eyes at him and he held up his hands.

'I said nothing.'

'You don't have to say anything, it's written all over your face.' Then she sighed. 'There's just no point in keeping at something unless it's the real thing. You might think I'm harsh, but I'm not. I'm just waiting for the *one,* you know?'

Max nodded slowly, his attention on the kettle that was now bubbling. 'Yeah. I know.'

She raised her eyebrows. 'You do?'

He filled the mugs with the boiling water and kissed Chloe briefly on the cheek as he left the kitchen, mugs in hand. 'Night, sis.'

His dad was setting up the sofa as a bed for Chloe when Max stepped out of the kitchen into the living room. He caught Max's eye, then crossed the room to him. Tonight, it seemed, was a night of interrogations. His dad ran one hand through his hair. Like Chloe's, it was dark, though it was a little longer than hers now, and the flecks of grey became more obvious every time Max saw him, in both his hair and the small beard that he'd let grow out a little in recent years. 'I, err, could hear your mother flapping.'

Max took a sip of the normal tea in his right hand. 'Yep. But that's ok, we're all used to it.'

His dad nodded, then rocked back on his heels. Always took the time to figure out what he wanted to say, his dad. 'I know it's not ideal, living with your parents, but I want you to know that we both mean it. There's always a place for you here, if you're not ready to go home yet, or else if you want to come back if things don't . . . work out, back there.'

Because he knew how it was meant, that his dad wasn't trying to push him into anything, Max clapped a hand on his dad's shoulder. They were almost exactly the same height. 'Thanks.'

He turned to go, but his dad spoke up again. 'Your mother just worries.'

'I know, Dad.'

'And look, she won't push—'

'But you will?'

'But she's getting to know a few people, the longer she's here,' his dad continued calmly, evenly. 'If you wanted to have a chat with someone, consider your options, I'm sure she could introduce you—'

'No, Dad.' It came out more sharply than he'd intended, and Max took a breath. 'Look, I'm sorry, but we've been through this. It's not that I don't appreciate it, it's just . . .' It's just that this was so repetitive, an echo of similar arguments they'd had when he was a teenager, his mother in particular wanting him to do things the way she thought was best – the medical career, especially. But he couldn't say it, not outright, not without offending one or both of them. So instead he settled with, 'I just have to do things my own way, ok?'

His dad stared at him for a moment, as if deciding something, then nodded slowly. 'Fair enough. As long as you're sure. Go and check on Erin before you go to bed, will you? It's rude to leave a girl like that without saying a proper goodnight.' He turned away, back to the sofa, so he didn't see Max's headshake. But really – *a girl like that*? As opposed to any other girl?

Still, he did just that, knocking on Erin's door a moment later. She opened it, already in her pyjamas but her face not yet stripped of cosmetics. He hadn't seen her without them in a long time – a privilege he'd given up when they'd broken up.

'I brought you tea,' Max said, lifting the mint tea that he'd made, hoping that it was still what she liked to drink before bed. An offering, he supposed – one to let her know that he was genuinely thankful she'd bothered to come out and see him, no matter what happened next.

She smiled, took it, and opened the door a bit wider. He stepped in, though he left the door open behind him deliberately. She was in the smallest room, but it was still plenty big enough. Her suitcase was currently open on a green and brown rug that he thought was hideous but his mother obviously liked, which was covering most of the spare wooden floor at the foot of the bed. The sight of her clothes neatly folded and piled there made him smile a little. No doubt she was ready to transfer them all to the drawers in the wardrobe, no matter that she was only here for three nights.

'You ok?' he asked. 'All settled?'

Erin nodded, blew on her tea and took a sip. He started to rock back on his heels, remembered his father doing just that and stopped, clearing his throat. Why could he suddenly think of nothing to say? It never used to be this awkward between them – even when they'd been recently broken up they'd always been relatively easy around each other. But for some reason this time it all felt forced, like there had been some irreversible change. Maybe it was just that six months had passed with barely any contact. That, and the fact that the last time he'd seen her he'd barely been functioning like a human being, clouded with the weight of something he'd been told time and time again was grief.

Erin set her tea down on the bedside table – Christ, his mother had put *flowers* there, yellow flowers, no less, Erin's favourite colour – and turned back to him, taking his spare hand, the one not holding his own tea, in both of hers. Her scent drifted over to him. She'd always smelled the same, ever since university, some kind of lavender scent which he presumed came from the same shower gel or whatever that she used.

'I've been so worried about you,' she said softly, with a fleeting glance at the open door.

'I know,' Max said, grimacing a little. 'I'm sorry. I should've been in touch more. I've just been a little ... distracted, I guess.'

She nodded vigorously, her hair, longer and lighter than when he'd last seen her, bouncing as she did so. 'I get that, I do.' But it was said in a way that made him doubt it. Feeling his shoulders tense, he pulled his hand from hers, then patted the top of her hand to make the action less abrupt. He just wished that she – that everyone – would treat him normally again, would stop tiptoeing around him. He'd decided to move on from it, as much as he could anyway; the least everyone else could do was respect that.

She stepped towards him, hooked her hands behind his head so that his mug of tea was pressed awkwardly against him, the steam of it coiling in the space between them. She tilted her head, the way she always used to, when gauging his reaction. 'I missed you.'

Her eyes were so blue. He'd almost forgotten that. He cleared his throat. 'I missed you too,' he said, because it was true. He wasn't sure he meant it in quite the same way, but he'd missed having her around. She continued to watch him, like she was waiting for some kind of decision. He hesitated for just a moment, then leaned in, planted a whisper of a kiss on her smooth cheek. He stepped away from her, lifted his mug in a kind of toast. The corner of her mouth crooked up.

'Night, Erin.' With that he closed the door behind him and let out a slow, long breath.

Chapter Thirteen

Max ran his hand along the side of the bridge they were currently walking across, admiring the feel of the cast iron. Though he hadn't spent much time here, he knew from an interest in the architecture of New York that this was Bow Bridge, and had been designed by Calvert Vaux and Jacob Wrey Mould, like many other of the key architectural features of the park. It was actually pretty fucking cool, though the egotistical side of him slightly resented that he'd not had the chance to design something like this, something that made it onto the 'top ten' lists – something that people came out just to admire. He sighed as he looked around him, a little bit in awe at the views from here. He was just able to make out some of the high-rise buildings of the city – a view that he imagined would become a little more obscured as the trees beefed up a bit in late spring.

'Jesus,' he said, shaking his head. 'I had no idea how big this place was.' He'd walked through bits of Central Park before now, but never purposefully just to enjoy it.

Chloe rolled her eyes at his statement, and he hunched his shoulders a little defensively. 'Well, it's been winter, hasn't it? And it gets bloody cold here, I'm hardly going to spend all my free time exploring the great outdoors.' Chloe, very deliberately, said nothing and looked the other way, swinging the picnic basket and apparently admiring the trees that were just starting to show their colours again, but at least Erin gave him a sympathetic shrug.

Max glanced down at the lake below, which, thanks to the sun's appearance, was glistening up at them, reflecting some of the green that was just beginning to blossom. There were even two rowboats coming up under the bridge, a couple in each of them looking delightfully pleased with themselves. It would be beautiful in the autumn too, he thought absently, with all the trees changing colours.

Chloe led them on a slightly meandering route towards what she called the 'heart' of Central Park – the Bethesda Fountain and Terrace. She held out her arms dramatically, picnic basket and all, when they caught the first glimpse of the big fountain in the middle of the lower terrace, water cascading around two circular platforms that held up an angel and down into a pond with lily pads dotted around its surface. Behind the fountain was the seemingly endless lake, where more people were rowing, or else sitting by the water on the sandstone two-tiered wall at its edge. The whole terrace was packed, a bunch of tourists with their cameras out and sunglasses on, despite the fact that, though sunny, it was far from shorts and t-shirt weather. He was certainly much more suitably dressed in jeans and a jumper.

The three of them walked across the orange-bricked

floor to find a space at the edge of the fountain. Then they all just stopped, staring up at it.

'It's called *Angel of the Waters*,' Max supplied. Erin and Chloe both nodded in a way that suggested they already knew this. He supposed, like himself, Erin must have done a bit of research into the architecture of the city, given she was an architect too.

Erin looked around, popping one hand on her hip. Max noticed a guy a few metres away give her an appreciative look, the red blouse she was wearing making her stand out amongst the crowd. 'I keep feeling like I recognise this from somewhere.'

'It's Central Park,' Max said, shrugging.

She tapped a foot, which was encased in a heeled boot that Max was surprised hadn't given her blisters yet. 'Yes, I know that, but it's like there's something more that I recognise, even though I've obviously never been here. It's been annoying me for a while.'

'Have you seen *Home Alone 2*?' Chloe asked. Erin frowned and shook her head. '*One Fine Day*?' At Max's raised eyebrows, Chloe shrugged. 'I did some googling – it's been in both those films.'

A woman, totally rocking the cowboyesque look of a checked shirt and tight blue jeans, came over and smiled at Max at that moment, holding out a camera. 'I don't suppose you'd mind . . .?' She gestured behind her to where a small girl, her hair in two plaits, and another woman with a cap on were standing by the fountain.

'Sure.' Max took the camera and took a few shots, smiling at the woman automatically when he gave it back to her.

'Come on,' said Erin, slipping her phone out of her handbag. 'Let me get one of the two of you.'

Max went along with it, knowing they'd just argue if he refused, though it gave him a slightly unpleasant jolt in the stomach, even as he smiled and put his arm around Chloe, because a distinct memory invaded his mind, of another girl with a different, more impressive camera, taking photos of him on the beach.

They found some space on the little wall by the lake, right in the corner by a big green flag, and under the shadow of one of the trees that was already looking bushy. Max leaned back as he sat down and nearly lost his balance, stopping himself just before he fell backwards into the water. He ignored the look Chloe gave him and stretched his legs out in front of him as she unpacked the picnic. He'd expected to be fairly ambivalent about the whole thing, only agreeing to the outing for Erin's sake, as she'd flown all this way, but it was actually a bit impossible not to absorb some of the atmosphere here, the feeling of the multitude of people out to enjoy some time in one of the most famous parks in the world, on a day that was definitely promising that spring was now here to stay.

'Is it always this busy?' Erin asked, accepting the picnic blanket that Max had declined and setting it down carefully on the stone before she sat, presumably so she didn't get those white trousers of hers dirty.

Max shrugged. 'No idea.' Chloe gave him a mocking headshake, and Erin looked between them, clearly deciding whether to tell Chloe to just leave him be. His sister was right though – not that she'd actually said anything. He should've done more while he was here; he just hadn't been able to find the energy to go out exploring on his own, even if he'd had the desire to.

Chloe handed round the canned drinks that their mum had packed, before opening up the Tupperwares. Their mum had insisted that they'd only get ripped off if they bought food in the park, and that it wasn't worth the money – and as she was the only one who'd grown up in New York, they'd decided to take her word for it.

'So,' Chloe said over a mouthful of mini-quiche. 'Where next?' She'd decided to take control of the day, apparently, and Max had decided to let her. 'We could do a bike tour?'

Erin looked uncomfortably down at her pristine outfit.

'Nah, not really feeling that,' Max said quickly, before Chloe could pick up on Erin's reluctance – and the reason for it – and make some sort of sarcastic comment. She might not mean anything by it, but she wasn't always great at noticing that other people still took offence at those comments, regardless of the fact she didn't necessarily mean it – and Erin was one of those people.

'Well what about the zoo?' Chloe pressed.

Max took one of his mother's smoked salmon sandwiches. She'd even cut the crusts off. 'The zoo? Are you serious?'

'Yes. Though actually, seeing the animals in cages might make me a bit sad.' She shoved a sandwich into her mouth whole. 'The castle!' Only it came out a little muffled. She swallowed, then tried again. 'Belvedere Castle. We definitely have to go there – apparently you can see pretty much round the whole city.' She frowned. 'Or maybe it was just round the whole park.'

Erin, who was still nibbling away at her first mini quiche, shook her head. 'How are you remembering all these little facts without looking it up?'

'I've got a photographic memory,' Chloe said, tapping the side of her head.

'Really?' Erin cocked her head. 'I never knew that about you.'

'That's because it's not true. Ignore her, Erin.' When Chloe only grinned, Max sighed. 'Look, if you're in planning mode, can you factor in that I have to go into the office at some point this afternoon? I've got that work thing on Monday night with these fancy clients, and I said I'd just double-check a few things.' He finished his sandwich, then frowned at Erin. 'I told you about that, right?' He'd added her as his plus one, being as how he could hardly just leave her at home with his parents on her last night in New York.

'You did,' Erin assured him. 'And I've got my dress ready.'

'You didn't tell me about it,' Chloe piped up helpfully. 'But that's ok, I'll make sure you have time to go to the office. Maybe I can come along too for the ride.'

Max raised his eyebrows. 'I doubt Liam will be there, it's the weekend.' He had to laugh when she pouted.

'And on that note,' Chloe said, 'I'm going to the loo. There's bound to be a public toilet around here somewhere, right?' She glanced round. 'I'll be right back.' Max watched her bound away for a moment, the leather jacket she'd put on to go with her black jeans well and truly suiting the short black hair and making her look like some kind of cute little biker chick. He refused to use the word sexy in relation to his sister. She fitted in totally with New York – there was no way you'd know from looking at her that she was a tourist.

Erin helped herself to a packet of strawberries, picking the stem off one before taking a small bite. Max watched her for a moment. She'd done her face subtly today so that she looked dewy and springlike – a bit like the trees surrounding them. She was so pretty; there was no denying that. Yet he didn't think he felt it, the usual punch of attraction he had around her. She looked up from the strawberries and saw him watching, smiled. He smiled back, wished it didn't feel quite so forced.

'So,' she said, tucking her hair behind her ears. 'I've been thinking.'

Max's stomach jolted, and if he could have grimaced without it being more than a little rude, he would have. He'd thought they'd be able to put off this moment or, best case, that maybe it wouldn't come at all. He cleared his throat. 'Right.'

'I know this year has been tough for you, but I want to be in your life, Max.' Direct and to the point, as always.

He took a sip of his drink – soda water – just for something to do. 'You are in my life,' he said, trying for easy and casual.

She kept her eyes on his face. 'You know what I mean.'

'Right,' he said again. Because he did. He tapped his fingers against his can. 'I thought you said we were different people now, that we'd be better off firmly as friends?' He cocked one eyebrow, kept his tone light. 'We were just too comfortable and that's why we kept coming back for

194

more. I'm *pretty* sure that's what you said.' He smiled to let her know he wasn't saying it resentfully.

She wrinkled her nose. 'I didn't say it quite like that.'

But she had said a version of it and he'd hated it at the time, had got all bent out of shape and stormed out of the room. He'd assumed that it was all coming from her, that she was just trying to get rid him. He'd shouted at her that they'd been through this all before, that she should just make up her damn mind one way or another, and told her he was fed up with being the one she came crying to when something went wrong in her life. Because he'd been offended that she was the one ending it, he hadn't even bothered to consider the fact that she was right. But then, over the last year, he'd realised that he'd been doing the same – he'd allowed her to be the one he always went running to, without even considering whether it was the right thing for either of them. And so he'd conceded, after learning not to do that, that she'd had a point, that they were probably better off as friends, because being together meant that they were always bursting at the seams a little – both of them growing as people yet unable to, because they kept pulling each other back to one another.

'This past year,' Erin continued, when it was clear he wasn't going to offer up his thoughts out loud, 'it's made me realise. It's made me think that maybe ... Maybe comfortable is good.' She took a deep breath, her chest moving with the action. 'I want to be there for you, Max.' He did actually grimace this time, but she shook her head firmly. 'I want ... Well. I just think that maybe we should give it another go.' And with that, she bit into a strawberry, though she kept looking at him, even when he wouldn't meet her gaze. He liked her directness – it meant you always knew where you stood – but it also made her particularly formidable at times, because she knew just how to go after things she wanted.

She offered the strawberries to him, and he took one. 'Surprised Mum didn't put in some champagne too,' he muttered, and to his relief, she grinned. She'd probably considered it, Max thought, and then remembered that he wasn't drinking at the moment.

He popped the whole strawberry in his mouth and she leaned back, tilting her face up to the sky and arching her back. 'I think you should move in with me, when you get back to the UK.' He choked a bit on the strawberry, but she only closed her eyes, apparently enjoying the feel of the sun filtering through leaves to warm her face. 'In Edinburgh,' she clarified, as if that were the main issue with her proposal. 'I know you don't have anywhere to stay.'

'Is that right?' Max growled, vowing to have a word with his mother when they were alone.

Erin opened her eyes, looked at him, and nodded. 'And the thing is . . .' She glanced over his shoulder and bit her lip. He wondered briefly if she'd seen Chloe. 'I don't mind if that's just as friends.' She huffed out a breath, looked back at him. He raised his eyebrows, and she elaborated. 'I'd rather it wasn't, which I'm sure you've gathered. But the offer's there either way.' She gave him a soft smile. She meant it too – she wouldn't say it if she didn't. She wasn't the type to play complicated games, and he didn't think she'd do that to him now. But even if it was just as friends, it was still fucking dangerous territory.

'So.' She shook back that long blonde hair. 'What do you think?'

Jesus, just like that, he was supposed to decide? He ran a hand across the back of his neck. 'Erin . . .' She was looking over his shoulder again, so he twisted slightly to look too. He'd been right – Chloe was weaving her way back over to them, and he was sure that neither he nor Erin wanted to leave the conversation open around his sister. He cleared his throat and twisted back to her. 'Erin, I—'

But he stopped, snapped his head back towards the fountain. He'd seen something there. Some*one*. He was sure of it. It'd only been a moment, but he had that face memorised. He frantically scanned the crowd, until he locked his gaze on a side profile. Warm brown hair, standing out like autumn in the spring, a small nose, full lips. Surely not. But he was already standing, already taking a step towards her, shifting position so as to see a little better. Shaking his head as if he couldn't be right about this. Maybe it was just because he'd been thinking of her earlier.

And then he heard the sound of her laughing.

'Max?' Erin's voice sounded dim somehow, compared to the thumping of his heart, the sudden blur of noise around him.

'I'll be right back,' he said, aware that his voice was clipped, almost a little panicked, and unable to stop it. He walked swiftly in the girl's direction, trying to keep his gaze locked on what was now the back of her head, cursing the multiple people who kept getting in his way. He felt a hand on his arm and whipped to it.

Chloe immediately let go, raising her hands as if in surrender. 'Whoa, what's up? Did it get that bad?' She punched her chest dramatically with one hand. 'Fear not, brother of mine, I'm coming back and I'll fend off any googly-eyed—'

'Just give me a minute, ok, Chlo?'

Chloe frowned. 'Hey, what—'

But he ignored her, quite literally running from her now, swearing under his breath when he couldn't locate the girl again. Surely it couldn't be her. He'd left her in London. Left knowing he'd never see her again. His head whipped around, scanning the area around the fountain. He just had to make sure, that was all. That was the only driving thought in his brain right now, even if he was, distantly, aware that it wasn't entirely logical. His heart was galloping as he jogged around the fountain, ignoring the curious-eyed looks, given he wasn't dressed for a run. He was a little out of breath already, making him realise how unfit he'd become in the last few months – he'd run the Edinburgh marathon two years ago, for Christ's sake, and now look at him.

Then he saw it, the flash of hair again, and reached out to grab the girl who was turning away from him. She glanced back, more than a little startled, and frowned. He dropped her arm immediately. 'Sorry,' he said quickly, and backed away as a man came up alongside her. 'I just . . . Sorry.' He took a breath, pulled both hands through his hair. The girl gave a little shrug, and, after a suspicious look from the guy, they both walked away.

Not Josie. Well, of course not. It was highly bloody unlikely, wasn't it? But still, the laugh . . . He hadn't

198

forgotten that laugh. Warm and uninhibited, the type of laugh that made you want to find something to joke about, just so you could hear it again. With one last glance around, he admitted defeat and walked back over to where Chloe and Erin were both standing, staring at him.

Chloe held both her hands out, palms up, as if to conjure up an explanation. 'What the hell?'

'Sorry. I just . . . I thought I saw someone.' They both continued to look at him, and Chloe's frown deepened. He really hoped she didn't press – she knew about his whirlwind romance at Christmas, but Erin did not, and given her little speech just now, he doubted she'd take kindly to it. He cleared his throat. 'It's nothing, don't worry about it. Just thought I saw a friend, that's all. Anyway, come on, let's go and find this castle, that sounds cool.'

He let out a silent breath when they both let the matter drop and turned to pack up the picnic basket. He wasn't sure he'd have been able to explain it anyway, not in a way that they'd understand. He wasn't even totally sure he knew what he'd been thinking himself. He only knew that, in that first instant, his heart had jolted at the thought that he might get to see her again and, for just a second, everything else had ceased to matter.

Chapter Fourteen

It was still just light as they pulled up outside the venue in Brooklyn, the sky turning a pale, purply blue, the lights down the street just starting to wink into existence. As he was nearest the car door on the pavement side, Max got out of the cab first, smoothing down the plain black jacket he was wearing over a navy blue shirt – having decided that, for something like this, you couldn't go wrong with simple and understated – then paid the driver through the window while the other three got out.

Chloe put her hands on her hips and stared at the building in front of them. 'It doesn't look like much, does it?'

Max huffed out a little laugh. 'What were you expecting?' It looked fine to him – it wasn't exactly a feat of architectural genius but it was solid, and the owners had clearly worked with what they'd got, preserving the archway to the ground floor and using traditional lettering with the name of the place. It was a tall, brick building, and Max knew that it was the first two floors that they'd be exploring tonight – a gallery-slash-bar that the owner, who also happened to be Max and Liam's client on an entirely different project, was hoping would be the next big, 'trendy' thing, where people could buy the 'cooler', more abstract type of art, and have a drink at the same time, appreciating the ambience. It sounded a bit pretentious to Max, but he and Liam had been invited to the opening of the place and instructed, firmly, by one of the senior partners that they must go along, because this guy could throw more work in the company's way in the future.

'I don't know. Something . . . cooler.' Chloe looked around, to where Liam was approaching on her right. Liam was wearing black trousers like Max, but that's where the similarity on outfits ended. Liam's grey jacket looked as though it had been made for him, and he'd added his usual splash of colour – never more than one thing at a time – in the form of a green polo shirt. Chloe hooked her arm through his. 'Come on then,' she said to him. And with that, she steered him straight through the entrance. Liam shot a slightly guilty look back at Max, who just shrugged as if to say, *You're on your own now, mate.* Out of the presence of their parents, and given they'd been sandwiched next to each other in the cab, Chloe and Liam seemed to have got over the ignoring you stage of the relationship. Max hadn't quite decided yet which was better, but as Liam had been there in the office on Saturday, despite Max's assumption of the opposite, and had invited Chloe to the 'shindig' himself, there had been nothing Max could do about it. It wasn't that he minded his sister having her fun, he'd just rather she didn't destroy his own friendships in the process – and he genuinely liked Liam, not to mention the fact that he was turning out to be a useful contact. Even if he didn't think he'd need Liam's help again, it was nice to have the option. Still, Chloe was only in New York for a week, which hopefully wasn't long enough for her to do any damage, and to be fair, Liam did seem to have his head screwed on about all this shit.

He and Erin followed the two of them into the building. Chloe turned and shrugged off her leather jacket to reveal a black dress with green dots over it, tight enough that it showed just how in shape she kept her body – and tight enough to make him want to wince, given the appreciative look Liam was now giving her. Max decided to ignore the way Liam's gaze dropped to her legs, which she was showing off in a pair of heeled boots. She handed the jacket to him and gave him a slightly smug smile. 'You sort the coats, Liam and I will get the drinks.' Erin raised her eyebrows at Max, but as Chloe was already walking away, Max reckoned it was easier just to go along with it. He saw Liam looking down at Chloe, all starry-eyed as they pushed into the 'gallery' part of the building, apparently finding her bossiness and entitlement incredibly endearing, and wanted to roll his eyes. At least he and Erin had always – for the most part – had their heads level around each other, even if they did find each other attractive.

They handed in the coats and followed Liam and Chloe into the gallery, which was dimly lit, with individual little lights to highlight each of the paintings, making them look, Max was sure, much better than they would do at home. Erin slipped her hand into his. It was warm and comforting, and he smiled down at her without even thinking about it. She smiled back in a way that made him a little glad when a waiter came up with a tray of some kind of red cocktail, because he had to ask which was the non-alcoholic version and it gave him an out from the moment. Yes, he definitely felt affection for Erin, but it was hard to figure out how much of that was friendship, and the lingering feelings of a long relationship, and how much of it was genuine for the here and now. And sure, she said she wanted to get back together, but she hadn't been so certain of that a year ago, so who knew how long that resolution would last?

She did look incredible that evening though, in a black dress, white stripes on the top half, with red painted toes pointing through her open-toed stilettos and a pendant hanging at her neck, just above her breasts. Her arms were bare and tanned in a way that, even if the colour was out of a bottle, made her look somehow more alluring, and she'd done her eyes in that way that made them look even more blue.

They shifted out of the way of another few people coming in, and Max took a sip of his drink, wishing it was alcoholic so that it would take the edge off, as he scanned the room for Chloe and Liam.

'I'm glad I'm here,' Erin said, and Max glanced down at her again to see that she'd put her drink on the ledge that ran along the wall behind them.

'I'm glad you're here too,' Max said. Because whatever else may be the case, that much was true.

Then she stepped into him, tilted her face up and kissed him. Her lips were firm, and sure, and tasted of lip gloss, like she always did. He didn't resist it – they'd been dancing round it the whole weekend, so why the hell not? It was just a friendly kiss. And yes, there was a familiar stirring there, signs that the chemistry hadn't gone away. Maybe it was impossible for it not to be there, given their history, the fact that they knew exactly which buttons to press.

She pulled away, smiled in that sure way of hers, then picked up her drink and set off into the fray. He closed his eyes briefly, then followed. It would be so damn easy just to slide into it all. To go with the flow this evening, have a couple of drinks, and end up in bed. It was her last night here, and she clearly wanted to. And, God, it had been four months now. Maybe it would even be easy to carry it on, to move in with her, settle back into each other. She knew everything about him – or pretty much – meaning he had a hell of a lot less capacity to upset her.

They did an obligatory circle of the artwork – they were all a bit too obscure for Max – then climbed the stairs to the next level, where they found Liam and Chloe by the bar. They ordered another drink each – all on the house this evening apparently – and Max tried not to think about the heat of Erin's arm, pressed next to his.

Liam took a swig of his beer. 'Well, look at us all, standing around in the new place to be in the up-and-coming part of town.'

'Think Brooklyn's been "up" for quite a while, mate.' Max accepted the fake gin and tonic that Erin handed him. 'And don't you live just around the corner?'

Liam made a face. 'Around the corner's a bit of a stretch. But either way, I have no shame – not all of us can afford to sponge off our parents.'

'Think that's a bit of an oxymoron?' Max cocked one

eyebrow at Erin in question, who allowed herself a little smile.

'Oh God,' muttered Liam, jerking his head almost imperceptibly towards the other side of the room. 'Incoming.'

Max swivelled in time to see Tim, senior partner, and Bradley, the owner of this place and Max and Liam's client, zero in on them. 'Well, better now than when you're all drunk,' Max said, making Chloe grin.

'Liam!' Tim exclaimed, budging his way into the circle and clapping Liam's shoulder, even though he had to reach up to do it. He pushed his glasses back on his nose and smiled benignly around the circle. 'I was just telling Bradley here what an excellent job I think you've been doing.' After muttering something to a nearby waiter with a tray full of glasses, Bradley stepped up, smiling on cue. Max knew full well not to be conned by that smile – Bradley was as sharp as they came, and seemed to have unerring focus on anything he dabbled in, despite the number of ideas he seemed to throw up. It was probably why he was still ripped, even though he was mid-sixties.

'Yes, yes,' Bradley said, nodding to Tim as if indulging a small child. 'I've been impressed by the work that Max and Liam have done so far, but let's see how it all looks when it's done, hey?' He gave the general circle a wink and they all smiled back obediently. Max wouldn't actually be at the company to see the final block of fancy, 'bespoke' apartments, but he was under explicit instructions not to mention that he was leaving, in case that caused any uproar.

'But yes,' Bradley continued, taking a glass of champagne that the waiter brought up to him, 'I'm glad you could all make it. I wanted all my people to see the kind of vibe I have in here, gives you a better sense of the type of thing I go for, you know.' He took a sip of his champagne, not so much as blinking at the use of 'my people'. Max arranged his face into something he thought indicated sage agreement, though he saw Chloe's eyebrows shoot up, and hoped she wouldn't say anything.

'It looks like a marvellous set-up,' Liam said, gesturing around, to which Tim and Bradley just nodded.

'Yes, I think so, but it all depends on whether it can turn a profit, doesn't it?' He looked away for a moment, scanning the room – presumably for someone more interesting or important. While his back was turned, Max mouthed 'marvellous' to Liam, with raised eyebrows, and Liam shrugged a little helplessly. 'Ah, here's my PR man,' Bradley continued. He waved someone over, then turned back to them, slightly blocking Tim from the circle as he did so. 'I wanted to get everyone in the same room, you know. It's good for business, isn't it? Always good to make connections, to celebrate the successes with the people that made them so.'

'Exactly right,' Tim said, nodding like Bradley had said something profound.

Bradley carried on as if Tim hadn't spoken. 'And Ollie here is actually doing the PR for this venue. Ollie!'

The man was already walking over to them, but doubled his pace at Bradley's shout, an action that was more noticeable because he was slightly shorter than average.

Ollie came into the circle, shook hands all around. His brown eyes lingered on Max for a moment. Max knew this guy, he was sure of it. It was the pixieish quality that he remembered, all sharp chin and slightly pointy ears. Josie's ex. An uncomfortable sensation brewed in his stomach, and he took a sip of his drink to try to quench it. Every now and then, Oliver's gaze flickered towards Max, in a way that suggested he recognised him too. Max realised he must be staring too hard when he noticed Erin looking up at him curiously, and tried to straighten out his features.

'Are you here alone then, Ollie? No colleagues along with you?' Bradley asked, clicking a hand in the air to someone at the same time. Again, Chloe wrinkled her nose, but said nothing.

'The others wanted to get in an early night, what with it being a Monday and all, so it's just me, I'm afraid.' Oliver raised his hands in a way that was clearly supposed to indicate apology, then took one of those hands up to smooth his already overly styled hair.

'No, no need to apologise,' said Bradley, taking a second glass of champagne from a tray that the waiter brought along and handing it to Oliver, who was apparently the only one in the circle who would be offered one. Liam shot Max a questioning look. So, his scowl had returned then. He gave a big shoulder roll, told himself to stop being ridiculous. He barely even remembered the guy, and hadn't given him a second thought since he'd met him. But he did remember thinking he was a dick at the time, and that thought seemed to have intensified now. Not helped by the fact that Bradley was just *fawning* over him – a couple of unintelligent, puffed-up peacocks.

'I did manage to drag my girlfriend along with me though,' Oliver continued.

'Is that so? Well, I'd be delighted to meet her . . .' Max

let Bradley's words wash over him for a moment. *Girlfriend*. The word thumped its way around his mind. It wouldn't be.

But then Oliver turned and beckoned to a woman, and Max's gaze shot over to her. And it was her.

Josie.

Josie, looking fucking stunning in skin-tight black jeans and heels to make her long legs look even longer, and a high-necked green, white and black top. She stood out more because she *wasn't* wearing a dress, and was now walking over to them as if she owned the room, smiling brightly at Oliver. She'd grown out her fringe, which suited her, and her hair was pulled up in some kind of elegant knot, studs glinting in her ears.

He saw the moment she clocked him. Her gaze darted from Oliver and around their little group, travelling over Chloe, Liam and Erin until it landed on him last. He saw her stride falter slightly, before she whipped her gaze away from him so fast he didn't have time to properly register the expression there. Those gorgeous eyes, ones that put the colour 'brown' to shame, stayed focused on Oliver as she came up to join them. Max found he was gripping his glass too tightly and flexed his fingers deliberately, trying to relieve some of the tension that had sprung through his entire body.

'This is Josie,' Oliver said proudly, gesturing towards Bradley. Josie's eyes were fixed on Bradley alone as she held out a hand, smiling, Max thought, a little tightly, her jaw locked into place.

'So nice to meet you.'

Bradley smiled. 'Is that another English accent I hear?'

He didn't give her the chance to answer. 'Charmed. She's a keeper,' he said to Oliver, even though he didn't know the first fucking thing about her. She hooked an arm through Oliver's and he wrapped his around her waist. Max couldn't look away, though she was refusing to look back at him, like she was deliberately trying not to. He wanted to clear his throat, to make her look at him, but what the fuck was he supposed to say when she did? She shouldn't even *be* here, in this city, and especially not with this prick. He'd cheated on her, for Christ's sake.

'Well,' Bradley said, clapping his hands together. 'It seems I'm surrounded by Brits! Max here is from England too, Ollie, he's been working on my little apartment project, so I'm sure you'll find lots in common.' Max tried and failed to pull his gaze away from Josie, aware that she must be able to feel it on her, that that was probably why she wouldn't return it. She had barely any makeup on, but she seemed to glow more in the dim lighting than either Erin or his sister. He took a deliberate sip of his drink. Lots in common, indeed.

Chloe cocked one eyebrow up, in a way that he'd taught her to do when they were twelve, and folded her arms. Max spared her a quick glance, checking for any warning signals that she was about to pipe up. She'd clearly taken offence at the fact no one had properly introduced her yet. Liam seemed to realise this at the same moment and said quickly, 'Can I also introduce you to Chloe, Mr Vane?' Oliver and Bradley both turned to look at Chloe as Liam indicated her, but Max saw Josie's gaze pass over Chloe to Erin before she quickly looked back at Oliver. *Look at me,* he pleaded silently with her. 'She's Max's sister,'

Liam continued, 'and English too.' Bradley spared her a perfunctory smile, and Chloe nodded politely, with a fleeting glance at Max as if to acknowledge that yes, he was indeed the dick Max had claimed.

But Max barely paid attention to any of that, because at the sound of his name, Josie had finally turned that gaze on him, as if she knew she couldn't avoid it any longer. And he'd given her every right to *want* to avoid it, hadn't he? His throat tightened as her lips twisted to form a smile that seemed painted on.

She cocked her head in that way he remembered. 'Hello, Max.'

Chapter Fifteen

Max cleared his throat, feeling like a complete and total idiot. 'Hi.' Jesus, what the fuck was wrong with him? Hi? *Hi?*

Josie nodded, then pulled her gaze away from him again, that fixed smile of hers slightly faltering as she flicked a quick glance up at Oliver, then around the room. Bradley looked from Max to Josie and back again, a mildly interested expression on his face. 'Oh, so you two know each other, do you? England really is delightfully small, isn't it?' He turned to Oliver, lowering his voice and leaning in, absentmindedly handing his empty champagne glass to a passing waiter. 'Ollie, I'll catch up with you in a bit, yes? I've just got to go and say hello.' Oliver nodded, his arm still around Josie, while Bradley waved a hand in the direction of two middle-aged men who had just appeared on the second floor. As soon as Bradley left, Oliver turned to stare at Max in a way that stopped ever so short of a glare, and his arm tightened enough on Josie that it seemed to force her closer against her side. So, he had placed Max, then. At the same time, Tim stepped in to take Bradley's place, manoeuvring it so that he was next to Liam and immediately starting up a stream of instructions to him. Liam nodded along, grimacing at Chloe apologetically.

His sister didn't notice, though. She and Erin were both watching Max, Josie and Oliver, clearly trying to work out the connection. Erin frowned. 'So, you two know each other then?' For some reason, Erin's Scottish lilt seemed particularly pronounced right now, when usually he hardly even noticed it.

Josie's bottom teeth came out to graze her lip in the way he'd seen her do when in London, when she was trying to think of what to say or trying to get out of a situation. She caught him looking and for a moment their gazes met. Her teeth retreated immediately, like she'd just figured out what she was doing. 'Yes,' Josie said, clearing her throat. 'We met at Christmas, in London.'

Oliver didn't seem to react to this, only skimmed his gaze over Chloe and Erin, like he was trying to work out their side of the puzzle. So, Josie must have come clean to him then, must have admitted that they weren't, in fact, long lost friends. He wondered what, exactly, she'd told him, how she'd made it sound.

Chloe's eyes widened a fraction and Max tried not to grit his teeth. She'd clearly cottoned on. He shot her a look, and in response she took a big gulp of her wine, then immediately fixed her gaze on Josie, eyes assessing her as they did a quick scan up and down her body.

Erin's frown lingered. 'At Christmas?'

Fuck. Max cleared his throat again. He'd make it sore soon if he didn't stop. 'Yeah.' He tried to smile at Erin like it was all no big deal. 'When I missed my flight, do you remember I told you about that?'

Oliver, who only came up to the bottom of Josie's chin, nodded vigorously at that, and gave a somewhat unconvincing grin. 'Right, I remember you now.' Max tried not to narrow his eyes at the prick. Pretending he'd only just figured it out – it was a boring trick. 'Didn't you come to the Christmas party?' Josie gave Oliver's back a little stroke, like she was soothing him. A movement that would probably have gone unnoticed, if Max hadn't been staring so hard. Josie and Oliver's eyes met for a second and when she gave him a small smile, he nodded back – some shared communication that no one else was privy to.

Oliver had got a job in New York, Max remembered. So was Josie just here visiting? He felt Erin's eyes on the side of his face and took a sip of his drink, looking very deliberately at it rather than at anyone in the circle.

Oliver turned his attention to Chloe and Erin, and Max thought that, when he spoke, his tone was overly jovial. 'What about you two then?'

'I'm Max's sister,' Chloe said easily. Josie's gaze flashed to her, and when Chloe grinned, Josie smiled in that same tight way. He'd made them speak to each other, hadn't he? Chloe had been all worried about Max going off the deep end, had been paranoid, thinking that being alone at Christmas would be triggering for him, so had been a little obsessive about pestering him to make sure he was ok. Did Josie remember speaking to her, he wondered? Not that he'd told her the ins and outs of it, had more just put her on the phone to make light of it all to Chloe, demonstrate the fact that he'd managed to find a pretty girl to hang out with while he was stranded.

'You both live here then?' Oliver flicked his gaze between Chloe and Max, seeming particularly interested in trying to connect the dots. Josie took a sip of her drink – white wine – but when he met her gaze over the rim of her glass, she looked away. Was she wondering that too? Wondering why he was here?

'Not really,' Max said. His voice came out a little husky and he wet his lips. 'I wasn't supposed to be, anyway – was just coming out here for Christmas initially.' He directed that last part at Josie. He wanted her to know that he hadn't been lying to her – about that, at least. 'But I got offered a short-term contract with Liam here at his architect firm, so I decided to stay on for a bit.' He gestured to Liam, who was only just returning to the conversation now that Tim was leaving. Liam nodded, glancing between them all as he tried to catch up.

'And I'm just visiting,' Chloe piped up. She glanced around. 'So do you reckon there are any snacks coming out?' No one answered her, though Josie looked around too, as if grateful to have an excuse to divert her attention elsewhere. Max ran a hand through his hair. Jesus.

'I'm visiting too,' Erin said firmly, inserting herself into the conversation. Max saw Oliver's eyes linger on her for a second, and he felt his free hand clench into a fist. Not because Erin was his or anything like that – she was beautiful, and other people were entitled to appreciate that – but because Oliver was with Josie, so he shouldn't even be sparing anyone else a second glance.

'You're from Scotland?' Josie asked, focused exclusively

on Erin and shifting her weight, making her earrings sparkle in the change of light.

Erin nodded. 'I met Max at university there.' She put her hand on Max's arm lightly, gave a little squeeze, so though she didn't actually say she was his girlfriend, it was heavily implied. Max saw Josie's eyes flicker towards Erin's hand, and knew she'd clocked it. He felt his body stiffen. He couldn't move away in case that offended Erin, but he wanted to, just so that Josie knew it wasn't like that. Or at least, it wasn't when he'd met her, anyway. He forced himself to let out a slow, silent breath. Fuck.

Josie nodded, cleared her throat. 'That's nice.'

Erin let her hand drop from Max's arm but shifted a little, so the side of her body brushed against his. 'And how did you two meet?'

Josie glanced up at Oliver, but though his arm was around her he was now doing a quick scan of the room. Clearly, whatever threat Max posed had been assessed and dismissed. Maybe he was just so confident in his and Josie's relationship that bumping into him was no big deal, a funny story they'd tell the grandkids. Prick. 'At work,' Josie supplied.

'Seriously, are there no snacks coming out?' Chloe blurted out. She gave Max a look as if to say *let's move*, clearly sensing the awkwardness. And she was the only one on his side of the circle that would understand why. He didn't want to move away yet though – what if Josie disappeared immediately after and he didn't get the chance to speak to her again?

He looked at Josie instead. 'So, how are you?' He took a sip of his drink, tried to make it casual. Tried not to let on that he'd been thinking about her since he left, wishing he'd said more in his note to explain. Or that he hadn't realised how much he'd regret it until he was on the plane and it was too damn late to change it.

She gave a little shrug of her bare shoulders. 'I'm good, thanks.'

'Still into your photography?' He was thinking of the photo she'd taken of him, the one on the beach that she'd given him for Christmas.

She nodded. 'Yep.' She let her arm slip from Oliver and curled a strand of her hair back into her bun. She paused, glanced at Oliver again. 'Actually,' she began again, her voice firmer now, 'I've started up an Instagram account for it, now that I've got the time.'

Oliver squeezed her shoulder, bringing his attention back to the group. 'She's taking the world by storm, my girl.' Max tried hard not to grit his teeth.

'Well, I'd love to see,' Erin said graciously – though whether she meant it or not, Max couldn't be sure. Josie hesitated, doing that lip-bitey thing again. Then she seemed to relent and got out her phone, showing it around to general compliments. The top photo was one in Central Park, posted yesterday, and it looked more beautiful on her phone screen than it had done in real life. So, it could have been her he saw, then. Not that he could ask – it would raise too many alarm bells for almost everyone in their little circle.

'Honestly, you don't have to keep looking, it's really not that exciting,' Josie said quickly, reminding him of when she'd shown him her photos on the beach, how reluctant she'd been to do so. But Erin kept scrolling down, with

Max and Chloe looking over her shoulder and Liam clearly trying to look interested. Josie shifted her weight a little awkwardly and he wished he could cross to her, squeeze her hand reassuringly, or just run a hand down her arm.

'The photos are incredible,' Max said, causing Josie to glance at him. 'You know, I've got a friend who's a photographer – I could introduce you if you like?' Chloe's eyebrows shot up and Max shrugged as if to say *what?* He was just being friendly, that was all.

'No thanks,' Josie said, a little too quickly. 'It's just a hobby really, I've got my freelance work in the meantime.'

'Well, they're cool anyway,' said Chloe, taking the phone from Erin and handing it back to Josie. 'How long have you been doing it?'

Josie seemed visibly relieved to have her phone back. 'Well, I started this account when I got to New York.'

'So you live here now?' Max asked, before he could help himself.

She nodded, and that same weird smile was back. 'That's right. Oliver and I moved out here in January.'

There was a beat where everyone seemed to be waiting for Max to respond, resulting in a slightly awkward beat of silence when he didn't. 'That's cool,' said Liam, stepping up. 'Are you loving it?'

Her smile seemed genuine this time, a hint of that open warmth he remembered from Christmas. 'I am. We've done all the touristy things and it's been so cool, right?' She looked up at Oliver, who once again had been browsing the room.

'Huh?' Oliver said. 'Right. Yes, that's right. It's been epic, right, babe?' *Babe?* Josie raised her eyebrows at him,

217

though whether at the 'babe' or at him just repeating the same question back to her, Max wasn't sure. 'Look, I'm really sorry all,' said Oliver, in what Max considered an overly pompous voice, like he was playing up the English for the American audience, 'but I've just got to speak to a couple of people – here for work, after all.' He gave a rueful headshake, like he wasn't just loving that fact.

'And I'm going to have to go to the ladies,' Josie said immediately, as if she'd just been waiting for the opportunity to get out of the conversation. To be fair, Max could hardly blame her – it wasn't exactly riveting conversation here. Oliver nodded, gave her shoulder one last squeeze, then strolled purposefully round the other side of the bar. Josie turned, hesitated, then looked back at Max. 'It was nice to see you again – sorry, I should have said that earlier.' She smiled a little, her gaze flickering quickly to Erin and back again. 'You're well?' She added it like an afterthought, and he could only nod. 'Well. I hope you all have a lovely time – and enjoy New York, if you're visiting.' She directed the last part to Chloe and Erin, like she was setting up stakes here and not just a visitor herself.

Chloe raised her glass to toast Josie. 'Cheers.'

Josie walked away with quick, long strides and Max watched her retreating back for a moment, downing the last dregs of his drink.

'Actually, I think I need to go to the loo too,' Erin said. She finished her drink, put it on the bar behind her. 'Be back in a min, ok?' She squeezed Max's arm as she swept after Josie. Max took half a step after her, almost thinking to stop her – what if she cornered Josie or something?

But Chloe swung round to face him, closing him, Liam and her off from the rest of the room.

'Who on earth was that, and why do you look so worried about it?' Max looked towards Liam for help, but he just shook his head, still looking faintly bemused. Fat lot of bloody help he was. 'She's the girl, isn't she?' Chloe pressed.

'What girl?' He set his empty glass down behind him. From the look on his sister's face, he knew he wasn't quite pulling off the nonchalance.

'*The* girl.' She nodded when he said nothing, his silence apparently answer enough, then folded her arms, tapping her fingers against one elbow. 'She's cute.' To Max's eye, 'cute' seemed like an incredible understatement for the way Josie looked tonight.

'Hang on,' Liam said. 'What am I missing here?'

When Max just shook his head, Chloe turned to Liam. 'He fell for this girl in London when he was stuck there last year, and then he just *left* her, and hasn't spoken to her since. That is said girl,' she added unnecessarily.

Liam's gaze flickered between Max and Chloe. 'Right,' he said. 'And, umm, why did you leave her, exactly?'

Max gave Chloe a *do not say anything* look, and she huffed out a breath. Liam looked between them. 'Right,' he said again. 'Well, I'll get us more drinks, shall I?' Max nodded gratefully. God bloody love Liam – he never pushed, not when it was clear you didn't want to talk about something. It was part of what made their friendship so easy.

His gaze shot to the corner of the room. Josie was coming out from where the loos were now. Was it just him, or was there more of a tightness to the way she was holding herself? He did a quick scan of the room, located Oliver chatting to another old guy in a suit, intently focused on what the guy was saying and apparently oblivious to Josie. Now was the time, then.

He'd barely taken a step, when Chloe swung round in front of him again. 'Do you really think that's such a good idea?' He said nothing. 'What are you going to say?'

He spared Chloe a brief glance. 'I don't know. I need to explain.'

Chloe huffed out a breath. 'She's with someone else now, there's no point in confusing the issue.'

Max scowled. 'That guy's a dick.'

Chloe scoffed. 'That's hardly the point. And what about Erin?' Max could only glare at her. Liam stepped towards them and handed them both a drink, looking very like he was trying to think of something constructive to say, which, in all fairness, was more difficult when you had very little idea as to what was going on. Chloe sighed. 'It's not fair, Max. To anyone. I just don't think you should open it all up again.' She tapped her fingers on the stem of her wine glass. 'Though you didn't have to make it so bloody dramatic when you left – what happened to the good old petering things out over WhatsApp?'

Max narrowed his eyes, then turned to Liam. 'Did I ever tell you about the time Chloe told a guy she actually had a twin, and the twin and her had been swapping with him and now she had to come clean – just to get him to dump her?'

Liam raised his eyebrows. 'A twin, hey?'

Chloe flushed. 'Look, it wasn't that bad, I just . . .'

And with that, Max took his exit. He caught up with Josie and reached out to take her elbow before she could clock him. She stumbled a little and when she looked up at him, colour flooded her face. She wrenched her arm from his a little forcefully.

'Sorry,' he said quickly. 'I just . . . Can I just talk to you for a second?'

She hesitated, studying his face like she was deciding something, then gave a single, jerky nod. 'Alright.'

She followed him to the nearest corner, one where the light barely reached. To lead her downstairs might be a bit too suspicious. Once there, she crossed her arms, waiting, and he cleared her throat. 'I didn't expect to see you here tonight.'

She raised her eyebrows. 'Well, that makes two of us,' she said.

'I just . . .' *Jesus, get a fucking grip, Max.* 'I wanted to apologise for how I left things with you.'

Her eyes stayed cold and even, but when she nodded slowly, her expression flickered. 'Yes. It wasn't ideal, I'll admit.' He winced at her tone.

'I just . . .' he tried again, but she shook her head to cut him off.

'Look, it's alright. It was just a bit of fun, wasn't it?' She sighed. 'And ok, maybe I got caught up in the romanticism of it all, but it was really just a fling, wasn't it?' She dropped her arms to her sides and straightened her shoulders. 'You don't owe me anything, so don't worry about it, ok?'

He scowled, tried to think of something to do with his hands that wasn't balling them into fists. He wanted her to be angry at him. Somehow, this ambivalence was worse – because if it had just been a fling, then why couldn't he get her out his damn head? He took a breath, tried one more time. 'I wish—'

'Look, Max, we've both moved on, haven't we?' She gave a pointed look across the room and Max saw Erin gliding over to Chloe, who was beckoning her over, clearly trying to keep her distracted.

Max looked back at Josie and frowned. 'You haven't moved on. You're moving backwards.' He was trying to get a rise out of her, but other than a slight tightening of her lips, he got nothing. He wanted to shake her, to snap her out of this weird composure and back to the real Josie, the one he'd met at Christmas, not this cardboard cut-out version who he couldn't get a read from.

Josie shook her head firmly. 'You might think that, but I don't.'

'What?'

She lifted her chin. 'I haven't moved backwards. I'm living in New York, aren't I?' She gestured around the room, then cocked her head in that way of hers. 'As I seem to recall, you thought I was secretly the adventurous type. So, maybe you were right.' The way she said it, it was like he could hear the shrug in her voice, but then their gazes locked and he wondered if she remembered that evening as vividly as he did. The cocktail bar, her eyes dancing in the candlelight. The taste of her when he'd kissed her later.

'Is that her?' Josie asked abruptly, glancing again at Erin, almost like she couldn't help herself. When Max frowned, she added, 'The girl who broke your heart?' He stared at her for a moment. Well, what had he expected her to think? He'd allowed her to think that he'd had his heart broken, as an easy and less complicated explanation for why he'd been so off with her at the start. He remembered it in excruciating detail, the weight of what he'd been feeling, and how she'd pulled him out of it, even though he'd been downright rude when he'd first met her. He started to shake his head, to explain that yes, she was his ex but no, she wasn't the reason he'd been like that. Out of the corner of his eye he noticed Chloe sneaking glances over at them, and he could almost hear her telling him to leave it alone. Then Josie raised a hand to someone across the room, smiled and nodded, and Max turned to see Oliver looking over at them. Just like that, his time was up.

Josie curled a strand of hair around her ear and took a step way. He saw her hesitate, turn back. She blew out a breath. 'Look, Max, I can't say it's not a little strange, seeing you here. But honestly, just so you don't feel bad or whatever, you leaving, in the way you did, was probably the best thing that could have happened to me.' Her gaze flickered over to where Oliver was waiting for her, then briefly to the ground before meeting his again. 'It made me realise what I had with Oliver,' she said firmly. 'Made me realise I wanted to give it another go.'

'He cheated on you,' Max said flatly.

'I'm well aware of that, thanks,' she said tightly, in a way that made him regret it. 'But everyone can make a mistake.' That head-cock again. 'Or are telling me you never have?' He said nothing because no, he obviously couldn't tell her that, could he? 'And I got to come out here,' she continued, 'and we've been going to Broadway and Central Park and everything – things I never would have dreamed I'd do, which has been just . . .'– she waved a hand in the air – 'amazing.' She nodded, like that was the word she'd been searching for. 'It's been amazing,' she repeated.

So maybe he'd just been a rebound – some fun that she needed to get out her system. He remembered that, on their expedition to that damn Winter Wonderland place, they'd run into Oliver, and it had been clear that the two of them had only just ended things. So then he'd thought there would be no harm – she was on the rebound, just looking for some fun, so why not have some himself? And the fact that she was gorgeous and intelligent and could make him laugh was obviously a plus. But then . . . He hadn't realised, until just now, that maybe it really *had* just been a bit of fun – for her.

Josie sighed, and he watched her chest rise and fall with the moment. 'So maybe,' she continued, 'maybe that's the reason fate or whatever made me run into you that day – because I might not have given this a go otherwise.'

Max shook his head, feeling suddenly weary. 'You really believe everything happens for a reason and all that bullshit?'

She raised her eyebrows at his tone, then shrugged. 'Not really, no.' Her face darkened a little at that, and some of her seemed to retreat inwards. He wondered if she was thinking of her parents and immediately wished he hadn't said anything. 'But it doesn't mean you can't appreciate it when things work out. So maybe I should be thanking you. But for now, I have to go, sorry.' She stepped away a little hurriedly on those spindly heels, and he reached out to grab her hand. She looked back at him, and didn't pull away. But he didn't know what the fuck he wanted to say, what his parting words should be.

He cleared his throat. 'I'll see you around?'

She pulled her hand from his, slowly, and he didn't take his eyes off her face as shadows in her eyes seemed to flicker. She blew out a breath, shook her head. 'Somehow I doubt that – don't you?'

And then, without giving him a chance to think of a response, she was walking away, back to her boyfriend, leaving him standing there alone.

He took a slow sip of his drink, saw that Erin was watching him now. She was frowning, and he couldn't blame her. Couldn't blame Josie, either – she had every right to move the hell on. She was right, it had been just a fling – because he'd made sure of that, hadn't he? He'd refused to allow himself to believe it could ever have been anything more, had convinced himself that they'd both be better off that way.

His drink tasted bitter on his tongue when he lifted it to his lips. Another cruel twist of fate, he supposed, that now he realised he wanted something more, it was too late.

Part Three: September

Chapter Sixteen

'Look, I'm here!' Josie turned her phone around so Memo could get a view of Dundas Castle out of the taxi window as it crunched its way up the gravel driveway. An actual, freaking castle, no question about it. The building loomed over them as they got closer to it, two circular turrets either side of what she presumed was the main area, then a further square turret further down. It was grey stone and looked like a drawing out of a medieval history textbook. To the right of it stood a few bushy trees, their leaves already welcoming autumn with a golden hue, which somehow made the whole thing look even more majestic. To top it all off, the sky was a bright, clear blue, and even with her stomach not quite settled at the thought of the weekend – with all the happy couples that weddings inevitably conjured up – she couldn't help loosening a breath at the sight of it all.

'Oh, isn't that just stunning?' Memo said, and Josie turned the phone back the other way, smiling at Memo's almost tearful expression. 'I just love Scotland. It's going to be such a beautiful wedding.'

'It is,' Josie agreed, trying to ignore the part of her that was dreading the whole thing.

'You will take photos, won't you?'

'Of course,' Josie said easily. Her camera was already sitting next to her on the middle seat, primed and ready.

'And you'll say hello to that lovely Laura for me?' Memo glanced up at something out of sight above the laptop screen on her end and nodded. Grandad, presumably.

'I will,' Josie promised. Memo had only met Laura once, but she had this uncanny ability to remember every single person in Josie's life, in extreme detail.

'And you'll be ok, there alone?' Memo seemed to peer in more closely, taking in, no doubt, the slight bags under Josie's eyes, the pale skin that she'd have to cover up later. She hadn't been sleeping all too well since she'd got back from New York, a constant whirr in her mind asking her what the hell she was supposed to do with her life now.

Josie hesitated for the briefest of seconds before saying, 'I won't be alone, I'll have Bia. And Laura.'

Memo looked up behind the screen, and smiled at something. Josie raised her eyebrows. 'Grandad said something about Bia, didn't he?'

'He says to say hello to her,' Memo said with another smile.

Her grandad muttered something inaudible as he came to sit on the red sofa next to Memo, one bushy eyebrow making itself known. Josie frowned, though Memo huffed out a laugh.

'What was that?' Josie asked.

'He said he expects you could do with the break from Helen right now, in any case.'

'I'm right here, Cecelia,' her grandad grumbled. 'I can speak for myself.'

'Well speak then!' Josie saw a slim hand reaching out to adjust the screen, and then her grandad's face came into full view. He leaned forward, holding a cup of something hot – black tea, no doubt – between his hands.

'Is she driving you mad, Josie? It's ok, you can tell us.'

'No, she's fine!' Josie lied. And really, yes, Helen *was* driving her slightly insane, but she knew she couldn't complain – she was letting Josie live there, rent free, while she tried to get herself back on her feet.

Memo moved the screen back to her side of the sofa. 'Oh we know just what she's like, my love. She's our daughter and we love her, but she was a total nightmare to live with as a teenager, and I swear she's hardly changed at all. She was always bossing your dad around; I tell you, it gave me a headache.' Memo smiled in a way that seemed genuine, but Josie wondered if she got that little jolt, every time she thought about the son she'd lost, just like Josie did, whenever she thought too hard about her parents. It was one of the things she loved about Memo, though – the fact she could talk about Josie's mum and dad with love rather than sadness. It made Josie able to do it too, when she was around her.

'She's getting me to help strip the wallpaper in her bedroom,' Josie admitted. Though, to be fair, she didn't have much else to do right now.

'Tell her to bugger off, Josie,' her grandad said, slurping his tea.

'Yes, and give her a cigarette if she complains,' Memo said.

Josie tried not to smile as her grandad muttered something under his breath. She caught the word 'encourage', but not much else.

'Anyway,' Memo continued. 'We'll try and come to see you both in Guildford soon.'

'Great!' said Josie. It had been too long since she'd seen them both.

Her grandad popped his head into view. 'Yes, and tell your grandmother I'm perfectly capable of driving, won't you, Josie?'

'He is *not*,' Memo said, before Josie could answer. 'His back's playing up again, and the doctor said he's not supposed to do anything strenuous.'

'Oh come on,' her grandad said, slinking back out of the screen, 'driving's hardly strenuous.'

'Is that my photo on the wall I see?' Josie asked. She'd long since learned it was best not to get in the middle of their bickering – both sides tended to ignore what she said in any case, so she was better off leaving them to it. It would be Memo who got her way in the end though, no matter how much she made Grandad feel he had a say in the matter.

Memo looked over her shoulder. 'Oh yes!' It was the photo Josie had sent them of her standing alone on Brooklyn Bridge, bundled up in a hat and scarf but beaming nonetheless. 'We love it, don't we, John?' Her grandad grunted his assent. Oliver had taken that photo, Josie thought, though the pang she felt at his name was barely there anymore.

The taxi came to a stop outside the castle as Memo looked back at Josie. Josie glanced at the taxi driver, but

232

he just gave her a wink as he got out the car. 'Did I tell you about the time your grandad took me to New York for our twentieth wedding anniversary?'

'Umm . . .' Josie glanced behind her to where the driver was now opening the boot and taking out her suitcase.

'We left your dad and Helen home alone and I tell you, the house was a *state* by the time we got back.'

'Memo,' Josie said, 'I'm going to have to go – the car's stopped.'

'Oh! Of course, my love, sorry.'

Josie cocked her head. 'Aren't you going to ask me about the quote?'

Memo smiled. 'I was trying to be nice and let you get on with your exciting weekend. But it's your turn, isn't it? Do you have one?'

Josie brought up the message she'd written to herself on her phone, and read out the quote she'd written down. 'The greatest trick the devil ever pulled was convincing the world he didn't exist.'

'Oh! Oh I know that one!' Memo flapped a slim hand across the screen. 'It's . . . Wait, don't go, I know it. It's . . . John!' There was thump and then a groan, and Josie was pretty sure Memo had hit her grandad.

'*The Usual Suspects*,' her grandad said from out of view.

'Right, that's it,' said Memo, smiling and slumping back down on the sofa. 'I would have got there eventually.'

Josie laughed as she turned off FaceTime, slipped her phone into her pocket and got out the taxi. She smiled at the balding driver as he handed over her suitcase – bigger than she'd usually take for just a few days, but necessary for the three separate formal occasions taking place as

233

part of the wedding. You had to admire Laura's vision for the whole thing, really.

'You going to be alright from here, lass?' the driver asked, hooking his fingers through the belt loop of his trousers, no sign that he was in any great rush. A far cry from the London or New York taxis.

'Yes, thanks so much,' she said, handing over the cash.

'Aye, you're welcome.'

She watched the car drive away for a moment, then let out a long, slow breath and crooked her neck one way then the other to relieve some of the tension. She turned a full circle to take everything in, allowing the slightly crisp morning air to caress her cheeks. The grounds were as epic as the building itself, seeming to stretch on indefinitely, though she didn't want to think about how many hours a day it must cost to keep the lawn that perfect.

She nodded to herself, squared her shoulders. She was here now and even if she *did* turn out to be the only single person the whole weekend, even if she *was* bombarded with endless questions over what had happened with her and Oliver, she was here because she loved Laura and so she would damn well make the most of it. Besides, she was lucky – she got to stay in the actual castle for three nights, Laura having deemed her close enough on her side to take one of the limited rooms here. And, really, you couldn't hope for a weekend in a more beautiful location – maybe it would prove to be exactly what she needed.

With that in mind, she put her suitcase to one side and picked up her camera. It was the perfect chance to capture the castle – there were two cars parked outside, but they were out of the way and easily hidden. Imposing, that was the right word for it. She supposed that was the point of it, originally. And the landscape was just glorious – blue skies, the sun causing reflections to dance in a few of the windows at the top of the turrets – though she imagined this was the type of place to look just as good with a moody, stormy sky in the backdrop. Still, she was glad of the weather, for Laura's sake. It was one of Josie's favourite times of year, September. You weren't *expecting* glorious weather, so when you got the tail end of summer it was even better.

After taking a few photos on her camera, Josie snapped one on her phone, then sent a WhatsApp to Bia.

The castle!

She got a line of heart emojis back, then *I'm SO excited. I'll see you tomorrow!!*

Josie smiled as she slipped her phone back in her coat pocket. Thank God Bia had agreed to step in as her plus one after Josie'd had to tell Laura that Oliver wouldn't be coming after all – she didn't think she could manage the whole weekend alone, pretending that she had absolutely no problem with being single in the face of her friend's marital bliss.

For a good minute, Josie made herself stand there, trying hard to be in the moment. She had to admit, something about the atmosphere here, the beauty of it, made her feel a little more peaceful than she thought she'd be. But not just here – she'd felt the same in Edinburgh. Almost the moment she'd stepped off the train, she'd decided she loved the city and was instantly sad she only got one night there. She'd never been to Scotland before – her grandparents had taken her to Wales a few times on holiday, but never Scotland – and now she was struggling to think why she'd never bothered to visit of her own accord.

After giving herself that moment, she grabbed her suitcase and wheeled it through the double doors – heavier than they looked – and into the main hall. It was quiet inside, almost eerie. There was a fireplace on the right, though no fire currently burned there, and there were a few candlestick holders dotted around, half-burnt-down candles dripping wax down their sides. There seemed to be an abundance of wooden furnishings, and the big rug made it feel like she was stepping back in time – it was the type of thing that might have been fashionable when Josie was a child. Still, she supposed that was all part of the charm.

There was a smartly dressed man, holding a clipboard and smiling politely in front of a blue table – was blue granite a thing? – with the biggest bouquet of flowers she'd ever seen on top of it. 'Hello, miss,' he said, his accent softer than the taxi driver's, his tidy appearance somehow giving the impression that he was too modern for a place like this. 'Are you here for the wedding? Can I take your name?'

'Josie Morgan,' she answered, still glancing around the room, trying to take in every little detail.

Clipboard Man nodded. 'You're in Buttercup.'

'Buttercup?' Josie repeated with a slight frown.

'The name of your room, miss.'

'Oh, right. Sorry.'

He came forward and took her suitcase for her. 'Shall I show you the way?' At her nod, he wheeled her suitcase ahead of her, leading her to the left, past a circular wooden table and four ornate wooden chairs, and up an epic staircase, wide enough to fit at least four people side by side. They passed a chair and table at the corner of the staircase, in case you wanted to have a quick sit down, apparently. Josie ran her hand along the banister, feeling little tingles run up her arm. People actually used to *live* here. She couldn't help grinning at Clipboard Man, who smiled back, as if he knew exactly what she was thinking.

As they neared the top of the stairs, there was the sound of voices, seeming to echo softly around the whole interior. 'Ok, well look, I don't need a microphone, I think that's too formal for this evening, but please make sure that— Josie!' Laura turned as Josie reached the top of the stairs. She had one hand in her hair, which looked both blonder and messier than Josie had ever seen it, and was standing with an older woman that Josie thought she recognised from a barbeque a while ago – Laura's mother – and two almost identical petite women, both also holding clipboards. Laura pulled her hand out of her hair and broke into a big smile as she came towards Josie. 'You're here!' She turned to Clipboard Man. 'Can you just take her bags up for her and put them in the room, leave the key in the door?'

Clipboard Man nodded. 'Of course,' he said smoothly. He turned to Josie. 'Will you be able to find your room?'

'Where's she staying?' Laura asked.

'Buttercup, I think,' Josie said.

Laura waved her hand in the air. 'No problem, I know where that is.' Josie smiled wryly. Of course she did. No doubt Laura had studied and memorised the floor plan weeks before. Laura shifted back to the other three women. 'This is my mum, Jose,' she said, proving Josie correct as she indicated the older, classy-looking woman. She smiled politely at Josie, like she recognised her but couldn't quite place her. 'And this is Tiffany and Abigail,' she said, gesturing at the clipboard women. Why did everyone need a clipboard? Josie wondered. Was it Laura instigating that, or something they just did here?

'I've no idea where John is,' Laura continued. 'He's off with some of his Scottish relatives somewhere, I swear there are more of them than I ever knew about, and every time he speaks to them he gets more and more Scottish. I swear *I* can't even understand half of what he's saying at the moment, so God knows how the speech will go.' She was definitely talking faster and slightly more erratically than usual. 'Anyway.' She gestured again towards the clipboards. 'We were just finalising the seating plan for this evening. I've put you on a table with Jess and Tom from work and Erin, one of John's friends – is that ok? He's sure you'll like her, though he only thought to tell me this *today*, of course and she *still* hasn't confirmed if she's actually bringing her plus one with her, but she's one of John's best friends, so.'

If Josie kept smiling like this all weekend, she swore she'd tear her facial muscles. 'Sounds great.' Even though she hadn't actually spoken to anyone but Laura from Peacock's since she'd left. A good thing, then, that it wasn't just the two of them and Josie – it meant that work couldn't be the only topic of conversation for the whole evening. And Jess and Tom, from the sounds of things, were minus plus ones tonight too. The thought of that made her relax slightly – maybe it would be genuinely nice to catch up with them, as long as they didn't linger too long on what she was doing now.

'Bia's not getting here until tomorrow, is that right?' Laura looked over one of the clipboard girl's shoulder at whatever was written there.

'Right. She's getting the sleeper train.' Since Bia was taking Oliver's place, Laura wouldn't have minded her crashing the dinner tonight too, but Bia now had a job as an estate agent – which by her own account she was quite good at because all you had to do was *persuade people, Jose* – and couldn't get out of a viewing last thing today, what with it being a Friday.

'Well, as long as she's here on time,' Laura said, tapping her fingers against her thigh. Laura and Bia didn't know each other that well, but they'd met a few times at Josie's birthdays and things like that, and Josie imagined Laura was thinking of the last party they'd been at together – Josie's leaving party before she'd moved to New York – where Bia had got the time wrong and showed up an hour late, thinking that she was half an hour early, with decorations for the table in the pub that she'd intended to put up to surprise Josie before she arrived.

'She will be,' Josie said firmly.

Laura huffed out a breath, looked at her mum. 'Could you do me a favour and try to find Dad? I just want to make sure he knows the plan today and tomorrow.'

Laura's mum – Andrea, Josie was pretty sure her name was – smiled, and stroked Laura's arm in a reassuring way. 'He knows the plan, love, but I'll go and get him, I think he's in our room.'

'Thanks.' She turned to the clipboards. 'I think that's it's for now, thanks.'

They nodded in unison. 'We're here if you need anything,' one of them said.

As soon as they'd departed, Laura dragged Josie down to sit at the top of the stairs. 'They're good here, you know,' she mused, glancing around their floor. 'I thought they were a pain at first, but they've actually done quite a good job.' It was high praise coming from Laura – Josie had no doubt she had the potential to be a total bridezilla, if only because she'd want everything to be done exactly her way and had so much experience putting things into action from being a publicist. 'It's been so stressful, trying to organise an outdoor wedding in *Scotland* of all places – the weather looks like it'll hold, but we've had to have a contingency plan just in case.' She tapped her fingers against her knees, currently covered in faded blue jeans. 'Anyway, distract me.' She looked at Josie. 'You're here early, I wasn't expecting anyone so soon.'

'Sorry,' Josie said immediately, 'I—'

But Laura waved Josie's apology away. 'No, no, I don't mean that – I'm more wondering how you did it.'

'Oh. Well I stayed in Edinburgh last night – didn't want to be late for the dinner or anything.' And trying to get the train and do it all in one day was a risk, in Josie's eyes. Plus, as much as she loved her aunt, an extra night on her own away from Helen was something she'd jumped on.

Laura nodded her approval – Josie knew that early was definitely better than late in Laura's book. She shook her head back, blonde hair almost down to her waist now, then eyed Josie critically. 'Why the hell haven't you been to see me?' Josie frowned and Laura waved her hand in the air. 'In London, I mean. Haven't you been back since, like, May?'

'June,' Josie corrected. Laura's brow furrowed and Josie gave her a little guilty smile. 'Well, June *technically*. The second is still June.' Laura made a 'hmph' noise and Josie gave her an apologetic look.

'How was it then?' Laura asked. 'New York?'

'It was . . .' Josie waved a hand in the air. She sighed. 'Do you know what, so much of it was great. We did everything you're supposed to – Statue of Liberty, Rockefeller Centre – everything. And I went to all these cool parties with Oliver.' It had been like something out of a film, Josie thought now. They'd arrived in an apartment provided by Peacock's that neither of them would have been able to afford on their own, only a forty-five-minute commute away from the centre of Manhattan, and had sat on their brand new sofa, drinking champagne that first night even though they were both knackered. The first month or so, Oliver had planned every weekend, determined to show her that he meant what he'd said about making it up to her, and had taken her to all the sights. It had been a total whirlwind in the beginning, and for a time she'd allowed herself to believe that she'd made the right decision in leaving London.

'And how was it then, with him?' Laura probed.

'Well, we broke up,' Josie said with a sigh. And she supposed it was only natural that people would ask about it. And it wasn't that she was still too raw or anything to talk about it – she'd had time, over the last few months, to realise that it was definitely for the best – but it still wasn't fun, admitting that your only serious adult relationship had crashed and burned, despite the fact that you'd moved to a different city together.

'I know *that*.' Josie could almost hear the 'you idiot' at the end of the sentence. 'But why?'

'We just . . .' Josie lifted a hand in the air, let it fall again. 'It just wasn't working, I suppose. We tried, but . . .' Laura nodded, and didn't push. The thing was, it really *had* been great at first. Josie had decided to give Oliver another chance after Max had left her – it had made her realise that if you wanted something to work, you had to really work at it. And at first, they'd *both* tried hard – she'd made the effort to go with him to all his work parties, he'd introduced her to everyone, he'd made sure he kept weekends free to do what *she* wanted to do, and she'd tried to be supportive of his career, no matter her feelings about Janice or the company. She'd managed to get over the Cara thing – pretty much – and had accepted that it was a one-off, a mistake that he deeply regretted, and that it didn't mean he didn't care for her. But after the first two months, things had become more difficult, and it had felt more like they were both trying too hard, that surely it shouldn't be *that* difficult. And then, she'd seen Max.

She still didn't know why it had been such a dramatic turning point, given nothing had actually *happened*. It had reminded her, she supposed, of how she'd been feeling when she first met Max, how she'd felt when he left her the way he had. She'd thought about it, and had tried to imagine how she'd feel if Oliver did the same thing to her. She'd be furious, of course, no question about that.

And she'd cry and scream and rage, and ask herself if it was *her* fault. All the normal things. But, when she'd looked at Oliver in that Brooklyn gallery, she'd had an uncomfortable feeling that maybe the emptiness she'd been left with after Max . . . maybe it wouldn't be quite the same with Oliver. She'd thought that maybe it would be almost a relief.

She and Oliver had ended up fighting that night, after they'd got home. Oliver had claimed that she'd been off the whole night, that she still wasn't over a guy she barely even knew, and that she didn't have an interest in him anymore. It hadn't helped that their sex life wasn't exactly great by that point. They hadn't officially broken up until a month after that, both of them admitting that all their efforts to spend more time together and make it work had actually had the opposite effect. She'd realised, in the space since the fight, that they just couldn't go back. They'd been distracted by a new city at first, and that had hidden the truth of the matter – they couldn't return to how they'd been before he'd slept with Cara, and she couldn't pretend that Max had never happened.

It had been surprisingly easy to leave Oliver, to say goodbye, and that, Josie thought, said it all. He'd driven her to the airport; they'd laughed as they had a last drink together. She was glad they'd left it that way, without any leftover resentment. Glad it had been a mutual decision, and not because one of them had hurt the other this time. But still, it wasn't exactly easy, admitting to herself that she'd thrown away her life in London and completely upped stakes for a relationship that was doomed to fail. Right after she'd almost given her heart away to a man who had treated her like a child treats their toys at Christmas – exciting to play with at first, then discarded as soon as they become boring.

'I'm sorry, Jose,' Laura said, putting a hand on Josie's shoulder and squeezing. Josie shrugged as if to say *it is what it is*. 'I still think it was brave, though. Giving it a go, going to New York. No one can say you didn't try.'

'Yeah,' Josie said, working up a wry smile. 'That's true.' And, on the days where she felt a bit more clear-headed about it, she allowed herself to think that too. She couldn't have necessarily known for *certain* that it was the wrong choice until she'd gone and tried – so at least this way, she wouldn't be wondering, wouldn't be chasing the *what if*.

Laura gave Josie a little nudge in the ribs. 'You could have at least stayed in New York until the end of the summer, though, then I could have come out and had a second hen do. I would've liked to go shopping there.' Josie laughed and Laura grinned. 'Where are you living now then?'

'Guildford.' She didn't add that she was currently staying with her aunt in her tiny spare bedroom. That she was temping and that both that and the living arrangements were already driving her mad. It was a severe backwards step in her life, and she needed to get her head around it before inviting the opinions of other people.

'I miss you in the office,' Laura said with a little pout. 'It's just not the same without you. No one to make fun of people with me, or work out ways to drive Janice mad.'

Josie gave a little huffing laugh. 'We never actually *did* any of those things.'

'Yeah, but it was fun thinking about it.' Laura glanced around, tapped her fingers on her knee again. 'Jose, I really want to catch up, but—'

'But you're busy,' Josie said, and got to her feet, Laura following suit. 'I don't suppose there's anything I can do?'

Laura pulled Josie into a hug. 'You're already doing it, by being here.' She eased back, angled her head. 'Just make sure you read the itinerary if you haven't already.' Josie laughed again and Laura waved a hand in the air. 'I know, I know, but even people who think it's ridiculous will actually be glad of it.' And it was hard to argue with that – Laura's itinerary was certainly helpful, including start times for each of the dinners, optional activities throughout the weekend, places to stay if you weren't in the castle, the dress code and what time she and John would be departing on the final night.

Laura gave Josie directions to her room, then called after her, 'John has some single friends, you know!' Josie looked back, raised her eyebrows. Laura gave her a wide, glowing smile. 'Just in case you're in the market for something.'

Josie shook her head and waved a hand at Laura as they parted ways, saving her grimace for when her back was turned. She knew Laura meant well, but she didn't think she could face being set up this weekend, what with all that entailed and the enthusiasm she'd have to fake.

She found her room, the key in the door as promised, and let herself in. Her first impression was of yellow, the second that it would be very suited to a woman in her seventies. The bedspread matched the curtains – yellow, a deeper yellow than the walls, with a blue pattern design on them – and there were six pictures

245

of different kinds of fish hanging on one of the walls. The bathroom was huge, including a full-length mirror and a bath that she definitely wanted to take advantage of later. On the vanity in the bedroom there was a computer set up, should you need it – a casual blending of old and modern. Josie decided in an instant that she loved it all.

Her suitcase was propped next to her bed, so she got out her camera and laptop, did a bit of editing then uploaded the best photo of the castle to Instagram – as with all the photos on her more 'professional' account, she included only a caption that explained where it was. Then she shut the laptop, took her camera, and went off to do some exploring of the castle.

Chapter Seventeen

When Josie got to the 'Croquet Room' there were already about forty people there, which, when combined with the tables – three circular and a long, L-shaped bench around one side and corner of the room – made it feel a little on the small side. She supposed that was, in part, the point – an intimate feel for this pre-wedding dinner, with a select sixty or so guests. Laura's family was small, Josie knew – no siblings and only one aunt and uncle – so presumably that was why she had a few more friends to fill her side. It was nice, Josie told herself firmly, that she was one of those friends. There was no reason to listen to the way her stomach was curdling ever so slightly as she shuffled into the room alone, as a few eyes she didn't recognise flickered towards her. No reason at all.

She turned her attention to the room itself, which had a light, bright feel: cream-coloured walls with landscape paintings dotted around sporadically, an open fireplace with a roaring fire despite the warm day, and candles on the tables as well as on the mantelpiece above the fire. The tables were covered in white tablecloths, the glassware almost seeming to sparkle, and they would be sitting on gold-backed chairs with blue cushioned seats.

Josie saw Laura by the fireplace, looking stunning in a black dress with bright blue and red butterflies, cinched at the waist with a slim, white belt and finishing just above the knee to show off her tanned legs. Her hair was down in soft, blonde curls – a more feminine look than she usually went for, perfect for a bride-to-be, but not overly simpering or virginal, which wouldn't have suited her in the slightest. She was with John, who had trimmed his beard, and who wasn't the only one in a kilt tonight, and a few others, deep in conversation. Instead of going to interrupt, Josie went in search of her name place, and found it on one of the round tables, next to an 'Erin' one side and a 'Graeme' the other. She bit her lip at the thought of being sandwiched between two people she'd never met.

She'd only been standing there for a second when she turned to the sound of squeals and saw Jess and Tom bounding up to her from the publicity and marketing team at Peacock's. The huffed laugh she let out was part relief at seeing people she knew. They looked exactly as she remembered them from last year – Jess, slightly on the short and plump side, was beaming, her round face a little pink already, and Tom was still as skinny as he always had been, despite starting up a protein-shake endeavour just before she'd left. A wave of nostalgia washed over her as she returned the hugs and the 'Oh my God it's been for ever's. She'd sat opposite Jess for two years, and even if her face had mostly been obscured by the computer screen during that time, they'd dealt with the same mood swings in the office, sat through the same meetings, had the same small talk every Monday morning. Strange that you went from seeing someone almost every day to them just dropping out of your life like that – a bit like a relationship, but one where it was expected to be transient.

A waiter, dressed smartly in a tux, came into the room and rang a gold bell, which caused Jess and Tom to smirk. 'Ladies and gentlemen, dinner will be served shortly, if you wouldn't mind taking your seats.'

'Don't think we'd mind, would we?' said Tom, pulling out his seat next to Jess, leaving Josie sitting awkwardly between two empty chairs as they waited for the other three people to join their table of six. It was all about the even numbers at weddings, wasn't it?

'So, where are you staying, Josie?' Jess asked, leaning across the table to be heard over the chatter of the room.

Josie eyed up the bread basket that a waiter brought out and wondered if it was too soon to help herself to a roll, given the table wasn't full yet. 'In Buttercup.' Then, when Jess looked blank, 'In the castle.'

Jess gave a little wistful sigh, while Tom pouted. 'We're in a hotel,' Jess explained.

'Yeah, and we're sharing a twin room,' Tom added. 'The height of glamour.'

'It was cheaper,' Jess said primly, 'so I don't know what you're—'

'There,' hissed Tom, nudging Jess sharply in the ribs and jerking his head. 'That's the guy. He's a plus one, I swear it, he didn't seem to know either John or Laura when I asked him about it.'

Jess sighed. 'You're being ridiculous. Stop.' She pushed his head back, then rolled her eyes at Josie. 'He's sulking because he wasn't allowed to add his plus one last-minute, even though we are *lucky*' – she put emphasis on the word and added a stern look at Tom for good measure – 'to be invited to the pre-dinner at all. Besides,' she added, fluffing up her hair, 'you only started seeing the guy two weeks ago, what did you expect Laura to say?' Josie felt a smile pulling at her lips, hours of office banter coming back to her.

Tom shook his head, helping himself to the bottle of sparkling water on the table. 'When you know, you know.'

'Are you also seeing someone, Jess?' Josie asked.

'Yes, but I decided not to bring him – it's only been two months, would have been a bit intense.' She gave Tom a meaningful look, but he only shrugged.

'Josie's with me, right, Jose?'

Josie decided that her safest option, at that moment, was to say nothing and the argument was effectively cut off by the presence of a rather fat man, in his fifties at a guess, looming over their table, then doing a slow lap, apparently unbothered by the fact Josie, Jess and Tom were all watching him do so. He stopped at the empty space on Josie's left, peered down at it, then nodded and pulled out the chair.

Jess and Josie exchanged a slight frown as he sat in the seat between them, forcing them both to move their chairs sideways a little to accommodate his bulk. He wiped his shining brow – apparently the effort of sitting down was all too much – and then turned his beady eyes, which looked smaller because of the rolls of fat on his face, on Jess then Josie in turn, without acknowledging Tom. 'So,' he said with an incredibly heavy Scottish accent, 'ye girls are my dinner companions then, are ye?'

Josie cleared her throat. 'Yes, I suppose so.' She became acutely aware of how posh her accent sounded. 'I'm—'

He frowned and leaned towards her, his chair audibly creaking with the movement. 'What's tha'? I cannae hear you, lassie, ye'll have to speak up, I've a bit of an ear infection.'

Josie shot a slightly alarmed look at Jess, which she tried to cover with a smile. 'Josie,' she said, more loudly than felt comfortable. He nodded, not making her repeat it, thank God. She glanced at the now two empty seats on her right. This man, surely, could not be John's friend's plus one – so that explained the last empty seat – but maybe he knew Erin somehow? It seemed a bit of an odd addition to the table otherwise, and Laura wasn't the type to assign people to tables randomly.

'I'm Graeme,' he said with a nod.

'And, err, how do you know the bride and groom?' Josie asked politely, disconcerted that his attention now seemed to be focused solely on her.

'John's uncle,' he grunted, helping himself to the bread on the table. Well, if he had, then surely she could too. But her hand was only halfway to the bread basket when Graeme's booming voice started up again. 'I was supposed to be on tha' table over there,' he said, glaring at the table in question, which was home to five people around his age, chatting away merrily.

'Oh,' said Josie. 'Right.'

'But my wife left me.' He was still glaring at the table, and Josie wondered which of those people was his wife. The petite woman who'd decided to own her greying hair or the friendly looking brunette with a glass of something in hand? Neither seemed a likely candidate.

'Oh,' Josie said again. She shot a glance at Jess, trying to bring her into the conversation, but she and Tom were deep in conversation about something, Jess pursing her lips at whatever Tom was whispering to her. Great. 'Well, that's . . . Gosh, I'm sorry to hear that.'

'Left me fer a younger model,' he said gruffly, his expression twisting in a way that actually made Josie feel sorry for him. He slathered his bread in butter, fixing Josie with a look as he took a big bite of it. 'Writer type,' he said, and a tiny piece of that bread came flying back out of his mouth, very nearly landing on Josie's cheek. She tried to edge away as subtly as she could. 'A total roaster,' Graeme continued. Josie nodded, having no idea what he meant by that, but presuming it was some kind of insult. 'No money at all. You just watch, she'll regret it. But I won't be having her back, ye hear me?' He glared at Josie, as if she'd suggested the opposite.

'No,' Josie said quickly. 'No of course not.' What the hell were Jess and Tom talking about? And where the hell was John's friend Erin? She'd gladly take anyone to get out of this conversation right now.

'Anyway,' Graeme said, narrowing his eyes again at the table he'd apparently been supposed to be sitting at. 'I told John I wouldnae sit over there with all of her friends.' So, maybe the wife wasn't even here? Josie didn't dare ask.

'I told him he had t' move me when I saw the plan for tonight.' Josie nodded, inwardly thinking how Laura must have hated the last-minute change.

A waiter came round with a bottle of champagne, pouring it into their glasses on the table, which thankfully provided Graeme with a brief distraction from Josie. She'd taken her first grateful sip of the bubbly liquid when a slim, blonde woman approached, wearing a dress of brilliant red, with lipstick to match, her blue eyes framed with gold eyeliner in a way that made them almost scarily blue. Josie choked on her champagne, and saw Graeme frowning at her.

Jess looked around Graeme to give her a quizzical look, but Josie's attention was on the woman, whose eyes were on Josie now. She raised one perfectly plucked eyebrow.

Fuck, Josie remembered this woman. Erin. Max's girlfriend. Fuck, *fuck*. She took another gulp of champagne. What were the bloody chances? She hadn't even *thought* it would be the same Erin – why the hell would she? Oh God. Her plus one. Josie felt a jolt and immediately looked around, her eyes still watering from her choking fiasco. She couldn't see him. So maybe it wouldn't be him after all – maybe they'd broken up since she'd last seen them, just like her and Oliver.

When she reached the table, Erin's full, sexy lips quirked into a smile when she saw Josie, though she only looked mildly surprised to see her here – or else she was better at hiding it than Josie. 'Hi all,' she said as she took her seat, right next to Josie. 'I'm Erin.' Unlike Graeme's, Erin's accent was all lilting and musical, and a quick glance at Jess and Tom told Josie that they were having the exact same thoughts that Josie had first had when she'd met Erin in New York – literally no one would be able to look at this woman and not think she was sexy. Graeme was staring at her, his glass of champagne halfway to his mouth, and Josie swore she wouldn't have been surprised if he'd licked his lips. She cringed internally, trying not to let it show on her face.

'My plus one's running a little late,' Erin said, indicating the empty seat. She shot a small smile at Josie, tilted her head. How could even *that* action just exude class? 'Nice to see you again.'

Josie forced out the words, 'You too,' at the same time as Tom grumbled, 'See, *she's* allowed a plus one.'

Graeme immediately engaged Erin in conversation, which Josie was thankful for, because it meant all she had to do was 'mmm' in agreement occasionally, whilst trying both not to study Erin and not to look around the room, waiting for her plus one's imminent arrival. Her body felt twitchy, unable to concentrate on anything, and she didn't realise she'd drunk a full glass of champagne until the waiter came round to top her up. The starters – asparagus and poached egg for the vegetarians, asparagus wrapped in Parma ham for the omnivores – were coming out and they were all talking about how they knew the bride and groom – Erin was one of John's best friends from school, apparently – by the time Erin's plus one arrived.

And there he was.

Max.

Max, of all bloody people, was here, at *her* friend's wedding. Here with his drop-dead gorgeous girlfriend, while she was so completely and obviously single, sat next to

John's fat uncle. She wanted to slam her head down on the table. She wanted to get up and leave, so she didn't have to face him, so she didn't have to smile and pretend that she was totally over him, that she had literally not given him a moment's thought since she'd bumped into him in New York, that *of course* he'd had nothing to do with why she'd come home again.

But she couldn't do either of those things. So instead all she could do was watch as he crossed the room towards them, looking uncharacteristically flustered, auburn hair a little messed up, the cuffs of his dark grey shirt not done up properly, his tie on a little wonky. He was thinner than when she'd last seen him, she thought, and his face was a little pale, like he could do with a good night's sleep, but other than that he looked just as handsome as ever, still moving with the long stride that she remembered so well.

'Cutting it a bit fine, aren't we?' Erin hissed as he sat down.

Max mumbled his apologies, straightened his tie – waving away Erin's help – then looked over across the table, directly at Josie. Their eyes held, and she felt her heart jolt, even as she refused to look away, refused to let on that she was thrown by it. The rest of the table could have been utterly silent or in full conversational flow, for all she knew in that moment.

Max gave her a small nod, then cleared his throat. 'Hi,' he said simply. He didn't look surprised enough to see her here, she thought bitterly. He was sitting straight, perhaps a little tense, but his gaze was measured on hers. Maybe he'd known she would be here, she thought, given whose wedding it was, whereas she could have had no idea. He'd met Laura and John, hadn't he? He would have known that she must be coming to Laura's wedding.

Josie nodded back. 'Hey.' Ok, good, her voice sounded even, casual. She took another sip of her champagne, trying to come to terms with the slight stumble of her heart, the automatic flare of her pulse against her wrist. Nearly five months since she'd left him in that Brooklyn gallery and she'd neither seen nor heard from him since – nor, to be fair, had she tried to get in touch herself. Why would she? They'd both been in relationships and even if hers had crashed and burned, his, apparently, had not.

Josie turned to Graeme, angling herself away from Erin and Max. Jess, legend that she was, had clearly picked up some sort of vibe, because she joined in the conversation with Graeme, taking over and merrily chatting away about what her job at Peacock's entailed, ignoring Graeme's interjections and allowing Josie to just 'hmm' occasionally, whilst trying *not* to glance over her shoulder, not to listen in to what Tom, Max and Erin were talking about. God, why the hell couldn't Bia have been here tonight? Josie felt her head throb and set her champagne aside, picking up her sparkling water instead.

As the starters were cleared away, Laura got to her feet in the middle of the long bench table, and everything went quiet. She smiled serenely around the room. 'Thanks, everyone. As you all know, the main speeches are tomorrow, but it's my turn this evening. I won't be saying a word tomorrow, because my only job then is to look beautiful.' A soft hum of laughter rippled across the room. 'I just want to thank you all for being here, and for my half of you, thanks for trekking all the way to Scotland.' She carried on with the thanks, made a few jokes, told of how she'd first met John at an event he was writing up for an online culture site. Her voice was smooth and confident, her posture relaxed – she'd always been good at public speaking, Josie remembered. If she'd ever been nervous about it, she'd never let on.

John was staring at her adoringly, and Josie tried to ignore the little wrench in her stomach at the sight of them. She didn't think Oliver had ever looked at her quite like that. She also tried to pretend she hadn't noticed the way Max kept glancing at her, rather than his girlfriend, and the way it was making heat travel along her skin, as Laura raised a toast to the love of her life.

They all clinked glasses, smiling, and clapped as Laura sat down. Josie wondered if Laura had known that Max would be here – whether she even remembered Max from the Christmas party. It wasn't like she could ask anyway – Laura had far more important things to focus on right now.

Erin started up a conversation around the whole table as waiters came round, offering them red or white wine, talking about the castle and its architectural history. Graeme was stating that all of them knew nothing, that given he had a good twenty years on each and every one of them – Josie thought a little more – he had the authority on the history of the place, like being older automatically meant you became more knowledgeable on *everything*. Max and Erin were bantering, arguing over one of the structures in the castle in an easy, friendly way, laughing at each other over having done the same research. So, she was an architect. Of course she bloody was. Smart and sexy, the jackpot. Josie took a sip of water, erring on the side of safety for this first evening – she didn't want to get drunk and say something stupid. She wasn't bitter. She wasn't. She also wasn't concentrating on the conversation, so that when Erin asked, 'What about you, Josie?' in an overly polite way, all she could say was, 'Huh?'

Max's attention had shot to her, almost like Erin addressing her had given him permission to look at her, and she couldn't help the quick glance back, even as she flexed her fingers on her glass. 'What do you think?' Erin asked, with a small head tilt. 'Edinburgh or London in terms of best buildings?'

She thought of Max admiring the architecture of Battersea Arts Centre and forced the memory quickly aside, looking very deliberately at Erin and not at him. 'Edinburgh,' she said, more confidently than she really should, given her relative lack of knowledge of what made a 'good' building. 'Pretty' was more what she was going for here. 'I mean, not that I've seen enough of Edinburgh to be sure of that,' she added, partly because she'd seen Erin's red lips open, and wanted to cut her off in case she was thinking of arguing. 'And London is incredible, obviously, and you've got all the iconic buildings there. But, well, I love the cobbled streets here, the way the city feels like it's its own little world – and the buildings are partly what makes that, right?'

She felt Max's gaze burning the side of her face as she spoke. He shouldn't do that. It wasn't fair for him to look at her like that with his girlfriend sat right next to him.

Tom raised his eyebrows; Graeme grunted, like what

she'd said had no value, while Jess was busy trying to get the waiter's attention for more wine. Erin paused, then shrugged. 'Well,' she said, glancing at Max from under long, full lashes. 'Just because one person agrees with you, doesn't mean you're right.'

Because of how they were sitting, Josie managed to avoid speaking to Max directly throughout the whole dinner, forcing herself to engage Graeme in more conversation than she would have liked, just so that there weren't any silences that had to be filled. She couldn't help comparing her and Max's situations – he chatting happily with Erin while she was stuck talking to Graeme – even as she told herself not to, that there was no point to it. She excused herself as soon as she feasibly could, right after the Eton Mess dessert. She timed it deliberately while Max was in the toilet so she didn't have to actively say goodbye, and ignored Jess's and Tom's pleas to stay up for 'just a few' shots.

'I want to be on form for tomorrow,' she insisted. 'And you two should think about that too,' she said, with a semi-scolding look at them both. 'Laura will notice if anyone's hungover.'

They descended into grumbles, but she could see from the look they gave each other that her comment had hit home. Erin gave her a distant little smile, nodded in a kind of regal way when she said goodbye. Josie made herself smile back, determined to be on her best behaviour. It wasn't Erin's fault, after all, that her boyfriend had had a brief fling with Josie nine months ago now. Wasn't Erin's fault that seeing him had made Josie realise that she still couldn't quite get over him, get over the way he'd ended it.

But what she could do, she told herself firmly, was accept how things were now. She could and would accept that he'd well and truly moved on, that he was with someone else now. She had to.

Chapter Eighteen

Laura and John stood facing each other, holding hands against the backdrop of the castle wall, the tops of trees just visible above it, their leaves a mix of green and golden-red, with a turret to their left. The soft sound of water running through the stone fountain, three tiers with four white horses at the bottom, whispered in the background. Josie could almost feel the history of the place, lives gone past colliding with the present in this stone courtyard. Her hands were clasped together, a lump in her throat as she watched the two of them, so complete in that moment, unconcerned about the two hundred people watching them.

Laura looked incredible – a dress of cascading white, tucked in all the right places, her hair pinned up at the back in curls, blue and white flowers in amongst the gold. She was like a real-life princess, getting ready to rule her castle. She'd clearly known what she'd wanted for this moment, and had gone for it. John was in a kilt, a smart black jacket on top, looking like something out of *Outlander*. And the weather, as promised, was holding, the sun warm enough that they didn't need jackets to sit outside. The photos of this moment were going to be incredible, Josie thought.

Bia was sitting on her left, her hair cut into a short, straight bob – she'd had to have it professionally straightened to achieve that – and now a dark purply-brown colour, and Jess and Tom were on Josie's right. Max was there, somewhere, with his perfect girlfriend, but she hadn't seen either of them, had deliberately not looked. At the end of the ceremony, when John and Laura kissed, Josie could do nothing to stop the tears from escaping, cutting twin paths through her carefully applied makeup. She let out a laughing sob when she saw Bia was crying too, her eyeliner – purple to match her hair – slightly smudged, and Bia grinned back sort of guiltily. Josie supposed it was impossible, unless you had a heart to match the stone wall, not to get emotional in this kind of atmosphere.

When the ceremony was finished, Laura and John, along with the rest of the wedding party, were taken away by the photographer, presumably to do some epic shots around the castle grounds, and the spectators were ushered to the front of the castle for the drinks reception on the lawn.

'Oh my God!' Bia beamed around when they got to the lawn, both her and Josie's heels – Bia's a good two inches higher than Josie's – sinking into soft ground. 'There are *stands,* Jose!' Well, she was right, Josie thought, you had to give her that. There were indeed various stands along the gravel in front of the castle, with different options for drinks – gin, whisky, something elderflower, from what Josie could tell. Bia and Josie split up from Tom and Jess to get theirs – Tom braving the whisky, Jess opting for

Pimm's ('Though it doesn't feel very Scottish, does it?') and Josie and Bia going for a gin.

It was at the gin stand that she saw Max making his way over. Josie gave Bia a meaningful look, and Bia's head snapped around, gin already in hand, to look at Max. 'Where's the girlfriend?' Bia whispered. Obviously, Josie had already filled Bia in on the whole ordeal. But Max was now too close for Josie to answer, so she worked up a smile instead. She'd decided last night that she would be cool, calm and serene whenever she had to interact with him. She would absolutely not let the bitterness shine through – especially not on her friend's wedding day. She saw Bia, however, had not quite got the memo.

'No scowling,' Josie hissed.

Bia rearranged her face. 'You're right,' she said, a little too loudly for Josie's liking. 'Blasé is better.'

Josie took a deliberate sip of her gin – with mint and berries and everything – as Max came up next to them. 'You look beautiful,' he said immediately.

She smiled, trying to make it a little cool. 'Thanks.' She'd gone all out today, because if you couldn't at a wedding at a castle, then when the hell could you? She'd carefully pinned some of her hair up and curled the bits that she left down so that they fell in ringlets around her face, the spiral earrings she'd chosen matching the style perfectly. She was wearing a dress that was navy blue at the top, sitting just off her shoulders and giving way at the skirt to a cream petticoat with navy stripes, which floated out when she walked. She'd gone for dark blue, strappy sandals to match the dress, had kept the makeup subtle but distinct.

Max turned his attention to Bia and did that polite,

charming smile that he used on people he didn't know. 'I'm Max.'

'So I've heard,' Bia said lightly. At Max's raised eyebrows and Josie's *look,* Bia smiled, held out a hand. 'I mean, hi. I'm Bia. Josie's best friend.' She put a bit of emphasis on the word 'best'.

Max nodded slowly. 'Noted.'

'Well, we're actually on the way to the ladies,' said Josie, deciding that avoidance was probably the best policy.

'Yes,' said Bia immediately. '*So* sorry not to be able to chat.' Jesus, Bia could at least *try* to be subtle.

They left Max standing there, and just in time – when Josie glanced back she saw Erin gliding over to him, perfectly swanlike, her blonde hair pretty much shimmering in the bloody sunlight. Josie must have made some kind of noise, because Bia frowned up at her, then glanced back too. 'Ah,' she said. 'So that's the girl.'

Josie sighed. 'So it would appear.'

'She's not *that* pretty,' said Bia, and Josie laughed.

'So convincing.'

Bia downed the rest of her gin in one. 'Well, regardless of what she looks like, I'm fully on board for hating her, don't you worry.'

Josie managed to avoid Max for the rest of the afternoon, and was grateful that, when the party moved into the pavilion, where everything was white, with fairy lights on the ceiling and flowers on each circular table, the seating plan had her and Bia on different tables to Max and Erin today. Different tables to Tom and Jess, too, and when Josie saw that both she and Bia were next to a guy each, Josie wondered if they'd been put on the obligatory singles table. A quick scan of the names told her that Graeme, at least, was not included.

Bia and Josie sat, Bia stumbling slightly on her heels, and Josie glanced around. From what she could gather, the majority of the two hundred or so guests were on John's side – the Scottish accents seemed to grow thicker, taking up more of the space. She was looking up when a guy with horn-rimmed glasses, hair with a copious amount of gel and a slightly protruding belly took a seat next to her. He gave a contented sigh, as if happy to be off his feet, though he had to be only in his thirties. He smiled at her. 'Well, hello there.' The accent was thick – definitely one of John's friends then. 'I'm Rob.'

Josie nodded politely. 'Josie.' She'd forgotten this about weddings – the endless introductions. She glanced round to see that Bia was already deep in conversation with the man the other side of her – a blond, tanned guy who already had Bia giggling. *Giggling,* for God's sake.

'So, Josie. What is it that you do?'

She took a sip of her elderflower and Prosecco cocktail, which she and Bia had moved on to after the gin. 'I'm, err, just in between things at the moment.' No need to mention that the 'in between' involved mindlessly answering phones at a car dealer reception. 'How about you?' she asked quickly, before he could press her further. And so he entered into the most mind-numbingly boring explanation of what he did, which was apparently something to do with 'statistical analysis' – something he seemed to feel the need to demonstrate with the frequent use of statistics. More than once, she tried to nudge Bia to get her attention, but Bia was oblivious, occasionally letting out bursts of high-pitched laughter – a sure sign that she was well on her way to being well and truly hammered – at something her guy was saying. Briefly, Josie wondered if this was the guy Laura had implied she should dress up for and, if so, whether she should be offended by that. Out of the corner of her eye, she saw Max on a nearby table, and tried not to notice the way Erin was touching his hand. Tried not to remember how his warm, strong hand had felt holding hers last December.

Bia finally turned her attention to Josie, just as Rob broke off his explanation of his job, to enter into a description of what he did for hobbies – which included rock climbing, something which Josie didn't quite buy, rock *collecting,* which she did believe, and butterflies. She wasn't entirely sure how 'butterflies' was a hobby, but decided it was safest not to ask. Bia gave Josie a look, but there was nothing either of them could do. 'And what about you?' Rob asked, in between a mouthful of venison that had been served with dauphinoise potatoes, and actually tasted impressive, considering the mass catering.

'Oh, I'm actually into the javelin.' Josie wasn't sure what made her say it – maybe it was the most recent glass of white wine – but it was out before she could think better of it. Next to her, Bia spluttered so hard that she started coughing, and had to take several gulps of water, waving off her guy's concern at the same time.

Rob seemed to notice nothing odd about that, and only raised his eyebrows fractionally. 'Really?'

Josie nodded. 'Oh yes. I've been in several javelin-throwing competitions, competing countywide.'

'She's come in first a few times as well,' Bia added helpfully.

'That's amazing,' Rob said, though whether or not he truly thought so was difficult to tell, given he used the same monosyllabic tone he'd used to describe his statistics.

'I also like designing marshmallow sculptures,' Josie continued, fighting to keep a straight face and refusing to look at Bia, who was grinning wildly.

Rob frowned. 'Marshmallow . . . sculptures?' He looked a little concerned by the idea.

'That's right,' Josie said with a smile. 'I'm actually in the Guinness book of world records for building the largest ever marshmallow tower – you should look me up.'

He nodded slowly. 'I'll do that.'

Josie and Bia exchanged a look when the speeches started, then swivelled to face the stage. John's speech managed to raise a few laughs, and Josie actually teared up when Laura's dad cried on stage himself as he gave his. The speeches were immediately followed by the first dance, and, true to form, Laura had clearly taken dance lessons before the day, so she moved elegantly across the dance floor, her usual quick, stamping stride nowhere in sight.

Bia's guy – Josie still hadn't got his name – stood as the dancing opened up to the rest of them, and held out a hand to Bia. 'May I?'

Bia bit her lip and glanced at Josie. 'Well, I—'

Josie shook her head. 'Go. I'll come and join you when I've finished this.' She raised her glass of wine. Bia hesitated, then took the guy's hand, who beamed down at her. She was barely as tall as his chest, even in those gigantic heels – not that that seemed to worry him.

Rob immediately focused in on Josie, pushing his glasses up his nose. 'So where did you grow up, Josie?' He blinked at her a few times, waiting patiently.

She tried to resist the urge to sigh, took a sip of her wine instead. Then she shrugged. 'Well, actually, I was raised in complete isolation in a forest for most of my childhood. What about you?' She cocked her head.

'Really?' Rob blustered, in a way that suggested he genuinely believed her. 'That's—'

He cut off as someone swept into Bia's vacated seat. Josie stiffened, and slowly looked up at Max.

'May I?' Without waiting for an answer, he sat down.

Rob and Max introduced themselves, shaking their hands across Josie's rigid body, then Rob waved a hand in her direction. 'Josie was just in the middle of telling me a story of her childhood. Did you know she grew up in complete isolation in a forest?'

Josie felt herself flush, and finished the rest of her wine to compensate. Max raised his eyebrows, his lips twitching in that way of his. She tried not to meet his gaze. 'Is that so?' he asked. She cleared her throat, nodded. 'Well,' Max said with a grin, 'tell us about it!'

Josie looked between them, then, deciding there was nothing for it, launched into a wildly invented story of her life in the forest, which included foraging for mushrooms and making traps, claimed that she knew how to start a fire with nothing more than just two sticks of wood, and that her grandmother was into dancing naked under the full moon. Rob kept shaking his head and saying 'Fascinating', and Max just kept asking more and more questions, getting really particular so that she had to come up with more and more obscure answers. It was a full twenty minutes before Rob stood up and excused himself. 'I'll be right back though,' he added. 'I want to hear more about this!'

Max and Josie watched Rob leave the pavilion towards the toilets, then burst out into simultaneous laugher. 'Oh my God,' said Josie, unable to stop and clutching her side.

Max grinned. 'You are really quite convincing. I wouldn't want to be on the other end of you lying.' For some reason, that had the effect of sobering her up, and the laugh died in her throat. She wiped at her eyes.

'Where's Erin?' She looked around, but couldn't immediately spot her.

Max waved a hand in the air. 'Around.'

Josie was tempted to ask him what Erin thought about Max coming over to talk to her, but resisted. They knew each other, she supposed, so maybe it was only natural that he'd make an effort to talk to her.

She caught Laura's eye on the dance floor, and when Laura beckoned her over, practically leapt to her feet, glad to have a real excuse to leave the table before Erin inevitably came along. She jerked her head towards the dance floor, turned away, then, feeling rude, looked back at him. 'Do you, umm, want to come and dance? With everyone, I mean,' she added quickly, because his green-gold gaze had turned sharp.

He shook his head, held up a glass of red wine. 'Nah, I'll sit this one out thanks.'

She nodded and went to join Laura, who pulled Josie into a circle with Jess, Tom, John and a guy she presumed must be John's friends. 'You're married!' Josie shouted over the music, making Laura laugh and pull Josie in for a hug.

Then Laura moved Josie to arm's length and held her there. She frowned. 'Why were you sat next to Rob?'

Josie raised her eyebrows. 'You did the seating plan, not me.'

'You were supposed to be sitting next to Stuart!'

Josie frowned. 'Stuart?'

'Yes.' Laura did a quick glance around, then pointed to the blond, tanned guy who was dancing with Bia, looking incredibly pleased with himself. 'Him.'

Josie snorted. 'Oops.'

Laura put her hands on her hips. 'You and Bia must have sat the wrong way round.'

'Ah well, at least Bia's happy. And it was still better than my dinner companion last night.' She gave Laura a meaningful look, and Laura grimaced.

'John's uncle Graeme?' Josie nodded. 'I'm so sorry, Jose, he literally left me no choice — he demanded to change table last-minute, and then had very specific requests on the type of person he wanted to be sitting next to, and John convinced me it'd be easier to just agree so Graeme didn't cause problems during the actual dinner and, God, you don't hate me for it, do you?' Laura sucked in a big breath, having apparently used up all her oxygen in that little speech. Josie got the impression Laura might be on her way to tipsy.

She shook her head, laughed. 'Laura, relax, I'm kidding. I can't even imagine how complicated it must be to pull something like this off — I'm hardly going to blame you for who I'm sitting next to.'

Laura wrinkled her nose. 'I'm still sorry. It's just, I knew you'd at least be able to handle him.' She let out a sigh,

270

glanced across the tent. 'And on the subject of handling yourself – I recognise that guy from somewhere. He's the Christmas guy, isn't he?'

Josie refused to let herself wince. Laura's day, she reminded herself. She would not lament. 'Yep,' she said easily. And then the song changed and everyone started dancing with more exuberance, effectively ending any conversations.

Josie danced with Laura for a bit, but when Erin came up to join John and a few others in a circle, all of them laughing and pulling each other round, she decided she'd made enough effort on the dance floor, so she grabbed her camera and snuck outside. She couldn't see Bia anywhere, though she could hazard a guess at where she might be, she thought with a small smirk. She sighed as she walked away from the lights and chatter, looking around. She wanted to capture the castle under moonlight, to get a sense of what it must be like when it slept in the grounds. She walked with no real purpose, stopping here and there to take a photo, the sound of voices faded until all she could hear was the music. The castle was lit up now, a bright yellow-gold, showy and classy at the same time. She wanted to see if she could capture that.

She was standing by the lake, looking out at the moonlit water, when she heard soft footsteps behind her. She jumped and spun around, then sucked in a breath when she saw who it was.

'Sorry,' Max said quietly. 'Didn't mean to scare you.'

Had he meant to follow her, though? She shook the question away, even if the alcohol swirling in her brain was making her think he was far more attractive than he had any right to be, all Heathcliff-like at the edge of the water. But it had been nine months now, she told herself for the millionth time. No reason to think about how they'd been naked together. No reason at all.

'Bored of the party already?' she asked as he came up next to her, looking out across the lake instead of at him.

'Just fancied some air,' he said lightly. 'You?' She lifted her camera in explanation. 'Ah,' he said.

The music was distant now, but she could just about hear it – there was a pop song on, potentially Taylor Swift though she couldn't be sure. The band were doing pretty well at alternating between Top 40s, cheesy classics, romantic classical and Scottish jigs – something for everyone. A cool breeze kissed Josie's bare shoulders and she shivered, just a little.

'You're cold?' Josie looked over to see Max frowning, reaching up to take his jacket off for her.

She shook her head. 'No, I like it. The breeze, the slight chill. There's something nice and, I don't know, real about it.' She cut herself off, wondering if that sounded stupid.

'You look like you're glowing,' he murmured. 'Like you're the one who just got married.'

Josie's stomach pulsed a little, but she tried to laugh it off, make it casual. 'I love it here,' she admitted. And it was beyond true. Somehow, everything seemed just a little bit better, walking under the moonlight with a castle just *there*. She laughed again, softly. She was sure it couldn't be just her who felt like that. His lip did that almost-smile thing as he watched her, maybe trying to figure out the joke, and his eyes looked light, absorbing some of the moonlight. They fell into silence and she felt that slightly awkward

272

need to fill it. 'I never even knew this place existed. *Any* of this, I mean.' She gestured with her free hand, trying not just to encompass the castle and the grounds, but beyond that, right to Edinburgh itself. 'But now that I've been here, I feel like it already holds a place in my heart. Does that make sense?'

He nodded. 'At least you know about it, all of it, now.'

She huffed out a laugh. 'And now all future weddings will pale in comparison to this.' But she felt her smile dim a little, and wrapped her arms around herself.

'Are you ok?' Max asked softly.

She nodded, her head feeling a bit too heavy on her neck. She hadn't had *that* much to drink, had she? 'Yes. I'm ok, yes, I'm just thinking.'

'About?'

'It's just, my parents,' she said, the words tasting a little thick and tingly on her tongue. Ok, so maybe she should have stopped one or two glasses ago. But then, what was the harm? He already knew about her parents anyway. 'It hits me every now and then,' she said quietly, 'the things they won't be here for. Like when I passed my driving test, when I graduated from Exeter. And I might never get married – who knows? – but if I do, they won't be here to see it.' She looked up to see his eyebrows pulling together, his eyes focused on her face. He opened his mouth to speak and she shook her head. 'I don't mean . . . It's sad, but it's just . . . An acceptance too, I guess. It's the type of sadness that's both more and less than the need to cry or sob or whatever.' She cocked her head up at him, tried a little smile. 'It's not going to ruin my night, I'm not going to break down about it or anything. It just . . . is, I suppose.'

'Josie . . .'

'I'm ok,' she repeated. 'Really. It's something I've learned to carry around with me, but in some ways I'm glad of that, because it means I loved them, and I remember them, you know?' She glanced up, and he nodded, though the light in his eyes had dimmed slightly. She sighed. 'And that part of me, it's part of what makes me who I am, and I can't hate that, because, most of the time, I don't hate who I am.'

He reached out, tucked a strand of her hair behind her ear. She should move away. She really should. 'I don't hate who you are, either.' His voice was almost a whisper. 'Any of the time.'

'To be fair, you probably don't know me well enough to qualify like that,' she said lightly.

He moved to step even closer and she took a deliberate step back, shook her head. She may be tipsy, but she knew perfectly well what would happen if he got even closer, and knew categorically that it was a bad idea. She took another step backwards, saw the way his expression changed, closed off to that poker face, as he slipped his hands into his trouser pockets.

'Goodnight, Max,' she said firmly, and turned to walk away from the allure of the moonlight, and back to the safety of the party.

Chapter Nineteen

Josie woke to the sound of banging at her door and groaned, rolling over to one side. The banging just increased. Bloody Bia. She hadn't come home last night, presumably off with her Scottish hunk, and had now probably forgotten her room key.

Josie threw off the covers, grimacing when her head pounded with the movement. She was frowning when she opened the door, and that frown only intensified, accompanied by a semi-painful lurch of her stomach, when she saw who it was. 'Max?' She raised her hand to her hair, which was matted from where she hadn't bothered to brush it out last night. 'What do you want?' It came out clipped and harsh enough that she blew out a breath. 'I mean, it's early – is something wrong?'

'No, sorry, I . . .' He rubbed a hand across the back of his neck and looked at her for a moment. Still saying nothing, he rocked back on his heels, his hair slightly damp, as if he'd just got out the shower, looking decidedly fresher than she felt. She folded one arm across her chest, only now noticing that she'd done the buttons up wrong on her flannel pyjamas last night, so her top was pulled all wonky. And she was sure she didn't smell as nice as him, all citrusy and enticing. He opened his mouth, shut it again, then raised his eyebrows. 'Early?' he asked, his voice too gruff to pull off the totally casual tone. 'It's nine a.m.'

Josie huffed out a breath. 'Yes, that's early. And that's not the point.' She shook her head, tried and failed to find something to look at that wasn't him. 'What are you doing here at all?'

'I, well, I have a proposition,' he said, his tone measured and even.

'A proposition,' Josie repeated slowly.

'Yes.' He took a breath. 'I want you to come out with me for the day.'

Josie stared at him, incredulous, then shook her head. 'And why on earth would I do that?'

'Because . . .' He ran his fingers through his perpetually rumpled hair, then dropped his hand to his side, where it seemed to hang flatly. 'Because you said that you loved Edinburgh, and I thought you might like to see more of it.'

She narrowed her eyes. 'I can see it myself, but thanks. Now, if you'll excuse me, I want to go back to bed and sleep for at least another two hours.' She stepped back, going to shut the door, but he moved to stop her.

He backed away just a step when she shot him a glare before she could help herself. She fought to even out her expression, even as the arm around her midriff tightened. 'Josie, look,' he began. 'I know you think I'm a dick.' She snorted derisively at that. 'And I know the way I . . . that what I did to you wasn't right. And I know that you've

276

moved on or whatever . . .' *He'd* moved on, more like. Not that she'd say it out loud, because she very much did want him to think she was just dandy. 'But I'd really like to make it up to you. Please. I've got somewhere I'd really like to take you.' His eyes searched her face as she stood there, considering.

She sighed, then shook her head. 'I just don't think it's a great idea, Max. Sorry.' She'd actually managed to half close the door this time when he reached out, grabbed her hand. She looked down at it pointedly and he let go.

'Please,' he said again. 'We're here together anyway this weekend, what have you got to lose?'

'We're not *together,*' she snapped, before she could help herself. A little grimace crossed his face before he nodded, smoothed it out. As for what she had to lose . . . There was nothing she could say to that, without sounding clichéd. But she'd given so much to him in December, more than she'd realised, and she wasn't sure she could face opening that door again.

'Where's Bia?' Max asked after a beat, peering into her room over her shoulder, as if expecting to see her lurking there. As if Bia would even be letting her have this conversation if she were in the room. 'She could come too?'

'I haven't even said *I'm* coming yet,' Josie said, a little tightly. But it made her think. What if Bia was caught up the whole day with her new conquest, and Josie was left to fend for herself, having to spend the day alone until dinner? And now, Max had guaranteed that she'd just be sitting here, thinking of depressing things, if that was the case.

'Where would we go?' she asked eventually.

His expression lightened a little. 'Edinburgh.'

'Yes. Where in Edinburgh – you said it was somewhere specific?'

He hesitated. 'It's a surprise. But I promise it'll be worth it,' he added quickly. 'And I'll make sure you get some good photos for that Instagram account of yours.'

She narrowed her eyes. 'How do you know I'm still doing that?'

'I saw the photo of the castle that you posted when you first got here.' She said nothing, though she felt her lips tighten. So, that was why he hadn't been surprised to see her here then.

'What about Erin?' she asked suspiciously.

'She's going to see some friends in Edinburgh, so she doesn't mind.' They just looked at each other for a moment.

Slowly, she nodded. Because if he was trying this hard to be friendly, then she would try too. Besides, she really *did* want to see more of Edinburgh, and she really didn't want to spend the day alone – and if she could get Bia to come too, then all the better. And it would be for today only, she promised herself. One day with him – maybe it would help her to move on, help her to see that she'd just been romanticising last Christmas, making it into a bigger deal in her head than it really was. 'Alright. But you can wait down in the entrance hall while I shower and change.'

His shoulders seemed to relax as he smiled. 'Thank you. You won't regret it.'

She shut the door, then sighed and rested her head back against it, closing her eyes but falling short of groaning in case he was still the other side. She straightened, crossed to the bedside table and picked up her phone, sending a quick WhatsApp to Bia.

Where are you? You need to ditch your hunk and come back to the room. Now. We're going for a day out with Max.

It didn't deliver. Well, that was just fantastic. Clearly her phone had run out of battery. She sank down onto the bed and briefly contemplated ringing Laura to find out which room Stuart was in – if he was even staying at the castle at all. But it really wasn't the kind of thing you wake newlyweds up for, now was it? So instead she sighed, and headed into the shower room to try and reverse last night's damage.

Josie got to the entrance hall about forty-five minutes later, deliberately not rushing. If Max wanted to drag her out on some mystery expedition, then he could bloody well give her some time to get ready. She hadn't managed to get hold of Bia, but had decided not to wait, because who knew how long it would be before she heard back from her? – she could be waiting half the day for all she knew.

What she wasn't counting on was Erin, standing next to Max in the entrance hall, admiring a painting of an old man. She looked immaculate, pulling off the ponytail in a way very few people can do and wearing a crisp blue blouse and white slacks. Josie slowed her pace, but Max had already seen her and was waving her over. Erin turned, smiled at her too, though Josie thought her smile was a little more reserved. Josie's eyes flickered between them as she stopped a metre or so away.

'Erin's plans fell through,' Max said, acting like it was no big deal, 'so she's coming too.'

Erin offered another small, slightly tight smile. 'I hope you don't mind me gatecrashing,' she said, with perfect courtesy.

'Of course not,' Josie said quickly. Because what was she supposed to say? This was her boyfriend, who was arranging a weird outing with a girl he'd slept with – no wonder her plans had magically fallen through.

'Come on then,' Max said, leading them outside. He looked easy enough, but his hands were tucked firmly into his pockets, making Josie wonder if he was being deliberately careful not to touch anyone. 'You've got your camera, right?' he added, a little redundantly given he was currently looking at the bag strapped across her shoulder.

She nodded, held the camera bag up. As they stepped onto the gravel, Josie glanced at the taxi, then at Erin, wondering if it was genuinely too late to come up with a reason not to go. But Erin was now sliding into the back seat, and Max was holding the taxi door open for her. So, trying to do so as gracefully as Erin had, she got into the taxi. She was fully expecting Max to shut the door and get in the front seat, but he got in the back too, so that Josie was stuck firmly in the middle between the two of them. She snapped her legs together, being extra careful that no part of her body touched Max, which was actually rather difficult, being as how she wasn't exactly tiny, and both Max and Erin seemed to take up the entirety of each of their sides, leaving her with no extra room. She put her camera onto her lap and crossed her arms firmly as the taxi pulled away.

'Edinburgh, that right?' asked the driver.

'That's right, thanks mate.'

Josie glanced at Erin, but either she already knew where they were going, or else Max did this kind of thing often enough that she was just used to it. Either way, she seemed relatively relaxed as she stared out of the window. Josie shifted, felt Max's leg press next to hers, and jumped obviously enough to make both Max and Erin look at her. She cleared her throat. 'So, everyone having a nice weekend?'

The small talk was forced and awkward, making it seem like the taxi was moving incredibly slowly – Josie actually glanced over the driver's shoulder at one point to check the speed. It was in one of those too-long silences, about fifteen minutes into the drive, that Max made everyone in the car start by practically shouting, 'Stop!'

The driver slowed, frowned at him in the rearview mirror, while both Josie and Erin looked out of Max's side of the window. For a moment, Josie assumed that they must have nearly hit an animal or something, but Max only said politely, 'Can you pull over here?' He indicated a lay-by next to a stile, which led to what, as far as Josie could tell, was just a big field.

The taxi driver, still frowning and looking at Max slightly suspiciously, pulled over, and Josie wondered if Max just had a desperate need for a wee or something. But he looked over to Erin and Josie. 'Let's get out.'

'What?' Josie and Erin said, almost exactly at the same time. Josie glanced at Erin, who gave Josie a little smile that almost seemed genuine. Nothing like the apparent insanity of a third party to bond you.

'What?' the driver said. 'You want me to drop you here? You'll have trouble getting a ride from here, lad, you want to be careful, aye?'

Max shook his head. 'Just for a few minutes, then on to Edinburgh. You don't mind waiting for us, do you?'

'Aye alright,' he said slowly, 'but I'll have to keep the meter running.'

'No problem.' Max glanced behind him through the window, checking the road, then opened the car door. 'Come on,' he reiterated to Josie and Erin, jumping out without waiting for an answer.

Josie looked back at Erin incredulously. 'Is this normal?'

She let out a soft little laugh. 'It used to be, actually.' For some reason, that fact seemed to please Erin and she smiled more widely at Josie. 'No point in arguing,' she said, gesturing for Josie to follow Max out.

Josie scrambled out of the car, taking care not to stand in a particularly muddy puddle, and followed Max over the stile and into the field. The pumps she'd put on this morning didn't really seem the ideal footwear for randomly setting off into wet fields, but at least they were better than Erin's heeled, suede ankle boots. 'What are we doing?' Josie called after Max.

He turned to her, spreading his arms to encompass the field. 'Making the most of it.'

Josie put her hands on her hips while Erin climbed the stile, seeming to take extra care so as not to slip. 'Of what, exactly?'

'Of *it*.' Max turned in another circle, stretching his arms to indicate the countryside. Josie felt Erin come up next to her and glanced at her, ready to exchange another incredulous look, but Erin was smiling at Max in such a tender way that Josie looked away quickly, feeling like she was somehow intruding on a private moment. She moved a couple of steps away from them both. It was beautiful, she had to give him that. The long grass came up to her knees and merged with the stems of flowers, their colours now muted ahead of autumn. It was still warm enough that there were insects and butterflies floating around and the end of the field gave way to woodland, which, because of the browns and reds, looked secretive and inviting, like you might find magical creatures there if you were lucky. She realised this had been part of what drew her to Max before, the slight unpredictability of him, the fact that he encouraged her to just go with it. She shook her head. Dangerous thoughts to be having right now, considering the circumstances. Especially as she was supposed to be convincing herself of the opposite.

'Let's take some photos,' Max announced.

She raised her eyebrows, then shrugged, taking out her camera. She started with Erin, who, of course, made an excellent model, then took a few of Max and Erin together, trying not to grimace when Erin tucked her arm around Max, rested her head on his shoulder. Rather than look at them, Josie focused in on the surroundings, facing away from the road to give the impression that there was nothing and no one for as far as you could see. There was a moment where a bird came from the direction of the woods, circling briefly above them – a bird of prey from the size of it, maybe a kestrel. She managed to get the photo of Max looking up at it, the bird in focus against the sky, Max almost in silhouette. She thought it captured both the wildness of the bird, the nature of it, and the awe they, as humans, felt when they got to watch something like it.

She stared at the woods for a moment after that, waiting to see if anything else would appear, which meant that she didn't notice Max coming over to her until he was practically on top of her. 'Amazing, isn't it?' She jumped, then laughed as she brought a hand to her throat. She nodded, glancing over to where Erin was now watching them both, her head tilted slightly. Before she could stop him, Max grabbed her camera from her, then held it above his head when she immediately swiped to get it back.

'Careful!' she said, her voice a little panicked.

He laughed softly. 'I promise I won't hurt it.' He held it gently, and she stared at him, scrutinising. 'I just want to get some photos of you.' She wrinkled her nose automatically. She hated when people did this, tried to make her the focus. That wasn't what it was about for her. 'You said your mother was never in any of the photos,' he pointed out.

'Yes, but I don't have kids.'

He shrugged. 'You might one day, and even if not, when you look back at your life don't you want to see yourself in it too?'

She pressed her lips together at that, and was distracted enough that he snapped a shot of her. 'Hey!' He laughed, took another one even as she frowned. 'Stop!' She stepped towards him and he darted away.

She heard Erin's musical laugh from behind her, and turned to see her smiling, apparently unconcerned about Max playing around. Indeed she looked *delighted* by the whole ordeal. She wondered if that was just because she was so secure – you'd have to be secure, looking the way she did after all. Erin walked over to Josie, still managing to look graceful even as her heels sank into the earth. She put a slim arm around Josie's shoulder, making Josie feel big and awkward next to her.

'Come on,' said Erin. 'Let's pose.' The first shots were weird and uncomfortable and Josie felt like she was smiling in that way children do for school photos. Then, somehow, through shouted encouragement from both Erin and Max, she and Erin were prancing around the field, striking ridiculous poses, both together and separately, with Max encouraging them with a fake photographer voice, saying things like, 'Fabulous, darling' and 'Love it, work it', until both she and Erin were laughing uncontrollably in a way that made Josie think that, perhaps, Erin wasn't actually a bitch. Josie ended up by grinning directly at Max, and he took one last photo before lowering the camera and holding it out to her.

They walked back to the car as a three, and, whether or not it was intentional, Max had certainly succeeded in clearing the air and relaxing everyone. When they were safely on their way again – Josie once again in the middle, like they had assigned seats – Josie flicked through the photos. She deliberately skimmed past the ones of Erin and Max together and deleted a few of herself surreptitiously, but stopped at one in particular. She was smiling at Max and though there was nothing to indicate it, you could tell, somehow, that he was on the other side, smiling back. Like they were the only two people in the field. She looked pretty, happy and carefree in that instant, and she knew then that she'd keep it, that years later, she'd want to remember the moment, and the lightness she'd felt in it. She glanced at Max, and saw he was smiling back at her. Then he took her hand, where Erin couldn't see, and squeezed it. And even knowing that she shouldn't, she squeezed back.

Chapter Twenty

The taxi pulled up on a side street in Edinburgh. You could just about see Edinburgh Castle in the distance, almost seeming to blend with the grey sky above, and Josie thought how the city seemed like a world of its own, like it could easily be gated off, the people inside living completely separately from the rest of the world. She loved the combination of the city-feel, the grandeur of it, combined with the sensation that it wouldn't take long to get to know it, to be able to walk the whole city without needing a map. Like you'd be able to find comfort in the small familiarity of the place, yet also be able to find secret nooks and crannies if you wanted to.

Erin glanced at Josie as they got out the car, then reached out to shake Max's arm. 'We should show Josie round Edinburgh later, Max.'

Josie twisted her lips. 'Am I that obvious?'

Erin smiled, and linked an arm through Josie's as they followed Max, taking Josie a little by surprise. 'I remember the feeling. I might be Scottish, but I grew up in Glasgow, and I still remember the first time I saw this city.'

'So do you still live here now?' Josie asked and Erin nodded. Josie glanced at Max, who was walking a little ahead of them. 'And you, Max?' she asked, raising her voice.

He glanced back at them, and his eyes seemed to flicker as he clocked Erin and Josie's arms, linked together. 'Huh?' he said with a frown.

'Do you live in Edinburgh now?' Josie pressed.

'Oh, no,' he said, looking back in front of him. 'I'm in Bristol at the moment.' Josie nodded slowly. So, he and Erin weren't living together then – she wondered what that meant.

Max led them to number seventy-two and rang the bell, Josie feeling a little uncomfortable with Erin's arm through hers. Either it was some weird girl power play going on, along the lines of keep your enemies closer, or else Erin was actually genuinely making an effort to be friendly, which made it decidedly more difficult to hate her. On top of that, the fact that Max wouldn't tell her what they were doing here, and that Erin seemed totally ok with the not knowing, was making her stomach curdle anxiously.

It was a grumpy-looking man, in his forties at a guess, who answered the door. He was a little scrawny, his beard and brown hair both peppered with grey. His face was brown, skin slightly leathery, like he'd spent a lot of time somewhere hot, somewhere other than Scotland. He narrowed his eyes, frowning with very bushy eyebrows. Those eyes, even squinted, were almost turquoise, the colour of the ocean on a bright day, and they travelled over the three of them suspiciously.

Erin smiled brightly. 'Hello again, Geoff.'

When the man's – Geoff, apparently – eyes only narrowed further, so much so that Josie was surprised he could still see out of them, Max sighed. 'I told you we were coming, no need to act so shocked.'

Geoff grunted. 'Right. Fine, fine, come in.' His voice was a little gruff, his accent difficult to place – Irish originally, Josie thought, but with hints of the north of England, and possibly Australia, that suggested he'd lived a somewhat nomadic life. He turned and walked away, moving with a grace that seemed at odds with the rest of his appearance, into the dim house, leaving the door open behind him. Max gestured Josie and Erin inside and shut the door behind them. Josie bit her lip as she followed Erin further in. Had Max brought her to see a friend, a relative? If so, why all the secrecy?

The house was a little stuffy, like no windows had been open in a while, the living room the man led them to untidy, stacks of books overflowing the bookshelf into piles on the floor, the wooden table in the middle of the room, between two mismatched armchairs, covered in coffee ring stains. There was no TV, though an expensive computer sat in one corner on a wooden desk, the keyboard buried under bits of paper. The walls were bare, apart from one photograph above the little fireplace – a murky river, surrounded in reeds, with the eyes of a crocodile just visible over the water, staring out at them. Josie felt a little shiver run down her spine at the sight of it – both for the photo and the moment of it, the intensity.

'Suppose you'll all be wanting a drink, will you?' Geoff asked, his voice practically a growl.

'That would be great.' Max seemed to be trying hard to make his voice overly friendly, a direct contradiction to his friend. He was good at it, when he wanted to be – that charm that he sometimes seemed to hide behind. 'Coffee?'

Geoff shook his head. 'Only got tea, and the straight kind. Coffee gives me an upset stomach.'

'Tea it is then,' Max said.

'I'd love a tea,' Erin said. Then all three of them looked at Josie.

'Yes, tea would be lovely, thanks.' She fixed a bright smile to her face, which Geoff didn't return. He didn't ask how they took it, only glided out through the door, into the kitchen presumably.

Max sat himself on one of the armchairs, slouching, looking completely at home, and Erin perched on the arm next to him, saying nothing. Josie let her gaze travel around the room, resting on two big, hardback books on the desk by the computer. The one on top looked like it was a collection of wildlife photography. Josie took a step towards it, and felt her phone buzz in her pocket.

I'm sorry!!! I only just plugged my phone in. Where are you??? I can be ready in five.

Josie shook her head as she read the WhatsApp, and was about to reply when Geoff reappeared, surprisingly quickly. He handed them each a mug – Josie's was the yellow one you got with the Mini Eggs Easter egg.

'It's black,' he said, in a voice that strongly suggested not to contest that. 'No milk in the house. I'm lactose intolerant.' He plopped himself in the other armchair, wrapping both hands around his own mug. With the only two seats now taken, Josie could only hover awkwardly. Erin shot her an encouraging look, though Josie had no idea why.

'Josie,' said Max, 'this is the friend I told you about. Geoffrey Gilligan.' He gestured to Geoff and Josie smiled politely, though she had no recollection of Max mentioning a particular friend to her. 'Geoffrey,' continued Max, 'this is Josie. The girl I mentioned.'

Geoffrey Gilligan . . . The name sprang to life in her mind, and her gaze snapped to the photography book on the desk, the crocodile eyes on the wall. A memory of that Brooklyn bar, of Max telling her that he had a good photographer friend, that he could introduce her, if she liked. Josie sucked in a breath, looked at the man. 'You're Geoffrey Gilligan?' She lurched towards him, stretching out a hand.

'That's what he just said, isn't it?' He took her hand, his grip firm and strong. He looked like he was still frowning, though she wasn't sure if that was just because of his bushy eyebrows, whether they always looked pulled together like that.

'I'm so sorry, I didn't . . .' She took a breath. 'It's so nice to meet you.'

'Not what you expected, am I?' he said with that slight growl.

Josie shook her head. 'No, I . . . I just meant Max didn't warn . . . Or that I didn't, I wasn't expecting—'

'It's the work that should be impressive, not the man – or woman – behind it.' He waved a hand to encompass his body. 'Doesn't matter what I look like.'

'No, of course not,' she said quickly. 'You caught me off-guard, that's all.' If Max had just *warned* her, then she wouldn't be coming across like a blundering idiot right now. And had Erin known? The way she was smiling made it look like she had, which seemed bloody weird in Josie's opinion. The two of them, teaming up in a show of let's be friends with Max's ex-conquest. She took a breath, fighting to claw herself back. 'I think you – your work, that is – is incredible. I saw the exhibition at Somerset House and I—'

But he waved his hand, cut her off, and looked at Max instead. 'You told me the girl had talent, Max, not that she was a fan girl.'

Josie felt herself flush, both at the words themselves and at the fact he was talking about her as if she weren't in the room. She wanted, so badly, to glare at Max, but Geoffrey was watching her now. She looked him straight in the eye, straightened her spine a little. 'I'm so sorry. I didn't ask Max to . . . Well. And I don't have talent, it's just a hobby, I play around with it, but I do really admire—'

He cut her off again with his hand. 'I'll be the one to decide if you have talent or not.' He held out that same hand, glancing deliberately at the camera she still had strapped across her.

She only gripped it more tightly. 'They're only of the last couple of days, and that's only been for fun, they're not edited or anything yet.'

He kept his hand out. 'Well, that way I'll be able to tell if you're any good, without you faffing around with filters or whatnot.'

Slowly, she took the camera out of its bag and passed it to him. He immediately turned his attention to it and she wrapped her arms around herself, not knowing what to do with her body. 'Really,' she insisted, 'I didn't ask Max, I don't want a favour, I'm not—'

'I know that.' His voice, though still gravelly, was more patient this time as he focused on her camera, not her. He flicked a glance to where she was standing, biting her lip. 'But Max here can be pushy when he wants to be, I know it. He got you here, didn't he?' Max only grinned, and at that, Josie's glare finally cut loose. Geoffrey laughed at that. 'Quite.' His expression softened a little, his eyebrows flattening out as he looked directly at Max. 'Though I'd say it'd be nice to see a little more of that pushiness coming through again – it's been missing for the last year or so, hasn't it?'

Max sipped his tea. 'It's coming back to me, every now and then.'

'Glad to hear it. Now be quiet.' He flicked through the first few photos, glanced at Max. 'I take it these are your work.'

Josie grimaced – the photos of her and Erin, in the field. 'Yep,' said Max, stretching out his legs. 'I'm discovering my talent late in life.'

Geoffrey made no comment, just kept looking through the photos. Josie let go of her arms, twisted her hands in front of her, knowing she was holding her breath but unable to stop. She felt unbelievably vulnerable, standing there while someone in the industry appraised her work, while Max and his bloody girlfriend sat there on the same chair, looking all smug.

Geoffrey looked up, grunted, and handed the camera back to her. 'Talent, yes.' He took a sip of his tea.

When it was clear he wasn't going to say anything else, Josie bit her lip. 'Umm, thanks.' He stared at her for a moment and though she felt heat creep into her cheeks, she didn't drop the gaze, sensing somehow that it was the wrong thing to do in that moment.

'Email me some of your best work,' he said eventually. He got up, crossed to the desk, and moved a couple of things around, then came back to her with a business card. She took it.

'I, umm, have an Instagram account.'

He shook his head and those eyebrows pulled together. 'No. I hate all that social media crap.'

Max rolled his eyes. 'Really, Geoff, you'd think you were ninety, not forty-five.'

Geoffrey huffed. 'Calling out my age in front of two pretty girls now, are we?' He stood, took Max's mug without checking to see if he was finished, then took Erin's when she offered it. Josie, realising she still had most of her tea left, hastily took a sip. 'No,' he said, looking at her. 'Take your time. I'll get the rest of us another, see if I can hunt up some biscuits.'

The moment he was out the room, Josie spun to Max, trying hard to control her expression, being as how Erin was currently sat between them. 'You could have warned me,' she hissed.

'But then you would have said no.'

She folded her arms, fighting the urge to throw a strop. Erin gave Max a look that Josie couldn't interpret, but Max only shook his head at her, then looked at Josie. 'I thought you'd be pleased,' he said.

Both of them were looking at her now. Jesus, talk

294

about pressure. She pulled a hand through her hair. 'I am, I suppose.' She made herself take a sip of tea, hoping it would settle her, though the liquid was more tepid than hot now. 'I am,' she repeated, and let go all intention of getting in a huff about it. Memo had always told her it wasn't an attractive quality. She glanced round the room again, sighed. 'It's seriously cool.' And she wished she had someone to tell, someone who understood the industry, who would understand just how seriously cool it was.

Geoffrey came back in, carrying a stool that she presumed must be from the kitchen, which she perched on, helping herself to a ginger-nut biscuit when he offered them round. After about half an hour of small talk, which consisted largely of Max and Geoffrey jibing at one another, while she and Erin sipped their teas politely, the three of them left or, more accurately, Geoffrey kicked them out. He stood in the doorway as they turned back to thank him.

'Email me,' he said to Josie, with command in his voice. 'I'll see if there's anything I can do to help.'

For once, she didn't protest that it was just a hobby. Instead, she asked something that had been playing on her mind a fair bit over the last few months. 'It's not too late? To start? I'm nearly thirty.'

He squinted his eyes shut, placed a hand dramatically on his forehead. 'Oh, the horror. You'll be decrepit soon enough.' He dropped his hand, looked at her. 'No,' he said evenly. 'There's no age limit. It's not like being a model.'

Josie smiled. 'No, and thank God I never wanted to do that. I like wine and cheese far too much.'

He cracked a smile at that, then nodded to Erin. 'You still looking out for him?'

'I am,' she said. Josie tried not to squirm as Geoffrey nodded.

'That's something, then.' He turned, clapped Max on the back. 'Two women, hey? Can't be that bad now, can it?' Max grinned, and Josie flushed, while Erin just prodded Max in the ribs, like she was in on the joke. 'Don't be a stranger, alright?'

Max returned the one-armed hug. 'I'll do my best, but no promises.'

'Can't say fairer than that.' And with a small salute, Geoffrey shut the door, practically in their faces. Josie led the way back to the street, feeling like a third wheel again. She frowned as she walked. She'd let herself be manoeuvred into this, even if she was pleased with the outcome. Was it a bad thing? Was this just another example of her being a massive pushover?

Josie heard Erin murmuring something to Max behind her, and felt the back of her neck prickle, even if she couldn't hear what it was. Then Erin split away from Max, came to link her arm through Josie's again. What the hell was that about? 'So,' Erin said. 'I think you deserve a drink after that, what do you reckon?'

Josie hesitated – a drink cosied up with Max and Erin was not exactly how she wanted to spend the afternoon. 'Well, we need to be back at the castle soon . . .'

'Oh, don't be silly,' Erin said breezily, tightening her grip on Josie's elbow. 'We've got tons of time.'

Josie resisted the urge to glance back at Max for help – but really, shouldn't he be on her side here? Surely he didn't want the three of them holed up together? Or maybe, if Erin's relaxed demeanour was anything to go by, he'd already told Erin about her, told her that Josie meant nothing, and that's why Erin was so laid back about the whole thing. Well, Josie thought, frowning slightly, if that was the case then she could be fine with it too, couldn't she?

'Ok,' she said out loud. 'But let's go for coffee – not alcohol. I don't want to turn up to Laura's farewell dinner already tipsy.' That, and she didn't think it was a good idea to have her inhibitions lowered right now.

'Deal,' Erin said with a nod, and proceeded to steer Josie through the city, down the famous Princes Street that was bustling with people, up a little slope and through some gardens, chatting away as she did so, apparently with a very clear idea on where she was headed. Five minutes into their walk, Erin seemed to realise that Max was still lagging behind and turned to demand that he caught up. She looked at Josie with those bright blue eyes – eyes that were hard not to feel jealous of. 'Honestly, you'd think we were forcing him to board the *Titanic* or something.'

Josie managed a weak smile, whilst a part of her wondered vaguely what would happen if Erin and Bia went head to head. Once Max came alongside them, Erin linked arms with him too and steered both of them onto a new street – Broughton Street, Josie read, partly because she was deliberately trying to pay attention to anything other than Max, now that they were close enough to touch, if it weren't for his tall, slim, beautiful – and, so far, *lovely* – girlfriend between them.

Erin carried on talking – either unaware or determined

to ignore the awkwardness – providing little titbits of history as they went. Personal history, rather than stuff to make the travel books – like where she and her friends had spent Ceilidh-Salsa dancing outside on New Year's Eve, or where Erin's friend had got so drunk she'd actually been sick behind the bin. It made Josie smile in spite of herself, picturing the city as something more than a beautiful tourist spot, but somewhere people actually lived, did stupid things, got into trouble.

Then, '*Voila!*' Erin announced, stopping abruptly outside a little café. 'We spent many hours in this place at university studying for our finals, Josie.' She smiled, a trace of something sad – nostalgia, perhaps – crossing her face. 'Do you remember, Max?'

Josie looked over at him to see him nodding, that half smile playing across his lips. 'I do indeed.' Oh great. A coffee shop that held nice, romantic memories for the two of them – wasn't that just perfect?

It was a small-looking café from the outside, tucked away, with a black staircase leading down on one side and a wooden sign over the red door that offset the grey exterior. Artisan Roast.

Erin released Josie's arm, and Josie took a subtle step away, pretending to examine the outside of the little building while Erin checked her phone. She heard Erin mutter, 'Damn', and turned around. Erin looked up, glancing between Max and Josie. 'I completely forgot, I said I'd grab a drink with a friend of mine today – she's having boyfriend drama.' Erin's cheeks flushed, ever so slightly, after she said it. So, Josie thought, maybe not quite as oblivious as she pretended to be.

'Which friend?' Max asked. Was it just her, or was there a hint of suspicion in his voice? But that was ridiculous – Erin was the one who suggested this, why would she be trying to get out of it now?

'Amy,' Erin said immediately. 'Remember Amy?'

Max just stared at her for a moment, then said, 'Fine. Invite her along. She can come for coffee.'

'Yes!' Josie agreed, perhaps a little too enthusiastically, from the way both Max and Erin looked at her. 'I mean, I wouldn't mind if your friend came, Erin.' That way, it wouldn't be just the three of them.

Erin frowned. 'Don't be silly, you don't even know Amy – and you don't want to hear all about her issues, trust me, it's enough to dampen anyone's mood. No, no,' she carried on, as both Max and Josie opened their mouths again, 'this is a celebratory coffee, Josie. You and Max go in and grab one and I'll go and see her for a quick drink down the road, ok? I won't be long – she works at a pub and is due back on her shift in a bit.' She gave them both a broad smile and, literally leaving them no choice, turned away and sauntered off down the road, blonde hair swishing as she went.

For a moment, Josie and Max just stood there, neither of them saying anything. Then Max cleared his throat, making Josie jump slightly. 'Well, shall we?' He gestured towards the red door.

Josie nodded. 'Right. Sure.' No need to feel awkward, she told herself firmly. They'd spent the whole morning together, for Christ's sake.

Not alone, an annoyingly superior voice whispered in the back of her mind.

Max held the door open for her, and she felt her arm brush up slightly against his as she stepped through. She snatched it back firmly. Who made doorways so damn narrow, anyway? It wasn't practical.

The café inside was intimate and classy – wooden flooring, lighting that managed to feel almost bar-like in quality, with a blackboard at the back of the room. The smell of coffee was gorgeous, with something else mixed in there too – something sweeter yet distinct, like ginger – and the sound of grinding coffee beans made Josie relax slightly. It was just coffee. Coffee in a well-lit, comfortably warm room. She slipped off her jacket, let Max get the drinks as she found a table – one of the round ones with little bar stools around it.

'Thanks,' Josie said as Max set down a fancy-looking coffee in front of her – in a tall glass like a latte, the milky brown of the top part merging with the almost russet brown of the coffee below.

'I didn't know what you wanted,' Max said almost apologetically as he sat down on the stool next to her – a healthy, safe distance apart, she was happy to see. And if the space between their knees seemed to hum, that was nothing, it was only the warmth of the air in here, that was all.

Josie took a sip and tasted the ginger she smelled in the air. 'It's delicious.'

'The house speciality,' Max said, his voice carrying more of that teasing tone she'd got used to. They both went quiet again, taking sips of their coffee. Josie made a show of looking around the café, noting that it was getting fuller by the minute, in an attempt to distract from the cringeworthy awkwardness. God, it hadn't been like this last night, out in the castle grounds. But then, she hadn't had those helpful glasses of wine today, and unlike a moment stolen in the shadows, here in the daylight, in a room full of people, it was all too easy to remember that he had left her – that he had left her, and that he was now with someone else, so nothing could happen between them again.

'So, what do you think?' Max asked. 'Will you drop Geoff a line?'

Josie winced as she took a too large swallow of her drink, the top of her mouth burning slightly. She looked away as she coughed. Nice, Josie. 'Yes,' she said. And saying it out loud made her realise the truth of it. She nodded, tilting her chin up a little. 'Yes,' she said again, more decisively. 'I will. Who knows what'll happen, but it's worth a try, right?'

He nodded. 'Couldn't agree more.'

She hesitated, then said, quietly, 'Thank you.' She looked him right in the eye, those gorgeous, two-toned eyes. 'Really. Even if nothing comes of it . . . Thank you. For thinking of me.'

His gaze lingered on her face in a way that made her nerves tingle. 'I do, you know,' he murmured.

Her breath hitched. 'What?'

'Think of you.'

What a thing to say. She wanted to be mad, to hate him for it. But their gazes met and held for a beat too long. And in that moment, Josie was back in the bar at Christmas, sipping cocktails in the corner, feeling his skin pressed against hers, hearing his voice as he whispered to her over the din of the music. The memory of it – of what happened later that night – flooded through her in a hot wave. She blinked, and was back in the coffee shop, a toddler crying in the corner, the coffee machine whirring. Taking a slow breath, she looked down at her coffee, wishing then that she'd asked for an iced tea instead.

'So,' she said, still not looking at him. 'You and Erin.' A way to remind herself, as well as him. There was no point in ignoring it, anyway, and better to get it out in the open.

Max rubbed a hand across the back of his neck. 'Yeah, look, Josie, about that—'

'I'm not asking for an explanation,' Josie said quickly. She didn't want him to think she needed one, not after so long. 'I just meant . . . She seems nice.'

'She is,' Max said, and for some reason, even though *she'd* said it first, Josie's stomach dropped a little. 'But it's just . . . Erin, she's . . .'

But what exactly Erin was Josie didn't get the chance to find out, because at that moment two ladies, one wearing a tartan skirt, the other a tartan cap pushed to one side like a fashion statement, came up to their table.

'Do you mind if we share your table?' the woman in the skirt asked. American, Josie noted. 'It's just, there's nowhere else to sit right now.'

'Oh,' Josie said. 'Well . . .'

'It's top rated on Trip Advisor,' the woman in the cap piped up, looking at Josie with such an endearing smile out of a slightly plump face, that Josie felt guilty for hesitating.

Josie glanced at Max. 'I guess?' She made it into a question.

'Great!' the skirt said, taking that as a firm invitation. 'We won't bother you guys, I promise, you enjoy your date.'

Josie grimaced. Then, when she saw Max making the same expression, laughed a little. His expression softened too as he met her gaze. The two women grabbed stools from a neighbouring table, and squished themselves round in a way that clearly indicated the table was not made for more than two.

'Do you mind just scooting up a little?' the woman in the skirt asked and Josie, politeness too ingrained, obliged, as did Max next to her. And with that, the space between them disappeared. Crowded round the little table, her elbows tucked in as she cupped her drink, Josie felt Max's leg touch hers – and, with nowhere to go, it stayed there.

Her skin prickled with electricity and she felt her heart pick up speed. Next to her, she was aware of Max looking down at his drink, refusing to look at her, even as the heat between their bodies pulsed. God, she could *smell* him this close, that mix of classy aftershave and something that was just all *him*.

Dimly, Josie was aware of the women at the table talking, something about the Royal Mile and whisky, but the exact words washed over her, like they were outside a bubble, and she and Max were alone inside it. The coffee machine, the toddler crying, the sound of people laughing – all of it sounded distant, separate, every inch of her body focused purely on the feeling of Max against her.

And then Max's phone buzzed. He jumped, and Josie sucked in her breath as he reached into his pocket.

'It's Erin,' he muttered, his voice slightly husky. 'She's outside.'

Josie nodded, and without another word, stood up. 'I'll just go to the bathroom, and I'll meet you out there.' Not giving him the chance to respond, she turned away and rushed towards the ladies' room. In there, she stared at herself in the mirror, taking slow breaths. *Get a grip,* she told herself. *And get over it.* Another deep breath, and she felt, if not ready, then as ready as she was ever going to be to face them both again.

The air was cooler outside the coffee shop than she remembered, the breeze fizzing off her hot skin. Erin and Max were right there, by the black metal stair barrier, but neither looked over as she closed the door behind her.

'Well?' Erin was saying. 'Did you tell her?'

Josie halted, her heart lurching.

'Give me a break, Erin, it's not that easy.'

'I'll take that as a no.' Erin's voice was clipped, harsher than the one she'd used earlier today. So maybe she wasn't quite as happy and easy-going as she made herself out to be. She wanted Max to tell her. Josie let that sink in for a moment. How far did it go? What commitment had they made to one another? She closed her eyes for a brief second. No. Best not to let herself go down that route.

'Josie.'

Josie jolted at the sound of Erin's voice, the harshness now gone, as if it had never been there. Josie looked at her, and Erin smiled. And she couldn't, even if she'd wanted to, hate this woman. Because even in the midst of this, Erin wasn't blaming her for it, didn't hate her for her history with Max.

'Hi,' Josie said, refusing to look at Max even as his gaze sought hers. She stepped towards them – just one step.

'I'll order us a taxi, shall I?' Erin said, pulling out her phone. No further mention of drinks, of celebration. And Josie counted herself lucky because of that.

The three of them stood awkwardly on the side of the road, Josie on one side of the shop, Max and Erin on the other. And when the taxi came, Josie got in the front seat, away from the two of them, before anyone could insist otherwise.

Chapter Twenty-One

Josie emailed some photos to Geoffrey, along with her phone number, as soon as she got back to her room at the castle, knowing that if she didn't do it right away she might lose her nerve, and not two hours later, when she and Bia were on the way to the final dinner, she got a call from an unknown number. She answered it with a cautious, 'Hello?'

'Josie?' It was a voice like a growl. 'It's Geoffrey Gilligan.'

'Oh!' Josie exclaimed. 'Hello,' she repeated. Bia, dressed in bright green to offset her purple hair, gave Josie a curious look, and she gave a little shrug.

'I've just had a look at your stuff, and I'm impressed – and I don't say that lightly. Now look, I'm running a course here in Edinburgh this autumn. The places are all full, but I'm willing to make an exception – partly because Max is a friend of mine, but mostly because I see talent, and from what Max has told me you are currently wasting said talent, which is a downright shame.'

306

'I'm not—' Josie tried to protest, but he stopped her.

'Let me finish. This would be a chance to develop that talent, to focus on your work exclusively. It starts in two weeks and runs until Christmas. At the end of it there's a student exhibition, which gives you the chance to showcase your work – we invite people in the industry, that kind of thing. There are no scholarships available, but I can offer some funding – enough to make a substantial difference, I'd say.'

Josie halted in her tracks, and Bia came to a stop too, now wearing a little frown as she tried to figure it out. Josie let out a slow breath. It was all a bit sudden, and she wasn't sure what to think of it. When she'd emailed him she was more expecting him to suggest a few competitions, that kind of thing. But to dedicate herself fully to a course . . . Could she really just up and move to Edinburgh? Commit to studying for the rest of the year, without any guarantee that it would lead to something? It seemed a little reckless, really, and more the type of thing she'd expect from Bia, she thought, glancing at her. 'I'm not sure, I . . . I need to think about it.'

'Alright, but think quickly. If I don't hear by the end of the week, I'll presume it's a no. Have a good evening, and hope to hear from you soon.' Josie kept the phone to her ear even after he'd hung up, staring at Bia, a little dumbfounded.

'What was that about?' Bia asked.

Josie filled Bia in on the way to the Auld Keep, where the last dinner of the weekend was being held. Predictably, Bia thought it was a wonderful idea and didn't see the problem with how Josie would make it work financially, simply shrugging and saying, 'You'll figure it out.' Josie was a little relieved when they got to the Keep, which somehow felt older than the rest of the castle, because it meant there was an excuse to stop talking about it.

They made their way to the Stag Chamber, where there was a stag head on one of the walls – hence the name, Josie supposed – though she tried not to look at the slightly glassy eyes. She'd never really appreciated the tradition of displaying heads of dead animals, once living, soulful things being displayed as nothing more than prizes, though she supposed it did add to the authentic feel of the place. As did the original stone walls, and she couldn't help sneakily running a hand along one. It felt rough to the touch and somehow colder than the rest of the room. There was a vaulted ceiling which curved above them, making it easy to imagine the room when empty, being imprisoned here perhaps, cobwebs in the corners and the steady drip of water leaking onto stone – the type of place where you could be left, and forgotten about.

There were two rectangular tables either side of the room, draped in black with a purple cloth running along the middle of them, with a smaller table at the top to join the two, where Laura and John would no doubt sit. There was a display of candlesticks on the tables, already lit, and lamps on the far wall that had been made to look like live torches, which combined gave the room a flickering glow.

Josie clocked Erin, nodding to her, as she and Bia made their way over to a table full of drinks, including actual mead, to help themselves. She couldn't see Max there, and tried to ignore the slight twist in her stomach. Maybe that was a good thing, she told herself. Maybe it was better if, after the coffee shop experience, she didn't see him again this weekend. And lots of people had gone home by now, unable or unwilling to take the extra day off work – including Stuart, according to Bia, and Jess and Tom, who had made their way back to London this morning. Jess had sent Josie a message saying that they must all meet for lunch when Josie was next in London, though Josie had no doubt that at least six months would pass before she saw either of them again. Dinner was therefore a smaller, more intimate affair, with seating for around thirty or so, the people left either close family or those who wanted to make a long weekend out of it. Josie had said she'd stay, because what did she have to go back for? Answering phones at a temp reception job, or else discussing the redecorating with Helen. And, of course, she'd wanted to be there for Laura.

Laura, who at that moment was standing near the stag's head, her face illuminated by candlelight, a soft, happy glow better than any makeup. Josie jerked her head towards Laura, and Bia nodded, following her. Josie felt the punch of guilt as they reached her. She'd stayed on, was considered close enough by Laura to stay on – the only work friend to get that honour – but she hadn't bothered to speak to her all day. Laura, however, didn't seem upset and beamed at Josie and Bia as they approached.

Josie pulled Laura into a hug, smelling a sweet perfume. 'You look beautiful,' she said as she eased back. 'Though I imagine you're fed up of hearing that, after how you've looked all weekend.'

Laura tossed back her head and gave Josie a look. 'No one, not even me, Josie, could ever get fed up of hearing that.' She smiled, looked around the room as the last few people joined. 'It's been good, hasn't it?'

'I'd say "good" is an understatement. It's been *amazing*, Laura.' Laura grinned. 'But how has it been for you, not too stressful?'

'No, once we got the ball rolling it all just sort of fell into place.' Though she didn't say it, Josie had the distinct impression that it was only religious planning on Laura's part that had caused it to do so.

'Well, you bloody nailed it,' said Bia with a grin, and gave Laura a hug herself. Laura squeezed Bia back.

'Glad you could make it.'

'Are you kidding?' Bia shook her head. 'Thank *you* for letting me gatecrash.' Neither of them made any mention of the reason Bia had to gatecrash in the first place, for which Josie was grateful.

John came over then, and pulled Josie into a bear hug. Josie smiled at him. 'Well, don't you look dapper? You should wear kilts all the time.'

'Ah, I would but she won't let me.' He put an arm round Laura, tugged her to his side.

Bia grinned at them. 'You guys are just picture perfect, aren't you?'

'Aren't we just?' Laura agreed, making Josie laugh.

'And how's the Boathouse treating you?' asked Josie.

'God, it's amazing,' Laura said. 'It's right on the lake, and we watched the sunrise over it this morning. You seriously can't get any better, even if the sun slightly disappeared after that.'

Josie raised her eyebrows. 'You were up at sunrise?'

John gave a mock grimace. 'Laura made me.'

Laura shook back her hair, down and straight this evening. 'Well, we put the rest of the morning to good use, didn't we?' John flushed and Josie and Bia laughed when Laura winked at them. John's parents came over at that moment, and Josie and Bia excused themselves.

Josie gave a little sigh and Bia cocked her head at her. 'I just can't believe it's already over,' Josie said.

'It's not over *yet* though. And I'm taking notes – I'm pretty sure I'm going to have my wedding here one day.'

Josie laughed. 'Now you just need to find the guy.'

Bia waved a hand in the air. 'A minor detail.'

'What about Stuart?' Josie asked with a smirk.

'Nah, that was just a bit of fun.'

Josie jerked to a stop as Max entered the chamber. He looked impossibly handsome in the glow of the room – *of course* he bloody did. It was a slightly more informal vibe this evening, despite the splendour of their surroundings, so Max was wearing black jeans and a fitted grey jumper. Erin waved him to her side of the room before Josie could decide if she should go over to him or not.

She saw Bia giving her a look, and frowned. 'What?' Bia took a sip of mead, raising her eyebrows over the rim. 'What?' Josie insisted as they took their seats – separated from Max and Erin by an elderly couple, presumably on John's side if the man's tartan kilt was anything to go by.

'I'm just not sure it's a good idea to go back there, given the way it ended last time,' Bia said.

'I'm not,' Josie said with a frown. 'Nothing's happened. Nothing's going to happen.'

'You spent the whole morning with him today,' Bia pointed out.

'Yes, and with his *girlfriend,* Bia.' The bit in between, she decided, she just wasn't going to mention. Because there wasn't anything to mention. Not really.

His voice rang out in her mind. *I do, you know. Think of you.*

Josie shook it off, focused in on Bia. 'And I was only with him because you weren't around.'

Bia ignored the jibe. 'You still have feelings for him.'

'I do not,' Josie said. But she knew that it came out a little too prim to sound convincing.

'Just be careful, ok?'

Josie sighed. 'Bia, I'm *always* careful.' But there was a little part of her that thought that, if that were true, she would have been able to enter into a fling with Max the way Bia had gone about it with Stuart.

Bia managed to distract her for most of the dinner, so that she barely paid attention to what Max was doing. The mead was slightly stronger than she'd planned for, so her head starting swirling pleasantly before she realised it, and she felt her voice getting louder, gesturing more emphatically when she and Bia discussed Big Ideas. As such, Josie was a little shocked when Laura and John started making the rounds to say goodbye to everyone.

Josie and Bia stood as they approached their section of the table. There were tears in Laura's eyes as she hugged them both. 'Don't ask me why,' she said. 'I'm just all emotional this weekend.' Because John was giving her a look, Laura prodded him in the ribs. 'It's normal, you jerk,' she said with affection.

Max and Erin were part of the little cluster that had come up round the other side of the table to say goodbye, and John turned to hug Erin, who gave him a friendly pat as they drew away. 'I can't believe you're a proper grown-up now,' she said with a sigh.

John snorted. 'You'll get there soon, I've no doubt.' Josie tried very hard not to look at Max. Would it be on the cards, she wondered? Would Max and Erin end up getting married, Josie no more than a story in Max's past? She pressed her lips together. *Let it go, Josie.*

The entire dinner party followed Laura and John outside to wave them off, but because they were walking to the Boathouse first to get their luggage, and because Laura wasn't wearing a wedding dress, it was rather less dramatic than the send-offs you saw in those romantic films.

'Thank God,' Bia said, as they gave a last wave. 'I've been needing a wee for about ten minutes.' She dashed off, and Josie headed back into the Chamber. She paused just inside the entryway. Max was sitting there, the candlelight bouncing in his hair. Erin was distracted, chatting away to someone on her other side, and Max looked up and caught her eye. And smiled at her in a way that should be reserved for his damn girlfriend.

Maybe it was the mead, maybe it was something Bia had said, or maybe it was the whole bloody weekend, the way he'd been acting like they had some kind of connection, that they were *something* to one another, but in that moment, she decided that she'd had enough. She turned on her heel and stormed away, practically barging into someone coming in the other direction. Screw him, she thought. Screw all the damn happy couples here.

She was out in the grounds when she heard him calling

her name behind her. 'Josie?' She ignored him and marched on further, the wind whipping past her face. 'Josie!'

She spun to him, glaring. 'What?' she spat out.

He jerked to a stop, frowned, then started walking slowly towards her, as if she were some kind of animal in need of taming. 'What's wrong?' he asked slowly. For a moment she just glowered at him. Clearly, he was under the impression that all of this was fine, that they were fine, that it was bloody *fine* to give her all these looks and take her hand when his girlfriend wasn't looking, because a countryside jaunt and a meeting with a famous photographer made everything just dandy.

She shook her head. 'What are you doing, Max?'

'What do you mean?'

'What are you *doing*?' she repeated. 'Why are you trying to worm your way back into my life?' She pulled a hand through her hair, felt the wind tug at it when she let go. There were no stars tonight, the night sky clouded above them. 'Or are you? Is that what you're trying to do – do you want to be friends? Is that what all of this is about?'

'No, I—'

'Then what!' Her voice erupted across the castle grounds. 'You bloody show up here out of nowhere, at my friend's wedding, where you have no right to be—'

'Hey, that's a bit harsh,' he said, still in that same careful tone of voice. 'I was invited, it's not like I did it deliberately to piss you off.' She shot him a glare, and his face tightened. 'This isn't ideal for me either, Josie, it's—'

'Oh yes,' Josie said, letting out a scathing laugh. 'I'm sure it's so hard being here with your gorgeous, intelligent girlfriend – whom I like, by the way.'

'I like her too, but it's not what you—'

'You were the one to leave *me*, Max,' Josie snapped. Her eyes were stinging now, damn them. She hunched her shoulders, wrapped her arms around them, trying to combat the chill that was clinging to her skin. 'You left me on fucking Boxing Day after I'd . . .' She took a deep breath, shook her head. 'Forget it. That's not the point, that's history.'

Max stepped towards her, his eyes dark like the clouds above them. They stared at each other for a moment, then Max took a breath. 'Look, I'm sorry, I never meant to hurt you—'

Josie gave a sour laugh. 'Oh, that's rich.'

'I tried to talk to you about it!' Finally, Max erupted too, something breaking whatever control had been keeping him in check. He pulled a hand through his hair in a way that looked painful. 'In New York. I tried to talk to you, to explain, and you just blew me off! And you seemed perfectly content with your new life there, I might add,' he added with a bitter tone. She only glowered. Of course she'd seemed content, hadn't she? She was hardly going to let on how much it had hurt, seeing him there, was she?

It was then that she decided that she didn't want to have this out after all, and turned to stalk away. He reached out, grabbed her hand, and pulled her back around almost violently. He let go immediately, like her skin burned him, and shook his head furiously. 'You think this is easy for me?' His voice was quiet, but each word held a punch that went straight through her. 'Wanting what I can't have?'

The words twisted in her chest, and she looked down at the ground to hide it. 'That's a ridiculous thing to say.

It's your choice, isn't it?' she said, before he could butt in. 'All of this – it's all on your terms.'

'In New York—'

'Screw New York. If you wanted me, then you should have tried to stay with me in the first damn place!' She was breathing too heavily now, but she couldn't seem to slow it. 'Or at least tried to stay in touch or *something,* instead of just abandoning me.'

Max winced, and for a moment, the fire that had flared up in her wavered. But then he spoke, and his voice was cold. 'You have no idea of anything, Josie.'

And just like that, the fire burned again. 'Well, no, because you don't tell me anything, do you? I've given you everything, I told you *everything,* and you give me nothing back.' She started to turn away again, not entirely sure where she was going. 'And maybe you blame me for that in some weird, twisted way, but I don't, and I don't think—'

For the second time that night, he reached out and grabbed her arm, pulled her to him so forcefully that the breath was knocked out of her. Their gazes locked, his eyes searching hers. Then he was kissing her, and she was responding without thinking about it. She pulled his shoulders towards her, needing more of him, and his fingers dug in at her waist. God, the taste of him. She hadn't realised until right now how much she'd been craving it.

'Josie?' The sound of Bia's voice catapulted them back to reality and they both sprang apart like they'd been shocked. Josie smoothed her hair as she turned to face Bia, who looked like a little fairy in the night, with the light of the Keep behind her. How much had she seen? Jesus, thank God it had been Bia and not Erin.

'I'll be right there,' Josie said, hoping that the waver in her voice was too light for Bia to notice.

'Is everything ok?' Bia's frown was moving between Josie and Max.

'Yeah.' Josie cleared her throat. 'It's fine. Go back inside, I just need a moment. I'll be there in a sec.'

Bia shifted her weight from one foot to the other. 'Actually, I was thinking of going to bed – I'm completely knackered.'

'Alright,' Josie said, as evenly as she could manage. 'You go ahead, I'll catch up with you.' Bia hesitated, but left, leaving Max and Josie alone. Josie turned to Max, and they stared at each other, their eyes glinting in the darkness.

Max shook his head. 'I'm sorry. I shouldn't have done that.'

Something crushed around Josie's heart, but she nodded, tight-lipped. 'No. I suppose you shouldn't have.' She took a single step away.

'Josie, wait, I didn't mean . . .'

But she'd had enough. She'd had enough of half promises, of the hints and looks and goddamn mixed messages. So when she spoke her voice was a hard line. 'No, Max. I'm done with this. You walked into my life, made me feel . . . I don't know.' She pulled a hand through her hair. 'Different. Then you walked out of it, without a second thought for my feelings. And that's fine, whatever, if you didn't want anything more. You could have found a nicer way to do that, but I can accept it.' She shook her head. 'But what I can't accept is this.' She gestured between them. 'Is you acting like nothing's happened, or trying to be friends, or hinting that you want something

317

more, and I can't . . .' She took a slow breath, trying to calm her voice down, wishing it didn't sound like it was on the verge of a sob. 'After this weekend, I think it's best if we don't see each other again.' Because what she'd realised over these last few days was that she couldn't be friends with him – not without wanting more. So if that was what he was asking for, she wouldn't do it. Better that he was out of her life completely, and then she'd be able to forget about him.

Max said nothing, just looked at her with an expression she couldn't quite make out. Her lips tightened, but she would not let her emotions get the better of her, would not cry. This time, it would be her turn to walk away from him. So she turned, holding her head high, and walked after Bia. And this time, Max did not follow.

Part Four: December

Chapter Twenty-Two

It was cold enough in the underground vault that Geoffrey had hired for the evening that Josie had kept her jacket on – clearly, they had not thought to ramp up the heating in the run-up to their little exhibition. The place had a cool, edgy atmosphere with mixed lighting, aiming to show the photography off at its best, and tables positioned strategically so that people were encouraged to stand and look at the work, rather than sit and drink.

Josie kept her hands in her pockets, partly from the cold but mainly to control the urge to constantly twist them together, as she watched people mill about, having put her glass of Merlot down already so that she didn't keep sipping it out of nerves. The students – twenty-one, including Josie – had been encouraged to invite people to this end-of-course 'Celebration', as Geoffrey had called it, and those were the people who, she was sure, made up the majority of the crowd, but she knew there were also some people from the industry there. She couldn't quite believe that it was *her* work being displayed up on the walls, that people were currently looking at it, cocking their heads curiously or nudging their friends to point something out. Across the room, she caught sight of Geoffrey, who only winked to where she was standing alone like a lemon before heading off to talk to someone else.

The theme was a celebration of Edinburgh. They'd been allowed to pick what they wanted that to encompass – people, buildings, landscapes. Josie had gone for landscapes – she'd known from the outset that it would be tough to do something fresh and original with that, but she was pleased with what she'd accomplished, and felt like she'd grown as a photographer for sure. It had, she would admit, been the most amazing two and a half months; it had been incredible to be allowed to indulge completely in what she loved doing.

She smiled as she saw Bia, who seemed fully delighted by the whole affair, chatting to John and Laura on the other side of the room, underneath a fellow student's portrait of two women outside a cafe. She felt a little warm and fuzzy inside, seeing her friends here for this, that they'd made the effort to come and not brushed it aside as something silly or insignificant, something she'd just needed to get out her system before she returned to the real world – as much as it felt like that to her, at times. The fact that all her confirmed guests were here didn't stop her from regularly glancing towards the door, however, her stomach pulsing uncomfortably every time she did so.

Having done a slow lap of the room, Helen, Memo and her grandad came back round to her. Josie smiled as Memo gave her another hug, breathing in her grandmother's smell of tobacco and cinnamon. Memo squeezed her shoulder with spindly fingers. 'This is amazing, my love.'

Josie beamed. 'I'm just so glad you all came.'

Helen scoffed a little. 'Of course we did, darling. What did you expect?' She was totally in her element, sipping her warm white wine like it was the most expensive champagne. 'And it's turning out to be quite the event, isn't it?'

Memo stroked Josie's hair, while her grandad gave her an awkward, one-armed pat – he'd never been one for overt displays of affection, but Josie could tell he was pleased, and he'd asked her a stream of questions about the different photos when they'd first arrived, which told her everything.

'We're just so proud of you,' Memo said. And they'd been so supportive when she'd told them she was going to do the course. Memo had offered to help pay for her accommodation, but Josie had refused – they were both retired and had better things to spend their money on, like bills. So she'd told them to come to the show at the end instead. For money, she'd taken a part-time job as a waitress in the evenings and weekends, which had been reminiscent of her teenage years, and shared a flat with two other girls, who she'd barely seen because she was hardly ever there, and when she was there she was holed up in her room sleeping. She didn't think she'd ever been this exhausted – or this happy.

Her grandad broke into a hacking cough and Josie frowned at him. 'Are you ok?' When he just waved at her, she pressed on. 'Is it a cold? Have you had your flu jab?'

'Oh, stop worrying,' he said affectionately, as the cough subsided. 'I'm hardier than I look.' But it was an uncomfortable reminder that they were both getting older – and something cold fluttered around her heart at the thought.

Memo brought her attention back around with a gentle squeeze on the shoulder. 'Your mum and dad would be proud of you too, my Josie.'

'I hope that's true.'

'Course it is,' grunted her grandad. 'They'd think you were brave, going after something you love.'

'Malcolm would have adored this,' Helen agreed. 'He was so proud of you when you rode your first bike – something every child accomplishes, so I can't imagine how awful he'd be here, showing off to everyone.' She flashed Josie a wicked smile over the rim of her wine glass.

Josie smiled at them both, even though her heart twisted ever so slightly. It was another moment where she wished they were there, to see what she'd chosen to do, to see the person she'd become.

'You must come and visit us soon,' Memo said, searching in her skirt pocket for something. Memo *always* wore skirts with pockets – it was something Josie had always admired. 'I know you're busy this Christmas, but after that.'

'I will,' Josie promised, trying to push aside the twinge of guilt. Her grandparents hadn't said anything, but she wondered if there was a part of them that was hurt or offended that she'd gone to Helen's rather than to them when she came back from New York. Helen hadn't asked her why either, had immediately said yes to the company, but the truth was Josie hadn't been able to bear the thought of spending that length of time there, even as she felt cowardly because of it.

'Right, I'm off to have a quick ciggy,' said Memo, and Josie frowned.

'You shouldn't. I thought you were giving up.'

Memo waved a hand in the air. 'The damage is already done, my love.' From the look on Helen's face she, too, wanted to say something to her mother about that, though Josie couldn't help seeing the irony there, given no one could tell Helen to stop indulging in the things she loved, either.

Josie watched Memo leave the room, wrapping her coat tight around her, while her grandad waved at Bia from across the room. Then Geoffrey descended on them with a flourish. 'Terribly sorry all, but I need to steal Josie away for a moment.' He grabbed her upper arm with a firm grip, as if daring her to argue. Out of the corner of her eye, Josie saw Helen, who was a good ten years older than Geoffrey, eyeing him up speculatively. To Josie's surprise, he didn't balk from the look, but gave Helen a little smile, bowed his head. Then marched Josie off across the stone floor.

'I want to introduce you to someone,' he said as they approached one of her photographs, then tapped someone – presumably *the* someone, on the shoulder. A woman, slightly older than Josie, tanned and with sun-streaked blonde hair, turned, raised one eyebrow. 'Charlotte – this is Josie.'

Josie smiled politely and offered her hand, trying not to display any outward sign of nerves as she wondered who this was. 'Hello.'

Charlotte took her hand and shook it in a brisk, efficient way. 'Hi there. I've been admiring your work.' Her voice was just like her handshake – cool and to the point. 'I work out in Botswana, and we're running a photography internship this year, partnering with one of the big lodges there.' She ran her gaze briefly over Josie, and Josie had the distinct impression she was being measured up. 'Geoffrey spoke highly of you and suggested you may be interested in wildlife photography.' It was a statement rather than a question.

Josie was wondering what 'spoke highly' actually meant, given the man had mostly been growling orders and criticisms at her over the last two months, but Geoffrey gave her a little nod. She met Charlotte's very direct gaze, tried hard not to bite her lip. 'Wow. That's amazing, thanks so much for thinking of me.' Though the woman hadn't actually said they *were* thinking of her, Josie realised, suddenly very aware of how ridiculous her hands must look, loosely hanging at her sides.

Charlotte handed her a card, which Josie took, looking down at it. 'The details of the internship are on the website there. You'll need to apply officially, but after having seen some of your work this evening I'd say the chances of you being selected for interview are high. You've only got another day to get the application in though – we've had to keep the selection process short and fast because the funding has only just been confirmed.' She smiled – efficient again, like she'd figured out just how much energy was needed for her face muscles to produce the desired effect, then nodded to Geoffrey and walked off, leaving Josie feeling slightly windblown.

She looked at Geoffrey, who was smirking at her, like he'd seen Charlotte produce this effect before. Josie shook her head. 'I'm not totally sure what happened.'

'Well, I *think* you've just been offered the chance at an experience of a lifetime, little grasshopper.'

She looked down at the card, then up at him, still feeling like she was playing catch-up. 'Is it inappropriate to hug you right now?'

He held up a hand, wrinkled his nose. 'I don't go in for that sort of thing.'

Josie laughed. 'This is so cool, and thank you so much for mentioning me to her . . .'

'But?'

She sighed. 'But I can't take an unpaid internship.'

He raised those bushy eyebrows. 'Whyever not?'

'Well . . . I'm not twenty-one anymore, for one.'

'Oh yes, I forgot that you're ancient.'

'Well, I *am,* in comparison to everyone else here.' He deliberately looked around the room, which included a fair few people her grandparents' age. She made an impatient noise. 'You know what I mean. And I've used up my quota of life breaks on this course, sadly.'

His eyebrows resumed their natural, frown-like position. 'Don't see what the big deal is. All your food and accommodation would be covered, and it's only for a year.'

She huffed. 'Yes, but I have no money, Geoffrey.'

'I think there's a pittance-like salary. Potentially. Besides, don't you have any savings? A girl like you's got to, surely.'

'What do you mean, a girl like me?'

'You know . . .' – he waved a hand in front of her face – 'organised, with a good head on your shoulders.' Josie pursed her lips, not entirely sure if he meant that as a firm compliment. 'Anyway,' Geoffrey continued, 'you don't have to decide now. Right now, you should just be enjoying the evening, given all the work you put in. Meanwhile, I have to do the rounds, I'm afraid.' He gave her an uncharacteristic squeeze on the shoulder as he left, and she went over to join Laura, Bia and John.

Bia grinned at her. 'Check you out! You're like, an actual photographer.'

John gave her shoulder a thump. 'Yeah, congratulations. We should have asked you to do the wedding photos.' Laura smiled and nodded at that, in a way that made Josie want to laugh. There was absolutely no way that Laura would have let an untested photographer loose at her wedding.

The door to the vault opened, and Josie snapped her gaze towards it automatically. But it was just a woman that Josie didn't recognise, holding the hand of a young boy. She turned back to Laura and Bia, to see them exchange a glance. 'What?' Josie asked, defensively.

'Looking for someone, are we?' Bia asked, bringing her wine to her lips.

'No,' she said, but the heat blossoming at the nape of her neck was giving her away. 'Alright, fine, I thought Max might be here. And it's not out of the realms of possibility, so don't look at me like that. He introduced me to Geoffrey in the first place, didn't he?'

'Hmm, I remember,' Bia said, in a tone that could have indicated disapproval, despite the fact that they were all in this room now only because of that introduction.

Laura glanced at John, who immediately went sauntering over to the bar, then turned to Josie. 'Did you invite him?'

She bit her lip. 'Well, no.' She'd thought about it, not

that she'd admit that to her two friends. Thought about it because she did, after all, owe him for this. And then decided that the safest bet was just not to go there. But despite that, and despite the fact that Josie had effectively told him she never wanted to see him again, she hadn't been able to help thinking that Geoffrey might have invited him, and that maybe he might have said yes to it. And, if she was being really, truly honest with herself, a little part of her had hoped for it.

Laura and Bia exchanged another look, clearly bonded over their disapproval of Max.

She sighed. 'I got flowers,' she admitted. A big, gorgeous bunch of blue, white and purple flowers, delivered to her flat this morning.

'From him?' Bia demanded.

Josie shook her head, stopped halfway through the action. 'Well, I don't know. There was no note.' Laura's eyebrows shot up, while Bia tapped her fingernails – painted dark blue, to go with her now almost charcoal hair – against her now empty wine glass.

'So you *thought* they were from him?' Laura asked.

Josie wrinkled her nose and said nothing, knowing there was no right answer to that question. If she said no, she was sure they'd see through it, and if she said yes, she wasn't quite sure what she was admitting. She'd assumed, at first, that the flowers were from Memo, but she had denied it when Josie had asked, and Josie hadn't been able to think of who else they might be from. And Max would have been able to find out her address from Geoffrey, wouldn't he? She pressed her tongue to the roof of her mouth. Stupid, letting herself go down that road. She'd

329

told him she didn't want to see him again – she should stick by that.

Josie and Bia were both watching her a little too intently, and she squirmed under the weight of their combined gaze. 'You need to message him,' Bia declared, after a moment. Laura frowned, but Bia nodded. 'Ask him if they were from him, and if so, then why. If they're nothing to do with him then at least you won't be wondering. You need closure, Josie.'

Laura's expression straightened out thoughtfully. 'Hmm. There may be something in that.'

'I don't need *closure,*' Josie said, trying to sound like she felt the idea preposterous. The problem was, Bia might be right. She'd known, really, that he wouldn't be here. And what had she been hoping for, anyway? That he'd broken up with Erin and would arrive with flowers, chocolate and champagne in hand, begging her to give him a chance, telling her that she was the love of his life? She almost let out a snort at the thought of it.

John reappeared at Laura's side, as if drawn by some silent signal, with four glasses of wine clutched in both hands. He dished them out, and Josie sipped her red automatically. Laura looked at her critically. 'I think the only thing to do,' she said, a little formally, 'is to get you good and drunk.'

Bia lifted her glass in agreement and Josie cocked her head. 'Hmm. There may be something in that.'

Chapter Twenty-Three

A week after the exhibition, which had marked the official end to the course, Josie was spending the last weekend before Christmas in her old flat with Bia, watching as Bia stood on a chair to straighten the gold star at the top of the Christmas tree. The tree was decorated mainly with silver, purple and, completely uncoordinatedly, red, this year, and Josie saw Bia had splashed out on some new decorations. She'd waited for Josie to get there to unpack the wooden swan, which Josie had placed on the tree in a rather ceremonial fashion. The flat looked almost the same as last year, with fairy lights around the window and on top of the fake fireplace, and tinsel hanging up over both bedroom doors.

Josie nodded back to the doorway of the flat as Bia got down from the chair. 'No mistletoe this year?'

Bia made a face. 'I had to take it down because Sarah and her boyfriend kept using it as an excuse to have loud make out sessions in the doorway under it and I kept getting stuck.' When Josie laughed, Bia sighed. 'Are you sure you don't want to move back in?' Sarah, Bia's replacement flatmate, had gone back home for Christmas already, so there was no danger of being heard.

'I don't have a job, sadly, and surely you can't kick her out anyway – doesn't she have a contract?'

Bia wrinkled her nose and said nothing, then glanced hopefully at the cupboard where the glasses lived. 'Wine?'

'Not until you pack, come on.' Josie practically dragged her to her bedroom, then sat on Bia's bed while Bia got out her stupidly large suitcase. Josie had already packed, given she'd come from Helen's and had only brought what she needed. She was kind of in between homes right now – she'd moved out of the Edinburgh flat, so most of her stuff was at Helen's, still packed. Still, she figured she'd think that through once she got back from Budapest, where she'd agreed to spend Christmas and New Year with Bia. They were due to fly first thing tomorrow.

Josie felt like she'd lived a rather nomadic life this past year – something she would have never thought herself capable of. It was almost impossible to believe a year had gone by. She supposed it always felt impossible, everyone said it every year, but particularly this year, given she'd gone from heartbroken in London to living in New York, to temping in Guildford and, finally, to playing at being a photographer in Edinburgh. After all that chaos it felt nice to be spending the last bit of the year in her old flat with Bia.

'What do you reckon?' Bia asked, turning around at her wardrobe and holding up a skimpy green dress.

Josie scrutinised it. 'I think you'll be freezing – it's *freezing* there right now.'

Bia pouted. 'It goes with my new hair though.' She ran her fingers through her hair – a coppery brunette as of two days ago – as if to prove the point.

Josie shook her head and crossed her legs to settle in. 'No. Put it away.'

Bia huffed but did just that, then flung several things from her wardrobe onto the floor behind her before doing the same thing with her drawers – a slightly unconventional method of packing. While she was doing that, Josie got her phone out and reread the email for the millionth time. When Bia looked over to her, she knew she wasn't exactly being subtle.

Bia, temporarily giving up on the packing, moved and plonked herself next to Josie so she could read over her shoulder, even though Josie had already read the email out loud to her – twice. 'Did you decide what you're going to do yet?' Bia asked.

Josie closed the email – it didn't change, no matter how many times she read it. 'No,' she said. After meeting Charlotte, she'd gone for it and applied for the internship in Africa, figuring that just applying meant nothing – she might not get selected, only one person did so the chances were low. But now she'd been offered the job. She'd actually *got* it after her interview a couple of days ago, and they'd given her a week to decide, given the placement started at the end of January. It all felt a bit much, making such a massive life decision in such a short frame of time.

'I really don't know,' Josie said, tapping her phone with her forefinger. 'I'm not sure I can do the whole living abroad thing – I always thought I'd be better off just staying in one place and settling.'

'You did it with New York,' Bia pointed out.

'Yes, but that was different – that was because of Oliver, because I had someone else there. It was a big deal, yes, but I knew I'd have one familiar thing. Besides,' she continued on a sigh, 'I proved my inability to hack it when I moved back to England, didn't I?'

'That was because of Oliver, not New York.' She prodded Josie in the ribs. 'Which you well know.'

Josie shook back her hair, looked at Bia with what she imagined was a sort of pained expression. 'It's just so ridiculous though, isn't it, going off to Botswana of all places for an *internship*?'

Bia shrugged. 'Doesn't seem so ridiculous to me, if you want to do wildlife photography. Surely you *need* to go somewhere like that.'

'Yes, but ... I don't know, isn't it the type of thing you're supposed to do at the beginning of your twenties? You know, go somewhere obscure to "find yourself" or whatever?'

Bia pursed her lips as she considered. 'Well,' she said slowly, 'maybe you're not going to "find yourself". Maybe you'd be going because you've finally found yourself.'

Josie stared at her, then broke into a smile. 'I quite like that.'

Bia grinned. 'Good, because I was worried it was going to sound ridiculous.'

Josie's phone rang in her hand, and Bia pushed off the bed to keep packing. Josie glanced down at the screen, and smiled as she answered. 'Hi, Aunty Helen. Sorry, I meant to text, I got here safely and we're just—'

'Hi, darling.' Helen's voice was sharper than usual and

Josie automatically tensed. 'Now, I don't want you to panic, but Memo's in hospital.'

'What?' Josie's spine turned rigid, and Bia turned to look at her, frowning. Josie's hand felt suddenly vice-like on the phone. 'Why? What's happened?'

'I'm . . .' Helen took a deep breath. 'She's had a heart attack – Grandad took her into A&E this evening, and they've admitted her.' Another breath, and this time it sounded like Helen was trying to choke back some emotion. That, above all, made Josie feel cold. 'She's ok – I've spoken to her on the phone and she's insisting she's fine, that everyone's making a big fuss, but they have to do some tests and keep her in for observation and, well, it's a heart attack. I'm on my way there now from Guildford. Dad just called me, but despite what Mum said he's a state so I said I'd call you.' *Dad. Mum. Not Grandad and Memo.* The slip made Josie's lips tremble.

'But . . . but she was at the exhibition,' Josie said, a little numbly. 'She was fine.' This made no sense. She'd seemed happy, healthy. Weren't you usually overweight or something when you had a heart attack? Wasn't there supposed to be some warning sign, something that meant they could prepare for this? She felt Bia sink back onto the bed next to her, rub her shoulder gently.

'I know, darling. I'm sorry.'

Josie shook her head. No. You only said *sorry* when someone was already dead. She moved her phone away slightly, checked the time. Not quite six p.m. yet. 'I'll get the train now,' she said to Helen. Surely there would still be one.

'Well, we won't be allowed in to see her overnight – we have to wait for visiting hours in the morning.'

'I still want to be there, with you and Grandad. What time is visitors' hours?'

'Nine a.m. tomorrow morning.'

'Well, we'll all go together then, from the cottage,' Josie said firmly.

'Alright, darling. I'll see you there. You call me if you get stuck.'

'I will do.' She got to her feet, needing to move, to do something immediately. *Heart attack*. The words reverberated round her brain and her throat tightened in response.

'And Josie? Try not to panic just yet.' Helen had control of her voice back, Josie noticed. 'Your grandad and I, we just wanted to let you know, just . . . just so that you know.' *Just in case*. The unsaid words hung in the space between them.

They said goodbye to one another, and when Josie hung up she just stared at Bia, who was still sitting on the bed. 'It's my grandmother,' she said.

'Oh, Josie.' Bia leapt to her feet.

'She's in hospital. She's had a heart attack. I have to go.'

'Shit, what?'

Josie didn't know if Bia was referring to the hospital or the leaving, but it didn't matter. She walked out of Bia's room to the living room, where she'd left her suitcase – thankfully she hadn't taken anything out yet. She quickly checked the train times on her phone – she could make the last train home if she left now; that way she could look after her grandad tonight and be there ready in the morning.

'Josie?'

Josie looked back at Bia. 'She's had a heart attack, B, I have to go. I have to get to the hospital.'

'I'll come with you,' Bia said immediately.

'No.' Josie took a step towards her, took her hands and squeezed them. 'We can't both miss the plane.'

'Shit, the plane.' Bia grimaced.

'Precisely. Look, you go. I'll ring the airline to see if I can catch a later flight if . . .' But she didn't want to finish that sentence, didn't want to say an 'if', because she wasn't sure what the end of it would be.

Bia shook her head. 'I can't let you go alone, Jose.'

'I won't be alone. I have Helen, and my grandad.' Where all this calm was coming from, Josie had no idea.

'But—'

'I forbid you to come, ok? Go to Budapest, start having fun. Meet some hot guy and get ready to introduce me.' She tried for a smile. 'You can't do anything anyway, and in all likelihood she'll be fine.' But despite her words, she was desperately trying to quash the gnawing in her belly that was hidden beneath her cool exterior.

She turned, grabbed her suitcase and wheeled it to the front door, closing the matter simply by the fact she was ready to leave, and Bia wasn't. She hugged Bia, who gripped her tightly back. 'Call me, please,' Bia whispered.

'I will,' Josie promised. 'It'll be fine,' she said again. And she really, really tried to believe it as she ran down the stairs, out of the building and towards the station.

Chapter Twenty-Four

After a thirty-minute drive from Josie's grandparents' place, Helen parked in the car park of the John Radcliffe hospital in Oxford and the three of them got out of her car, Josie reliving her teenage years by hopping out of the back seat. She and Helen had both stayed overnight with her grandad in her grandparents' cottage, Helen insisting that Josie slept in her old room while she took the sofa. Not that any of them had had much sleep, each of them waiting for a call, waiting to be told something worse had happened.

Josie hadn't cried yet. She felt like she'd been in a constant fight to control the tears from the start of the three-hour journey – a train then tube from Streatham to Marylebone, waiting at the station, a train to Oxford, and then a taxi. Even after she got to the cottage, she hadn't given in to the urge to cry and the result was that she was fluctuating between a calm stillness and an intense burning behind her eyes.

They arrived at five to nine, all of them having been up

since the early hours, filling the morning with small talk until it was late enough to leave the cottage. Now they walked in relative silence, across the car park and through the glass doors of the hospital. She was in the cardiology ward, according to Josie's grandad, so they followed signs through the hospital and ended up in a small waiting room.

The nurse at the reception desk there smiled, putting on big, round glasses when Helen asked where Cecelia Morgan was. She glanced briefly at something behind the desk. 'She's just through the doors to your right, then take the first left and you should see her. I can only let two of you through at a time though,' she added. 'Hospital rules, I'm afraid.' She slipped off those glasses, smiled benignly at them.

'You two go first,' said Helen. 'I need to pop to the loo anyway.'

So Josie followed her grandad through the doors, trying to keep her stride relaxed for his sake. They knew nothing, she reminded herself, and people didn't always die from a heart attack. *Some did, though,* a dark voice in the back of her mind said.

Memo was propped up against two cushions on the ward where they found her, the two beds either side of her also occupied. She smiled as Josie and her grandad approached, and though her face looked a little paler, and more lined than usual, her grey bob unnaturally unkempt, she seemed ok at first glance. In all honesty, her grandad looked worse than Memo, dark purple circles under his brown eyes, like he hadn't slept for days.

Memo held out a hand for her husband, who went to her side immediately, stroking back her hair in a tender gesture of the kind he never usually liked to perform in public. She held the other hand out to Josie, who went to her, making sure to keep her smile in place. Neither of her grandparents needed to see her cry right now.

'How are you?' croaked Josie's grandad.

'Oh, I'm fine, like I told you,' Memo said reassuringly. 'It's a bit odd, what with all these doctors and nurses prodding about, and they want to keep me here a while to *observe,* and really this gown does nothing for my complexion, but apart from that . . .' She smiled at each of them in turn, though Josie felt her own smile falter. Because the thing was, even if she was in a lot of pain, there was no way she would say anything – this was the woman who had once brushed off a broken arm as 'just a minor inconvenience when you're trying to do the shopping'.

'Have they said anything about how long you have to be here? Or what happens next?' Josie asked, glancing around to take in all the other patients here. It was quite a big room and had that peculiar smell – disinfectant mixed with hidden body odour – and Josie found it strange how a room so bright and white could feel so incredibly claustrophobic.

'Well, they drew me a diagram this morning, and said something about eighty-five-per-cent blockage, but, really, they just need to run some tests and scans and the like so they can tell us what to do.' This time when Memo smiled, it seemed a little more strained. Josie caught sight of a nurse across the other side of the room – blonde, with creamy skin, and younger than Josie – bending over one of the patients. She had the strongest urge to go up to her, to tell her, tell *someone,* that her grandmother wasn't usually like this – she wasn't old and sick, she still went for bike rides at the weekends, she baked terrible biscuits and hosted a book club every month, even though she failed to finish the damn book every single time. She was a person, not just an old, sick lady. She took a slow breath, returned her attention to her grandmother, and tried to join in the idle small talk – it was clear that Memo wanted to be distracted, that she didn't want to go over and over what had happened or what might be about to happen.

After thirty minutes, Josie went to switch with Helen, who jumped to her feet in the little cardiology waiting room, having been staring at a magazine on her lap. 'She seems ok,' Josie said before Helen could ask, and Helen let out a slow breath, nodded.

Then Helen looked Josie up and down. 'You should go back to the cottage,' she said. Josie shook her head, opened her mouth to protest, but Helen cut her off. 'Darling, I know there is absolutely no way I'm going to get your grandfather to leave once visiting hours are over, and there's no point in us all just waiting around here, so you should go home – one of us should, at least. I need to be here with him,' Helen added, when Josie started to try to say that Helen should go, in that case. Helen gave Josie's arm a little rub. 'You'll only be thirty minutes away, so you can come right back. You can take my car if you like.'

Josie hesitated. Thirty minutes seemed like a long time to her right then, and it felt wrong, leaving them here. But she was reading between the lines and knew Helen wanted the rest of the hour to be with her parents, and, in truth, Josie wanted the chance to break down a little herself, out of sight.

'Alright,' she agreed. 'But I'll get a taxi so you have the car if you need it, and please call me, the moment you know anything.'

Helen stroked her hair. 'Of course, darling.' She gave Josie some cash to cover the fare without even asking, and, given she was currently broke, Josie took it.

When she got out of the taxi at the cottage, for a moment Josie just stopped, her breath steaming out in front of her, and stared at her old home, looking at it properly in daylight. She hadn't noticed in the dark last night that it looked smaller, somehow, even than when she'd last been here a few years ago. It was a semi-detached cottage, flower pots surrounding the front door, the small front lawn neatly mowed, hanging baskets below the one second-floor window you could see from the front of the house and, she knew, the two at the back. All her grandad's work – he was the gardener. There was a black gate to the left of the cottage, which led to the back garden – that was the way she used to let herself in after school, on the rare occasion that one of them wasn't home, because they'd never bothered to lock the back door. They hadn't used to worry about that sort of thing back then, not out here in their little village.

Her parents had lived on the other side of the village – to get some semblance of independence, Josie supposed, so that they weren't living on top of her dad's parents. Close enough, though, that they could access their help when they needed it, and could pop round once a week or so. She imagined that had been the plan, anyway. As a teenager, she used to go and stare at her parents' old house sometimes on the sly, would take a detour on the way home from school, get off at a different bus stop and just go to look at it, to try and remember what it looked like on the inside, and to get a glimpse at the family who lived there now, their daughter too young for Josie to know. But despite that, it was this cottage that she stood outside now that featured most prominently in her memories of growing up.

She used the spare key – it was always in one of the plant pots, without fail – and let herself inside. She crossed through the living room and saw a photo from her exhibition – the one of Silverknowes Beach with a grey, moody skey, hanging in pride of place on the wall. Memo had bought it, telling her she wanted to be her first customer, and seeing it there almost made Josie break down. She took a breath and carried on walking through the house.

When she reached the kitchen she just stared out at the back garden – bigger than you'd imagine from the front of the house. There had been a swing set there when she was younger. Even before her parents died, her grandparents had put it in for her, but they'd got rid of it when she'd become a teenager and had declared she no longer used it, given it to another family in the village, she thought. Behind her was the kitchen table that they'd all had dinner round and she even had the whisper of memories of her parents being here too, the five of them squeezed round a table built for four.

She set to work on washing up the tea and breakfast crockery from this morning, then closed her eyes very

343

briefly, her hands in the soapy water. A heart attack. The words just wouldn't go away, even though she'd just seen her, had seen that she'd been awake, and talking. But this wasn't supposed to happen yet. She couldn't lose her grandmother – she wasn't ready. She was supposed to have a handle on her life before that happened, was supposed to be settled with a husband or something, supposed to have her own family to lean on. She wasn't ready yet to lose the parents who had raised her after her own died – she didn't know how to go through it again.

There was a knock at the front door and Josie switched off the tap, determinedly swallowing the lump in her throat even though her mouth was dry.

When she opened the door, she just stared, then blinked several times. She thought fleetingly that maybe she'd passed out from emotional exhaustion, that this was some weird dream.

He stared back at her from the doorstep, his gaze flickering over her face, as if trying to gauge her reaction. In the cold sunlight, his eyes looked a crisper, darker green. His face was paler than usual, like it was absorbing some of the cold, and there were pockets of shadows under those eyes. His expression was that carefully neutral one, like it was ready to go either way, depending on what she said to him in that moment. She glanced behind him, to the taxi that was now pulling away from the gravel driveway, then shook her head when she looked back to his face. 'Max. What are you doing here?' Because of all the people she might have expected to see, he had not been one of them.

One corner of his mouth crooked up – not really a

smile, more an expression of solidarity, of understanding. That damn burning behind her eyes started up again.

'I spoke to Bia. She thought you might be able to use a friend. But if you don't want me here, I can go. Just say the word, Josie.'

His eyes sought hers with such tenderness that she had to press her lips together to stop her bottom lip from trembling. And in that moment, despite the fact that she'd told him she never wanted to see him again, despite the fact that he *shouldn't* be the one person she wanted to see right now, somehow he was. So when he stepped towards her, a little tentatively, and rested a hand on her arm, she gave in and leaned against him, breathing in the smell of him and allowing his arms to come around her in comfort.

Chapter Twenty-Five

Josie sat curled on the sofa while Max made the tea, brought a mug over to her. She cupped her hands around it, craving the heat – it was toasty warm in the cottage, thanks to her grandparents' generous heating, but she still felt cold to her core. Max sat down next to her as she took a sip of milky tea.

'How are you doing?'

Josie sipped her tea again. 'I don't really know, in all honesty.' She glanced at him. 'Bia told you what happened?' It seemed so like Bia to have told him that she didn't even question it.

'She said your grandmother had a heart attack, yeah. I'm guessing she's still in hospital?'

'Yeah. My aunt Helen and my grandad are with her. I just got back from the hospital and she seems ok, she was up and talking like normal, but I'm not sure if she was putting it on. The doctors have apparently just said that she needs to be there for observation, and they're doing some scans or something today, but I don't know what's normal – how long is it usually after a heart attack, before you know if someone's going to be ok?'

'I don't know. I've never known anyone who's had one before.'

Josie shifted position so she was resting her head on his shoulder, feeling almost guilty that it felt so easy to do so. 'How are you here, Max?'

'Well, I got a train, then a taxi, being as how I can't drive at the moment, and—'

Josie shook her head. 'You know what I mean,' she said quietly.

He shrugged slightly, keeping the movement gentle so as not to dislodge her head from his shoulder. 'I told you – I spoke to Bia and—'

Josie sat up, stared at the side of his face until he met her gaze.

He sighed. 'I just wanted to be here for you, Josie.' He reached out to tuck a strand of hair behind her ear.

Josie sat very rigid. 'And Erin?'

He shook his head. 'I'm not with Erin. We were always just friends, really. I'm sorry for letting you think otherwise – I should have made that clearer.' Even as something in Josie loosened, ever so slightly, he took a breath. 'I'm really sorry, for how things have been with us – for all the mistakes I keep seeming to make. And if you want me to leave, I will. But it's your choice.' His lip quirked into half a smile. 'It'll be on your terms this time.'

She stared at him for a moment, and he didn't balk from her gaze. 'Stay,' she said with a little sigh, giving in and resting her head back on his shoulder. In that moment, she decided she didn't really care if she was being weak,

347

allowing him back in her life. The fact that she so easily slipped back into wanting him there told her that it was no use anyway – he had a place in her heart whether she liked it or not. And right now, she was too damn tired to process this on her own, so if he wanted to be here then she'd let him. Later, once her grandmother was out of the woods and she had the energy for it, they'd have a proper conversation.

Max rubbed his hand along her arm soothingly. 'How was your show?' he asked, and Josie half shrugged.

'Good,' she mumbled. She hesitated, then, because she would keep wondering if she didn't, said, 'I got flowers.'

The hand stroking her arm stopped briefly before continuing again. 'I hope you don't mind?'

She sighed. 'No. I don't mind.'

They were quiet for a moment, drinking their tea, then Max looked outside the window. 'It's actually a really pretty day.' Josie grunted a little. It didn't matter to her that it was blue, frosty and bright outside – why should it? Gently, he took her tea from her, set it down on the table to his right. 'Come on, I think we should go for a walk.'

She pulled back, frowned at him. 'What?'

'You can show me the village where you grew up, I'd like to see it.'

Josie pursed her lips. 'I don't really feel like it.'

'I know, but sitting around here waiting for something to happen or waiting for the test results or whatever is going to do you no good – from what I know of her I don't think your grandmother would like to think of you doing that.' There was enough truth in that – in both parts of what he'd said – to make her agree to it. She was sure

348

she could use the distraction, given there was no way she was going to be able to rest right now.

So, after changing into a slightly warmer outfit from her Budapest suitcase, they headed off out into the cold, the sun doing its best to dissolve last night's frost, and walked towards the village square. The Christmas lights were up, though not quite as majestic in daylight, and there was a huge Christmas tree in the square, decorated all the way to the very top, the colour scheme a little different every year, if it was still the same as when she was a teenager.

'I used to help decorate this tree,' Josie said, gesturing. 'Well, not *this* tree per se, but the tree they put up every year here.' Max looked down at her, his shoulders hunched against the cold. 'Everyone used to get involved,' she continued. 'And my grandparents were big on tradition. As were my parents,' she said with a little sad smile. She had a fleeting memory of her dad on a ladder, being one of the few to brave decorating the top of the tree while the rest of them looked up, the children playing with sparklers, the adults drinking mulled wine.

'How about you?' she asked as they walked towards the tree to stare at it.

'Me?'

'What were your Christmases like, growing up?'

'Well, my mum, being American, is very into Christmas.' His lips twitched as they started walking again, a few more people coming out now as the handful of shops started to open, supporting local businesses by doing what shopping they could here. 'She went big on the decorations – inside and out – on the house where we grew up in Bristol, though nothing could happen until the first of December. And we did everything – eggnog, Christmas cookies for neighbours, the lot.'

Josie smiled. 'Sounds nice.'

'It was. I think Mum tried to enforce Thanksgiving on us too, before I can remember it really – Dad said she gave up in the face of our Englishness, so she had to focus all her efforts on Christmas instead.'

Josie surprised herself by letting out a small laugh. 'And now? You still all spend it together?' She remembered last year, how he'd been on his way to see them all.

'I think that was my mum's plan, but they've only been living in America for a few years, so we'll see if it holds. When my parents sold the house I grew up in,' he added, 'me and my sister, being the adults we are, threw quite a strop – no more Christmases there.'

Josie chuckled, the action, tired as it was, warming her a little. 'Sounds like a reasonable—'

'Josie? That can't be you?' Josie frowned and looked towards the sound of the voice. A dark-haired woman wearing a red coat, heavily pregnant from the looks of things, was beaming at Josie as she stepped towards her from the local shop.

It took Josie a moment. The woman had shorter hair than she remembered and her face was rounder, smiling rather than scowling, and without the thick layer of makeup she'd worn without fail during their secondary school years. 'Beth?' asked Josie.

'Oh it *is* you,' Beth said, resting her gloved hands on the bump underneath the coat. 'I haven't seen you in so long! I see most of the others every year at least, but you don't usually come back for Christmas, do you?' She'd almost forgotten this, Josie thought, the fact that you couldn't go anywhere here without bumping into someone you knew.

'Not usually,' Josie admitted, trying hard to keep her smile in place. The thing was, even at school she and Beth hadn't been the best of friends, more like friends by association – they'd hung out in the same group and were from the same village, but really, they'd never done anything one-on-one unless by accident. Still, a wave of nostalgia hit Josie – she hardly ever saw anyone from school these days, the last few years proving more and more difficult to arrange regular meet-ups, what with them all dotted around and busy with their own lives, jobs, partners.

'You're back for Christmas then?' Josie asked, knowing the small talk was mandatory when you bumped into someone like this.

'Oh, my husband and I actually moved here about a year ago,' she said, her eyes twinkling a little as she said 'husband'. 'He's set up his own construction company, you know.'

'That's nice,' said Josie automatically, although having no clue who her husband was made the information fall a little flat.

'And we're expecting our second child,' said Beth, running her hands protectively over her stomach.

'Second,' repeated Josie, a little dumbfounded. 'Wow.' Memo had told her Beth was pregnant, Josie remembered vaguely, but hearing about it and seeing it were two different things.

'I know.' Beth beamed again, looking much happier than Josie had ever thought she could. 'Neil's at home with Lucy

351

at the moment, I just popped out to the shops for my mum.' She raised a shopping bag to emphasise the point. 'Anyway, it's so good to see you,' Beth continued, when Josie didn't immediately think of something to say. 'And we were all so sorry to hear about your grandmother – I really hope she'll be ok.'

Of course everyone would know, Josie thought. Though it didn't make her feel annoyed – in lots of ways it was nice that people knew, and cared. 'Thanks,' she said. 'Me too.'

Beth nodded sympathetically and Josie marvelled at how different she'd turned out to be. She didn't feel any different herself from the slightly shy, rule-following teenager she'd been – but maybe it was hard to tell, with yourself. 'And is this your husband?' Beth asked politely, indicating Max, who Josie realised she'd left standing there, watching the conversation in a slightly bemused manner.

The question reminded Josie so much of Beth at school – her direct way of speaking, which had so often got her into some kind of trouble – that she laughed a little. It was nice to know that some things, at least, did not change. 'This is Max,' she said. 'A friend.' For want of a better – or more complicated – word, anyway.

Beth glanced down at Josie's left hand, almost like a reflex, and seemed a little disappointed. 'Well, that's ok,' she said reassuringly, 'there's still time to meet someone.'

'Actually,' said Max, speaking for the first time, 'they're trying to stop you doing that now – they don't want you to meet anyone new after you turn thirty.'

Josie and Beth both frowned at him. 'They?' Beth asked.

'The government,' Max said promptly. 'They did some

research on it – turns out it's bad for our mental health, meeting someone so late in life, so they're introducing all these measures to encourage everyone to settle down in their twenties.' His face was deadly serious, even as Josie stared at him incredulously. 'It's supposed to increase social cohesion and lead to fewer mental health problems, especially depression, meaning we can divert funding elsewhere. It's all going back to Durkheim's original research on suicide, you know.'

Beth's frown only deepened, while Josie shook her head at him, amazed that he could say it all so convincingly. 'I didn't see that anywhere,' Beth said. 'Was it on the news?'

Josie elbowed Max hard enough in the ribs to make him wince. 'He's being an idiot, Beth, ignore him – it's his idea of a joke.'

Beth had a half smile on her face as her eyes flicked between Josie and Max, like she was trying to figure out the punchline. 'Anyway, we're doing gingerbread-making now at my mum's house – you should come! Unless you have plans right now?'

'Oh, I don't—'

But Max cut Josie off. 'That sounds amazing. I love gingerbread.' He settled the matter by taking Beth's shopping bag from her to carry, then gesturing for her to lead the way.

Josie remembered Beth's house from her teenage years, when she'd spent a few group sleepovers there, but she wasn't prepared for the wave of familiarity that hit her when she stepped into the warmth. They stripped off hats and coats and Beth's parents came out from the kitchen, both of them wearing matching aprons.

'Josie Morgan, that isn't you?' Beth's mum exclaimed, coming up to her with sparkling, delighted eyes.

'I bumped into her on the way,' Beth said. 'Thought we could use a hand.'

'Oh, we certainly could. We were so worried when we heard your grandmother was being taken to hospital last night, weren't we, Simon?' Beth's dad, completely bald now, nodded obediently. 'That's why you're here?' Josie nodded, getting the distinct impression that this was the reason she and Max had been brought along for ginger-bread-making at eleven in the morning. 'Well, try not to worry, distraction is the best thing, I'd say. Beth was right to bring you along.'

'Thanks, Mrs Cope.'

'Oh, come now, Josie, you're not a child anymore – you go ahead and call me Pippa.' She brought her into a hug, then pulled back, and to Josie's surprise those sparkling eyes looked a little tearful. 'You look so much like your mother, do you know that?' She'd been told that before, of course, mainly by Memo, but it always gave her a little jolt, hearing it. 'She used to do all this, you know,' said Pippa as she led them into the kitchen, where there were a few racks of gingerbread men already cooling, the kitchen pleasantly steamy, smelling of cinnamon, ginger and spices, flour on every surface as far as Josie could tell.

'The gingerbread, you mean?' Josie asked, glancing back at Max to check he was ok. He was already in conversation with Beth's dad, nodding along to something.

'Yes, that's right,' said Pippa. 'It's for the Christmas tree, you know – decorations, but we always put them on last minute, because obviously they all get eaten. And for the annual bake sale to raise money for the homeless – you remember that, of course?'

'Right. Yes, I do.' Her grandparents had taken her along as a child, though they'd stopped making her come as a teenager, when she insisted she'd be happier at home reading. They'd brought her something back from it every year though, and Josie felt a slight tightening in her stomach at the thought, at how she'd so adamantly refused to get involved in any of the traditions after her parents had gone. And there was another flash of memory now, one she'd forgotten or buried, of her mum in their orange-tiled kitchen, with trays and trays of gingerbread surrounding her. Her hair tied back in a bun, wearing a red polkadot apron covered in flour, telling Josie she was only allowed to sneak away the misshapen biscuits to eat. It was nice, she realised, to get that back, to know that she still had those memories tucked away somewhere, just waiting for the right trigger.

A few more helpers arrived over the course of the morning, and together they mixed the batter, rolled it out, cut into shapes, set the timer, and put the biscuits on racks to cool, like a little, very relaxed, assembly line. She was laughing along as Max got dough stuck all over his hand, as Beth's dad – Simon – nearly burned his fingers because he wouldn't listen to Pippa, as Pippa told her stories of people sneaking out at midnight to get the gingerbread off the tree because it was just so damn good. Pippa put Christmas songs on in the background, and though Josie exchanged a grin with Max at that, for once she didn't hate the sound of the music, rather found herself humming along with the tunes.

At lunchtime, Pippa offered around mulled wine — saying that it being a Monday was cancelled out by the fact it was Christmas time — though Josie declined and was given a peppermint tea instead. Max opted for the tea too, potentially just in solidarity. He was sitting down now, having insisted that being stood up around all these beautiful women was making him lightheaded, and making them all coo in response.

Pippa seemed to have an endless amount to talk about saved up inside her, but it never seemed forced, rather felt easy, almost soothing to listen to. 'A psychological thriller this time,' she was saying now, about Memo's book club. 'It's very exciting, I'd be surprised if Cecelia doesn't manage to finish *this* one at least.' Then, when someone brought up the last badminton game of the year, happening tonight at the local village gym, Pippa piped up with, 'Oh yes, Simon will be going to that, won't you, Simon?' Simon nodded. Josie glanced at Pippa from where she was hovering by the oven, with her oven gloves on, ready and waiting, and Pippa smiled. 'Your dad used to go to badminton all the time, you know. Malcolm was always on the winning team, wasn't he, Simon?' Another nod.

And so, instead of it making her sad and bringing up memories of the crash, instead of being haunted by the thought of her parents' lives here, Josie felt comforted by it all, being surrounded by people who knew them, who had memories of them, who knew that they'd been real people, just like they knew her grandparents.

It was thinking about her parents that made her realise she hadn't written her letter yet this year. She'd been planning to do it in Budapest, but obviously that wasn't going to happen now. Being here, around people who knew her parents, made her think that now was the perfect time to do it, so she slipped off the oven gloves, set them on the side. 'Pippa?' Pippa looked over to her from where she was showing Max precisely how she wanted the biscuits iced. 'I don't suppose I could borrow a piece of paper and a pen, could I?'

'Of course, love. Down the hall and to the left – Simon's study is in there.'

Josie brushed a hand over Max's shoulder as she left. 'I'll be back in a sec.' He smiled up at her and nodded, then went back to concentrating on the decorating, his tongue poked out in concentration. It made something flutter in her heart, seeing him there, willing to get involved in things like this, just to stay with her and make sure she was ok.

She found the study and helped herself to paper and pen, then sat down to write the letter.

Dear Mum and Dad,

I'm missing you, as always – maybe more so this year, because I'm back home. But it's nice, being here, and knowing I'm not the only one thinking of you. I should have come back here at Christmas before now, I know, but I hope you know it wasn't because I didn't want to think of you both on the day you died – it was because I was too scared to.

Memo is in hospital – maybe you already know that. I hope so much that she'll be ok, but whatever happens, I promise I'm going to try harder to come back here. I don't want to lose this place, or lose any part of you both.

Merry Christmas and lots of love,

Josie

Josie pressed her lips together, but it felt somehow cathartic, writing a slightly different letter, and she knew she wasn't about to cry. She found an envelope, sealed it, and tucked it inside her coat on the way back to the kitchen.

An hour or so later, most of the gingerbread was finished and Josie and Max took their leave. Pippa gave them a gingerbread man each, wrapped up so they could eat them later. Josie hugged Pippa and Beth, and when she promised Pippa that she'd come back to visit soon, she meant it.

Josie hadn't realised it had started to snow while they were inside, and she gasped slightly at the sight of a very thin layer covering the pavement. As they walked, tiny snowflakes nestled into Max's hair, like flecks of blue ice in the fire. There had been no word from Helen all morning – Josie had texted a few times, but knew that she'd hear if anything drastic happened, one way or another. Still, now she was outside, away from the distraction of people and baking, the fear was starting to creep back in.

She took Max's cool hand in hers and he squeezed it. Without telling him, she led him towards the same post box she used to run to as a child, the same one to which she'd delivered her letters to Santa. Because he already knew about it, she didn't have to explain when she slipped the letter inside, and this time neither of them said anything at all – it was enough for Josie just to have him with her. She couldn't help wondering, briefly, if this was the start of a new Christmas tradition – delivering her letter with Max, every year – and knew that the hope that squeezed her heart at the thought was potentially a dangerous thing. Now was not the time to think too much on that, though, so she said nothing as they turned and walked hand-in-hand back to the cottage.

Chapter Twenty-Six

Josie sat curled up on the sofa once more, toasty warm from the fire. There was something comforting, and a little mesmerising, about watching it eat away at the wood, sparking occasionally as it did so. Memo and Grandad's red stockings hung above the fireplace as part of the Christmas decorations – sticklers for tradition, they did one for each other every year. She knew they would have kept doing one for her too, if she'd ever spent Christmas here.

Max was in the kitchen, insisting that he fix her a hot drink and a snack, even though he had no idea how to work the appliances, so she caught the occasional hiss or grunt as he tried to figure it out. While he was busy, she rang Helen.

'Hello, darling.' Her voice was a little tired, but it didn't sound too panicked or emotional, which Josie took as a good sign.

'Hi. Have you heard anything – is there any update at all? Have you been allowed back in to see her?'

'Not yet – the afternoon visiting hours are about to stop, but she's been in for another scan, apparently. I don't think that's a bad thing though – it means they're looking after her, right?'

'I guess,' Josie said slowly, not liking the idea of Memo being wheeled around the hospital with no one to keep her company.

'There's talk of surgery, I think.'

'Surgery?' Josie's heart jolted. 'That doesn't sound good.'

'Well, I don't think it's necessarily bad if it helps her, and it's not right away – there's a waiting list, apparently.' There was a long sigh. 'Anyway, I don't think there's anything we can do for now, darling. It's a waiting game until we know any more.'

'Are you staying there? Maybe I should come back.'

'I don't think so, darling – you might as well get some rest there, then come back in the morning. I'm going to try and convince your grandad to leave too, if we're not allowed back in in the next hour. There's no point in us all sleeping overnight here.'

'Alright. But don't you need anything from the cottage? You or Grandad?'

'No, it's fine, I came back for a bit today actually – you were out.'

'Sorry,' Josie said immediately. 'I went for a walk with . . . Max is here.' She glanced into the kitchen, but he still seemed distracted.

'Is that so?' To Josie's surprise, Helen didn't ask who Max was – clearly he'd made a big enough impression at the time to lodge himself in Helen's memory.

'Umm, yes.' She wasn't sure how to explain exactly what

was going on between them, being as how she didn't really know herself.

'Well, I'm glad of it.'

Josie frowned. 'You are?'

'Yes, I'm glad you're not alone. Has he . . . talked to you about anything?'

Josie glanced at him again, then quickly away. 'Not yet,' she said, really hoping Helen wouldn't go into it now.

She only sighed. 'Your grandad is off trying to find one of the doctors, so I think I'd better go and find him, darling. He's not doing very well with the sitting and waiting.' No, Josie thought, he wouldn't be.

'Alright. You promise to call me the moment you hear anything?' A bit of optimism couldn't hurt, after all.

'I promise. I'll text you, let you know when we're on the way back.'

Josie hung up as Max came back with a plate of scrambled eggs on toast, which he handed over with a sort of apologetic grimace. 'You're not having any?' she asked as he sat down next to her.

'I'm not really hungry, but you should go ahead, eat.' He glanced at her plate. 'If you're generous enough to call that food.'

She ate in relative silence on the sofa, barely even tasting the food. But she ate it all, her stomach feeling better because of it, and set the plate aside. Next to her, Max was holding a mug, staring at the fire as she'd been doing. He looked just as tired as she felt, pale and drawn.

'So,' she said. 'No New York for Christmas this year then?'

He looked at her, and hesitated before speaking. 'No,

well, my parents are actually in the UK at the moment – we're having Christmas all together at my sister's flat – she even managed to get the day off work.'

Josie bit her lip. 'And now you're here with me instead.' Two days before Christmas, no less.

Max shook his head. 'Don't worry about it. I want to be here and they understand.' She wondered what, exactly, he'd told them when he'd left at the drop of a hat to come to her – his parents had never even met her, and she doubted her brief encounter with his sister in New York had left a positive impression.

Josie let her head drop companionably on his shoulder and felt a tingle across her scalp as he stroked her arm. Needing the warmth, the comfort, she tilted her face up so she could kiss him and he returned it, soft and gentle, in a way that made her sigh. He stared into her eyes as they broke away. He was the only person she'd ever met who had ever looked at her like that – in a way that made her feel like he was looking at *all* of her, and still liked everything about her.

'Josie,' he began, tucking her hair behind her ear. 'I know this isn't really the right time to say this . . .' She felt herself tense next to him, waiting for the blow. He ran his hand down the back of her neck, left it there. 'But I love you.' His lips did that small, half smile – the one she knew he truly meant.

Josie felt herself holding her breath as she searched his face, the words he'd spoken not quite feeling real. She reached her own hand up to rest it on his, and took a breath. 'Max—'

But before she could finish he closed the distance

between them and kissed her again softly. Like he knew that she wouldn't be able to say it back – not yet. Like he understood that she was worried she was just too emotional to mean anything she said right now, and was too scared that he might leave her again if she did say it. So when he pulled back, she just closed her eyes and rested her forehead against his.

'Will you stay with me tonight?' she asked instead.

His lips curved. 'Of course.'

She led him up the narrow staircase to her old bedroom, figuring the scandal of her sharing her single bed with a man would be overshadowed by more pressing matters at the moment. Her grandparents had barely touched her room since she'd moved out, all those years ago. They'd kept it hers even though she hardly ever used it, hadn't changed it into an office or a gym – it wasn't even a spare room, couldn't be, with all her things still there, her teenage posters still on the wall, a line of cuddly animals on the top of the bookshelf, the ones she'd kept resolutely all the way to eighteen.

Once they'd each used the bathroom, Josie slipped into her pyjamas, he stripped down to his boxers and they got into the single bed together, wrapped so tightly together that they fitted as easily as one person. Despite how tired she felt, her body was still tense and rigid, on high alert as she waited for a call. She didn't think she'd be able to stop it, was sure that she had another sleepless night ahead of her, but Max stroked her back in a slow, soothing rhythm and she felt herself start to drift. She fell asleep listening to the rhythm of his heart.

Sleep didn't hold her for long though. She woke in

the middle of the night and immediately reached for her phone. Two messages – one from Helen, one from Bia. She opened the one from Helen first. *Couldn't get your grandad to leave until we know more. Don't worry – no change. See you tomorrow morning. Xx*

She let out a slow breath, then read Bia's message. *Is Max there?*

He is, she typed back. *I hear you sent him.*

She got a message back immediately, making her wonder what Bia was doing, to still be awake at this time. *Sort of. Are you ok?*

Sort of.

I'm here when you need me, ok?

I know. In the meantime, have fun for the two of us, ok?

She got out of bed and slipped on an old dressing gown, not bothering to care how she looked. It was dark outside, but there was still a layer of bright white snow in the garden, and the moonlight bounced off it, taking away some of the blackness.

Her stomach was churning with anxiety again, so she left Max sleeping and tiptoed down the creaking stairs. She was sitting in front of the dying embers of the fire when he came down to join her, not long after. She glanced up. 'Sorry – did I wake you?'

'No,' he said softly. 'I've just got a bit of a headache is all.'

She got up and found some paracetamol in one of the kitchen drawers, handed it to him along with a glass of water. Then they went back to the sofa, sitting in companionable silence for a little while, Josie becoming so lost in thought, in worries over Memo, that when Max spoke, it made her jolt. 'Do you have any candles?'

She frowned. 'Probably, why?'

'Let's find them.' It didn't take long, knowing her grandparents as she did, and she came back with a selection, along with some matches. He took one – a big, cylinder candle – and twisted it in his hands. 'In some places, they have a tradition at Christmas where they light candles for lost loved ones.' He looked at her, the orange glow of the embers reflected in his eyes. She bit her lip, then nodded.

She lit two candles for her parents and placed them on top of the fireplace, watching the light flicker. The flame was so fragile – one single breath and it could be put out. He lit one himself, and placed it next to hers. They watched them for a moment, then Josie glanced at him. 'Who's it for?'

He hesitated. 'Someone who died, far too young.'

She remembered how he always seemed to get it, that weight you carry when you lose a loved one. 'I'm sorry,' she whispered, realising that she was apologising in the way everyone did when she told them about her parents. But there wasn't another word that was right, she realised now.

'That's ok.' He took her hand. 'I was angry for a while, but I'm not now.'

Josie closed her eyes to banish the burning. 'I just can't bear it,' she whispered. 'What if I'm lighting another one for my grandmother next year?'

He turned her to face him, ran his hands down her arms in a gentle caress. 'Do you remember what you told me at Laura's wedding, in September?'

She sniffed a little, thinking specifically of how she'd

366

yelled at him, how they'd ended up kissing. *I think it's best if we don't see each other again.* Apparently, she'd been wrong. 'I probably told you more than one thing.'

The corner of his mouth crooked up before his expression grew soft again. 'You said that you were glad of the sadness, that it meant you remembered your parents, that you loved them, and that it makes you who you are today.' She nodded, finding it slightly amazing that he'd remembered so exactly. 'So if the worst happens, you'll be sad, but that will mean you loved her and remember her.'

She pressed her lips to stop the sob, her control almost wavering, but nodded again. It was better, so much better, that he wasn't trying to offer false promises, to tell her it would be fine when no one could know that. And she believed what she'd said to him, even though, right now, it was hard to think there was a time when she'd feel like that again, if the worst were to happen.

Max cupped her face, lifted it so that her gaze met his. 'Josie,' he began slowly, and the look in his eye made her stomach twist painfully – she got the impression she was not going to like whatever was coming next. 'There's something I want to talk to you about.' He took a breath and her stomach started to churn again. 'Something I should have told you last December.'

Before she could answer, her phone rang and she jumped, then scrambled for it. Her heart picked up speed and her palms felt immediately cold and clammy. It was three in the morning – there was only one reason Helen could be calling her right now. She answered on the third ring.

'Darling, they're taking her in for surgery – they found

something, I don't know . . .' There was a gulp of air. 'She's going in for a triple bypass now, we haven't been allowed to see her first.' Max's face seemed to drain of colour to match how Josie felt. 'It's not . . . They haven't said it means anything terrible, just that it needs to be done but, well, it's open-heart surgery and she's been bumped up the waiting list and . . .'

'I'm on my way.'

Chapter Twenty-Seven

They got a taxi to the hospital. Helen was waiting outside for them, her face illuminated by the almost fluorescent lighting, her cheeks and nose pink from the cold, a blue and gold scarf wrapped tightly around her neck. Josie's throat was too tight to speak as Helen smiled tightly at them both, then gestured inside.

They followed, and Josie dimly noticed that they were going a different way to last time. Everything seemed too bright, too clinical, as they walked along the corridors. 'She's in surgery now,' Helen said, answering Josie's silent plea for information. 'I can't understand half the garbage the doctors are telling us and they refuse to stand still long enough to explain everything properly. She got bumped up the list for surgery is all I know – they needed to get her in there.'

Josie nodded, though she pressed her lips together to stop herself from speaking. *That doesn't sound good*, is what she wanted to say, but she refused to let herself say anything that would make anyone worry more. Helen led them into the ICU waiting room.

'It's where she'll be once she's out of surgery,' Helen explained, when she saw Josie looking around. Helen led them towards Josie's grandad, who was standing so still it looked unnatural, staring at the glass door. It had no distinguishable handle anywhere, but was presumably where they'd be going once Memo was out. *When,* Josie told herself. Not if.

Josie sank into the nearest chair, preparing herself for the wait. Her body felt rigid, like it was locking in place to keep her together, and her mind felt strangely blank. At some point she was aware of Max coming to sit next to her, rubbing her shoulders reassuringly.

After a while, Helen stepped outside to take a call, though Josie had no idea who she could be speaking to right now. Max did two separate coffee runs, and at one point brought back several bars of chocolate. No one touched them, though her grandad had given him a weak smile at the thought, from his position closest to the glass door. Later, Max went out and reappeared with more pain-killers and a bottle of water for himself, though adamantly refused to leave when Josie suggested he should. She was drifting in and out of bleary sleep, her head on his shoulder, when, towards nine in the morning, just as official visiting hours were starting, Helen jumped to her feet.

Josie sat up immediately, Max giving her hand a little squeeze, and watched as an older man, with grey hair and a slight bulge at his belly, walked towards them. He smiled at her grandad.

Smiled.

Josie's body started to melt, her hands began to tremble in relief, before the doctor even spoke to them.

Josie stood when he reached them, she, her grandad, Helen and Max forming a tight little semicircle. 'She's ok?' Josie demanded.

'Well, she's got a long recovery ahead of her,' the doctor said calmly, 'and we need to keep her here for a few more weeks, but she came through the surgery ok, which is a really positive sign. She's coming around now, if you'd like to see her.'

Josie's grandad nodded, swallowed, and stepped towards the glass door ahead of the doctor. Josie went to him, squeezed his arm, and he managed a weak smile back at her. He looked terrible, and she hoped she'd manage to get him home at some point soon to eat a proper meal and sleep. She glanced back at Max as they were led away by the doctor, through the door which he had to open with a special pass.

Max was rubbing his neck as if it were sore. 'You go ahead, I don't want to crowd her.'

Josie frowned. 'Are you ok?'

He smiled then, though it looked a little stiff. 'Yeah, it's just this headache. I'll go and get some fresh air and walk it off, and I'll pick up coffee for everyone on the way back.' Josie hesitated, biting her lip. 'Honestly, I'll be fine. Go and see your grandmother, and I'll be . . .'

Josie cocked her head. 'Outside?'

Max blinked, then nodded. 'Right. Outside.'

She hesitated again, unwilling to leave him if he was in pain, after what he'd just done for her, but the doctor was still waiting for them and she had to see Memo. She couldn't think of anything to say to him that encompassed what she felt in that moment, the fact that he'd stayed with her, had seemed to know exactly what she needed without being told. Instead, she nodded, and mouthed, 'Thank you.'

Helen, however, turned to walk back to Max, even though, in Josie's opinion, now was hardly the time to interrogate him on his intentions. Josie only caught a bit of their exchange before she turned the corner with the doctor and her grandad – Helen seemed to be saying something, and when Max shook his head, Helen rested a hand on his arm. Josie frowned slightly, but her attention was immediately diverted by the doctor, and when she looked over her shoulder, Max was walking away.

In the hospital room, Memo lay there, looking more fragile than Josie had ever seen her, her hair a little greasy on the white pillow, her hospital gown overly large on her thin body. Josie took a slow, steadying breath. The doctor had smiled, she reminded herself. Then Memo's eyelids fluttered open, as if she'd heard the footsteps, and one side of her mouth crooked into a smile. 'The way you're all looking at me, you'd think I was some kind of miracle,' she croaked, the words sounding like they hurt her to get out. Next to Josie, her grandad let out a sob, and crossed the room to take her hand as the doctor did some quick checks. Helen came in behind Josie and they went to the other side of the bed, Helen putting a hand on Josie's back as if to reassure them both. Though her aching facial muscles protested, Josie worked up a smile for Memo. She was standing firm on her oath not to cry in front of her – she didn't want to let her know how terrified they'd all been.

'How are you doing, Mum?' Helen asked softly.

'Oh peachy,' Memo said, her voice even hoarser the

second time, and a little slurred. 'You know, for someone who's just had their chest cut open.'

Josie blinked away the tears, but Memo still seemed to notice because she reached out, her movements stiff, and Josie took her hand, squeezing it as gently as she could. Outside, there was the sound of a commotion, someone being rushed through the corridor, reminding Josie just how close to death Memo had been.

'I've got a quote for you' Memo croaked.

Josie frowned. 'What?'

'Faith is believing in things when common sense tells you not to.'

The breath Josie let out was more like a sob. *'Miracle on 34th Street.'*

Memo grunted, her purpling eyelids fluttering closed again. 'Thought I'd have you there. You don't like those Christmas films.'

Because the tears were starting up again, Josie backed away, trying to swallow the lump in her throat. Her grandad, too, looked too grey and tired to say anything, but Helen came to the rescue, piping up, talking about the lack of good food in the hospital and downloading all the research she'd done on the best diet to start Memo on once she was out of hospital. Josie wasn't sure exactly how long had passed before she realised that Max still hadn't arrived. She cleared her throat and the other three looked at her. 'I'm just going to go and find Max,' she said quietly. 'Let him know we're all ok.' She nearly added *for now* at the end of the sentence but stopped herself in time.

'Oh, he came with you, did he?' Memo croaked, her breathing growing heavier. 'That's nice.'

He wasn't there when she got to the waiting room, so she headed out to the front of the hospital, in case he was still outside. It was cold and fresh, her breath misting in front of her, but there no sign of him there either. She was frowning when she retraced her steps. There were a few more people in the waiting room now, but none of them were Max.

Josie saw Helen coming out from ICU and crossed to her. 'I can't find him,' she said, trying to control the hint of panic that was creeping into her voice. Had he disappeared on her, again? Surely not, not after what he'd told her.

But there was a faint ringing in her ears, and her nerves felt jittery. *There's something I want to talk to you about.*

'Didn't he say he was going to get coffee?'

Josie nodded, but bit her lip. The other two times he'd been, he'd been back in moments, and she'd passed the coffee machine when she went to look for him outside.

'Maybe he went to the toilet,' Helen suggested, but she was frowning too.

Yes, thought Josie. That would be it. She hadn't checked there, obviously, but if she waited for him here then surely he'd be back any minute.

It was then that two more people came out from the ICU. One of them was the young, blonde nurse Josie had seen yesterday, and it was her who gestured towards Helen and Josie. Josie's heart stuttered and she looked at Helen, seeing the same panic reflected in her face. The woman the nurse was with, who was wearing blue scrubs, a look of authority marking her out as a doctor, nodded, then walked over to meet them.

'What is it?' Helen demanded.

'You came in with a man, is that right?' Her voice was far too even, far too calm.

'Which man?' Josie asked, even though she knew, somehow. She understood that this woman had come looking for them in particular, that she was talking about Max, and that whatever the reason, it wasn't good. A chill descended on her body.

'A Max Carter?' The way her voice turned gentle around his name made Josie want to hiss.

'Yes,' she said instead, almost snapping it out. 'Has there been some kind of accident?' Had he made a faux-pas, taken too many painkillers or something? She knew that was wrong, knew it was more than that from the way the doctor was looking at her with a practised face. But her body wouldn't believe her. It remained chilled, and numb.

The doctor glanced around the room. You wouldn't know it was Christmas Eve in here, Josie thought numbly. Nothing to mark the festive period, like celebrating a festive holiday was somehow wrong, when surrounded by so much death.

The doctor indicated one of the seats in the waiting room, and ushered Josie and Helen towards it. But Josie stayed standing. 'What happened?' she whispered. She needed to know. Needed to know *now*, needed this doctor to tell her.

'Can I just ask what your relationship is to Max?'

'I'm his . . .' Josie hesitated, trying to figure out the right word. There wasn't one, she realised. But the doctor didn't need to know the details right now. 'I'm his friend.'

The doctor nodded, and took a breath. 'I'm so sorry to tell you this, but he's passed away.'

Josie just stared at her. That couldn't be right. There'd been some kind of mistake, obviously. Max was *fine,* he'd been here five minutes ago. He'd made gingerbread with her yesterday, he'd come with her to the hospital. You didn't just keel over and die after that. Something cold seized her heart as she thought for a moment that they'd meant to come out to tell her that something was wrong with *Memo,* because they shared the first letter of their names, before realising that she was the only one who called her grandmother Memo.

'No,' she said firmly. Her voice was sure, confident. She even looked around the room again – ready for Max to come up to them now, to make some joke that only he would understand about the mistaken identity.

'What happened?' Helen whispered to the doctor, and Josie jolted, turning her attention to Helen. *Nothing happened,* she wanted to tell Helen, because there was no way they were talking about Max.

'He had a brain aneurysm. There was nothing we could do. He collapsed here, in the waiting room, but by the time we got him to—'

'No,' Josie repeated. But her voice sounded lumpy and wrong now.

The doctor looked directly at Josie now. 'He would probably have got a bad headache at some point in the last few hours, but he would likely have thought nothing of it, because of the tumour.'

Headache. That one thing, that one word, made everything feel distant. Her ears were ringing and the words the doctor was saying faded to nothing. This wasn't real. It wasn't real, it was some horrible nightmare – maybe she was still back at the cottage, maybe she'd never woken and was still asleep in Max's arms right now.

Helen's grip was vicelike on Josie's arm. Josie didn't notice that the doctor had walked away to give them space until she saw her on the other side of the room. She blinked, trying to bring the world back into focus as Helen steered her to a chair, made her sit down.

'Brain tumour?' Josie repeated thickly. It didn't make sense; it wouldn't fit together in Josie's mind, like pieces of a puzzle that you couldn't jam together no matter how hard you tried.

Helen was crying. *Helen* was crying. Josie watched the tears fall onto the top of her lip, watched her wipe them away with her sleeve. Those tears didn't look real, either. 'He had cancer, Josie,' Helen said, her voice choked.

'No, he didn't.' Because Josie would have known, wouldn't she? That wasn't the type of thing you just didn't tell someone.

'It was terminal. A brain tumour. He was expecting to . . .'

'No.' But the pressure behind her eyes, in her throat, was building. 'He would have told me.'

'I think he was going to,' she said softly.

'How do you know this?' Josie demanded.

'He told me,' Helen said, her voice hitching.

Josie shook her head. That didn't make sense. Why would he tell Helen, and not her? 'But they said aneurysm.' It was all she could do – focus on the straight facts, on what had been explicitly said. Because it didn't make sense. Where was he now? Where *was* he? If he was really dead, then why were they telling her out here? Why not take her to him, let her see for herself?

'I know. And he couldn't have known about that, from what the doctor said – they come about very suddenly. So I don't think he was expecting it to happen . . . now.' Josie was shaking her head, over and over, the room swirling out of focus again. 'Look,' said Helen, clearly making an effort to sound more like her usual self, for whatever good that would do, 'stay here, I'll go and find out the details.' Josie looked at her. She didn't want details. The details didn't matter, not if it was true.

But instead, she just said, 'Ok.' Her voice sounded numb, cold and empty. It didn't sound like hers, just as her body, in that moment, didn't feel as if it belonged to her.

'And we need to call . . .' Helen looked at Josie, shook her head, blinked back tears. 'I'll sort it. I'll come back. This isn't . . .' But she didn't finish. She just squeezed Josie's shoulder so hard that it hurt, though Josie was grateful for that, because then all she had to do was focus on that one part of her, on the dull pain there, instead of on how she felt like she was being ripped apart, like parts of her body were attacking one another.

It wasn't real. It was all she could think as she watched Helen at the desk, speaking to the receptionist, then searching for something in her handbag. Max wasn't dead. Her grandmother . . . her *grandmother* had been the one who was ill, not Max. Surely he couldn't have had a tumour, couldn't have hidden that from her. How had this happened in a matter of moments? She felt she should be crying, screaming, shouting, demanding answers, but instead her body seemed to be slowly shutting down the more she thought about it, so that she couldn't so much as blink.

When Helen came back to her, Josie saw that she was clutching something in her right hand. A letter, Josie noticed dimly.

Helen sat down next to her, rested one hand on her shoulder, and lifted the letter in another. 'He gave me this to give to you,' she said softly. Josie shook her head, but she took it when Helen pressed it on her, only noticing when she saw the paper shaking that her hand was trembling. She set it down in her lap, stared at it. Her name was on the front, in Max's handwriting. *Josie.*

Josie looked back at Helen, shook her head. 'I don't understand.'

Helen's eyes were wet, her chin was wobbling. 'He rang me,' she said softly. 'To explain everything, and to ask my advice.' She took a breath. 'I suggested waiting until after Memo got a bit better, because I was worried how you'd handle it, but I . . .' She hitched in a breath. 'I'm so sorry, my darling.'

Josie wished she wouldn't say it. *I'm sorry.* She knew first-hand why people said that, what it meant.

'Can I get you anything?' Helen asked.

'Water,' Josie croaked, not because she wanted it but because she wanted to be alone right now. Helen nodded and got to her feet. Josie watched her cross the waiting room, then looked back at the letter in her hand. But she didn't open it. Because if she opened it, she knew, then that would make it real.

Chapter Twenty-Eight

Three Days Earlier

Max stared down at the page, wondering whether to screw the paper up for the fifth time and try again. Nothing he'd written sounded right. Because how the fuck were you supposed to explain something like this in a letter?

He took a sip of his coffee, strong and black the way he liked it, and stared out at the Bristol street below from where he was perched at the windowsill in his sister's tiny flat. His parents had chosen to stay in a hotel, thank God, after deciding to come to England for what would be, he was sure, his last Christmas. He took a breath, held it, then blew it out again. He'd come to terms with that, and he'd had longer than the doctors had initially thought to do so. Six months, they'd given him, when he'd found out just over a year ago. Right before he'd met the girl he'd fallen in love with, the girl who would make him wish, more than anything, that he had just a bit more time.

He looked over his shoulder to see Chloe shuffling into

the room, her dark eyes bleary. She always looked like this in the morning – softer, somehow, when she first woke up, as if it took her a while to build up that front she so often hid behind. She glanced down at the crumpled papers on the floor.

'How's the letter faring?' she croaked. His heart gave a painful tug. His baby sister. She was the one he was most worried about leaving, because he knew that she had tried the hardest to keep it together, to keep things normal, since he'd got his diagnosis. He was sure she'd go on like that until the end, because she knew it was what he needed, no matter what it cost her.

'I'm not sure. I'm not very good at letters.'

She grunted, shuffled to the adjoining kitchen to switch the kettle on. 'Just write what's in the heart or . . . something like that.'

He tried for a cocky smile, neither of them wanting to break in front of the other. 'Thanks, o wise one.' He glanced towards her bedroom. 'Liam still asleep?'

She yawned, nodded. 'Nothing can wake that man, I tell you. This one time—'

Max held up a hand. 'If this is something to do with sex, then I'm telling you now, Chlo, I don't want to hear it.' She grinned, just the smell of coffee seeming to wake her up. Against all the odds, Chloe and Liam had actually hit it off, and had managed to make the long-distance thing work. Liam had proposed a few weeks ago, and Chloe was rushing to have the wedding in February. She said it was because she wanted to just get on with it, claiming haughtily that she didn't want to live in sin when their mum questioned her, but Max knew the real reason. He knew it was also why Liam had proposed so soon. After they'd been together a few months, Chloe had told Liam about the tumour. He knew that his friend and his sister wanted him to be there at the wedding, and they were hoping that February would cut it.

He was grateful when his phone beeped on the windowsill next to him. A text from Erin. She still did a lot, just to check in. She knew, just like his family did, that it was only a matter of months, but instead of stepping back and keeping her distance, she was making sure that he knew she was there, as a friend, whenever he wanted to talk.

When he'd got back to the UK, he'd stayed with her for a few weeks in Edinburgh, but just as friends. He hadn't known, then, if the treatment he'd been getting in New York at the beginning of the year, the new clinical trial that his mum had insisted he at least try, would work, and Erin had been choosing to believe that it would, to believe that having a long-term relationship with him would be an option. But even before he'd found out the opposite, he'd known it wasn't right to get back with her. And she'd actually accepted that. Had proven herself to be a total legend of a friend, trying to make him come out and do things. She'd invited him to the wedding, even though he hadn't actually decided to go until he'd seen Josie's photo of the castle on her Instagram account, and known she'd be there.

He stared down at the paper again. He should have told her then, in September. But seeing her had made him feel light again, and it had been easier to let her assume that Erin was the problem, not to put the weight on that weekend, at her friend's wedding. He'd hoped that maybe it was one-sided – just because he hadn't been able to shake her, didn't automatically mean that she felt the same. And if she wasn't that attached to him, then there was only so much he could hurt her. But it was wrong, to hope for that, to think that he was protecting her by not telling her. That feisty little friend of hers had told him as much when she'd sent him an angry Facebook message after she'd caught them kissing. He'd thought it safer not to reply to her, but it had made him think.

He read the letter one more time, grunting his thanks when Chloe put a second coffee down in front of him. Deciding it would have to do, he picked up his phone and dialled.

The voice that answered was somehow bouncy. 'Hello?'

'Hi, is that Bia?'

'It is.' The voice turned suspicious. 'Who is this?'

'Max Carter. Look, I know this is—'

'Max? As in Josie's Max?' *Josie's Max.* Not right, and wouldn't ever be true.

'Yes,' he said, knowing what she meant. 'Look—'

'How did you get this number?'

He huffed out an impatient breath, glanced up to where Chloe was watching him, eyebrows raised. 'From John, who got it off Laura. Now will you just let me finish? I have a favour to ask you.'

'Well, I won't be doing *you* any favours,' she said primly.

Sometimes, blunt was best. 'Bia,' he said flatly, 'I'm dying.' He couldn't, or wouldn't, look at Chloe when he said it.

There was a pause at the other end of the phone. Then, 'What? What do you mean?'

'I mean what I said,' Max said evenly. He was more used to saying it now – what did it mean, when you came to accept those two words, *I'm dying,* as just a natural part of conversation?

'No,' she said. 'I mean, God. I'm sorry. What . . . For how long . . . Does Josie know?'

'No, and that's where I need the help,' Max said. 'I need to get a letter to her.'

'A letter? You want to tell her that you're *dying* in a letter? You can't do that, it'll kill her.' *Jesus.*

'There's nothing else I can do now,' he said quietly, noting the slight pleading edge that had come into his voice. 'I know I shouldn't have got into it with her.'

There was the sound of chattering in the background at Bia's end of the phone, followed by Bia swearing. 'No,' she said. 'You shouldn't have.' She sighed. 'No, look, I'm sorry, ok? It's just . . .' And then Bia told him, about Josie's grandmother, about the fact that she was there alone. Two minutes later, he'd convinced Bia to give him the address, along with Josie's aunt Helen's number – he didn't want to risk getting there only to not get past that barrier. As soon as they hung up, he grabbed the letter from the windowsill and strode to the spare room where he'd been staying for the last few months. Chloe stumbled after him.

'What are you doing?' she demanded.

He didn't even glance back at her. 'I have to go, Chlo. I have to see her again.' He shook his head at himself. 'I have to at least try to explain it – I owe her that, I owe her more than a letter.'

He shoved a few things in a bag, then turned to see her standing in the doorway, hugging her arms around her and looking impossibly young in that moment. Her lips were trembling. He crossed the room, put his arms around her and felt his own throat tighten. 'I'll be back,' he whispered into her hair, even knowing that there was only so long he could keep telling her that. 'But I have to see her before I . . .'

Chloe pulled back, dashed a tear away under her eye. She nodded. 'Go.' She took a shaky breath. 'Tell her – if she doesn't kick you out before you explain, that is – that if she ever wants to look me up, now or in the future, then she's welcome to.' She tilted her head and a small smile played around her lips. 'I'd like to get to know that girl of yours.'

He walked to the front door of the flat, Chloe following him. *Girl of yours.* And she was, Max knew, even if she had no idea just how much she'd captured his heart. Captured it when it was already too late, when he had no right to take her heart the way she'd taken his. He'd tried to stop it, but it was too late now, too late to stop the fall, so all that was left was to make the best possible decision in this moment, and not be a coward about it.

He turned back to Chloe. 'Fill Mum and Dad in, will you?' They'd only worry and try to stop him going if he told them himself. Chloe nodded. He brought her in for one last hug and felt her chest sob against him. He kissed the top of her head. 'I love you, you know.'

'I know that,' she whispered. 'I always will.' She pulled back, blinked up at him. 'Now, go get the girl before it's too late.'

Chapter Twenty-Nine

Josie stared at her name on the envelope. Her heart was thumping a steady rhythm of *not real, not real, not real.* Helen was still the other side of the room, getting her water. Around her, there was the humming of various noises, all blended in together – the whirring of a machine, the sound of footsteps, the murmur of conversation.

Not real, not real, not real.

She lifted the letter, the paper feeling soft and fragile in her fingers.

Not real, not real, not real.

With aching slowness, she opened the envelope, her body moving as if without her mind's instruction. Then, unable to put it off any longer, she read.

Josie,
I hope I get the chance to tell you all this in person, but we both know first-hand that life doesn't always play out the way we want it to. I don't want to ruin your Christmas by telling you this now, but I want to make sure I don't leave

you without an explanation. So this is for after Christmas, just in case.

When I first met you last December, I'd just found out that I had terminal cancer. An inoperable brain tumour. They couldn't give me an exact date of when my time would be up, just that it would be, at some point, possibly in as little as six months. I was on my way to New York to see my parents, yes, but also because, being the optimistic doctors that they are, they wanted me to go into a clinical trial there, which was supposed to increase both my quality and length of life. I didn't mean to get close to you. I certainly didn't mean to fall in love with you — knowing that there could never be any future between us. And as I got to know you, I hated the idea of you suffering too — I didn't, and don't, want to give you another person to grieve.

That's why I left you that way last year — I let myself have those few days with you, but I thought it would be better for both of us to cut ties. I never thought I'd see you again, but I'm so happy that our paths were destined to intertwine. I've been selfish, allowing myself to see you, coming to the wedding just to be near you, because having you in my life, even just as a small part of it, has made this last year more bearable and has given me reason to hope, when I thought that was lost. I've been trying to work up the courage to tell you this all year.

The treatments haven't worked and I've come to accept that there is no way out of this for me — I'm nearing the end. But you've given me moments of joy in this last year, where otherwise I would have had only darkness, and I want you to know how much that means to me, how grateful I am to you. I nearly gave up twice in the last year — once last December and once this September, and both times you gave me a spark of something back.

The doctors have told me that things will get worse from here. There might be some personality changes, I'm going to get more noticeably ill, and soon I won't be able to hide it from anyone. I don't want you to see that. I want you to remember me as you've known me, rather than as someone ill, confused and dying. It's selfish, and it's another reason I've put off this moment – hoping that I would go quickly and quietly, without you having to be a part of it. If that happens, then know that that's the way I would have wanted it.

I'm so sorry, Josie. I'm sorry that I put you through this, I'm sorry that I couldn't stay away from you.

But I'm not sorry for loving you. I could never be sorry for that, and I hope you're not sorry for it either.

We might not have had for ever together, but I meant what I said last year – I will be forever glad I met you. I love you, Josie, and I hope your life is full of amazing, unexpected, brilliant things that shine just as brightly as you do. Know that if I had the chance, I'd choose to spend my life with you.

Forever yours,
Max.

Helen was there when Josie put the letter down in her lap and looked up. The hot tears that were running down her cheeks were silent. 'He didn't say goodbye,' she said numbly.

'Oh, darling. I think he's been trying to say goodbye to you since he met you.'

With that, Josie curled into a ball on the chair, and, finally, she wept.

Part Five: January

Chapter Thirty

Josie stood in the background of the small crowd that had gathered in Bristol, near to where Max grew up, her black heels sinking into the wet grass, her breath misting in front of her. The tears stung her eyes, but the cold breeze dried them on her face as they fell, as she listened to the minister's words about how much he would be missed, about what he meant to everyone here, how he had been taken from this world tragically young.

Tragically young. At that, Josie's breath hitched and she felt Bia's hand tighten on hers to her left, felt Helen step in a little closer, rest her hand on her shoulder on her right. Memo couldn't be here, though she'd wanted to be, because she was still recovering in hospital. A blast of hot pain sliced through Josie. She shouldn't be here, either. *He* shouldn't be here, not in that coffin, not about to be put in the ground where no one could see him. Where she couldn't see that almost smile or take his hand or lay her head on his shoulder. It wasn't right. It wasn't *fair*. It wasn't fair that he had lost his life, and that he had been

391

taken from her. It wasn't fair that he hadn't told her about it, that he'd known, right from the beginning, that they'd never have a future together. She took a deep, slow breath, trying to let go of the feeling. It wasn't right, to be mad at him. Not on this day.

After the funeral ended and people started to disperse, Josie caught sight of Erin. Erin who had not, apparently, been Max's girlfriend – or at least not this past year. Erin whose blue eyes were now bloodshot, as she looked over to Josie. Her face was pale, lips pressed tightly together as if to keep the emotion in. But she smiled, a trembling, uncertain smile, and moved towards Josie, who, for a moment, considered backing away, turning and bolting. Because she wasn't sure if she could face it, wasn't sure if she was ready to talk to someone who knew him, to make it a real and undeniable fact.

Next to her, Bia gripped more tightly, but Josie shook her head and whispered, 'It's alright. I'll find you in a bit, ok?'

Bia hesitated and Helen murmured, 'Are you sure, darling?' just as Erin came to a stop in front of them, her sleek, blonde hair pulled back into a neat bun.

Josie nodded, and the two of them left without further argument. She was glad of it – this moment, it belonged to people who knew Max, who really *knew* him. 'How are you doing?' Josie asked softly.

Erin shrugged. 'Oh, you know.'

They looked at each other, then Josie shook her head. 'I'm trying to think of the right thing to say and I just can't.'

'I don't think there *is* a right thing to say.' Tears sparked in Erin's eyes and Josie felt her own tears match them.

They both looked away, and Josie imagined that Erin, too, was trying to get herself together. 'I loved him so much,' Erin breathed, looking down at the grass, where her heels were sinking slightly into the soft ground.

Josie's throat tightened so it was almost painful. 'Me, too.'

Erin nodded, met Josie's gaze once more. 'I know. I saw it, in Edinburgh.'

Josie hesitated. 'I didn't mean to . . . I thought you were together, then.'

'I know,' Erin said again. 'We weren't,' she added. 'But I guess you've figured that out by now. So when I say I loved him, I just mean . . .'

'You don't have to explain,' Josie whispered. She knew how Erin felt. If Erin had seen how Josie felt about Max then the reverse was true too – they'd loved each other, and the fact that had changed from romantic love didn't change anything.

'He let you think it though,' Erin said quietly. 'I knew what he was doing, trying to hide behind me. And I tried to get him to tell you the truth, but he . . . I don't think he could face it, then. Could face how it would change the way you might look at him.'

Erin and Max, standing outside the coffee shop in Edinburgh, Josie remembered with a jolt to her heart.

Did you tell her?

Give me a break, Erin, it's not that easy.

Josie closed her eyes against the burning there, and when she opened them, she allowed a few tears to fall. Erin stepped forward, took Josie's hand in one of her own, and squeezed. 'I'm sorry that he didn't tell you sooner.'

Something bitter wanted to swell in her at that, at the

fact he'd kept it from her, had allowed her to fall in love with him. But there was a part fighting that, something that she knew would be there after the grief settled, after she fought her way through the impossibility of these few weeks – and that part was glad of it. Glad that she'd met him, glad that she'd known him, had fallen for him. If he'd told her when he'd first met her, when he was still reeling from the news, that day she'd run into him on her bike, would she have allowed herself to fall for him? She doubted it. She wouldn't have had the courage. And then she would have missed out on something that had the power to change her life.

So she shook her head now at Erin. 'I know why he didn't.' It wasn't quite forgiveness – that would have to come later. But understanding, that was a start.

Erin looked over Josie's shoulder and Josie turned to see Max's sister, the one she'd met in New York – Chloe. She started towards Josie and Erin, looking nothing like Max, with short dark hair that framed an attractive face. But when she smiled through her tears as she reached them, Josie saw it there, the same softening expression that Max had. It made something hard rise up in her throat and for a moment she struggled to breathe. In the distance, birds were chirping, unaware of what had happened here, and the sound of a far-off car horn seemed to punch through Josie, a harsh reminder that the world was still out there, still carrying on.

Erin and Chloe smiled at each other, some sort of understanding passing there. 'I'll see you around, Josie,' Erin said. She let her hand trail over Josie's shoulder in a farewell gesture.

'I hope so,' Josie said, and meant it.

Chloe watched Erin walk away for a moment, then looked at Josie. 'I'm so glad you came.'

His *sister*, Josie thought. What did she say to his sister – his baby sister, as he'd once told her? 'I'm so sorry that—'

But Chloe shook her head, like she knew what Josie was going to say. That she was sorry Max had been with her, in his final moments. That she was sorry she'd taken him away from them – even though she *wasn't* sorry, because she selfishly wanted those moments to herself. Wanted them, and moments she would now never get. 'He would have wanted to be with you,' Chloe said softly. She glanced over her shoulder, beckoned someone over, then took a breath and squared her shoulders as she faced Josie again.

Two more people were now coming to join them. A woman with the same auburn hair as Max and a man who had Chloe's face, though a slightly wider framed body. Max's parents. Josie took a shaky breath.

'Josie,' Chloe said, 'this is Valerie and Roger. My parents.'

Josie felt her chin wobble as she looked into Valerie's eyes. Max's eyes, though with a slightly softer edge. 'I'm so sorry for your loss,' she said, her voice not as steady as she was aiming for.

Valerie shook her head, stepped up to Josie and took both her hands in hers. 'Our loss,' she said firmly, with the hint of an American accent. 'If you're Max's girl, then it's our loss.'

Josie nodded, and felt the tears, never far away, start up again.

She talked to Max's parents for as long as they all could bear, and promised to stay in touch. Chloe hovered for a moment longer when Roger and Valerie left, ready to accept more condolences from friends and family. 'So,' she said. 'How's the photography?'

'Oh.' Josie lifted a hand to tuck her hair behind her ear. 'Alright, I guess. I did a course.' It felt wrong to be talking about something normal, something mundane, in the face of what had happened.

Chloe angled her head, the action almost birdlike. 'I know. Max told me.'

That made Josie smile, just a little. 'He did?'

She nodded. 'He also told me about Botswana. Geoffrey,' she added at Josie's questioning look. 'My brother was good at getting information out of people.' The smile on her face shook, but held. Someone called Chloe's name – a tall, muscular man with deeply tanned skin – and Chloe nodded over her shoulder. 'I have to go and do the rounds, so to speak.' She blew out a breath, shook her head, and tears glistened in her brown eyes. 'Sorry,' she breathed, and Josie shook her head.

'I'll let you go,' Josie murmured, noticing Bia already on her way over, like she'd noticed that Josie was about to be left alone. Like she knew that she'd break if she was.

Chloe grabbed her hand before Josie could leave. 'What I meant to say is, and I don't know if this will make it better or worse, but he hoped you'd take it.'

Josie frowned. 'What?'

'Botswana,' Chloe said. 'He hoped you'd take the job there.' She paused, then smiled, her gaze going distant for a moment. When she looked back at Josie, her eyes were brighter. 'He thought it might make you realise how much you shine.'

Part Six: December Again

Chapter Thirty-One

Josie sat on the sand around the fire, her knees to her chest and arms around her legs. The fire was sparking as it heated up, getting ready to barbeque – or brai, as they called it here – the boerewors. To her right, Charlotte was chatting to one of the rangers, and on her other side the two helicopter pilots were laughing at something on one of their phones. For a moment, though, she was content just to sit, to let the sounds of the people around her mix in with the sounds of the night birds just beginning to stir, as she watched the African sun set. The colours were incredible here, glowing orange that seemed like it was scorching the sky, fading to pink like it was being slowly extinguished. They'd picked a point tonight, for their Christmas brai, higher up than usual – though still in the safety of the park where no curious leopards could wander in – so they could watch it right until the last moment.

She took a sip of her ice-cold Savanna, allowed it to slide down her throat, grateful for the relief it brought after the intense heat of the day. Charlotte caught her eye and smiled, cocking her head as if to check Josie was ok. Josie smiled and nodded, and Charlotte went back to her conversation.

Josie stretched out her arms behind her. She was browner, slimmer and fitter than she'd been last year, but despite that it was hard to believe she'd been in Botswana for nearly a year now. Bia and Laura had both been out to visit her, and Helen kept threatening to do so. Josie had been worried about leaving Memo so soon after heart surgery, but after a three-month recovery, Memo had proven her determination and, by all accounts, was pretty much back to normal. The internship was nearing an end, but she had another month to figure out the next step, and she wasn't worried. She'd found what she loved doing – even though she still had to pinch herself that she was doing it here, of all places – and she knew she'd find something similar, in time. She'd started to put the feelers out, and she knew Charlotte would give her a good reference. But some of the best things, as she knew first-hand, came from the gaps in life, so if she ended up with nothing for a few months then it wasn't the end of the world.

One of the helipilots moved away from the group, calling his goodbyes, and Josie set her Savanna down, then got to her feet and jogged to catch up with him, her t-shirt sticking to her back with sweat. 'Off to the airport?' she asked.

'Yeah, some guests coming in and I've got to pick up some supplies.'

She linked her arm through his, walked alongside him. 'Can I ask you a favour?'

400

He grinned. 'Anything for you, gorgeous.'

'Can you put some letters in the post for me over there?'

He nodded, held his hand out for the two letters she slipped out of her shorts' pocket. They were a little crinkled, but she didn't think the recipients would mind, given the circumstances. He frowned as she handed them over. 'You've forgotten the addresses, Jo.' She didn't know why, but everyone here insisted on shortening her name as much as possible.

'I know. They don't need them.' She shook her head when he raised his eyebrows. 'Don't ask.'

'Alright then.' And he set off, heading towards his helicopter and back to civilisation for a few hours. She smiled a little to herself, standing still for a minute to look out at the setting sun. Who would have thought that this would be how she was fulfilling her Christmas tradition this year? With one difference now, of course – two letters in place of one, three people forever in her heart instead of two.

The sky was turning orange – the sunsets here were like nothing else, surrounded by the African wildlife. She stayed there a moment longer, breathing in the warm air, tilted her tanned face to the sky, just a little, and smiled, just in case anyone was watching. Then she flipped her ponytail over her shoulder, and went back to the others to welcome in Christmas.

Dear Mum and Dad,

I'm writing to you from Africa this year, would you believe it, and it's Christmas again already. Things here have been busy, hectic and amazing. I know you'd have loved it here. Memo is doing well, and the doctor thinks she'll be ok, thank God for that. I've promised to spend Christmas with them next year at home, no matter what I end up doing next, and I'm already looking forward to it.

I still miss you both, and I always will, but I'm so proud of where I am now, and I know you would be too.

Merry Christmas and lots of love,

Josie

Dear Max,

Almost a year exactly since I last saw you and I feel both that so much time has passed and that none has passed at all. There's a part of me that still expects you to just show up out here in Africa, in that way of yours, and I'm not sure if that will ever pass. Maybe that's because you're still with me, in a way that will never change.

I've been Skyping your sister from out here — she's not much into letter writing, she says. After you died, she and Liam rearranged the wedding, and they're due to get married next June. It's going to be in the same castle as Laura and John's wedding, because I told Chloe about that weekend, about how happy you'd been when you were there. She's invited me and I'm going to go. I'm going to go, and I'm going to dance out under the stars there, and think of you.

I wish you would have told me what was happening to you, Max, but I understand why you didn't — though that part has taken some time, I'll admit. I know that you were just trying to protect me from it, but you should have known that would never have been possible. Because as much as you said that I made your life brighter, you were the light in mine when you were there, and so many times when you weren't.

I wish so many things. I wish you hadn't felt you had to

go through all that alone. I wish this hadn't happened to you, because I know in my heart that had we had the chance, we would have been together for ever. I wish I'd got to know you sooner, so that I could have known you for longer. But I'm learning that you can't change what was, so instead of wishing, I'll use this letter to thank you. These past two years have changed my life, and that all started with you.

You helped show me that I could do things I never dreamed I'd be brave enough to try, you showed me that it's worth holding on until you meet that one person that makes you feel complete, but most importantly, meeting you meant I had the courage to be those things by myself. Part of me feels like I'll never truly be complete without you, but this past year I've made a pretty good start. I've been bitten to death by mosquitos, I've been unable to sleep because of the heat, I've been scratched to death by bushes. I've slept out under the night sky, I've seen wild lions, giraffes, leopards. Best of all, I've captured it all on camera. I never would have done any of that if I hadn't run into you, quite literally, on that cold, December day.

So I'll say now what I wasn't brave enough to say in person, and please know that if I'm ever lucky enough to feel this way again, I'll make sure I'm brave enough to say it then.

I love you, Max.

Now and always.

Josie

Acknowledgements

Any credit I deserve for writing this book should be equally split with my amazing, smart and talented editor, Sherise Hobbs, without whom this book would quite literally not exist. From that very first conversation in a café, Sherise has been relentlessly brilliant and incredibly generous with her creative thoughts, encouragement and attention to detail, and has helped me shape this book into something I'm truly proud of. So, Sherise, thank you.

Thanks too to Bea Grabowska for being on team #AlwaysinDecember (and thank you for telling me the book broke your heart, which I choose to take as a compliment, even though I'm not totally sure what kind of person that makes me). Thank you Katie Green for a brilliant copyedit. In the US, thanks go to Hilary Teeman for some brilliant last editorial suggestions, which helped elevate the book further, and to Caroline Weishuhn.

Emma Rogers is to thank for the absolutely beautiful cover – a cover that I really hope everyone judges the book by. Thank you to Nathaniel Alcaraz-Stapleton and

Rebecca Folland for your hard work and securing some truly champagne-worthy rights deals. Team Marketing & Publicity always have a special place in my heart, so thanks to Ellie Morley and Emily Patience (Emily gets extra credit for sharing my name).

Outside the publishing force, Charlotte Levens deserves enormous thanks for coaching me through this book, for brainstorming ideas about Christmas dates (in the middle of July), for answering my research questions about hospitals, and for many forced coffee/wine chats about this book. Char, I'm pretty sure you know this book as well as me by now, but look, now it's published and it was worth it! I will thank you with more wine, preferably on a beach with some horses around.

Lastly, thanks to my lovely older sister, Jenny, for letting me stay in her beautiful house to write this book (and to Tom, her husband, because by virtue of staying in her house I am also staying in his . . .). And thank you to my nieces, Lily and Ella, for helping/distracting me and making me take breaks from staring at my laptop all day to play zoos/The Floor is Lava/puzzles and, in Ella's case, to put this story aside to help her write stories of her own, inevitably about a girl called Jane and a horse called Daisy.

If you've read this far then you, reader, also deserve thanks. Thank you for reading this book – it makes it all worthwhile.

We hope you enjoyed reading
Always, in December.

Read on for an extract from
Emily Stone's heartwrenching novel

The
Last Gift

2012

Chapter One

A grey-haired man in an anorak held the pub door open for Cassie and she smiled at him gratefully as she ducked under the low wooden beam and stepped into the warmth, her hands full, clutching a tray of mince pies. Logs cracked in the fireplace in the corner, and the smell of mulled wine, sherry, pine and cheese all rolled into one. She walked towards the rustic bar, nodding to a few people as she passed, the chatter of what must have been nearly the entire village washing over her. It made her smile – everyone out together on Christmas Eve.

She caught sight of Tom, leaning against a stone wall and laughing as he threw his head back. His blond hair flopped to one side, evidence of the fact he'd let it grow far too long recently. He didn't notice her coming in, chatting away to someone who had their back to her, beer in hand. Someone with messy dark brown hair, a relaxed posture, wearing a black jacket that showed off those impressive shoulders. Her stomach gave a little lurch, and she nearly stumbled straight into the old oak bar, clutching the tray she was holding and throwing it out in front of her to save the mince pies.

'Watch out, Cassie love – we don't want to see all your hard work ending up on the floor!' Linda, landlady of *The Red House, appeared on the other side of the bar, having come* through the double doors that led to the kitchen. She tucked a tea towel through the belt on her jeans and crossed to where Cassie was standing, reached out from across the bar to grab the mince pies, then set them down by the coffee machine behind the bar.

'Sorry, Linda,' Cassie said quickly, slipping out of her coat. 'I know I'm a bit late, and I—'

Linda waved her apology away, her many rings glinting in the light from the candles Cassie had helped set up earlier today. 'Don't be silly. You're a doll for making them. In fact, they look so good I might have to sneak one away before the rabble get their hands on them.' She did just that, grabbing a coffee saucer and setting a mince pie down on it, using a teaspoon to take a mouthful. She closed her eyes and groaned in what Cassie thought was slightly overdone pleasure. A crumb of the pastry stuck to Linda's red lip gloss, and Cassie wondered if she should tell her. 'I swear, your baking gets better every time I try it. And what's that I taste? Something orangey?'

'Cointreau,' Cassie agreed with a nod, feeling wonderfully mature. She'd started experimenting with different ingredients, and had spent a while trying out different liqueurs in the mincemeat, though it had taken a few attempts to get it right, being as how her experience with liqueurs, and what they all tasted like was, admittedly, somewhat limited.

The door to the pub opened again, letting in a blast of cool air that managed to reach even the bar. Cassie looked over to see Hazel, her best friend since the beginning of secondary school, coming in with her mum. Hazel spotted Cassie and her eyes – green, not hazel – sparked as she closed the distance between them in a few long, elegant strides. Cassie clocked the heels that Hazel was wearing and tried not to wrinkle her nose. They always looked ridiculous together when she did that because of the height difference – Hazel tall enough to be a professional model, and Cassie short enough to still occasionally fit into child's clothing. Honestly, Cassie had told Hazel that they looked like some kind of double act and that they should be trying to *reduce* the difference in their heights rather than accentuate it, but Hazel didn't care. She was confident in her height and, when some guys went so far as to call her 'giantess', she simply claimed that men weren't worth it. She was sure her height was going to come in useful one day, if only so she didn't have to get married just so she had someone around to reach the top shelf.

'Happy Christmas Eve!' Hazel gave Cassie a hug - bending down to do so - then stepped back and pursed her lips as she studied Cassie, who twirled a strand of her hair back into place behind her ear. Hazel nodded approvingly. 'The dress works,' she said decisively, and Cassie felt relief wash over her, as she tried very hard not to glance at the head of messy brown hair behind her. She'd bought the dress – black, tight-fitting, with silver snowflakes on it – especially for tonight.

Hazel's mum, Mel, joined them at the bar, nearly as tall as Hazel, and smiled at Cassie, showing perfectly straight teeth. 'Bet you're glad to be this side of the bar tonight.' Cassie smiled and nodded – she'd offered to work but Linda had insisted she had it off, so that she could welcome in Christmas with the others.

Mel and Linda kissed each other on the cheek to say hello, then Mel glanced down at the tray Cassie had brought. 'Are those mince pies?'

'Cassie baked them,' Linda said proudly, like she was showing off a picture a young child had drawn her, one she wanted to stick on the fridge. 'Here,' Linda shoved a mince pie under Mel's nose, 'try one.' Mel dutifully did as she was told, then raised her perfectly plucked eyebrows.

'Well, I have to say, that is delicious. Better than M&S!' Hazel rolled her eyes behind her mum's back at Cassie, who tried to hide her grin. 'And what's that I taste? Brandy?'

'Cointreau,' Linda and Cassie said together.

'My, my,' Mel said. 'That's rather posh, isn't it? Well, it works, I tell you. You teach her that, Linda?'

Linda shook her head, her brunette bob swishing with the movement. 'You've seen the menu here, we're all ice cream and straight-down-the-line brownie, and we're damn good at it. But Cassie's far more talented than me, destined for greater things.' Linda winked at Cassie, who felt herself flush a little. Linda might be her boss, but she was more than that too – someone who had her back, she knew, no matter what. She'd started out working in the kitchen at *The Red House,* washing dishes and helping make the coleslaw, before she was old enough to work behind the bar. Tom had done it before her, so had got her the job. Linda had been the one to get Cassie into baking, asking her to help out with the pub deserts, and though Cassie worked front of house now, she was still playing around with the baking in her own time, seeing what happened when you mixed different flavours or combined recipes – with mixed results, admittedly.

Mel saw someone she knew at that point, waved, then crossed the room to join them, leaving Hazel to pull Cassie aside. 'Well,' she demanded immediately. 'Have you talked to him yet?' Hazel could be quite intense when she stared down at you like that, so Cassie took a step back on her spindly stilettos – another purchase just for this evening – and huffed out a breath.

'I only just got here! I came separately from Tom because I was bringing the mince pies and I wasn't ready.' Wasn't ready, because she'd taken over an hour changing her hair and doing her makeup, trying to find *just* the right look, the one that said she was an adult now, not just Tom's little sister.

'Well come on,' Hazel said, shaking back her dead straight black hair – hair that she dyed to make *more* black, even though Cassie honestly couldn't tell the difference. 'No point standing around here with longing stares when he's right there.' And before Cassie could tell her not to, Hazel marched straight over to Tom and Sam, leaving Cassie scurrying behind, trying to look both graceful on her heels, and keep up with Hazel's long stride.

Tom grabbed Cassie as she reached him and gave her a one-armed hug, leaving his arm around her shoulders. 'Here's my girl, and her sidekick.' Cassie smiled while Hazel stuck her tongue out.

'I'm no one's sidekick, Rivers.' True, Cassie thought. She often felt like a sidekick to Hazel, rather than the other way around. Tom grinned, dropped his arm away from Cassie and gave Hazel a quick, hard hug. Cassie, meanwhile, tried hard not to look at Sam directly for too long, even though she could feel his gorgeous blue eyes on her, assessing, while he stood there with his thumbs looped through the belt loop of his jeans, casual as you like.

'How's the land of university treating you?' Hazel asked.

Tom wrinkled his nose. 'Annoyingly hard work this year.' Tom was in his third year, and Cassie had been treated to many a phone call already, lamenting all the work he was having to do, rather than being able to keep exploring the night life of Manchester. 'Well,' he clarified, 'for some of us anyway. Sam here seems immune.' Sam shrugged, and Cassie shifted to face him, relieved to have an excuse to look at him. She smiled, and he nodded back.

'Looking good, Cass.' Cassie felt heat rise in her face, and she did a sort of shrug-nod thing in acceptance of the compliment.

Tom rolled his eyes. 'She ought to, the amount of time she spent with that bloody hair rod.' Cassie flushed more, and really hoped it wasn't as obvious as it felt. She shot Tom a glare, which he ignored.

Hazel came to Cassie's rescue, giving Tom a friendly punch on the arm. 'It's Christmas Eve, you idiot, we are *supposed* to dress up and look pretty.'

'Well, you do,' Sam said, looking at Cassie. God, it was just impossible to look away from those eyes. 'Look pretty, that is.' He glanced at Hazel, almost like an afterthought. 'Both of you, that is.'

Hazel shot Cassie the briefest of glances that Cassie didn't dare return, even though the back of her neck was

416

sparking with heat. 'Well Rivers,' Hazel said, 'I think it's about time you bought me a welcome home drink, isn't it?' She cocked her head in that way that made all of their teachers go pale.

Tom raised his eyebrows. 'Surely if it's me who's coming home, *you* need to buy the welcoming drink.'

Hazel pffed. 'Details, details.' She walked away on those long legs and Tom, with a slightly helpless glance back at Cassie, followed, leaving Cassie alone with Sam. She suddenly wished she'd thought to get a drink when she first came in, because then it would have given her something to do with her hands. As it was, she didn't know what to do with them – they felt useless and awkward by her sides.

'So, umm, how was the trip back from Manchester?' she asked, shifting closer to the wall as a few people passed them in the crowed space. Tom and Sam had stayed up there a few weeks after term ended, getting up to God knows what, and had only got back a few days ago.

'Ah boring, you know,' Sam said with a shrug. He'd filled out even more since Cassie had last seen him over summer.

'You staying with your mum?' Sam nodded. 'How is she?' Cassie liked Sam's mum – she was quiet, but there was something so warm about her.

'She's great,' Sam said, and those blue eyes softened, just a little, in a way that made Cassie's heart flip, even as she told herself to get a bloody grip.

'And . . . your dad?' Cassie asked hesitantly.

Sam narrowed his eyes, and the softness was instantly lost. 'No idea,' he said hardly. 'Last I heard he was off in Sri Lanka surfing or something.'

Cassie twirled that same lock of hair that kept wanting

to escape her carefully styled half-up half-down look. 'You haven't heard from him?'

'No, and I don't want to.' He said it in a way that effectively closed the subject off and Cassie bit her lip, wishing she hadn't brought the subject up in the first place. She knew how Sam felt about his dad, but had wondered, what with it being Christmas and all . . . She glanced at the bar, to where Hazel and Tom were still in a queue – too much for Linda to handle solo, as Cassie had predicted.

'Anyway, how are you doing, Cass?' Cassie glanced back at him to see that the tension was lost, chased away like it had never been there – back to his easy, casual self. She'd had a crush on him for as long as she could remember – it was the reason she hadn't gone out with anyone at school even though George Haycock had asked her out and he was actually quite cute, if a little short, according to Hazel. But last summer, she, Tom and Sam had hung out a lot together, just the three of them because Hazel had been away, and something had changed, and that had decided it for her. He'd started flirting with her too, holding her hand when Tom wasn't looking, and she'd been sure, then, that it wasn't just a one-sided crush. He'd left for university in September, but now he was back and Cassie had decided – this was the night. She was going to be brave and kiss him. Or, at least, she was going to work up to flirting enough that he kissed her first. She hadn't decided which one yet.

'I'm good,' she said, trying for an easy tone to match his. 'Finished sending off all my university applications last week.' She said it deliberately, reminding him that she wasn't that much younger than him, only a few years.

'Oh yeah?'

'Yeah,' she agreed. 'Business studies.'

Sam frowned. 'Really? That doesn't seem—' But he broke off as a group of four vacated the sofa table through the archway, then grabbed her hand, linking his fingers through hers, and sped towards it, tugging her along behind. She laughed at the urgency as he pulled her down next to him on the sofa, her hand still in his. She was still smiling as he shook his head. 'Can't let a spot like this go to waste, Cass.'

It was one of the best tables, she'd give him that. Right by the crackling fire, the Christmas tree that Cassie had decorated herself in the corner, a lone candle on the low wooden table, surrounded by empty glasses from the group before. There was another group of young people – a year or so above Cassie, she thought – sitting on stools on one of the high tables next to them, and one of the girls was eyeing Cassie and Sam with disgust, clearly having hoped to bag the table herself.

Cassie laughed again as she looked back at Sam. He was sitting very close to her, she noticed, their legs pressed against one another's, hands still linked together. He reached out, tucked that errant strand of hair behind her ear, where it stayed, listening to his touch where it had not listened to hers. She held her breath, her heart fluttering.

'You really do look beautiful, you know,' Sam murmured, his eyes not leaving hers, and Cassie felt her skin spark.

'Excellent, you nabbed us a spot.' Cassie jumped at the sound of Tom's voice, and Sam dropped her hand. She let her breath out on a whoosh as Tom and Hazel sat down on the sofa opposite. Hazel handed Cassie a vodka and lemonade with a little smirk, like she'd seen the whole thing.

'So, what were you guys talking about?' Hazel asked, the picture of innocence. Cassie narrowed her eyes at her, though the effect might not be as severe as she'd hoped, given she still felt flushed from the 'beautiful' comment.

Sam shrugged. 'Cassie was just saying she'd been applying to uni.'

Tom made a disgusted noise in the back of his throat. 'Yeah. Business.' Sam raised his eyebrows at Tom's tone of voice and he shook his head. 'She'll hate that.'

'Hey!' Cassie exclaimed. 'Right here, remember?'

Tom turned to her. 'Well, you will. Don't know why you don't do cooking or something.'

Cassie snorted. 'Cooking? At university?'

Tom waved an impatient hand in the air. 'Baking. Food tech. Whatever. Something you love.'

Cassie sighed. 'It's a hobby, Tom.' She angled her head at Sam. 'You really want to tell me you're doing law because it's your true passion?' She couldn't say the same thing to Tom – he really *did* love geology, though he managed to get away with it and not slip into nerd territory because he was also sporty, good looking, and charming.

'Nah, but I'm going to be rich, Cass, and then I'll be able to do whatever I like.' Sam grinned, first at her, then at Tom, who grinned back in solidarity whilst Cassie and Hazel rolled their eyes.

Once they'd finished their drinks, Cassie and Hazel went to the loo together, ignoring Sam's comment about synchronised weeing. Cassie checked her face in the bright fluorescent light of the bathroom, reapplying mascara and lip gloss. She glanced at Hazel who was doing the same in the mirror next to her. 'Well?' she asked. 'What do you think?'

Hazel gave a firm nod. 'He is definitely flirting with you.'

'He *is*, isn't he?'

Halfway between the bathroom and their sofa table, Hazel got pulled over by her mum. Mel pouted, her eyes a little glassy in a way that suggested she was definitely well on her way to being hammered. Not that Cassie minded – it was easier to get drunk if the parents were wasted. 'You haven't talked to me all night,' Mel said to Hazel. 'Come on, give me five minutes, it's Christmas!' Hazel rolled her eyes at Cassie, then sighed, as if to say that she might as well get it over with now. 'Where's Claire, Cassie?' Mel asked.

Cassie shrugged. 'Probably in bed by now. She's not really into Christmas.' Not really into socialising in general. Mel gave a disapproving 'hmmm' in response, then leaned into Hazel to give her a big hug, whispered something in her ear. Hazel grimaced over Mel's shoulder at Cassie, and though Cassie laughed, she couldn't help feeling a little pang as she waved and walked back to Tom and Sam. At least Hazel had a mum to come here with. Mostly, she thought she had a handle on it, the fact that she was, technically, an orphan, but there were times when the loss of it flared up, and Christmas was one of those. There was always such an emphasis on family, and Claire, though Cassie thought she did her best, was hardly one for the festive holiday spirit.

Cassie smiled at Linda, who was holding up an empty

tray where her mince pies had been, then turned the corner to the sofa table. She stumbled to a stop, her stomach clenching painfully. Tom was there, leaning against the back of the sofa and scrolling absentmindedly through his phone. But he was alone. Because Sam, it seemed, had found other company, and instead of sitting with his best mate, he was up by the high table. Up by the table, and pressing the girl who had given them the dirty look against the wall. His hands all over her, their faces locked together.

Cassie felt sick, physically sick, and she felt her eyes start to sting, even as she told herself, repeatedly, to calm down. The alcohol certainly wasn't helping, but then, what the hell was he playing at? He didn't even *know* that girl. And he'd told *Cassie* she was beautiful, not this stranger.

Tom looked up, saw her, and gestured her over. She went to him, a little numbly, because what could she do? She could hardly run out in floods of tears in front of everyone. Talk about overdramatic.

'Hey,' Tom said as she sat down. 'What's up?' He knew, of course he knew. She'd never been able to hide her emotions from Tom.

'Oh, nothing,' she said, trying as hard as she could to keep the break out of her voice – and trying very hard not to look over at Sam, even though he was right in her eye line. Had she been stupid, thinking he might kiss her tonight? Had she been reading into things? No, she thought firmly. She wasn't an idiot, she knew when someone was flirting with her.

Tom prodded her in the ribs, and she batted his hand away automatically. 'What's wrong?' he pressed.

'Just . . . ' She hesitated. No way could she tell him the

truth. 'Just emotional, you know. It's the last Christmas properly at home, before I go to university.' Tom pursed his lips but nodded, seeming to accept that as an answer. She knew Tom only came back home for Christmas – for all the holidays – because she was still there. He and Claire got on in an amicable sort of way, but they weren't close. And so, when Cassie went away too, would they both stop coming back home, without someone to draw them back? Cassie didn't like to think about it, the thought that she might not have a base to spend time with her brother.

Sam had broken away from the girl, though he was running one hand up and down her arm. Cassie gritted her teeth. She was such an idiot! What must he have thought, leading her on? Had he been playing with her over summer? Was that why he'd done it out of sight of Tom, so that there was no proof, nothing Tom could get mad about?

'Hey, I know what will cheer you up,' Tom said, bringing her attention back to him.

Cassie sighed. 'Do you now?'

Tom nodded, a wicked grin spreading across his face. 'I've got a cracker of a treasure hunt planned for you this year.'

Despite herself, Cassie laughed, as Tom must have known she would. It was something he'd done every year for her since before she could remember, something that had made Christmas feel extra special as a child – a series of clues that she had to solve, following a trail that led to her present. 'What's at the other end?'

Tom shook his head in mock horror. 'I can't tell you that, it would spoil it!'

Cassie was still smiling when Sam looked back over at them, like he was checking they were still there, still waiting – like he wanted the option to do whatever the hell he liked. So, even though the smile wanted to drop off her face, even though she wanted to scream or cry or storm out of there, Cassie made sure that the smile stayed in place as she gave him a sarcastic nod, then turned to Tom to talk about the first thing she could think about, being damn sure to laugh – loudly – at every break in the conversation. And she vowed, then and there, that she would not let Sam Malone know how much he'd got to her. She was done with him, she decided. Done with him for good.

The Last Gift

Emily Stone

Every year since Cassie was small, her big brother, Tom, has left her a trail of clues leading to his Christmas present to her. It's been only the two of them since their parents died and they were taken in by their grandparents, and Tom has always loved seeing his sister's face light up when she finds the gift at the end of the trail.

Years later, their tradition remains. To Cassie, Tom has always been her rock. So when she gets the news, just before Christmas, that Tom has been killed in a climbing accident, her world is shattered.

After the funeral, Cassie is stunned when she finds a hidden note from Tom in her flat. It's the first clue that will lead her to his Christmas gift this year; he must have set up the treasure hunt before he went away. A heartbroken Cassie decides to follow the clues and find her brother's last gift – not realising she is about to discover more than she ever realised about her brother and their parents . . . Or that the trail will lead her to love, in the very last place she expected to find it . . .

Available to order

REVIEW

Bookends

When one book ends, another begins...

Bookends is a vibrant new reading community to help you ensure you're never without a good book.

You'll find exclusive previews of the brilliant new books from your favourite authors as well as exciting debuts and past classics. Read our blog, check out our recommendations for your reading group, enter great competitions and much more!

Visit our website to see which great books we're recommending this month.

Join the Bookends community:
www.welcometobookends.co.uk

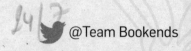 @Team Bookends 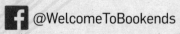 @WelcomeToBookends